THE
SHORTEST
ROAD

ALSO BY DAVID L. ROBBINS

Souls to Keep
War of the Rats
The End of War
Scorched Earth
Last Citadel
Liberation Road
The Assassins Gallery
The Betrayal Game
Broken Jewel
The Devil's Waters
The Empty Quarter
The Devil's Horn
The Low Bird
You Are Your Own Always (collection of essays)
Isaac's Beacon: The Promised Wars: Book One

FOR THE STAGE

Scorched Earth (an adaptation)
The End of War (an adaptation)
Sam & Carol
The King of Crimes

THE
SHORTEST
ROAD

THE PROMISED WARS: BOOK 2

DAVID L.
ROBBINS

WICKED SON

A WICKED SON BOOK
An Imprint of Post Hill Press
ISBN: 978-1-63758-765-2
ISBN (eBook): 978-1-63758-766-9

The Shortest Road:
The Promised Wars: Book Two
© 2023 by David L. Robbins
All Rights Reserved

Cover Design by Matt Margolis

Post Hill Press
New York • Nashville
WickedSonBooks.com

Published in the United States of America
1 2 3 4 5 6 7 8 9 10

For Lindy, who helps me get through.

AUTHOR'S FOREWORD

All principal events in *The Shortest Road* are based on the historical record. While several actual persons appear in this novel, the central characters are completely fictional. The exception is reporter Vincent Haas, inspired by the exploits and reportage of I. F. Stone and Kenneth W. Bilby, both journalists for New York's *Herald Tribune*.

For the whole Arab world, the struggle is religious. It is for them a matter of Jewish religion against their own. The masses are gripped by widespread fervor. The men are keen to enter the fray as the shortest road to Heaven.
King Farouk I of Egypt
1948

THE CHARACTERS OF *THE SHORTEST ROAD*

(In order of appearance)

Gabbi, Rivkah's younger sister, Palmach

Vince Haas, American journalist for the *New York Herald Tribune*

Malik, a Bedouin

Barja, Malik's older sister

Rivkah, Austrian immigrant to Israel

Tarek, commando jeep driver, born of Yemeni immigrants

Moshe Dayan, commander of the Eighty-Ninth Commando Battalion

Red Yakob, prisoner in Transjordan, Palmach

Benny, rear gunner in Gabbi's commando jeep

Mrs. Pappel, Austrian immigrant to Israel

Jonny, commander of Gabbi's jeep company

King Abdullah Husseini, Hashemite king of Transjordan

Hugo Unger, German plumber, survivor of Buchenwald, immigrant to Israel

Pinchus, commander in the underground dissident group Irgun

David Ben-Gurion, prime minister of Israel

Hillel, machine gunner in Gabbi's jeep company

Elam, a driver in Gabbi's jeep company

Count Folke Bernadotte, the UN's envoy to Palestine, member of the
    Swedish royal family

Naftali, Romanian engineer on the Burma Road

Menachem Begin, leader of the Irgun

Major Keisch, officer in the Alexandroni Brigade of the Israeli Defense
    Force (IDF)

Abner, gunner in Gabbi's jeep company

Pelz, Dayan's second in command

Rabinowitz, young mechanic in the Eighty-Ninth Commando Battalion

Michael, Irish loader in Gabbi's armored car

The mayor of Lydda

Schwimmer, Palmach captain

Shmulik, PIAT operator

Cohen and Spiro, members of underground dissident group, the Stern Gang

CHAPTER 1

GABBI

May 14, 1948
Massuot Yitzhak
Arab Palestine

With her good right arm, Gabbi swept every dish, teacup, and saucer off the shelves. She threw pots and pans through the windowpanes.

By the light of a bonfire outside, she knocked the clock off the mantle and ground the bits under her boot. She smashed three lamps, the glass screen of a lantern, and that was it. There was nothing of real value in the small house, no antiques, no keepsakes or art. The Jews of Massuot Yitzhak had all come to Palestine empty-handed. Here on the edge of the Negev, they were the last of their lines, and the first of their lines.

Gabbi went out to sit on the porch step of her sister's house. Not long ago this had been Gabbi's home too. She might die today. It seemed a fine place to wait.

Tables and chairs burned nearby, near enough to feel the heat. Two young men with axes hacked the last of a rocker and a bed frame. Everything in her sister's house that would burn had been dragged outside, demolished, and set alight, to deny the Arabs even the firewood. Inside, a farmer with a knife ripped apart mattresses and cushions. When the wreckers were done, they went elsewhere.

No one sat on the step with Gabbi; she wanted no one's conversation. The bullet wound in her left shoulder talked enough.

The first light of dawn light washed the bare Judean hills rosy. Blood crusted in Gabbi's uniform where the bullet had passed through. Blood had dried black on her wrist. Below Massuot Yitzhak, thirty Arab trucks waited in the wadi.

Using one hand, Gabbi raised a palm-sized rock. She smashed the barrel of her rifle until it bent. Her wound raised tears, but she pushed into the pain until she had ruined the pistol, too. Gabbi left both useless weapons beside her on the porch so the Arabs would see them when they saw her.

✳ ✳ ✳

Three hundred armed Arabs entered Massuot Yitzhak. They came cautiously, dashing from cover to cover before they would step into the open. They seemed suspicious that the Jews might work some last-minute perfidy.

A dozen *fellahin* came to collect Gabbi. She stayed seated while they formed a semicircle. The men were peasants in dark robes dusty at the chest and knees, grit in their beards from lying under Jewish gunfire for three days.

The Arabs ogled Gabbi, curious. She stayed motionless while they kicked through the ashes of the bonfire and rummaged through Rivkah's house, until one Arab gestured her to rise.

She cradled her hurt arm. At gunpoint, the Arabs walked Gabbi to the cistern in the center of the kibbutz; there, the surviving defenders of Massuot Yitzhak were being corralled. Twenty out of the two hundred were wounded, some borne on doors used for stretchers. All the walls of the kibbutz were pockmarked by bullets. Bloody handprints smeared a whitewashed fence.

Gabbi stumbled through the gathered soldiers and farmers to a spot near the cistern's pump. She collapsed to her knees beside the low stone wall. Gabbi held no romance about living or dying on her feet. She was simply too tired to stand.

Arabs stomped about the kibbutz looking for pillage, but the houses, barns, workshops, clinic, kitchen, and dining hall had all been gutted by its people, just as every weapon had been spoiled.

The Jews hunkered under the early sun, waiting for no clear fate. Those nearest the cistern passed around cups of water while the Arabs set fire to the orange orchard, the olive grove, and the fields of fodder.

For an hour, one *fellah* after another stamped up to the Jews to fling worthless rifles and broken clocks at their feet. Gabbi and the defenders had spent three days of battle prepared to die. That resolve did not fade around the cistern but passed among them like the water; they sipped from it and refreshed themselves against the fear that they would be murdered. They held hands and assured each other with nothing but the faith that whatever was going to happen would happen to them all.

As the sun climbed, smoke from the burning orchards and crops blew high past the cistern. At no particular signal, without a trumpet or curses, a dozen fellahin stepped side by side and leveled their weapons at the seated Jews. The dozen Arabs became a muttering fifty. One young settler, a boy as blonde as hay, was the first Jew to stand. Then all two hundred put their feet on the ground.

Gabbi turned a slow circle, listening to the settlers pray in many languages.

None of the Jews spoke Arabic, they could only guess what the fellahin were saying. The Arabs raised voices at each other and jabbed gun barrels at the Jews. The Arabs seemed rudderless, even as they grew wild-eyed, as if some alarm had gone off and they needed to take action now or lose the moment.

From behind, other fighters, not peasants but soldiers of the Arab Legion, rushed forward to push down the guns and shout in the faces of the fellahin. The legionnaires wore khaki instead of peasant robes, moustaches not beards. They gestured east towards the Jerusalem road and to the rumble of engines climbing the slope, past the quarry. The legionnaires shook their heads and slapped their thighs as if disappointed.

Quickly, two ambulances and three buses roared into the center of the kibbutz; each bore the scarlet emblem of the International Red Cross. Out of the buses streamed dozens of nurses in grey smocks and white mobcaps. Five men in shorts and safari hats followed from the ambulances. One tall and wide-shouldered woman strode through the thick of the Arabs to stand with the Jews, nearest to Gabbi. In commanding Arabic she announced something. When she was done, she spoke in English to Gabbi.

"You are a soldier?"

"Yes."

"The Arabs are going to take your people to Transjordan. We will guarantee your safety."

"Where are you from?"

"Sweden. And you?"

"Austria."

"You're hurt." The nurse plucked at the blood-stiff threads at Gabbi's shoulder. "You come with us. We will evacuate the wounded."

"I don't want to go."

"And so you may die. This wound will get infected. I would not expect mercy in Jordan.

Decide quickly."

The nurse strode off to find some Arab in charge.

✳ ✳ ✳

The defenders of Massuot Yitzhak insisted Gabbi leave with the Red Cross and the other wounded. Go, they said, keep fighting.

In the late morning, a Red Cross doctor put Gabbi's arm in a sling. She boarded a bus filled with other wounded and the smells of antiseptic and gauze. All eyes were plastered to the chicken-wire windows as the Arabs loaded the rest of the defenders onto black trucks. The fires in Massuot Yitzhak's fields and groves were finished; the final smoke drifted across the white hills east to the Dead Sea.

After the Arabs had crammed one hundred seventy captives onto their trucks, a dozen nurses boarded the second bus; this one followed the convoy out of the kibbutz. The trip east into Transjordan would take less than an hour. The remaining nurses and doctors took seats on Gabbi's bus among the bandaged.

The tall Swedish nurse sat with Gabbi. The wounded raised fists to Massuot Yitzhak as the bus began to roll.

The nurse said, "A few stitches. A week to ten days. You'll be fine, with a pretty scar to talk about."

At the bottom of the slope, between the heights of Yellow Hill and Rock Hill, the quarry road met an intersection. The Arab convoy with the prisoners of Massuot Yitzhak turned south for Hebron. Gabbi's bus and the ambulances turned north, for Jerusalem.

Gabbi asked, "Why aren't we going to Kfar Etzion? There's wounded there. My sister is there, she's pregnant. You can bring her, too."

The nurse fidgeted on the bench seat, uncertain whether to touch Gabbi before she spoke.

"No, dear. There aren't."

Gabbi's shoulder stabbed, as if her wound knew something before she did.

"What do you mean?"

"You don't know." The Swede glanced about the bouncing bus. Some realization made her jaw drop. "My God. None of you know."

Gabbi squeezed the nurse's wrist.

"What happened?"

The world collapsed into Gabbi's heart, which could not hold it.

"What happened?"

"Yesterday. The Arabs killed everyone in Kfar Etzion."

Gabbi's grip on the Swede faded. The nurse said, "That's why we came today. To protect the rest of you. We thought you knew."

Gabbi held a breath, not knowing whether to scream or hold it forever. She spent it on a word.

"Everyone?"

"I'm terribly sorry."

Gabbi rammed her face against the chicken-wire window. A mile away, on the highest hill of the Gush, Kfar Etzion had not been burned. Gabbi slid her wounded arm out of the sling to hook both hands into the crosshatch wire and pull as hard as she could. The wire didn't give.

She shoved the tall nurse out of the bench seat; the woman tumbled into the aisle. Gabbi leaped for the front of the bus. The nurse grabbed her ankle, almost tripping her. Gabbi kicked to escape. She would jump off the bus, run to Kfar Etzion, live or die by what she found there.

She tore at every nurse who rose between her and the door. The bus sped north for Jerusalem.

CHAPTER 2

RIVKAH

Hebron
Arab Palestine

Rivkah awoke in darkness, to a call of her name. Rolling over to face the bars, a great figure stood before her cell.

Malik's arms came through the bars. She rushed off the cot, into his grasp.

"Forgive me." He pulled her tight against the iron between them. "I could not come before now."

Rivkah did not smell on Malik the desert, no sun or sand, not the stink of his camel. Only guns.

He released her sooner than she'd wished. Rivkah stepped away.

"Where have you been?"

"With the other prisoners of the Etzion bloc."

Rivkah backed away to sit on her mattress and not risk her legs failing at whatever news Malik brought.

"All of them?"

"All of them. The Red Cross arrived in time. The other three settlements were allowed to surrender."

"Did you see Gabbi?"

"Yes. She was wounded."

"Is she…"

"Your sister walked out of Massuot Yitzhak, a bandage on one arm. The Red Cross was allowed to evacuate her. I could not speak with her, you understand."

"Yes. Thank you."

"Your villages have been looted and burned. They are no more. This is what has begun."

On impulse, Rivkah covered her stomach. She had secreted something, a child, away from Massuot Yitzhak and Kfar Etzion before they were razed.

"Where will I be taken?"

"Into Transjordan. You will be interrogated in Amman. After that, a prison in Umm el-Jimmal. You will all stay there until the war ends."

"What will happen then?"

"The Jews will win this war, but it will not be quick. Your baby will be born in Transjordan. There is a doctor among the prisoners. It will be well. Come here."

Rivkah rose. Malik reached inside his deep sleeves for a matchbox. He struck a flame, the brightest thing in her cell for three days.

Malik moved the match closer and pointed at Rivkah's hand.

"In Amman they will take that ring from you. Give it back to me."

She slid the silver band off her finger. Palming it, Malik blew out the match. He kept the scorched stick to leave no evidence of himself.

"When the war is done, I will go to Missus Pappel and give her this again. I have something for you."

From inside his robes, Malik pulled a folded page of the *Palestine Post*. He handed it to her.

"You cannot be found with this."

Malik struck another match.

"Read it to me, child. Whisper."

He burned more matches while she read and whispered. Listening, Malik's hand went to his breast.

Rivkah returned him the sheet.

"Tell him I'm alive. Find a way."

"I have no way to find him. There is a war."

She reached through the bars to touch his billowy sleeve where he'd hidden the page.

"Try. Please. The paper says he's in Galilee."

Malik nodded.

"Tell him Chayim for a boy. Chaya for a girl."

Behind his black beard starry with grey, Malik said, "Life. It is a good name. One day I will bring a poem for your child. Farewell, Rivkah."

The dark feathered around Malik. He retreated facing her and did not turn his back until far away from her cell. Rivkah lay on her cot, hands over her kicking belly.

CHAPTER 3

VINCE

May 16
Samakh
Jordan Valley
Israel

In a trench beneath a copse of date trees, forty young fighters slept in shifts, their hands as pillows. They wore misfit uniforms, mostly their own clothes and boots mixed with military wear, a wool cap, an olive sweater. One in five had no weapon. Vince did not sleep so that he might see the start of the war.

At midnight, the Arabs arrived. Five miles west, a pearly string of headlights appeared beside the Yarmouk River. Once the first Syrian trucks rolled across the border at al-Hama, they became invaders.

The mile-long Arab convoy rushed across Israel's borderlands. A few hundred Jews in their path were the first soldiers of Israel in two thousand years, young men and women who'd hoped for one peaceful night, their first as citizens of their own nation. They aimed guns into the dark, unsure what might come out of it.

Two miles away, the invading convoy left the road, climbed a hill, and shut down.

Vince was older than the others in the trench. They asked him, "Will the Arabs come tonight?"

"Dawn."

His answer was passed down the trench; the Jews pulled in their rifles. Those who could go back to sleep did. A few stayed on watch.

Vince walked to the end of the trench where he lay down alone. He didn't want to talk, to ask questions or answer them. He'd hurried here to Samakh to get in the way of the war.

❊ ❊ ❊

At sunrise, the shelling began. The Syrian artillery was random and inaccurate; rounds exploded in an avocado orchard and the open fields, shells overshot the village to fall in the Galilee. The Syrians managed to blow up a few mud huts in the village.

During the barrage, an Arab infantry company moved into the buildings of an animal quarantine station two hundred yards south of the village. They laid low while the cannonade continued another hour, still with little effect. When the big guns stopped, the Syrians made no charge at the Israeli force, just satisfied themselves with patrolling the road in armored cars.

The sunlight became pleasant on the banks of the Galilee. The battle took on the feel of deadlock, even reluctance. In midafternoon, Israeli reinforcements arrived, a hundred Haganah from Tiberias. They were a professional-looking bunch in matching uniforms, each with a weapon. They dug in alongside Vince and the platoon. The Arabs watched and did not shoot, saving their ammunition.

At dusk, in ocher light, the Syrians finally pounced. An artillery salvo did little damage to the Jews' dug-in positions. In the van of the Arab assault, a trio of armored trucks clattered toward the village, firing their stub cannons.

When the armored cars had rolled within a hundred yards of Samakh, the Syrian infantry broke into the open. To a trumpet fanfare and ululations, the hundred Arabs in the quarantine station charged at Vince and the young soldiers under the fig trees. Three hundred more

Syrians launched themselves at the mud huts and stone walls of the village.

The defenders in the trench around Vince turned steely. One called to him, "You should go now."

"I'll be okay."

The boy pointed to Vince's press armband, a white "P" on a black field.

"The Arabs can't read that."

Syrians flooded over open ground or loped behind their battlewagons. They fired wildly and bellowed their resolve as they advanced. The Haganah and farmers pressed their cheeks to their rifle stocks and picked out one Arab each to kill, and laid out grenades at their knees.

The armored car in the lead thundered at a squat stone house on the eastern rim of the village. The house vanished behind the blast but when the smoke cleared the walls had held. Before the Arab gunners could reload, the house answered.

From a window, a 20mm autocannon unleashed a powerful burst, five rounds per second, each bullet larger than a finger. The Jewish gun chewed through the battlewagon's armor plating; the gun crew let the destruction of the truck be long and terrible to make a point. Their rounds punched through the Syrians' steel with screeches that drew every eye and ear. The assault paused as the riddled truck sparked and shook, all four tires popped. The vehicle collapsed on its rims the way a dying beast might fold its legs.

Behind the ruined armored car, the second and third Arab trucks reversed, wanting no part of the Israelis' autocannon. But a trumpet sounded again and the infantry moved around the retreating vehicles. The foot soldiers stepped into the road, out from cover. The Israelis opened up on them.

The first rank of Arabs fell; behind them, a hundred dropped to their knees and bellies to shoot back. The hundred infantrymen from the quarantine advanced against a withering fire to fight within fifty yards of the village. Every step was costly, trading grenades and rifle fire. By the dozen, Arabs fell in the road and on the stony open ground. The battle cries of the invaders became the wails of the wounded.

If they had surged, the Syrians might have won the battle, might have overrun the trenches and swamped the village. But the Jews emptied their weapons and their last-ditch hearts, and the Arabs hedged.

The blare of another bugle turned the Arabs around. The Haganah and the farmers stopped firing while the Arabs helped their hurt off the battlefield and dragged their dead off by the boots.

CHAPTER 4

MALIK

May 17
Hebron
Arab Palestine

Malik raised his hands in mock surprise, as though a puff of smoke had come out of the goat stew.

"*Wallah.*"

Barja waited beside the table, hands on broad hips. She and Malik had inherited their father's great size. Malik had grown tall while Barja grew stout.

She asked, "Is it spicy enough?"

He tasted more, then tapped the spoon against his temple as if to jar his thoughts.

"There are no words that can describe this meal." He licked his lips where a fire smoldered; the stew was seasoned too hot. "Sit, sister."

Barja pulled out a wooden chair. She wore a pale cotton *thob* she'd embroidered in blue cactus flowers, and a turquoise headscarf. Barja's husband was dead. Her son had left the house yesterday and she did not know where he was.

Malik dug into one more mouthful, then set the spoon aside.

"Give the rest to a beggar. It will give him hope of God."

The white tiles of the kitchen floor gleamed, spotless. The next room over was a small den where Barja greeted her embroidery clients and the religious men who brought her monthly widow's stipend. Every night, she made up the sofa and slept there; she let her son Hadi have the one bedroom.

Malik pushed his hands inside the sleeves of his black robe.

"I must leave for a while."

Barja lay both palms on the table. She wore four gold rings, gifts from Malik. On his hidden hands he wore ten.

As children, Barja had defended him. She lacked soft ways both then and now.

"With a war started? You go?"

"Allah's will."

"You have no idea what Allah's will is. Where will you go? Back to your desert?" She said this as if the desert were a barren place.

"To Galilee."

"Galilee? What is there? Are you going to fight?"

"No."

"Then why?"

"A friend."

"I don't care."

"Careful, sister."

"Your place is here, protecting us. Not someone in Galilee. We are your family."

"You'll be safe."

Barja muttered, "*Feh.*"

"But you must do something."

"I will not take instruction from you. Not if you are leaving."

"You must keep Hadi here."

"Why?"

Malik said, "He is wild."

"He had a wild father."

"The Jews killed his father. And they will kill Hadi. Listen to me. The street is full of fools shouting how easy it will be to win this war.

Hadi is seventeen. He and his friends are the first ones who will accept a gun from anyone and get on a truck. They will not come back."

"That is why you must stay."

"Keep him here."

The sun would set in an hour. Malik had never been north beyond Jericho. His camel's feet had not touched a paved road except to cross it. Galilee, a sea he had not seen, lay a hundred miles away.

Rising, Malik touched fingertips to his chest, to his lips, then his forehead.

"*Habib Albi.*"

As he left, Barja did not respond that she loved him in return. Malik had done nothing but upset his sister. He had only tried to make peace. He might have lied but had not. Perhaps he should have.

✳ ✳ ✳

Malik fed and watered his camel. The beast ate greedily, grunting and burping at the trough so loudly that even children who knew camels laughed.

Malik headed east through the outskirts of Hebron. He would camp tonight in the hills north of al-Shuyukh, tomorrow at the oasis outside Jericho. After that, he would follow the River Jordan north to Galilee. Vince had written his last column from Samakh, a village beside the sea. Malik couldn't be certain he would still be there, but Vince was famous and people would know of him.

On the edge of Hebron, the houses became small and threadbare, the trees short and wind-bent. The setting sun cast gold on the hills of Judea and charcoal in the clouds. Malik and his camel padded by a well where women gathered for their evening wash. His ambling camel blinked long lashes at them, but Malik kept his own eyes on the east.

Ahead, before the dirt lane faded to pebbles, then sand, three soldiers emerged from the last cinderblock building. They wore moustaches and fezzes. Malik marked them as foreign.

All three threw up hands as if they knew Malik and understood he would be difficult to stop.

Malik reined in short to make the three foreigners walk to him. The camel, with an ugly disposition, spit.

The soldiers wore the uniform of the Arab Legion.

Malik slid hands inside his sleeves. "*Salaam'alaikum.*"

The shortest, skinniest legionnaire lowered his hands. He left his rifle on his back while the other two leveled their weapons at their waists.

"Where are you going, friend?"

The camel chuffed like it understood the question.

Malik said, "About my business."

The little one rested hands on his hips. "What business is that?"

"My own."

The little soldier exchanged glances left and right. The two flanking him shifted their stances, one foot in front of the other.

The little one said, "Maybe it's best if you stay in Hebron until the war's over."

"Friend, I know those hills better than you know your mother."

The little one seemed unsure if he'd been insulted.

"We'll need to take your rifle."

"You have your own."

"We're disarming all the local militias."

"Ah. I see. But don't you believe the Palestinian people should fight for themselves?"

"We will do a better job of it for them."

"I am not in a militia. I have business elsewhere. I will keep my rifle."

The little one crooked a finger at Malik's holstered long gun. One soldier took a stride. Before he could take a second step, he stared into the bore of a pistol Malik drew from his black sleeve.

The second legionnaire twitched as if he might come to his comrade's defense. Malik stilled him with a second pistol whipped from the folds of his robe. The legionnaire stopped so quickly the tassel of his fez swung across his forehead.

From high on the grumbling camel, Malik said to the two in his sights, "Pull the magazines out of your rifles and toss them."

The little one barked, "Don't."

They ignored him and rid themselves of their rifles.

Malik spoke down to the little soldier. "Where were you three days ago?"

"What?"

"Were you in Gush Etzion?"

"I don't have to tell you anything."

The small legionnaire was a mean man, but he was not under one of Malik's pistols. Malik asked one of the soldiers looking into his guns, the one he deemed the youngest of the three.

"Were you there? In Kfar Etzion?"

"Yes."

"Were you there for the killing of the Jews?"

The youngest soldier could not guess Malik's intent.

"Yes."

"All of you?"

"Yes."

"What is your tribe?"

"Howeitat."

"All three of you?"

"Yes."

"I am of the Tarabin. You are not my brothers, my cousins, or my friends."

Malik swung the pistols away from the Jordanian boys to the little, mouthy one. With both guns he shot the fellow in the center of the chest, so he could die watching Malik ride away.

CHAPTER 5

RIVKAH

Amman
Transjordan

The interrogator wore a white headscarf, black skirt, and jacket. She was matronly and thin.

Referencing Rivkah's bloody shirt, she asked in English, "Are you hurt?"

"No."

The small, windowless room held only a wooden table and two metal chairs. In the center of the cement floor a drain would allow the room to be hosed down. The one door was steel, with a slit at eye level.

The interrogator asked about Kfar Etzion. When Rivkah was finished describing the ordeal, the woman called Rivkah a liar. She did not shout.

"No massacre happened in Kfar Etzion. There was a battle. The Jews lost."

Rivkah didn't insist.

The interrogator asked questions Rivkah could not answer well, about the defenses of the Etzion bloc and the plans or abilities of the Haganah. Rivkah repeated her opposition to war; each time the woman shrugged to imply Rivkah's opposition came too late.

After a half hour of fruitless tension, the interrogator pointed to Rivkah's bulging belly. Rivkah sat with her legs spread, the only way to be comfortable. She needed to urinate; the baby was pressing on her bladder.

"When are you due?"

"Three months."

"May I?"

Rivkah said, "Yes."

The woman laid a hand on Rivkah's bump. The interrogator gazed at the back of her own hand, blinked, and smiled privately, some wish or woe. Rivkah tried to lay her own hand over the interrogator's, but the slit in the door closed and the woman withdrew.

A tall man entered: handsome, clean-shaven, the eyes of a crow. He wore a business suit and a red-checked keffiyeh. He carried no weapon in his large hands.

The woman stood; the new occupant of the room slid the vacated chair further away from Rivkah. When he sat, he crossed his long legs at the knee. The woman faded against the cinderblock wall.

In Hebrew, he said, "You're not a soldier."

"No."

"You're a kibbutznik."

"Yes."

"What can you tell me?"

"Only what I've seen."

"I'm sure that is already too much. How is your child?"

"With me."

"Of course."

The interrogator crossed his arms to behold Rivkah.

"Do you believe you'll give birth under your olive grove in Massuot Yitzhak?"

"I understand it has been burned."

"It has."

"We will plant another."

"You won't. You will not see Gush Etzion again. You will not win this war."

"No one will."

"It may appear that way at first. Driving out the Crusaders took us two hundred years. We are in no hurry."

"And we have nowhere else to go."

"Why should that be an issue for the Palestinian people?"

"It should be an issue for all people."

"Sophistry. You think that is why you should take land that belongs to others? Because you are desperate?"

"I believe we can share the land."

"Too few Arabs and Jews agree with you. So there is war."

"And if there is war, our backs are to the sea."

The interrogator got to his feet. He had no more to ask, only more to say.

"Fifty years ago, my father sold land to the Jews. Why shouldn't he? The Jews should have homes, as you say. They were my father's boyhood friends. The Jews and my father worked together, broke bread together. He thought of you as cousins, you share the same patriarch in Abraham. Then you came to Palestine in greater numbers, you bought more land. What you did not buy, you claimed, as if the ground was just waiting for you. In this war, what you have not purchased or claimed, you will try to take."

The interrogator strode to the door. With his hand on the doorknob, Rivkah spoke.

"Tell me."

He turned.

She asked, "Why isn't it a good thing that we're here? Can't we add to each other's wealth? Why not build a better nation together?"

The interrogator released the door. He did not sit again in the hard chair but strode in front of it to bend at the waist. With arms buttressed on his knees, he spoke to Rivkah as if to a child.

"There is a slogan in Europe and America. The Zionists use it to raise money to bring Jews to Palestine. Do you know it?"

"No."

"They say Palestine is a land with no people, for a people with no land."

The interrogator stood to his full height, hands pressed at his chest. "As if I am not standing here. Do you hear the erasure of me?"

"Yes."

"This is the argument of all colonists. The natives who were there before you were just backward nomads in a wilderness. Do you hear how condescending you are? My grandfather planted a thousand hectares. My father taught me to read Latin. Arabs do not need Jews to build us a better nation."

"I'm not a colonist."

"No, you're not. You're something worse." The interrogator aimed at Rivkah's belly. "We let in one Jew. Now there are two. You are the reason it is *our* backs to the sea."

He indicated Rivkah's crusted tunic.

"The people who did this. Did they shout Deir Yassin?"

"Yes."

"Know this. Your great-grandchildren will hear the same shout."

The man exited quietly. He seemed not to be wicked. Perhaps his father was dead. Perhaps he had his own child at home to explain the world to.

CHAPTER 6

GABBI

May 19
Tel Aviv
Israel

In a dream, Gabbi flew over a desert above a thousand Arabs. Soaring, she cast a shadow, fleet, undulating over the dunes. Like a fingertip down a dewy pane, Arabs disappeared in streaks where her shadow touched them.

She awoke in her room and sat up. The other hospital bed was empty. Across the hall a soldier moaned, someone else finding sleep hard. The hospital had sent most of its pain medication to the front and had little left for the soldier or Gabbi, only antibiotics.

She slid her left arm into her sling, put on a cotton gown, then wandered barefoot to the nurses' station. Quietly a radio played on the desk of the midnight nurse.

The woman asked, "Can't sleep?"

"Can you turn the radio up?"

"I don't want to wake anyone."

"Just a little."

The nurse nudged the volume. The program was American band music broadcast from Cairo.

Gabbi tapped her bare toes; the nurse drummed fingers on her desk until she looked up with a brightened face. Gabbi turned to the sleepless soldier who'd come out to join them.

He'd wrapped himself in a royal blue terry robe and slippers. Black coils covered his crown, his beard was long like a religious man's. His skin was dark and his sage green eyes seemed out of place.

Gabbi said, "Sorry if we woke you."

He stuffed one hand in a pocket. With the back of the other, he batted away her apology.

The soldier measured her, then padded back to his room.

✳ ✳ ✳

In thin morning light, the soldier entered her room. He sat on the empty bed and took from his robe pocket an orange.

Gabbi sat up against the wall. With her good right arm she reached for the orange.

He said, "I'll peel it for you."

The soldier drove his thumbs into the navel of the fat Jaffa, then spread the slices apart like petals. He lay them in Gabbi's lap so she could pluck them.

Deep in the city, an explosion boomed. The Arabs shelled Jerusalem through the night and past dawn to keep the Jews awake.

The soldier produced a second orange and set to trimming away the rind.

"What's your name?"

"Gabbi."

"I'm Tarek."

She indicated his hands, dusky around the bright orange. "Are you African?"

"My parents are *Teimanim*." Yemeni. "I was born here in Tel Aviv. Do you want to hear a story?"

It seemed odd, to sit as a stranger, present an orange and tell a story after last night when he hadn't spoken at all. Perhaps by this morning he'd grown lonely enough. Tarek's eyes were not serene but sea green and stormy.

"Okay."

"When my mother was nineteen, she heard about a rich Jew in England giving away land in Palestine. She walked two hundred kilometers from Sana'a to the Red Sea, to get on a boat. When she passed through my father's village, he asked where she was going. He was nineteen, too. He ran back to his home, packed a bag, kissed his parents and caught up with her. He had a valise in one hand and offered the other hand to her. She took it."

"That's lovely."

"And you?"

"Austrian."

"Where are your parents?"

Gabbi shook her head.

Tarek said, "I'm sorry. Forget I asked."

She ate another slice of orange. Gabbi didn't want to reward Tarek with her sadness for the treat and the tale he'd brought into her room. Oddly for such a poor first impression, he seemed to enjoy talking now. Gabbi pointed to the gauze wrap under his terry robe.

"Ribs?"

"Fractured two."

"What happened?"

"I came home on leave for a few days last week, just in time for the Egyptians to bomb Tel Aviv. A shell hit my father's shop."

Tarek tugged at the collar of his robe. "He brought me this yesterday. And the slippers. The nurse said you can't keep your eyes off them. You want them?"

"I'm leaving tomorrow."

"Where to?"

"I'm not sure."

"Why not?"

"No one knows I'm alive."

Tarek cocked his head. "Where were you hit?"

"The Etzion bloc."

"You're a farmer?"

"No."

"Soldier?"

"Palmach."

Tarek covered his heart and dipped his brow. It was the sort of respectful gesture Malik might make.

Gabbi said, "The Arabs murdered my sister at Gush Etzion."

She'd not said this in five days.

"I'm so sorry."

He knit his hands in his lap and tapped the pads of his thumbs.

After moments, she said, "Tarek."

"My mother." In the silvery light he looked up with rimmed eyes. "She was in the shop when the bomb hit. The place was on fire. I got my father out, then went back in for her. A timber fell on me."

He said no more of what happened inside his father's burning store, as she'd said little of Gush Etzion, or her mother and father. The rest of these stories spoke of themselves.

Tarek said, "I've got an idea."

"What?"

"My battalion's standing up a commando force. Jeeps with machine guns. Fast and nasty. We'll hit the Arabs behind the lines, then scoot off into the desert. Can you drive?"

"No."

"Can you shoot?"

"Yes."

"These ribs are supposed to keep me here a few more days. I can talk my way out a little early. Come with me."

"Can I do that?"

"Why not? You're dead."

Tarek sat on the edge of her bed. He extended a hand, dark like the shadow in her dream.

Gabbi rested her palm in his.

CHAPTER 7

VINCE

Samakh
Israel

Artillery jarred the Israelis awake. Vince scrambled outside the mud hut where he'd slept.

The bombardment was short-lived. As dust settled, the chink of tracked vehicles scrawled through the dirt lanes of the village. Vince dashed to the trench to get a better view of the Syrians' return to Samakh.

He jumped in among the Haganah under the date trees, so early in the morning that their shadows stretched behind him. From the east advanced three dozen armored vehicles. At their head rolled ten Renault two-man tanks. Behind the French light tanks marched three hundred Arab infantry belting out loud as they marched to the blats of bugles. They shouted, "*La ilaha ill Allah wa Muhammad rasul Allah.*" There is no God but God, and Muhammad is the messenger of God.

The Arab infantry didn't repeat their mistake from two days ago; now they stayed behind the cover of their rolling armor. The Israelis' anti-tank cannon announced itself as it had done before, singling out a battlewagon to make an example of it. But after only a few flaring rounds, the gun jammed and quit.

This left the Jews nothing to counter the Renaults. The tanks gained boldness and speed; they drove up behind the blasts and smoke rings from their short cannons, driving hard ahead of the cheers and tooting bugles of their infantry.

The ten French tanks stood off at three hundred meters and tore up the village. They struck at the Israelis' dug-in positions, every bunker and standing structure. Everywhere the Jews took flight.

A runner arrived at the trench.

Panting, the boy shouted, "Retreat," then sprinted off.

All the Israelis leaped up and ran. Vince ran with them.

They bolted away from the Syrians, west through a kilometer of plowed land to the neighboring fishing village, Degania Alef. The soil underfoot was loose and slowed the routed Jews' retreat. Syrian shells and bullets hounded them.

A hundred Haganah fled on all sides of Vince. There should have been two hundred but they were felled in the fields and were left behind.

Degania Alef

Vince walked among weeping Jews. They cried as they rammed shovels into the ground, deepening foxholes, filling sandbags. He captured none of it in his notebook; how could he be seen scribbling about the soldiers left in Samakh's rubble and cratered fields? The young defenders of Degania were certain they would join their dead friends and die tomorrow in battle, in this place where the Jordan flowed into the Galilee.

At sundown, two jeeps pulled in from the west. They came in quick since they'd entered the range of the Syrians' cannons. Vince followed the arriving delegation into a stone house.

Around a large table sat a soldier and five members of the Degania council. Vince pressed his back to a wall. He took out his notebook and pulled the pencil from behind his ear.

That morning, five settlers had rushed south to Tel Aviv to plead with the government for reinforcements to save their kibbutz. At the table now with them sat a one-eyed major, a native son of Degania Alef, the new commander of the Jordan Valley's defense. He wore a black silk patch over his left eye socket. His name was Dayan.

Dayan asked the first question. "What did Ben-Gurion say?"

The first settler to answer wore a grimy white shirt and suspenders. Vince supposed he'd appeared like that before Israel's prime minister.

"Ben-Gurion said there aren't enough guns or men to go around. The whole country's a front line."

"So he's not sending reinforcements."

"No."

"Did he give you any orders?"

"He said hold our ground."

"Did he happen to specify how?"

"Yes."

"And?"

The settler glanced about at the others who'd been there when the prime minister spoke. The farmer seemed to want assurance that he'd heard Ben-Gurion right. Another kibbutznik held out a hand, to say go ahead. Tell him.

"He said to wait until the Syrians are on top of us. Then fight."

This did not jar Dayan. He asked, "What else?"

Vince jotted in his notebook how the one-eyed Jewish major who'd been ordered to die in place asked, What else?

"He's sending some cannons. Four of them."

"What are they?"

"Mountain guns."

Dayan repeated, "Mountain guns."

"Ben-Gurion said it was all the artillery the Haganah had."

Another farmer spoke up: "He wanted them to go to Jerusalem. We changed his mind."

Dayan chuckled and patted the table with one hand. He didn't explain himself, but he knew these mountain cannons and they made him laugh.

"When will they get here?"

"Noon tomorrow."

Dayan stood to conclude the meeting.

"Then it seems our task is to still be here at noon. Gentlemen."

Before Vince filed out, Dayan asked him to remain.

"Mister Haas."

"That's right."

"Thank you for everything you've done for Israel."

"Just reporting, Major."

"Do you have questions for me?"

"How many soldiers were left behind in Samakh?"

"Fifty."

"How many have you got left?"

"Seventy in Degania Alef. Eighty in Degania Bet."

"You got enough guns?"

"Every fighter has a weapon now."

"Against three hundred Syrian infantry and two dozen tanks."

"Mister Haas. I understand you were in Samakh."

"I was."

"Then I assure you, you have seen the first and last victory of the Syrian army."

Vince set down his notebook and arranged the pencil beside it, neat like a table setting.

"How do you figure?"

The major leaned forward. Vince had an urge to cover one eye, to see how Dayan saw.

"That is the wrong question to ask."

"Okay."

"The armies of five Arab nations have invaded Israel. Do you know what they are fighting for?"

Dayan wanted to provide his own answer. Vince shrugged.

"I don't believe they know, either. Certainly, they hate us. But to hate a Jew in Cairo or Amman, in Beirut or Baghdad, that is one thing. To carry that hate across a border, to invade a place where the Jews pose them no threat? To risk your own life for hate? That is more abstract. The question you must ask is this: Will the Arabs' hatred be enough when Israel fights back?"

Dayan motioned for Vince to follow outside the small house.

Under a waxing half-moon, the digging continued around Degania Alef. Dayan cocked an ear to it, pleased.

"Five Arab armies have come with thirty thousand troops. Why do you think they brought so few, Mister Haas?"

"They don't figure you stand a chance."

"Of course. How can the Jew stand against the armies of five Muslim nations? What are we to them? Half a million surrounded by seventy million?"

Dayan issued a hiss, a *fah*. "To them, the Jew is a merchant. A money handler. A violin teacher. But do you realize, four of the five Arab armies who invaded us have never fought in a war? Only Transjordan's Legion has been blooded, and they are just five thousand. We have thirty-five thousand soldiers in the field. That number grows every day Israel exists."

Dayan waggled a finger above Vince's notebook, insistent that Vince take notes.

"The Arabs believe they are seeing the rise of the Jewish warrior. They are not. They are seeing his return. And remember this, Mister Haas. We are not five different countries with monarchs and a hundred tribes. Israel is one. We will act with one purpose."

"What is that purpose exactly?"

"Survival. I assure you, I will not lose Degania Alef. Shall I tell you why?"

"Yeah."

"Because I was the second child born in this kibbutz."

Dayan rested a hand on Vince's shoulder.

"I will have a car take you somewhere safe so you may write that we will win."

Vince donned his straw hat and slid the pencil into the hatband. "That's okay. I'll see you tomorrow at noon."

CHAPTER 8

VINCE

May 20
Degania Alef

Before sunup, a Haganah crier banged tin plates to rouse the defenders of Degania Alef: "Get in your holes!"

For the first time in days, Vince sat up on a mattress instead of the ground. He poured water over his head from a bucket he'd brought in the little house last night before retiring. He donned his straw hat and walked out under a blue-black sky. Soldiers and settlers jogged to their positions, bootlaces dragging.

Vince squashed his long legs into a foxhole, then pulled his knees up under his chin.

The pan-banger quit; he, too, had gotten under cover. Minutes later, in the first inky light, the Syrians opened their assault. Mortars and artillery quaked the ground, concussion waves coursed above Vince's straw hat. He plugged his ears with his fingers.

✳✳✳

When the all-clear sounded, Vince climbed from the foxhole. He shook the grit out of his hat, knocked the dust off his shoulders, and stretched his back. On every side of him, fresh craters smoked. Vince took a moment to be aware of his luck, standing in the middle of so many smoking holes. But Rivkah might be dead, and he hated himself in the moment for thinking his luck was good. Vince hurried across a paved road to a trench, to bury himself again in the war. A Haganah fighter lent him a pair of binoculars.

A half kilometer to the east, Vince counted another dozen Renault tanks with the sun low on their steel backs, rumbling out of Samakh. Fifteen armored cars trailed the tanks. Every cannon and machine gun pointed at Degania Alef.

Vince returned the field glasses. He asked the young fighter, "You want to say something for the newspapers?"

The soldier said, "We'll hold."

Vince sprinted to a lemon grove. A squad of Haganah lay hidden under the yellow-green fruit. On the short road from Samakh, their dozen guns were the Jews' first line of defense.

Three hundred meters away, the leading Syrian tanks reached Degania's perimeter fence. Behind the Renaults advanced two hundred Arab infantry skirling battle cries.

The first tank squashed the perimeter fence; far behind it, Arab infantry yelled bravely. The rest of the Renaults followed through the wires. In a wedge they rumbled over the fields.

The first tank lined up against a concrete pillbox at point-blank range. The cannon fired twice; both salvos pounded the hardened walls. The Renault idled while smoke billowed across the ruined face of the pillbox. The tank seemed almost to gloat.

Then out of the pile emerged a dozen boys. They didn't run away from the Arab tank but scurried right at it and the two tanks flanking it. Quick-footed, the boys lit the rag fuses on several Molotov cocktails. Three of the boys ran close enough to smash burning bottles against the first Renault's armor.

Flames swarmed around the hull and in the undercarriage. The tank's hatch was flung open; the two-man Arab crew bailed out before they were cooked alive. Another tank took a Molotov to the face, then turned from the battle with fire licking its turret like a tea kettle. A third tank threw a track after several grenades erupted under its belly. Empty-handed, the boys galloped across the cropland without a shot fired after them. In Degania Alef, every Jew cheered.

From a limestone house on the rim of the kibbutz, a 20mm autocannon, hidden until the right moment, cranked up. The gun made a racket like hammers beating chains, striking a trio of armored cars behind the burning tanks. All three Arab battlewagons shuddered, riddled by armor-piercing rounds, then came to a standstill.

The Syrian assault hesitated but did not halt. Nine more Renaults and a dozen armored cars rattled across the plowed fields. Arab mortars in Samakh found the Jews' autocannon; within moments, the stone building that housed it vanished under the thunder of three direct hits.

A hundred Syrian infantrymen edged closer behind the tanks. Several Renaults came within fifty yards of the Haganah's forward trenches. In Degania's bunkers and in the lemon grove, the Jews held their fire.

One Arab tank raced into the middle of the kibbutz. It paused, exhaling black fumes, with many targets to pick from. Its short cannon flashed first at the nearest stucco house and blew a hole in the wall. Five Haganah fighters limped out and scattered.

A defender popped up in a foxhole twenty yards on the right flank of the tank. From the hip, like a gunfighter, he fired a PIAT anti-tank weapon. The report knocked him backwards, down again into his hole. The shell exploded against a bogie wheel, causing the tank to howl then halt.

Another boy leaped out of the same foxhole. Bolting straight at the disabled tank, he flung a burning Molotov against the driver's slit. Gasoline-fed flames gushed across the tank's front as more defenders in other holes bounced up. The Renault tried to withdraw but with a terrific screech threw a tread and could only go in a circle.

The tank stopped. The hatch opened but the Haganah fighters in the lemon grove peppered it to make sure the Arab crew stayed inside their deathtrap. More fire was splashed on the tank; in the center of the kibbutz, with the engine running, the Arab tank became an inferno.

Then all the defenders of Degania opened up.

The shooters under the lemon trees pinned down the Arab infantry. More Jews zigzagged in the open with burning bottles, flashing like fireflies. The boy with the PIAT kept popping up in his foxhole, firing from the hip. The Arabs' mortars continued to bombard Degania, but the Israelis did not take a step back.

The Syrian advance into the settlement stalled; only the burning tank had made it past the lemon grove and the trench.

An Arab trumpet declared itself over the battlefield.

The Syrians turned their backs on Degania.

✳ ✳ ✳

In the afternoon, the Israelis rearmed, broke out their rations, and wrapped their wounds. Six dead Haganah were taken away in jeeps while the Sea of Galilee sparkled. In the kibbutz, Vince borrowed a farm truck. He wanted to go take a look at the only four artillery pieces in all the Israeli army. The ones that made Dayan laugh.

A mile and a half west of Degania, Alumot Ridge was steep, not tall. On the western side of the Jordan, the crest rose a hundred and fifty feet above the river valley. Vince shifted gears to keep the old pickup climbing.

On top of Alumot, crews from a five-truck convoy maneuvered four mountain cannons to face the Syrians. The 65mm guns looked like field pieces from another century, just four-foot-long tubes mounted between wooden wheels.

Vince approached, tapping his press armband. One gunner waved him over. Vince pointed with the eraser of his pencil.

"What the hell is this?"

"This is *Napoleonchik*."

"Will it work?"

The gunner repeated: "Will it work?" In Russian, he said, "*Yob tvoyu Mat.*"

With the back of his hand, the Russian shooed Vince back several steps. All the crews wrestled their vintage cannons into position to fire over the sea.

The Russian said, "We have no gun sights. So, we get range over water. Like so."

He clapped his hands over their ears, Vince did the same. The mountain gun woofed a gout of flame but the recoil was surprisingly soft. Far out over the Galilee, a fountain marked the shell's landing. The Russian and his crew conversed, then opened the breech to shove in a second round. The next crew in line fired out to the blue water to pinpoint their own gun's aim.

The cannoneer patted his artillery piece. "This one I call Sultan Kebir."

"What does that mean?"

"Lord of Fire. It is what the Egyptians called Napoleon."

"How far can these things reach?"

The Russian said, "Four miles." He pointed east to the Syrian army encamped in the fields outside Samakh. "They are two."

✳ ✳ ✳

The gunners on Alumot fired gleefully, ramming shells into their cannons as quickly as the barrels could let fly. All the muscular boys had a sheen and were roundly deafened.

Beyond the river and the Deganias, the Syrians found out they hadn't brought the only artillery to Galilee. Through binoculars Vince watched explosions walk across Samakh; the Arabs pinballed around, looking for shelter. Ten minutes after the bombardment began, Syrian vehicles began to bolt further east to get out of the range of the Jews' old artillery on Alumot.

The gunners, powder-stained, dark as coalminers, shouted with every report as though they might speed the shells on their way. The accuracy of the 65s was impressive, even without gunsights, and their power was unquestionable. The four crews fired in broadsides like a warship. One lucky round from a *Napoleonchik* set off a fireball in the center of Samakh, a boiling blast that echoed over the Jordan Valley.

The smiling gunner said, "Ammo dump."

Once Samakh lay in heaps, the Alumot gunners turned their heated barrels on the Arab tanks and infantry camped in the fields.

The first volleys set three armored cars on fire. Flames crept into the crops then spread to the Syrian infantry's tents. The Alumot gunners didn't slacken but fired more, cracking craters in the earth in front of the retreating Arabs, nipping at their heels.

When they were done, the four mountain guns rested; heat mirages wriggled above their barrels. Samakh had been wrecked and deserted; the open fields smoldered with no Syrians moving in them. The Alumot gunners divvied up cigarettes. Vince left them to their moment and drove away; they'd earned the right not to share it with him.

Arriving in Degania, a soldier hailed him down. Vince pulled over.

"What is it?"

"We captured an Arab. A Bedu. He walked straight into the village. He says he knows you."

CHAPTER 9

MALIK

Degania Alef

Vince jumped out of an old truck. He needed to eat, change clothes, and stand in the rain.

Malik opened his arms for Vince to step into them. He squeezed, then pushed Vince out to arm's length to give him a good shake. A pair of Jewish guards inched forward.

Malik said, "Tell them we are friends."

Vince, still in Malik's grip, informed the soldiers that this was his very good friend; the guards filtered away into the remains of the kibbutz.

Vince looked a wreck, lank and scanty. The grey stench of gunpowder laced his clothes, hunger stained his breath. The scarecrow who'd already seen too much had seen more. Malik, as he'd done for Rivkah, had arrived just in time.

"It is good to see you, Vince."

"And you. It's been, what, six months?"

"A long time."

"How'd you find me?"

"You are not so hard to find."

From a billowy sleeve, Malik handed over the last column Vince had written for his American newspaper. The date was five days ago, the place: Degania Alef, Jordan Valley.

"You are Vince Haas."

"How'd you get here?"

"I followed the river north for three days. I camped last night outside Beit Yerah and waited. When the shooting stopped, I walked in."

"Where's your camel?"

Malik pointed west. He didn't know.

He moved to the remnant of a stone wall. Malik could ride a hundred kilometers but he'd just walked three and wanted to sit.

He stroked his beard to buy a moment, so he might speak his mind cleanly.

"Vince."

"Yes."

"I have always liked saying your name. It is like lemon in tea. Vince."

"What are you doing here, Malik?"

"I came to find you. I have something to tell you. But before I do, I see I must ask you the same. What are you doing here, Vince?"

"My job."

Malik gestured at the near-complete destruction of Degania Alef. Jews dug through the ruins for the bodies of their kind. Others limped or lay in the open for medical care. Fire guttered in the crannies of an Arab tank in the middle of the village; even a shallow breath brought the wrenching odor of burned flesh. On the road into the settlement lay many Syrian corpses, more sprawled in the scorched fields. The battle had been terrible, and narrowly won.

"Is this indeed your job?"

"What are you getting at?"

"I see no other journalists. Were they here, too? The British, French, even Israeli? Why only Vince Haas in Samakh and Degania?"

Vince patted knuckles into a palm, then pulled off his tatty straw hat. He combed fingers through hair still the color of maize but flecked with grey. A pencil stayed behind his ear.

Vince had begun to heat under Malik's words. Malik eased up, a lesson from the desert, to move slowly in the sun.

Vince said, "I haven't seen you in half a year. You show up out of nowhere and you won't tell me why. Has something happened?"

"Vince."

"Goddammit, just tell me, Malik."

Malik got to his feet also, to help Vince understand it would be unwise to swear again.

Vince turned a labored circle, looking for something in the scarred world. He may have found it by the time he circled back to Malik, for he returned to his seat on the busted wall.

"Look, you came a long way. Through a war. I appreciate it."

Malik remained standing. "I am your friend."

Vince hung his head. "I know."

He pointed a jeweled finger at Vince's chest.

"You are trying to hide from Rivkah. From your grief. You are stabbing yourself into this war like a knife. Careful, my friend. It may stab back and kill you."

Vince's head hung, perhaps under the crowning weight of Malik's truth. More likely his grief.

Malik said, "Lift your head. I have, indeed, come too far not to see your face."

Malik would have put a hand under Vince's chin if Vince had not raised it himself.

"Rivkah is alive."

A great and invisible grasp plucked Vince to his feet. "What?"

"She survived the massacre of Kfar Etzion. Five days ago I visited her in jail in Hebron. By now, she will have been taken to Transjordan. She asked me to tell you that your child will be named Chaya for a girl. Chaim for a boy."

In the desert Malik had seen many men stumble across the short span from life into death. Vince reeled over this bridge, too, though he came the other way. Malik caught him by the shoulders.

CHAPTER 10

RIVKAH

May 21
Prisoner-of-war camp
Umm el-Jimmal
Transjordan

Rivkah found it hard to bear more sun. Only the tents had shade, and inside them it was always sweltering.

She stood in line for a tin plate of vegetables, grains, and a cup of water. All day the ground drank heat and, like any drunkard, let go of it slowly. Rivkah worried that every drop of sweat robbed the child.

When they had their plates filled, the two hundred Jewish prisoners gathered on the heat-seeping earth. Rivkah took her food to her tent to eat and perspire alone.

She sat on her steel cot, one of eight mattresses. The canvas turned the light sallow while heat spooled in the tent's peak. Over her food, Rivkah cried in warm privacy.

When Red Yakob entered with his plate, she stopped her tears. He sat on the next bed.

He asked, "Are you alright?"

"It just got to me, that's all."

Red Yakob gave Rivkah his cup of water. He looked around, curious for differences from his own tent. He shrugged; the privations in the camp were similar enough for men and women alike.

"I've got something."

He set his plate on the sandy floor. Yakob wore the olive khaki tunic of the Haganah with no insignia. From a pocket, he pulled two creased pages. He rattled them before handing them over.

Rivkah spread them open. Tight handwritten columns covered the first sheet, front and back.

Yakob said, "This is every name in the camp. Three hundred."

"Did you do this?"

"Took me four days."

On the second page, Yakob's scrawl covered only one side.

"This is a list of the dead at Kfar Etzion. One hundred and twenty-nine."

Rivkah asked, "What are you going to do?"

"Escape. Publish these."

"What if they catch you?"

"I speak Arabic."

"You look nothing like an Arab. You're the color of a firetruck. We're sixty miles from Jerusalem. They'll kill you. No questions."

Yakob stood so she wouldn't argue. "People need to know we're alive. My mother needs to know."

"What can I say to you?"

"Be careful, maybe. Don't get shot."

"Yakob, be very careful."

"Like always."

"How will you do it?"

"Dig under the wire. Bribe a guard. I'm not sure yet."

"Yakob, you can't tell anyone else."

"I won't."

"You shouldn't have even told me."

He held up the paper of the murdered. "You were almost on this one."

When he was gone, she lay on the cot, beneath the child who, without a name, would have been on neither of Yakob's lists.

CHAPTER 11

VINCE

Degania Alef

Malik said goodbye to his camel.

The animal lowered the parabola of its neck to Malik's eye level. Malik spoke softly in Arabic while tapping between the camel's wide, tufted nostrils. The camel listened without blinking.

Vince waited, propped on a fender of his rental car, a Vauxhall, a former British staff vehicle that he'd stowed days ago in a garage in Beit Yerah.

Dayan leaned beside him, cross-armed.

Malik finished admonishing the camel, then threw his bedroll over a shoulder. He slid his long rifle from the saddle and brought it to Dayan.

"I assume I may not keep this."

"No."

"You will feed him, yes?"

"The farmers will take care of it."

"Do not try to ride him." He touched his forehead, then his heart, to Dayan. "*Shukran.*"

Malik said to Vince, "I am ready."

Vince opened the Vauxhall's passenger door first so Malik would not fumble with it and embarrass himself in front of Dayan.

✳ ✳ ✳

Jezreel Valley

Malik thrust his arm out the window to let his sleeve riffle and snap. Vince tried to talk with him but Malik seemed too amazed.

The Vauxhall whipped past cultivated fields and citrus orchards that walked up hillsides. In the broad spaces between settlements the Jezreel Valley opened to pastures of wildflowers. The war felt remote.

An hour west of Degania, Vince crossed the plain of Megiddo, the treeless tableland where the Bible said good and evil would stage Armageddon. Vince explained this to Malik, who reeled in his arm out of respect for the old faiths.

The road rose to a hilltop forest. When it descended, the tilled lands were worked by Arabs. Vince slowed to enter a village where children ran and women in hijabs carried baskets. Malik waved at some boys on donkeys to show he was in a car, but this was nothing special to them.

Vince pressed on southwest. The Jezreel was the breadbasket of the Jews, fertile and peopled, with room for much more. Malik took it all in with closed-lip wonderment. Never had he moved this fast, journeying a day's camel ride every hour.

Nearing the coast, Vince drove between two settlements, one Jewish, the other dead. South of the road, the village of Hadera pulsed with trucks and mule carts, ringed by vineyards and groves. Settlers moved in the streets like blood through a heart. Just across the road, barely fifty yards, lay a town half the size, without traffic. The fields were untilled and not a single sign remembered the place's name. Surely it had been Arabic. A few Israeli soldiers walked the village as though measuring it.

Malik said his first words of the trip. "Take me to the sea."

A mile later, Vince stood with Malik high above the Mediterranean on a yellow cliff. A hundred feet below, the water rolled itself white onto a small beach. A family sat on a blanket. Southward, the coastline turned rugged, the black rocks were pocked like sponges.

Malik balled his hands on his hips. Vince and he stood halfway between Haifa and Tel Aviv; each city was thirty miles away. Both skylines were dimly visible through the coastal mist.

Malik spoke above the blue water. "I had no idea."

"About what?"

"I have seen the Jews in the Negev. In Gush Etzion. In the desert towns, Bethlehem, Hebron, Beersheba. The Jews are so few in Palestine."

Malik put a large palm out to the wind as if to stop it, but it blew through his fingers.

"Now I have seen them in Israel."

On the horizon, a cargo ship plowed north for Haifa. Malik turned his back to it. He faced Vince, and behind Vince, a new nation.

"This," Malik said, "is where I must live."

CHAPTER 12

GABBI

Ruhama Badlands

Gabbi almost flew out of the jeep.

Tarek shouted for her to fire, but his madcap driving made her choose between holding onto her machine gun or shooting it.

She planted her boots hard on the floorboard while Tarek swerved through red poppies and yellow mustard. Behind her, standing fast in the rear of the jeep, burly Benny burned through his first ammo belt; brass casings tinkled around his boots. Gabbi took aim at nothing, just wild-flowers and desert clumps, and pulled the trigger.

She absorbed the recoils into her good shoulder. Racing across the uneven wadi, Gabbi loosed a dozen rounds from the dash-mounted weapon. Because the jeep could have no windshield, green and gold bits speckled Tarek's brown cheeks.

He yanked the wheel hard left and stomped the brakes, almost unseating her again. The jeep skidded sideways, opening the field to Gabbi's gun. She swung the machine gun, shifted her finger to the bottom of the trigger to fire on full automatic, and chewed through the rest of her ammo belt, fifteen rounds per second. Sizzling shells bounced off her lap.

Together with Benny's roaring gun overhead, Gabbi raked a patch of crimson poppies.

CHAPTER 13

MALIK

Neve Sha'anan
Tel Aviv

Vince showed his identification papers to Israeli guards blocking the road. They asked Malik for papers. Vince said, "He's with me." The car was impressive. Vince reminded the guards that his credentials were those of an American. He didn't wait for the guards' reaction and motored on. Malik patted him on the shoulder.

"The Jews call that *chutzpah*."

Vince took the big car down streets wide like canyons. Here, people lived and worked on top of each other higher than anywhere he'd ever been—windows over windows, balconies at dizzying heights, steel and stone built taller than temples. The desert towns Malik knew were a thousand years old, cut from stone carved out of the ground nearby. Tel Aviv was modern and foreign, made from nothing of the land under it, as if the city had been brought here from afar and assembled.

Vince drove by a crowd. People peered inside the passing car. He stopped beside a toppled streetlamp. Pale powder coated the pavement, the sidewalks, the trees, and many Jews.

Vince said, "The bus station's one block away. I'm going to take a quick look and be right back."

"As you say."

Vince donned his straw hat. "Stay in the car."

"Where would I go?"

"I'm serious, Malik. Leave the door locked."

Vince leaped out, locked his door, then disappeared into the throng. Every kind of Jew flowed past the parked car, young men in uniform, businessfolk in dusty suits, old men in suspenders, women in slacks, men behind beards dark as Malik's, boys in dungarees.

Two Jews, one small man with jug ears, the other in a skullcap and vest, approached. They stopped strides away and pointed into Malik's window.

They cried out to the crowd: "Here is an Arab!"

People clotted around the car. Some pedestrians came close enough to rap on the windows. A few more shouted, then more. *Arab.*

Someone pounded on a fender, another stood on the front bumper. Scarlet faces crowded the windows. The car swayed, tossing Malik side to side. He did not know what the Jews wanted, though he was certain what they were capable of. Any minute a rock or a brick would be thrown through the glass, hands would reach for him. The crowd had the cowardice of the nameless and many.

A grey-eyed man with a moustache pushed his nose against the glass. He screamed, "Egyptian!"

The car rocked harder. From his sleeve, Malik freed a *jambiya*. The grey-eyed man shouted, "He's got a knife!"

Malik could wait no longer for Vince.

He unlocked the car door. The swaying stopped. The grey-eyed man moved back. Malik pushed the passenger door open to step into the street.

None of the hundred Jews matched Malik's height. All of them smelled of charcoal and concrete dust.

Malik thrust out both arms, the curved knife firm in one fist. His robes reared with him, they made him appear giant and dark.

He showed the knife first to the grey-eyed Jew in the front rank, then drew the blade slowly across all their eyes as if slicing the air. Malik showed the crowd that another step would cost more than his own life.

The grey-eyed man spread his arms as if he might hold the others back. A woman did the same. Unsettled moments passed, moments that might tip one way or another.

At the rear of the crowd, the people parted. Above their heads, Vince shouldered forward, rushing like a horse through a wheatfield.

"No," he belted, "he's with me!"

The Jews made way. Out of breath, Vince asserted himself into the center of the faceoff between Malik and the crowd.

Vince huffed, "Get in."

Malik set the curved knife at the feet of the grey-eyed man.

"I am no Egyptian."

He climbed in and shut the car door. Malik slid his hands into his sleeves where he had other knives.

※ ※ ※

Driving off, Vince barely kept his eyes on the road.

"Didn't I tell you to stay in the car?"

Malik did not treat this as a real question.

White buildings coursed past, packed tight like teeth. Green, red, and striped awnings jutted over the sidewalks against the sun. The people of the city went in and out, up and down. Their time outdoors was their time between structures.

Malik spoke no more on the drive. The consequences of his decision to get out of the car would have been his alone, so he owed Vince nothing in the way of explanation. Vince seemed to swallow his annoyance, though he cast Malik many glances.

After ten minutes, Vince stopped the car in a courtyard between five bland buildings. These had been barracks; now they were a hospital. This was a cleverness of the Jews, to create what they needed from what they were left.

Vince said, "Stay here. I mean it. Stay here."

He entered the nearest structure and returned quickly. When Malik stood from the car, Vince said, "Walk behind me. Right behind me."

"I am no child, Vince. And if I am, I am not your child."

Vince blinked as he drew and expelled a breath through his nose.

"I'm protecting people from you, my friend. Please."

"As you say."

Vince led the way into one of the buildings. Inside, on tables and rolling beds, in rooms and in corridors, lay wounded soldiers.

Vince took hurried strides. Malik's dark robes brushed across the bandaged boys on their beds in the hallway. The wounded did not speak, only raised their heads to see him pass.

Malik followed Vince to a small ward. Curtains hid several beds; one window at the end of the room let in the day. Vince whispered with a nurse, then pulled aside the last curtain.

Malik was pleased that Mrs. Pappel was nearest the window.

CHAPTER 14

VINCE

Army Hospital No. 5
Ramat Gan

Vince held back the hospital curtain so Malik could enter first.

Mrs. Pappel sat upright in bed, her back against pillows, a book in her lap. At the sight of Malik, without taking her eyes from him, she set the book aside. Mrs. Pappel pulled her long braid in front of her.

"Hello, Malik."

He did not move forward until she beckoned him.

She said, "Hello, Vince. Thank you."

Vince followed into the small space and dropped the curtain. He'd spent the day in a car with Malik, watched him gaze over the sea and stare down a mob. Not for a moment had Malik appeared so grand as he did before Mrs. Pappel.

Color flooded her face and her shoulders came off the pillows. Vince hadn't seen Mrs. Pappel in two months. The absence of her left foot under the hospital blanket seemed to have worked no change in her.

Malik said, "I have a poem."

She said, "Yes, please."

He turned up both his palms in presentation:

"The legs of a bird are small.

The steps of a bird are small.

Why would a bird walk at all
when it can fly?"
Mrs. Pappel beamed. "Was that for me?"
Malik gestured as if to lay the poem beside her.
She said, "That was perfect. When did you write it?"
"When I entered and saw you."
"Vince, go borrow some chairs."
When he returned with two metal folding chairs, Mrs. Pappel was breathing hard into her hands. She spoke through her fingers.
"Rivkah's alive."
Vince arranged the chairs, giving Mrs. Pappel time to collect herself. He sat, Malik stayed standing. Malik would not sit while Mrs. Pappel was crying.
She wiped her eyes on the bedsheet, then waved Malik into the chair.
Vince said, "I'm going to go see her."
"How? She's in Transjordan."
"I'll get an interview with King Abdullah."
"Can you do that?"
Malik said, "He is Vince Haas."
Mrs. Pappel blew a small kiss to Vince. "Give that to her for me."
Vince asked, "How are you?"
"There's no infection. I still have most of my calf. The doctors tell me I can get a false leg, like a sailor."
"When will you leave the hospital?"
"Three weeks. They'll fit me for a prosthesis first. Then I have to learn how to walk with it."
"Get out of Tel Aviv as soon as you can. I'm not sure the city's safe. On the way here, I stopped at the bus station the Egyptians bombed. Forty people were killed. They're digging more out."
Malik raised one finger to Vince, to advise him to keep the afternoon's events between them.
Vince asked Mrs. Pappel, "Where will you go?"
"I have some money left. I'll buy a small place."
"Where?"

"I think Zichron Ya'akov. It's a lovely village, fifteen miles south of Haifa. We should be alright there."

"We?"

"Rivkah and the baby."

Mrs. Pappel broke off to give Vince a chance to speak. When he did not, she said it for him. "You, too."

"Does Hugo know you're in here?"

"I don't know. He hasn't visited."

Malik rose.

"I must return something."

Mrs. Pappel seemed to know what it was. She held out a hand while Malik twisted a silver band off his pinky. He placed the ring in her palm; she slid it over her thumb. Mrs. Pappel wore it admiringly for moments, then returned it to Malik. He slipped the band again onto his pinky finger.

He said, "I will safeguard it with my life."

"That's a bit dramatic. Let's hope there's no need."

Malik dipped his hands into his sleeves and drew himself up. For the first time ever, Vince heard him clear his throat.

"Missus Pappel. You cannot live in the desert. I mean no disrespect."

"None taken."

"I have never lived in a city, or a village. But I know how to live."

"Yes, you do."

"I will teach myself. To do as you do, inside walls. Under a ceiling. It is time."

"Oh, dear." Mrs. Pappel lifted hands to her cheeks. "Is this for me?"

"I have seen I cannot do it inside your country yet. Not while our peoples are fighting. But I will stay near you. I will become accustomed. Vince?"

Vince was so enthralled that it startled him to be called on.

Malik asked, "What is the nearest Arab city to Missus Pappel?"

"Lydda."

"How far?"

"Eight miles."

"How many Arabs live there?"

"Twenty thousand."

Mrs. Pappel, still astonished, asked, "What will you do there?"

"Woman, do not forget. I am a merchant. I have bought and sold guns from Germans, English, Turks, Arabs, Jews. I have done this in the Negev. I will do it in a city. There is war now. I do not worry."

"Do you need money?"

Malik held up both thick hands, studded with his gemmed rings.

Other than laying the one ring in her palm, Malik and Mrs. Pappel had not touched.

"When peace returns, I will come to Zichron Ya'akov. There we will see what is possible."

Mrs. Pappel blinked at Malik as if a wind blew off him.

"I wish for that."

He touched his lips, then his heart, to seal the promise.

Mrs. Pappel asked, "Must it be guns?"

"What do you mean?"

"Can you buy and sell anything else?"

"What else?"

"Food, perhaps?"

"If you ask. Missus Pappel?"

"Yes?"

"May I steal?"

Plainly the question made her happy.

"Malik."

"Yes."

"Have you ever had a wife?"

Malik spun on Vince.

"I will speak with her alone. Thank you. Bring Rivkah home."

Vince stood. He kissed the top of Mrs. Pappel's head and patted Malik's wide shoulder.

"Keep out of trouble, my friend."

"I cannot promise."

"Why not?"

"Trouble may come for her. Or for you. My friend."

With the slightest of shoves, Malik propelled Vince through the curtain.

CHAPTER 15

GABBI

May 23
Kibbutz Gevim

On her third try, Gabbi took apart and reassembled an MG 34 machine gun faster than Tarek. The rest of the company let him hear it.

Following that, she taught the company's twelve drivers how to read the stars if they were in the desert without a compass. Her Palmach brothers had taught her on many nights atop Yellow Hill at Gush Etzion.

In the afternoon, Jonny gave the jeep company permission to wash. Gunner Hillel, a whippet-lean and freckled lad, pretended to be Gabbi in the shower. He pantomimed how she might go about it. The joke was harmless and done in front of her. The company hooted as Hillel teased, and Gabbi laughed with them. Tarek snickered, too, even tossed the water from his glass on Hillel to watch him smooth it around. When the time came for her to shower, Tarek stood guard outside the bathhouse.

At dusk, before the evening meal in the barn, Jonny called for everyone's attention.

He was a barrel-chested South African, a former British officer. Jonny possessed the South Africans' love of meat. At every meal he traded Gabbi his eggs, vegetables, soup, or pie for her poultry or goat.

Jonny left the barn doors open; the evening air slipped through pleasingly. The company lounged, Gabbi slouched with the boys. Hillel

made a game of mimicking her exact pose as if he were still imperson-
ating her. Gabbi winked and the boys at his table shoved him around in
his chair.

Jonny let their play fade on its own. The company quieted, but it
dawned on them that something important had come. Jonny was being
gentle with them, like a last cigarette.

"Lady and gentlemen. The balloon's gone up."

The commandos came out of their slouches. Some prodded the fellows beside them, *here we go*. At Jonny's back, the sun dissolved into the
sand and, not far beyond that, the sea.

"Early last week, the Egyptians took a swing at the first two Negev
settlements in their way, Nirim and Kfar Darom. Both held out. Then five
days ago, they went after Yad Mordechai on the coast road. The Egyptian
army can't move any further north until they take the kibbutz. They've
thrown a thousand men and fifty tanks into the battle."

Benny asked, "How many defenders are in Yad Mordechai?"

"Twenty Palmach. A hundred and thirty farmers."

The commandos whistled.

Eli, a driver, said, "I know these farmers. I trained some of them.
They're old ghetto fighters. Poland and Russia. Trust me, they won't go
down easy."

Jonny continued: "Yad Mordechai's done everything it can do. The
fighting's been bad. Yesterday it was hand to hand. Half the settlement's
dead or wounded. They're out of ammo and water. Last night, they radioed that they're afraid of another massacre like Kfar Etzion. Tonight, Yad
Mordechai's going to fall."

Jonny shook his clasped hands at his company. He seemed excited
for their first combat mission; the gesture looked like prayer, too.

"Commandos, we're going to go get them out."

✳ ✳ ✳

The jeeps raced at fifty miles per hour, north by full lunar light.
They ran blacked-out through the desert on a vague ribbon of road.

Gabbi had no passenger door, no windshield, nothing to grab onto but a swivel-mounted machine gun that swung at every bump and curve. At one sharp turn it almost dumped her over the side before Tarek snagged her arm. Gabbi rammed one boot against the floorboard, the other on the dash, and dug her fingernails into her seat.

The night land whizzed by, quicksilver fast, knobby with scrub and thorn bushes. Out front of the twelve fleeting silhouettes, Jonny's jeep climbed to sixty. The Egyptian front line lay four miles away.

At seventy miles an hour, the blood danced in Gabbi's veins. No one had goggles; Gabbi's eyes watered. Benny whooped. He was a squat and thick boy with a low center of gravity, and over all terrains he never lost balance.

The jeeps slowed as they approached the medical station at Gvar'am, three miles shy of Yad Mordechai. Across the dark wastes, the dozen commando jeeps tested their weapons. The desert flashed as Gabbi racked her charging handle, checked the ammo belt, and loosed a clean three-second burst.

In Gvar'am, the jeeps loaded up on bandages, tourniquets, and medical tape. Benny walked alongside Gabbi, both carrying boxes.

He asked, "Can I tell you a secret?"

"Sure."

"If I see a really bad wound, I'm afraid I'm going to faint."

Benny's face angled down as if ashamed. Gabbi set her boxes in the back of the jeep, then unloaded his armful.

"It's hard. At the first one, you might even turn away. But Benny. Benny."

She waited until the burly boy lifted his head.

"You'll turn around. You'll put the wounded and the dead on your big back and you'll carry them out of there. You'll do that, Benny." She touched his arm. "And we'll see you do it."

Jonny gathered the commandos around his jeep. He pointed to five crews, Tarek's jeep last.

"You five are on me. We'll go into Yad Mordechai. The rest of you will keep the way in and out clear. Engage only when you have to. When you do, go in hard. It's a big moon tonight, so there's no secrets. Any questions?"

Jonny let the commandos' resolve set in, let them elbow each other, tap one another on the back.

"Mount up."

The company clambered into their vehicles. Benny hopped over the tailgate to stand on the sandbags that protected him from land mines. Tarek took the wheel, Gabbi her machine gun. The three of them leaned together to touch heads once.

Jonny led the dark company overland into the kibbutz, staying off the paved road. At thirty miles an hour, the jeeps went into an arrowhead formation to keep out of each other's dust. Tarek drove second in line on Jonny's left, ten yards back. The first mile of the Negev hummed by.

The convoy dipped into a shallow wadi. Jonny ordered six jeeps to stay on the bottom of the gully out of sight, then powered up the short slope to lead the rest of the way into Yad Mordechai. Tarek got right behind him headed up the wall. Gabbi planted her feet and clung to her machine gun. The six jeeps crested the wadi; a mile east, battered Yad Mordechai stood on its hill.

A bright moon marked the commandos by their dust tails. The first shots came from some unseen Arabs in a trench or a crater ahead. Benny answered blindly with his first combat rounds while Tarek sped across the hardpan under a milky light.

A Palestinian rocket scuffed across the stars to explode overhead into a shimmering emerald light. Two more flares followed; all three bathed the desert in blinking garish green. The six lit-up jeeps dashed the final half mile to Yad Mordechai through small-arms fire. The green flares faded and the Negev receded again into moonlit grey.

Fifty yards from the kibbutz's breastworks, Jonny halted the jeeps. He shouted the password, "*Masada*." Above the defense berm, a voice called for them to come ahead. Jonny led the commandos inside the perimeter, past a fortified trench into the heart of the settlement.

Dark figures scuttled about, just fifty defenders still able to move and fight. Egyptian artillery had stripped bare the land surrounding the kibbutz; any Arab assault would have had to cross a wide-open killing field. Dugouts, tunnels, and sandbagged caves provided the defenders cover to ride out the barrages.

Jonny dismounted. He called to the defenders of Yad Mordechai, "Bring out your wounded."

Gabbi leaped from Tarek's jeep, Benny landed nimbly beside her. Tarek and the other drivers stayed at their wheels, engines running. Gabbi tore open a box of bandages. She pushed Benny in the back.

"Go."

With a stern nod to himself, the broad-shouldered boy strode towards the figures lurching from jagged buildings, trenches, and a dugout bunker. The ground was scorched and gouged; the whole ruined place smelled of fire and busted concrete. Thirty wounded moaned as they staggered into the moonlight, dirty as if they'd climbed from their own graves. Benny and the gunners jogged to help or carry them to the jeeps. Gabbi stayed with the jeep and the bandages.

Benny returned quickly with a Haganah boy who wore a sock hat pulled low over his right eye. Even on Benny's strong arm the boy stumbled. Gabbi helped lift him into the passenger seat. She pressed the back of her hand against his feverish cheek. The boy had used his hat as a bandage.

"I'm going to take this off you."

The jittery boy said, "No."

Benny held down his arms.

Gabbi peeled away the sock hat. The young soldier trembled and grunted while the blood crust broke. Gabbi took a close look at the wound: a bullet had scored a trough along the boy's skull above the right ear. The smell of sepsis turned her head. She dug into a box of gauze while Benny bared his teeth, stayed in place, and held the Haganah boy still.

She wrapped the soldier's head in fresh gauze; this eased the odor. Benny arranged him in the back of the jeep, then climbed up to stand over him, hands on his machine gun grips. The other five vehicles were still loading wounded and corpses.

Tarek said, "Let's go."

"Shouldn't we wait?"

"I can go faster alone. Let's get this kid out of here. We'll make it back that much faster."

Benny said, "Go."

The Haganah boy added his own weak voice. "Go."

Gabbi hopped in. Jonny didn't call to them as Tarek spun out of Yad Mordechai.

Tarek maneuvered into the stark no-man's-land. He sped straight east, not retracing the convoy's loop into Yad Mordechai but making a beeline back to Gvar'am.

With no headlights, only the moon to light their way, Tarek could not run flat out, but he pushed as fast as he might. Every bush and sparse tree that brushed by made Gabbi squirm.

The winding of the jeep's engine drew another round of flares; the Egyptians were everywhere around Yad Mordechai. The rockets burst red this time; Tarek laid on speed, able now to see the crimsoned landscape. More rifles cracked; a round flinted off the jeep's hood. Gabbi peered hard ahead for anything but the wind to move.

A mile out of Yad Mordechai, with two miles to go, flare after flare began to streak into the sky. The light on the desert turned dawn-like.

Suddenly, a chorus of machine guns blared behind Gabbi and the rushing jeep.

Tarek shouted, "It's the rest of the company!"

The other six commando jeeps had leaped out of the wadi, into the fray to yank the enemy's attention from Yad Mordechai to them.

Though no bullets whizzed past Gabbi, she swung the MG 34 searching, Benny too. Tarek leaned into the wheel like a jockey.

In the desert ahead, among the gnarls of brush in the bloody light, two clumps seemed to move. Tarek saw this, too. He swung the jeep to chase after them.

The outlines of two camels and riders emerged in the red night. The camels galloped west towards Jonny. Tarek cut a wide circle around the figures, keeping Gabbi's and Benny's guns on them.

Neither rider did anything belligerent, but both held rifles. Tarek told Benny to fire over their heads. He did.

The Arabs fired back.

Gabbi shoved her shoulder into the gunstock. She squeezed the trigger on automatic and cut down the camels. The straining engine, the weapon's bark, nothing could bury the squall of the beasts' dying. The camels didn't fold but keeled over and spilled their riders. Another red flare popped, well-timed for Gabbi to pump a clean burst into the two Arabs' backs as they ran away.

She tilted the smoking muzzle upwards. Benny asked something of Gabbi, but she paid no attention.

Tarek drove past the bodies. The camels had died with their necks stretched as if to finish a race; their fellahin riders lay spread eagled. They might have been innocent, just Bedu in the wrong place. Tarek turned east. Benny knelt to hold onto the Haganah boy while the jeep zipped over the desert.

Tarek leaned across the gearshift to Gabbi. He said, "That was for your sister."

She said, "My sister's dead. That was because Jonny said to keep the road open."

CHAPTER 16
MAY 30

AMMAN
TRANSJORDAN
By Vincent Haas

Herald Tribune News Service

King Abdullah Husseini of Transjordan accepted my request to pay him a visit.

I'll be the first correspondent in the Arab-Israeli war to cross battle lines and return.

At an airport outside Tel Aviv, I board a U.N. plane. We fly to Kalandia air strip in the hills north of Jerusalem behind Arab lines. A driver takes me east over the Jordan River, past the Dead Sea, past Jericho.

An hour later, I'm in Amman. The capitol of Transjordan is not a showplace. Like all things left in the sun, it can't hide its age. The city sprawls with languor, with little fresh blood to make it vital. There are as many shops as mud huts, as many donkeys as cars. It's a shoddy site for the throne of the Hashemite king.

My guide takes me to the fusty Philadelphia Hotel. I'm told to have lunch while the king finishes his nap.

In the middle of my first course, the driver reappears. It seems Husseini is eager to speak. I'm driven to a brownstone palace overlooking the city. In a conference room lavish with Turkish carpets and wall hangings, the king beckons me to a settee opposite his big chair.

The king is a short, lean-faced, dignified man with a tight goatee. He wears white robes and turban and, though he is royalty, crosses his legs and smokes like an American.

First, these are the rules: I must file all my copy through Arab censorship, I must seek no military information, and I will report impartially.

Husseini begins with an hour-long oration on the successes of his own Arab Legion. They've won every battle against the Jews. The war is going well for Transjordan. But he questions his allies, Syria, Lebanon, Iraq and Egypt. He reserves special disdain for the Egyptians. Since the time of the pharaohs, he says, they've suffered one military failure after another.

Husseini asks my own take on the war. I tell him the Lebanese and Syrians in the north, the Iraqis and his Arab Legion in the middle, and Egypt in the Negev, have between them not captured a single major objective. A few Jewish settlements have fallen after tough defenses, but Arab fighters are primarily occupying Arab villages and towns.

Meantime, the strength of Israel grows every day. Volunteer fighters and pilots from sympathetic Western nations flood in. Sizeable arms shipments are unloaded each night somewhere in the new nation.

The king says the Jews are breaking the terms of the United Nations' embargo on the import of weapons and immigrants into the conflict.

"The patrons of our Arab countries have been America, Britain, and France. All are members of the U.N.'s Security Council. None will defy the embargo to sell us what we need. In the meantime, the Israelis, clients of no one, stock up on black market surplus from the war."

Then Husseini says admiringly, "The Jews are well-accustomed to dealing in the shadows. For two thousand years they have survived beneath the feet of giants. They are a tenacious and resourceful people."

I tell him of an Arab friend who refused to give up his rifle to Husseini's Legion soldiers in Hebron. My friend killed one of them. Why are Transjordanian soldiers disarming Palestinians? Doesn't Husseini want the Palestinians to fight for themselves?

"No."

"Why not?"

"I am fighting on their behalf."

When the Arabs and Jews are done with their war, Husseini—who traces his lineage to the prophet Mohammad, whose ancestors ruled in ancient Mecca—intends to extend his kingdom west of the Jordan. He will add one million Palestinians to his subjects. Husseini will seat the new capitol of Transjordan in Jerusalem. He doesn't want the Palestinian people to feel they've won their own struggle, but that he has done it. On top of that, Husseini doesn't want the Palestinians to be well-armed just in case they prove to be less than grateful to him.

"After we annex what remains of Arab Palestine, we will live peacefully alongside the Jews in their own homeland. If they will stop seizing territory."

The king claims says that Transjordan didn't start a war to destroy the new Israeli state. Nor does he have any intention to restore the Palestinian people to their own homes. He admits that he and the other invading Arab leaders plan to keep all Palestinian lands they might conquer.

With this, Husseini admits to me that the Arab invasion of Israel is a land grab, at the expense of the Palestinian people.

He adds, "My advice to the Jews is to be more reasonable. My advice to the Arabs is to accept the logical."

This is a remarkable break with history. Husseini knows it. He's telling the Arab world to accept a Jewish state, an abhorrent idea to them for centuries. He tells the world, too, that he will be a king in Palestine.

I retire to the palace library to type this column. I'll file it later at the Western Union in Amman. After two hours in Husseini's library, I submit the copy to the king's censors. We wrangle for another hour; they don't like the king's candor about his allies, or the blatancy of his scheme to add the Palestinian people and Jerusalem to his domain.

Husseini weighs in with the censors. He tells them to leave everything.

"In order," he says, "to see what the Jews will do."

Reporting from Amman, Transjordan.

CHAPTER 17

RIVKAH

May 31
Prisoner-of-war camp
Umm el-Jimmal
Transjordan

The guard wore a moustache, with no beard, and a fez. Like all the guards, he was secular; a devout Muslim would not walk this close to strange and overt women. He carried no weapon inside the wire.

The gate and blockhouse stood at the far end of the camp. Rivkah followed the guard's quick steps; he moved like a pigeon, unnerved to be among so many Jews.

They strode past a hundred tents, all packed together. The tent rows foiled any breeze, the air in the camp stayed still and stale. At night, Rivkah listened to the snores and nightmares of her neighbors on all sides. The ground was dust, so dry it did not make mud when it rained.

At the blockhouse, the guard held the door open for her, then opened a second door to a room with bars across a single window. The guard followed inside.

Vince was on his feet before a little table, both chairs pushed in. He'd not sat while he waited.

Vince spoke to the guard. "Get out."

When the Arab did not move, Vince unfolded a heavy sheet of paper from a coat pocket. The guard glanced at it, returned it, then spun on his heels out of the room.

Rivkah asked, "What is that?"

"A letter from his fucking king."

She shook her head at him.

"You are Vince Haas."

They faced each other. Vince didn't approach. She did not extend her arms. The distance between them was short but immeasurable. Rivkah wanted to tell Vince, "I have seen so much," even knowing he might say, "I have seen so much." She was a prisoner, he was free. In a way, though, he was not free, because she and the child were his, and they were here, captured.

She asked, "What's in the letter?"

"You know what's in the letter."

"Vince."

"What."

"I can't go with you."

"You can. Just walk out of here with me."

"These are my people. I belong with them."

"Do you know how that makes me feel?"

"Yes."

"And you said it anyway."

"Yes."

"What about the child? That's my child."

"It's theirs, too."

Vince shifted his boots on the concrete floor as though readying to take a punch.

"Just say it. I'm not a Jew."

"Can you know how it makes me feel to have to say that?"

"No."

"It tears me apart. I love you."

Vince rushed at Rivkah. The distance between them collapsed, but the barriers did not. He could not push them out of the way, but he pushed so hard against everything that held them apart that he brought it all with him, crushed it between them, and held her.

CHAPTER 18

HUGO

June 1
Mugrabi Square
Tel Aviv

Hugo asked for a table away from the street, under an umbrella.

The young waiter sniffed at his particularness. "Can you wait?"

"You have no idea."

The lunchtime crowd had settled in at the sunny café. *Alte kachers* in their Tuesday klatches filled half the place, the rest was taken up by soldiers. Some boys were clean-shaven in spotless starched uniforms. The others, tired, slat-eyed, looked like they'd just slapped the desert off themselves and sat.

Hugo wasn't going to get the table he wanted so told the waiter he'd take any spot available. He was led to a two-top beside a group of young soldiers. The boys said nasty things to the waiter, derided him for not being in uniform. On leave from the front, they played at indifference and meanness, but they were fooling themselves. They remembered every awful thing, like Hugo. They eyed Hugo next. He spread his calloused workman's hands, his plumber's inky nails, to welcome anything they had to say. The boys returned to their beers.

Hugo reached into his jacket for a kerchief. Before dabbing his brow, he sniffed the kerchief to make sure it wasn't one of his plumbing rags. If it was, he didn't want it touching his face.

Pinchus appeared in the middle of Hugo's second beer. Hugo had told the waiter to leave the empty glass on the table; Hugo wanted Pinchus to see how late he was. He had no wristwatch to tap at Pinchus; if he wore a watch, he'd break it at least once a day crawling under someone's building, slinging wrenches, routing clogged pipes.

Pinchus wore a brown suit and vest, a watch fob, and his over-large spectacles. He was pale as ever, contained, a discreet man you'd forget as soon as you looked away.

Pinchus had no more need to live underground. But he held too many secrets. He was still more vault than man, and vaults stayed hidden.

The young soldiers paid Pinchus no mind when he sat.

Hugo said, "One day, I want to see you in a yellow shirt. Shorts and sandals and a straw hat with a big brim."

Hugo raised a hand for the waiter to come. He wasn't sure the waiter would notice if Pinchus did it.

Pinchus told the server, "A beer and an egg salad sandwich, please."

"Am I paying?"

"You're a working man now."

Pinchus slouched, hands folded across his vest and watch fob.

He leaned his head back and closed his eyes. He seemed to listen, or smell, or both.

Pinchus said, "On a day like this, it's difficult to remember we are at war. Though, to be honest, I can't recall a day when we were not."

"How's it going? I don't keep up."

Pinchus sat upright, alert now. He rattled a finger beside his head. "Some of us don't have that luxury."

"You've had other luxuries."

Pinchus lowered his hand, answered well by Hugo. He clapped lightly and spread a napkin across his lap, a show of gusto.

"The war. Let me see. Transjordan's Legion has advanced to Lydda ten miles to our east. The Egyptians are at Isdud, twenty miles south.

They are both attacking Jerusalem." Pinchus raised an empty hand as if he held a beer for a toast. "So, let us enjoy lunch."

Hugo left his own glass sweating on the table.

Pinchus asked, "How are you?"

"I sleep well knowing I won't see a noose in the morning. Or you."

"To that point, then. Why have I asked you to meet?"

"Should we discuss that now? I might not pay for your sandwich."

"I will eat it anyway, then fade away."

"What do you want this time, Pinchus?"

"The same thing I've wanted every time. To serve the interests of the Jewish people."

"You mean the interests of the Irgun."

"By that, I mean the Irgun."

"There's no Irgun anymore."

"Not entirely true. Tomorrow, in fact, we will sign an agreement with the government to disband and merge with the *Zahal*." This was the nickname of the newly formed Israeli Defense Force, hammered together out of the Haganah plus the dissident groups Irgun and Stern Gang.

"You're joining the Zahal. That's good. Yes?"

"But we will retain our Irgun force in Jerusalem."

"What for?"

"Jerusalem is not officially a part of the state of Israel. The United Nations has assigned it free-city status. So, we've taken advantage of that to exempt our force there from our agreement with Ben-Gurion. A few hundred will continue to fight under the Irgun flag."

"That can't make Ben-Gurion happy. He's going to accuse you of trying to keep your own private army."

"But we are not. Not at all. We have a Jewish homeland now. In Israel, we'll be builders and soldiers. We'll respect the government because it's our own government."

"Then why keep fighting as Irgun?"

"So that we will not be forgotten or swept aside. Our name, Hugo. Our legacy. We can't let this government silence us. Irgun did too much, paid too much, to bring Israel into the world. *You*, Hugo, paid too much."

Pinchus's beer arrived on the table. One of the soldiers at the neighboring table reached for it; Pinchus snapped his fingers in the boy's face. That was all it took for the lad to withdraw.

Hugo said, "You're a terrorist."

"I have been."

"A Zionist. You might be a fascist."

"I think of myself as a revolutionary."

"And you're a liar."

"True. How, specifically?"

"This isn't about legacy. It's another of your plays for power. You had more of it when Ben-Gurion was hunting you down. Now there's a war on and everyone's on the same side. I know you, Pinchus. You're not good at living in plain sight."

Pinchus eyed Hugo over the rim of his beer. He sipped, then set down the glass to wipe foam from a grinning lip.

"Plain sight, indeed. Nicely done, Hugo."

"Surviving you over and over gives a man insights."

"In truth, this is indeed about influence. But remember, my friend. With influence comes privilege. You'll be remembered."

"Don't remember me. Just keep my checks coming."

"Certainly."

"So why are you here? Now?"

The waiter set down Pinchus's egg salad sandwich. Pinchus didn't untwine his fingers in his lap but examined the sandwich, then the patio and all its patrons, the surrounding buildings, a great clock tower above Mugrabi Square, the trees and green patches, parked cars and traffic. It all seemed of a piece in Pinchus's gaze, as if he might still plant a bomb somewhere in it.

"Ben-Gurion is considering a truce with the Arabs. The Irgun disagrees. We oppose any halt in the war until Israel controls Gaza, the Negev, and all the land west of the Jordan."

Pinchus took a bite of egg salad, a reward for his own frankness.

Hugo said, "That's politics. You know I'm not political."

"But you are Irgun. That has been burned into you. And that is why you will say yes."

"Yes to what?"

"One more time. I need you."

"To do what?"

"To be an Irgun presence where there is none."

"The last time you said that, it turned out to be Deir Yassin."

"This will not be so treacherous."

"Are you lying again?"

"Alright. Perhaps it will not be so treacherous."

Pinchus took another bite of his sandwich while Hugo waited. Pinchus chose the oddest times to pause. The habit was a holdover from his life underground, the need to change habits, alter routes.

"The Arabs are blockading the road to Jerusalem."

"From Latrun. I know this."

"As long as there has been a Jerusalem, the road from the sea has run through the same east-west valley. That valley, you know, winds beneath the hill at Latrun. The Arabs have returned to the old British fortress there. From that height, they dominate the road. No Jewish convoy can reach Jerusalem under their guns."

"I've ridden that road, Pinchus. Have you?"

"No. And I may not have to. It turns out, there is another way into Jerusalem."

"Where?"

"A few kilometers to the south, there is a second, parallel valley. The hills keep it out of sight from Latrun. For two thousand years, this valley has been unpassable by all but shepherds and goats. Soon, it will be traveled by Jewish trucks. Then we will save Jerusalem."

"And me?"

"A secret road is being constructed. They're calling it the Burma Road, after one the Americans built during the war in the Pacific. Ten days from now, there will be a truce. After that, all work on the road must stop. I need you there, Hugo. I will not have it said the Irgun had no hand in the rescue of Jerusalem. I require your expertise."

Pinchus dabbed his napkin to his lips, interrupting himself again.

Then Pinchus said, "I want you to drive."

CHAPTER 19

MALIK

Lydda
Arab-controlled Palestine

The young husband petted the dray horse. Malik had given the animal no name.

The husband shouted after his wife as she walked back to their small house: "Bring everything I've set out. I won't carry it."

The husband wore a gold-embroidered kufi cap. He also wore his best suit, perhaps so he would not have to carry that out of Lydda. He'd wrapped an onyx string of masbaha beads around one hand to help him track the names of God. He looked to be a minor official or a small businessman. His house was in the Hara El Gharbiye, the western quarter of Lydda, on a good, cobbled road. The old bricks were clean on this street swept by the wives.

The husband said, "This is a fine horse."

Malik flicked at the notion like he might a fly. "This mule pulls my cart. I will shoot it when I am done."

"That is no way to treat an animal, brother."

Malik would not shoot the horse. He was playing a role. He appeared harsh to some, pious to others. For this fussy fellow, he acted the hard merchant, whatever would get him the best price. In the Negev, if a man could not adapt, he would not live. The city was child's play.

Malik stroked the pink nose of the nag. "I once had a horse. A magnificent beast. He was a grey, with a white mane so long that when it blew across your knuckles it felt like you were sliding your hands under a woman's dress. Eh?"

The husband chuckled behind his tight beard. He said, "Yes," though he'd likely never done such a thing.

Malik asked, "Where will you go?"

"Ramallah. The Jews won't take Ramallah."

"Why not?"

"The UN promised it to the Palestinians."

"Did the Jews make this promise?"

The husband snorted as if Malik were ignorant. He was of many things. Not of the Jews.

The husband rummaged through Malik's cart, laying hands on clocks, skillets, cutlery, anything with too much weight and too little value for the Palestinians to flee with.

"This is quite the haul."

"I stay busy."

"Are you Bedu? You look Bedu."

"I am."

"Then you've come to the city."

"I have."

"Why? To speculate on people's misery?"

"Friend, if I sell you food, I speculate on your hunger. If I sell you guns, I speculate on your fear." Malik spit in the road for the man's naïveté.

The wife came out of the house with an armful of pots and pans and a velour-lined case of silverware. Malik examined the goods fleetingly, then told the woman to dump it on the cart. The good old horse did not twitch.

Malik didn't haggle but paid what the man asked because the man had asked too little. He and his wife would be gone from Lydda within the hour. They had no vehicle, so on foot they would shamble east thirty kilometers to Ramallah. The walk would take them two days, perhaps three. Malik would circle back this afternoon and enter their little home.

He'd take whatever else the wife did not bring out. Or he might stay in their house for a bit; it was pleasant enough on a clean street.

Mrs. Pappel could not upbraid him. Malik paid a fair price for his wares. Whatever he removed from houses later had already been abandoned. That was not stealing.

Mrs. Pappel was right to tell him to deal in something other than guns. There were plenty of weapons in Lydda; two hundred legionnaires, plus a local militia. But a hundred citizens left the city every day. Pots and pans, knives and forks and clocks were lying about in abundance. Guns were not.

Later, Malik would sell his items to arriving refugees, those poor, tired, or scared ones who could get no further than Lydda. People running from the war, from burned fields and desolation, from villages conquered and occupied by the Jews then given Hebrew names. The ones straggling into Lydda would pay Malik twice what he doled out to the husband and wife.

Malik clucked his tongue beside his horse and cart. He called up the street, "*Shira'. Baya.*" Buy. Sell.

CHAPTER 20

VINCE

Tel Aviv

Vince stepped out of the UN plane onto the sunny tarmac. The slowing propellers blew heat backwards at him. He carried only a small overnight bag; the big Vauxhall waited in the airport lot. His room at the Kaete Dan across from Tel Aviv's beach awaited with a shower and a mattress.

A burly civilian in khaki slacks got out of a black Peugeot parked beside the runway. The man intercepted Vince on the way to the parking lot.

"Mister Vincenz Haas?"

"Yeah."

"The prime minister would like to see you at his residence."

"When?"

"Now, sir."

"Friend, I just got back from Amman. I slept on box springs in a bad hotel. I haven't had a shower in two days. I smell. Tell Mister Ben-Gurion tomorrow, okay?"

The man extended a thick arm towards the Peugeot.

Vince said, "Fuck."

He tossed his little luggage in the back of the car. Vince's shirt was wrinkled and sweat-stained; he set his straw hat in his lap. The driver made no conversation on the ride from the airport, likely a concession for how tired Vince looked.

Ben-Gurion's private home stood a block from the sea. Though palm fronds shaded his street, the sidewalk leeched summer warmth. The prime minister's house lacked soft angles and charm, just a grey two-story cube. The driver stayed with the Peugeot.

A young woman, perhaps an aide, answered the door. She ushered Vince through a humble sitting room. Ben-Gurion shouted down the staircase, "Come up, Mister Haas."

Vince had only met David Ben-Gurion once, weeks ago. Then, the prime minister was a frazzled leader readying for a war that by all military thinking was hopeless.

The squat old man at the top of the stairwell offered an assured handshake. He led Vince into a book-lined study. The spines were in Hebrew, Latin, and French. Vince had hardly taken a seat before Ben-Gurion said, "Off the record."

Vince tucked away his notepad and pencil.

The prime minister rolled his wooden office chair from behind his desk. His halo of white hair made him look like an overcast moon.

"Did Husseini really say he would live beside a Jewish state?"

"He did."

"Provided he has Jerusalem as his capitol."

"He said that, too."

"I gather from your column that Husseini is already tired of the war."

"He sounded that way."

Ben-Gurion laced hands over his belly then leaned back. The spring of his office chair squeaked. The prime minister's shoes tiptoed the rug.

"After reading your piece, I decided to remind the king that this is a war he started. Yesterday I sent three planes over Amman to bomb his palace. Eleven were killed."

"I know. I was in Amman. And you knew I was there."

Ben-Gurion smiled. "It would have been a tragedy. But see here."

The prime minister raised a finger as he shifted his round girth; he scooted his short legs forward to put his shoes flat on the floor.

"Our poor Husseini is in a trap of his own making. Him, Farouk, al-Quwatli, all of them have allowed their people to be caught up in a frenzy. In Cairo, Beirut, Baghdad, on every Arab street, Jews are despised. Their leaders claim to despise us, too, but in truth they are simply opportunists. They invaded claiming to support the Palestinians, but the facts lie elsewhere. They are in Israel only to stop each other from grabbing more than their share. And now, Mister Haas, they have grasped the ears of the tiger. You see?"

"I don't."

"They cannot hold on. They cannot let go. Have you had your afternoon tea?"

"No."

Ben-Gurion knelled a small bell from his cluttered desk. His aide poked in her head, took his order for tea and biscuits, and disappeared.

He said, "In this war, we are all young nations. Egypt has been independent for thirty years. Iraq, fifteen. Lebanon, Syria, and Jordan, less than five. When they invaded Israel, we were one day old."

The aide returned with a plate of white cookies. She left and came back with a kettle and cups on a platter. Vince accepted a filled cup. The cookies proved lackluster, but he'd foregone breakfast in Amman.

"The Arabs wish to increase their land and power. I completely understand. In this, we are alike."

Ben-Gurion took a quiet sip of tea.

"I'm told you left someone behind in Transjordan."

Vince set down his tea. He produced the list Rivkah had given him, prepared by Red Yakob.

"Here's all the prisoners from the Etzion bloc. This list is the dead from Kfar Etzion."

The prime minister took the pages. "You snuck this out? That took some balls."

"You'll publish the names."

"Immediately. Thank you. I'll see what I can do."

"About what?"

"About your friend. I'll send word to Husseini."

"She won't leave the others behind."

"Then we'll see about the others. Thank you for coming. I realize you must be done in."

"I am."

"I have one more question. The UN is sending an envoy to enforce the truce. A member of the Swedish royal family. Bernadotte's his name. You will meet him, I assume."

"If I can."

"I will appreciate any insights you may provide."

"When does the truce start?"

"In ten days."

"Why wait 'til then? Start the truce now."

Ben-Gurion set aside his teacup, then rocked out of the chair. He stood easily, spry and suffused. This was the head of a new little country that did not fold when the Arab world came crashing down on them.

"We have a little more land grabbing of our own to do. We will speak again, Mister Haas. My aide will see you out."

Ben-Gurion rang the bell.

CHAPTER 21

GABBI

Outside Kibbutz Negba

Tarek lay in the bottom of the wadi.

Everyone else kept their seats in the jeeps. The commandos had been out patrolling the roads since midnight. No one had much left in their canteens. Even at daybreak, the sand was warm, but Tarek preferred to snooze stretched out.

Benny used a boot knife to clean his fingernails. Gabbi drizzled water over her scalp and rubbed it in to have one place on her body that felt cool and clean.

Tarek lay face up, boots together as if he were in a grave. Benny nudged Gabbi and they shook their heads at him. She imagined lying beside Tarek on a sandy beach. Gabbi had never lain next to the sea. In Israel, she'd gone to the desert to find her sister and had not left it.

Benny climbed down to lie near Tarek. Gabbi nestled between them.

The sand vibrated with the pounding of Negba, even from four kilometers away. Every five seconds, another blast from an Arab howitzer battered the kibbutz's hundred and fifty defenders. While the earth shivered, Gabbi dozed holding the hands of both boys.

✳ ✳ ✳

All ten jeeps leaped out of the wadi. Tarek shifted fast and gunned his motor to tighten up behind Jonny; the rest formed up on Tarek's tail. Benny rode out the bumps and speed on his feet, Gabbi clung to the dash. Tarek stole a fast nod at her. Rushing into a battle, he was with her more than when he'd been lying next to her in the wadi.

Negba resembled a Bible scene, a place God chose to destroy. Plumes of dust hung over the settlement and did not drift away. Only a water tower stuck its head above the haze.

Out of the south, eight Egyptian tanks and five armored battlewagons approached kibbutz Negba, firing their cannons and machine guns as they came. Jonny sped the commando jeeps in a wide arc around the tanks, intending to avoid the Arabs' armor in order to get at their infantry.

The ten jeeps jounced over brush and uneven land. The Egyptian infantry was easy to spot, three hundred of them tramping in ranks a mile behind the tanks. The foot soldiers, too, looked biblical, an army walking in the Negev. Gabbi checked her ammo belt and charged the bolt of her MG 34.

Out front, Jonny raised a fist. Tarek did the same; every driver followed suit. The signal was given: the attack was on.

The commando jeeps sheered away from each other. Small-arms fire zipped over Gabbi's head; the Egyptians shot high, surprised.

Tarek swooped down on the infantry's right flank, rushing forward behind Benny's and Gabbi's braying machine guns. Two jeeps jetted up on either side, Hillel tail-gunning on the left, Shmuel on the right. All three jeeps trailed rooster tails. Their six machine guns howled with enough sudden firepower to stop the Arab infantry in their tracks. The Egyptians dropped to their knees. Jonny and two more jeeps jackknifed in from the left flank; the rest of the company circled and blasted away on their own, dipping and pecking at the Egyptians like seabirds.

The halted infantry set up automatic weapons, their Vickerses and Brens. Tarek and all the drivers wheeled away to scurry out of range of these bigger guns. Gabbi and Benny quit shooting, the Egyptians faded too far away to be worth the ammo. The Arabs fired at the commandos to keep them at bay, but their shots at the rabbiting jeeps sailed wild. The company carved dusty rings around the infantry who seemed content to stay put, defend themselves, and let their tanks handle the battle for Negba. This was the point of the commandos' assault, to sever the infantry from the armor. This made the Egyptians' tanks vulnerable.

Jonny sped up beside Tarek; he motioned for both Tarek's and Hillel's jeeps to pull over.

He shouted, "Either of you have grenades?"

Hillel did not. Benny had plenty. He heaved a heavy sack over to Hillel.

Jonny said, "See if you can cause some trouble for the tanks. We'll keep the infantry busy."

Jonny flashed away. Hillel's driver took off in the lead. Tarek asked Gabbi, "How's your throwing arm?"

"Good enough."

"Benny?"

Benny swatted the top of Tarek's head.

Tarek popped the clutch to see if he could send Benny tumbling out the back. He made Benny sit, that was all.

✳ ✳ ✳

The battlefield of Negba was flat, open land. Here the Negev began to lose its hold; the soil was rocky but held promise. The vista to the east and south was blank and endless. The farmers of the besieged kibbutz had watched their hard-won crops squashed by Egypt's tanks. Gabbi roared into the battle sowing Negba's soil with spent casings.

Side-by-side, Tarek and Hillel's jeeps knifed into the heart of the melee on the plain at the doorstep of the kibbutz. Both jeeps rushed first at a tracked armored car; two Arab gunners rode its open back, firing a Bren machine gun. The vehicle paced back and forth, protecting the flanks of an Italian light tank working over a concrete bunker on Negba's perimeter.

As the jeeps closed in, the tank fired at the bunker's face. The explosion sent concrete bits spinning through the air; Gabbi felt the concussion on her cheeks as she raced past. The Jews inside wouldn't be able to stand many more hits like that.

Both jeeps circled the armored carrier at fifty meters, trading rounds and betting on their speed. The hood of Tarek's jeep took punctures but so far the bullets had missed anything vital in the engine. Tarek meshed gears and kept the growling jeep skipping around the Egyptians.

Hillel's jeep slowed. Tarek zoomed past. Gabbi swung around to look back.

Tarek asked, "What the hell is he doing?"

Hillel's jeep bled speed fast. Something was wrong; maybe their engine had been hit?

Tarek wrenched the wheel hard. "Hang on!"

Gabbi clutched the gun mount to stay in her seat. Even Benny crouched. Tarek powered through his own dust cloud to reach Hillel's braking jeep. Gabbi and Benny fired nonstop to keep the Arab gunners focused on them. Blistering casings sprayed on Gabbi's legs and between her thighs, but she would not let go the trigger to shrug them off.

The tank blasted the bunker again. Hillel rolled off the back of his jeep, which zoomed away without him.

Tarek yelled at Gabbi and Benny, "Cover him!"

Through the battle haze, their twin machine guns struck sparks against the Bren carrier. On top, the two Arab gunners ducked behind the armor gunwales; they didn't see Hillel running up from behind. The boy's freckles gushed red as he dashed ahead, a grenade in each hand.

Tarek mashed the pedal to dash in front of the Egyptians, to lock their eyes on him. Benny's gun barrel yammered above Gabbi's head, the heat from it glowed on her neck. Tarek careened to stay out of the stream of bullets spurting from the Egyptians' Bren. Dirt kicked up in front of the jeep, Tarek slewed out of the way. Not for the first time, he caught Gabbi's arm to keep her in the jeep.

The Arab tank clanked closer to the bunker to finish the job. Across the battlefield, another tank, a British Locust, noticed the close-in battle with two pestering, swirling jeeps. It clattered their way. Benny slapped a fresh belt into his machine gun and continued to pepper the Bren carrier. Gabbi clipped a pair of grenades to her belt.

Hillel ran right to the backside of the armored car. He pulled the pin on one grenade then bowled it between the squealing metal tracks. The other grenade he armed, then flung up into the laps of the Bren gunners.

As Hillel turned to sprint away before the explosions, the machine gun of the oncoming Locust tank barked. Hit, Hillel spun to the ground.

The crump of the first blast was muted between the Bren carrier's tracks. The armored car rolled only a few more meters before grinding to a halt with a mechanical sigh. Hillel's second grenade detonated in the open top. A steel helmet flipped like a coin into the air.

Gabbi motioned Tarek to slow. "Let me out."

He shook his head, no.

Benny yelled down over his machine gun, "Let her out!"

Tarek said, "Gabbi," and nothing more. He speed-shifted down to second gear. Gabbi grabbed the jeep's doorframe and stepped out; she galloped alongside until she could keep her feet under her, then let loose. Tarek pulled away.

Hillel writhed in the dirt, clutching his leg. The motionless Bren carrier, gutted by the boy's grenades, belched smoke.

The Italian tank paused its onslaught of the bunker. The tracks churned to turn from the bunker, the cannon turret rotated towards Hillel. Eighty meters off, the Locust tank rumbled closer. Gabbi unhooked the grenades from her belt.

Smoke pulsing from the Bren carrier blew across the face of the defenders' bunker. Out of a tunnel entrance, one Israeli fighter emerged carrying two Molotov cocktails; both rag fuses were aflame. The man wore the clothes of a farmer, pants held up by suspenders, boots made for the fields, but he had a hard look, likely one of the Polish ex-partisans. He darted straight for the Italian tank that had turned its back to him.

The farmer smashed the first burning Molotov onto the engine compartment, down into the air intakes. Instantly the petrol ignited; gasoline-fed flames swept over the tank's motor. Wiry and quick, the farmer bounded to the front of the tank. He broke the second bottle across the driver's slit, blinding the tank with fire.

The treads stopped spinning, then the turret. The farmer, stunned by his own actions, stood still, chest heaving, to admire the results. Gabbi ran up close to roll one of her grenades under the hull. Seconds later, the grenade blew; the tank jumped like a kicked animal.

On top of the turret, a steel hatch raised. One Arab tanker scrambled out, then another. The farmer reached to the small of his back for a Mauser pistol. Striding forward, he emptied the magazine into the two Egyptians even as they jumped down through the flames. The tank had a crew of four. The others were left to burn inside.

Across the battlefield, the Locust tank closed relentlessly on the twin girders of smoke pulsing from its comrades. The Negba farmer cast a dulled look at the bodies, then dipped his head at Gabbi and Hillel before disappearing inside the pocked bunker.

Hillel said to Gabbi, "Get out of here."

She kneeled beside him to examine his wound; the bullet had drilled a clean channel through his left calf. Hillel wouldn't die from it. The tank coming their way wouldn't give him the time.

"This is going to hurt."

The boy grunted while she dragged him behind the Bren carrier. Gabbi leaned him against a bogie wheel. She stood clutching her last grenade.

Hillel said, "No, no. Stay here."

She leaned out from behind the inert Bren carrier. The Locust tank closed to inside fifty meters.

Hillel's jeep flashed across the parched battleground. Dust trailed it like a comet's tail, tearing straight at the British tank to intercept it.

Tarek and Benny roared up to the Bren carrier. Tarek slid the jeep sideways, spraying Gabbi and Hillel with pebbles.

"Get in!"

Benny jumped down to help Gabbi lift Hillel into her seat.

Tarek said again, "Get in."

"Get him to Gevim, then come back for me."

She tapped Hillel's shoulder. The freckled boy was grimacing so hard he'd shut his eyes. She poked him again. "Hillel."

"Ahh, what?"

"Reach in that sack. Give me another grenade."

With quaking hands, the boy pressed the grenade into her palm.

Tarek stomped the clutch. "Be alive when I get back."

Gabbi stepped aside as Tarek spun out in four-wheel drive. She watched the jeep go, Benny solid in the rear, Hillel holding on, Tarek driving off angry.

Flames engulfed the Italian tank. The haze it spilled was heavy, oil smoke. Gabbi pulled up her bandana across her mouth and nose. She would hide inside the black haze while the Locust drew near the burning Bren carrier, the Italian tank, and the bodies.

Forty meters away, Hillel's former jeep continued to dodge the guns of the approaching Locust. The driver, Elam, flipped grenades in the tank's path; none landed true, and the Locust screaked closer to Gabbi.

At thirty meters, she stepped from behind the Bren, a grenade in each hand. She crouched inside the dark boiling coils of smoke. Kotzer, the front-seat gunner in Hillel's jeep, blasted away while Elam tossed another grenade. They kept the Locust occupied and buttoned up. When the Locust had rolled within twenty meters, Gabbi pulled the pins on both grenades. She blinked away tears from the smoke coursing around her.

At fifteen meters, a fireball gushed beneath the Locust. With the sound of a struck anvil, the tank reared up onto one track, then came back down hard. Its diesel engine powered down while the tank seemed to gather itself. Gunner Kotzer bounced more rounds off the armor, Elam sped past but missed with another grenade.

The tank peered almost dumbly at the two blazing vehicles. It might even have seen Gabbi standing in the smoke, holding two grenades. The tank shuddered once, then a clatter came from deep in its frame; the Locust backed away in reverse, wary of rolling over another land mine.

Hillel's jeep gave the Locust a wide berth and let it go. Gabbi stepped out of the smoke so Elam could spot her. Further south, more Egyptian tanks and armored cars turned their tails and decamped from Negba. Gabbi threw away both live grenades under the burning tank.

✳ ✳ ✳

One at a time, the jeeps returned to the wadi east of Negba. Gabbi climbed to the crest to watch for Tarek.

Nine vehicles parked on the hardpan bottom of the wadi. Most were unscathed; a few had taken some Egyptian rounds. Hillel had been the only casualty among the commandos. Jonny took a radio message from Gevim that Tarek had gotten Hillel there safely; the boy would keep his leg. After that, no one knew where Tarek and Benny were. Soon after, another message came through. Jonny shared it with the company: Negba had held out, only eight defenders killed. The Egyptians lost a hundred.

Gabbi couldn't see Negba. A grey cloud had descended over the kibbutz; the Egyptians were exploding smoke shells to mask the retrieval of their wounded and dead off the battleground.

Jonny climbed the berm beside Gabbi. He handed her a pair of binoculars.

"You can stay one hour. I'll tell Elam and Kotze to wait with you."

Minutes later, eight jeeps of the company rolled out of the wadi. Elam and Kotzer spread a tarp out from their jeep to recline in shade out of the noon sun.

Gabbi lay on the lip of the berm with Jonny's binoculars. The glasses were no use. The Egyptians' smokescreen obscured all of Negba and the plain. The chemical fog crossed the wadi and settled in the basin. Gabbi raised her kerchief; behind her, Elam and Kotzer coughed and profaned.

She trained her ears out into the shifting grey haze. Nothing issued through the veil. The high sun ironed down any wind on the desert. The smoke hung in place as if painted there. Gabbi breathed through her kerchief.

An hour marched around her watch face. Elam and Kotzer left her alone. Every passing minute increased her dread that Tarek was dead.

She would have to abandon Negba soon. The two boys in the bottom of the wadi were folding up their tarp. Gabbi stood on the lip of the wall; something pricked her ears.

The distant noise of a laboring engine wended through the blowing smoke. Gabbi raced down the berm.

She ran over wild plants and desert rocks, towards the jangling motor. Visibility inside the mist was poor; Gabbi searched for any shape, any blot that might be Tarek. She came to a standstill to listen, let the sound grow closer. Through the wisps, the clanking sounded like a machine crawling.

Something moved in the haze, a grey form grew closer, darker. Gabbi called out to Tarek. The figure angled towards her, then took a firm shape in the drifts.

Gabbi's first step was a stagger backwards. Tarek sat at the wheel of a jeep that had been shorn in half. The rear was gone: no tires, fenders, or mounted machine gun. No Benny. In four-wheel drive, the front half clawed across the desert. The severed jeep plowed a rut, dragging itself to bring Tarek back.

Gevim

After dark, Tarek rode off with Jonny and Elam to find the place on the battlefield where Tarek had struck the mine.

They returned with Benny's body and laid him on a table in the mess hall. A candle was lit at his head. Benny lay without a sheet over him. The jeep was more ruined than he. All his wounds were internal. He appeared smooth and pale as the sand.

Thirty commandos made a *minyan* and said *kaddish*. Tarek and two others pulled boards off a barn and scrounged for nails to build a coffin. Gabbi sat a three-hour vigil with Benny until Elam took her place.

In the dark garage, Gabbi climbed to her loft above Gevim's two farm tractors. As always, the garage smelled of grease. Her tunic and hair reeked of the Egyptians' smokescreen and her hands stank of cordite. Gabbi didn't wash or strip off her clothes but lay on the mattress with odors of the farm and battle.

Tarek entered carrying a lantern. Without a word he climbed the wooden ladder to Gabbi. She scooted to make room.

She showed him a page from a Jerusalem newspaper dated a week ago. Jonny had brought it to her. In the paper was a list of all the victims from the massacre at Kfar Etzion, plus the names of those kept prisoner presently in Transjordan.

"My sister's alive."

Tarek kissed her lightly. She'd cried over Benny, then for the news of Rivkah.

He blew out the wick in his lantern and lay facing away. Gabbi was just as drained as him, smelled the same. She drew close to lap an arm over Tarek.

She held him tight; that was what he'd come for. Gabbi asked no questions, said nothing to soothe him, nothing for herself, Benny, or Rivkah. Tarek's breathing evened out. Sleep sealed the silence in the bed.

Late in the night, Tarek thrashed. She held him, the way he held her from tumbling out of the jeep. Tarek seemed in his dream to know she was there and quietened.

CHAPTER 22

VINCE

June 5
King David Hotel
New City
Jerusalem

A crackle from the Old City caused a long echo. Bernadotte peered off the hotel patio, across the ravine that was no-man's-land. The shade of an oak looked well across his outdoorsman's face, his thin lips and crinkles beside his eyes, sleeked hair, skin the color of cognac.

For afternoon drinks with Vince, Count Bernadotte had donned the smart khaki uniform of the Swedish Red Cross, the organization he formerly ran. Pinned with service medals, in short pants, he crossed long legs and rested a palm on one knobby knee. It seemed a purposeful gesture, a way to appear unflappable.

"Is that gunfire?"

Vince said, "Yes."

A waiter returned with Campari and soda and Vince's beer. Count Bernadotte did not acknowledge the waiter or the drinks. His glass came without ice; the Arabs had blown up the water pipes into Jerusalem. No one on the King David's patio had food, only beer and lukewarm liquor.

The count stayed fixed on the panorama of ancient walls a half mile east. Husseini controlled the Old City's center and north; Egyptian forces were encamped in the south. All day, Jerusalem popped and pinged like a cooling engine.

"Have you been to Rome, Mister Haas?"

"No."

"For the devout, Rome is the only city in the world with a view comparable to this. It, too, was built on hills."

Bernadotte aimed at the Old City a cigarette he'd poised between two fingertips.

"The Mosque of Omar. Solomon's Temple. The Wailing Wall and the Church of the Holy Sepulcher. The Garden of Gethsemane."

"You've been here before."

"I have not."

"You know Jerusalem."

"I am studious, Mister Haas."

"Do you mind if I take notes?"

"Take all that you require."

Vince pushed aside the beer to lay out his notebook. He hadn't removed his straw hat; no one on the King David's patio was fancy today but Bernadotte. He slid a pencil from behind his ear.

"Count, let me ask first. What makes the UN think they can stop this war?"

Bernadotte eased the cigarette to his lips. He smoked regally.

"The UN is the proper authority. Great Britain has ceded the mandate for Palestine."

"Do you think that authority's going to make much of a difference between the Jews and the Arabs? When it comes right down to it?"

"I do not."

"What else has the UN got?"

"I understand this will sound both naïve and proud. The United Nations has me."

Vince copied the quote in his notebook.

Bernadotte continued: "Certainly, I am aware of the difficulties. The Arabs reject a Jewish state, whatever borders it may have. The Israelis use their superior military strength to ignore the partition boundaries and conquer all the territory they can command."

"That sounds on the money."

"It does not help that America and Britain are not fully aligned. The United Kingdom needs oil more than it needs Jews. However, in the States, there is a fountain of sympathy for Israel. The gallant, plucky little underdog. I imagine you share the sentiment."

"My opinion isn't news. You don't?"

"I'm not certain you know my record. Please indulge me. During the war, I was instrumental in the release of twenty thousand inmates from Nazi camps. I was selected for that role of mediator for one reason. That reason was my compassion. I have not come to Palestine as a judge, Mister Haas. I am here to relieve the greatest amount of human misery that I can."

Bernadotte finished his cigarette with an elegant draw. He stubbed out the remains, then aimed both fingers at Vince's notebook.

"Please add that codicil to your notes."

Vince tapped the end of the pencil against his temple.

"Don't worry. I got it."

The count sipped, then swirled the highball as if it had ice. He set down his glass, gingerly.

Vince said, "You negotiated with Himmler."

"I did."

"That won't make the Jews happy. You sat across from the head of the Gestapo. You bargained with their executioner."

"To save Jews."

"They won't like it. Not even to save Jews."

Bernadotte ran a knuckle across his lips. The back of the hand was veined. Though he was an orchestrated man, he came across as hardy.

Bernadotte smiled privately.

"Did you know I have an American wife?"

"I didn't."

"She tells me I am single-minded. I believe she means it as a complaint. I do like to think well of people. Mister Haas?"

"Yes."

"The UN has offered independent states to both the Palestinian Arabs and the Jews. The Jews have accepted this. The Arabs have not. Why, do you think?"

"There's a million and a half Arabs here. The UN's map gave them forty-five hundred square miles. There's just half a million Jews. But they got fifty-five hundred square miles."

"A result of the West's sympathy for the Jews' plight?"

"They don't call it a plight. They call it a holocaust. And probably, yeah."

"But surely the Jews would surrender some land for peace."

"I think Ben-Gurion might."

"Then why will the Arabs not even negotiate?"

"They're convinced there has to be a war."

"I don't understand the sense in that."

"The way the Arabs figure, if they go to war and Israel wins, the Jews get their state. Fair enough. If Israel loses, they don't get a state. Either way, there has to be a fight."

"Why?"

"Because you can't ask the Arabs to accept Israel without trying to stop it first. That would be shameful. The Arab street wouldn't tolerate it. No Arab leader would survive it. They've preached hatred of the Jews for a long time. They've put themselves in a spot where the decision's got to be made on the battlefield."

The count hoisted a hand to beckon the waiter, though his attention was again on the Old City.

When the bill for the drinks arrived, Bernadotte was unfamiliar with his Palestinian money. Vince picked up the tab.

On their feet, Bernadotte stood an inch shorter than Vince. He extended a hand for a shake. His grip showed some muscle.

Vince said, "You'll be careful."

"Of what, in particular?"

"There's lots of lead flying around. Try to stay out of the way."

Bernadotte had not yet released the handshake. With his free hand, he pressed Vince's arm.

"As my American wife will tell you. I'm single-minded."

Bernadotte put on his hard-billed green hat, adjusted it, and strode away.

Vince stayed put at the shady table with a fresh beer and his feet up on the patio wall. He passed some time watching Arab snipers scurry along the rooftops of the Old City.

CHAPTER 23

HUGO

June 6
Beit Mahsir
Burma Road

A rockslide shoved Hugo's bulldozer sideways, towards the cliff.

Stone bits and sand showered him. Hugo covered his head, then shut down the big diesel. He climbed off the machine on the side away from the piled-up rocks. Stepping down, the tips of his boots traced the ledge; loose shingles skipped down the sheer slope. One more meter, one more good-sized boulder nudging the treads, and he would've been in the driver's seat when the dozer barrel-rolled into the valley.

He scooted along the skinny shelf to the rear of the dozer until he was safe on the road. Hugo rested hands on his hips to survey his good luck. Others rushed over to gush over his close call.

He was thirsty, hungry, dusty. The little avalanche was well-timed; noon brought the end of his seven-hour shift. Hugo turned for the long, sweltering trek down the stony, tight path he and three hundred others were forging. His hands buzzed as if ants crawled through them. Twenty shovels and pickaxes went to work to clear the rubble so the next driver could climb on the dozer and keep making the Burma Road.

Above the valley on the sere ridges, Israeli sharpshooters kept watch over the horde of men and women who'd come to build this secret lane to

Jerusalem. They worked rakes, sledges, and pry bars. The men wore sun-hats, the women kerchiefs. They sang in German, Polish, and Hebrew.

They all knew Hugo the driver. When he walked past, they called to him their relief that he'd not been hurt.

Hugo plodded down an incline that was sharp enough to pain his knees. A few craters marred the valley floor where Arab cannoneers in Latrun had blindly fired at the Burma Road and missed.

The workers' camp lay two kilometers to the west, among scrubby knolls where the road began its long rise into the Jerusalem heights. Some of the slopes were so steep that pack mules had to be whipped to get up them.

Dehydrated and testy, Hugo reached the workers' camp. A laborer poured him one cup of water and handed over a bread slice drizzled in honey. Hugo dragged a rag across his grimy face and neck, then ducked into a communal tent to lie on a canvas cot. He lay down to the rattle of trucks ferrying more laborers and tools up to the switchback where his dozer had gotten stuck.

"Hugo, get up."

One of the road engineers, Naftali the Romanian, stood over Hugo's cot, a cigarette stuck on his lower lip.

"What?"

"The *pizda* who drove the tractor after you. He has got it stuck again. We cannot free it."

"What do you want me to do about it?"

"Take another bulldozer. Push it off the road."

"What time is it?"

"Three o'clock."

"It's still hot out. Get someone else."

"No." Naftali wagged the cigarette in Hugo's face before pointing it. "You."

"Why?"

"You are the best driver. And—"

"And what?"

Naftali squatted to bring his unshaven face down to Hugo.

"Everyone knows this. When you want something wrecked, you call Irgun. Come on."

✳ ✳ ✳

The night's digging stopped. The chink of mauls and the scratch of rakes hushed and every motor idled. The Burma Road went quiet, which it never did.

On the slope, around a hairpin curve, a hundred laborers raised a hundred lit lanterns in an aquiline row. Hugo sat on the seat of a bull-dozer, Naftali stood beside him on the track. Both sipped apple brandy from Naftali's pocket flask.

Out of the west on the Burma Road came a sound like an army on foot. A dome of lamplight yellowed the dark from behind a hill. Then the first porters rounded into view.

They walked three abreast in a hundred ranks. A hundred lanterns swung with their gait. Every man and woman bore a stuffed pack, a flour sack, or a net bulging with foodstuffs across their shoulders. Each back was bowed, every head was up in the column marching past Hugo's bulldozer. The Burma Road's workers cheered and held their own lanterns high.

"Look at them." Naftali raised his flask.

These were not soldiers or farmers, but Tel Aviv office workers and dockworkers, teachers and government hands. Burdened, they climbed the last parts of the hidden road still not ready for vehicles. Lorries waited on the paved road two kilometers ahead at the top of the canyon. The trucks would carry the supplies the rest of the way into Jerusalem. Tonight, ten tons of food and ammunition would break the siege, enough for one more day.

Hugo reached for Naftali's flask, took a pull, then handed it back. He climbed off the dozer.

Hugo stepped into the human stream and quickly found a man smaller than himself. The fellow was bent over under his pack, as if searching for something lost.

Hugo said, "Hello, friend. Mind if I carry that a bit for you?"

On the lamplit road, the little man clamped his teeth. He didn't seem to believe Hugo's offer. Hugo reached for the straps. "Here."

Hugo aided him out of the pack; in turn, the two porters who'd been walking with the little man helped Hugo heave into the straps.

Hugo asked, "What's in here?"

"Tinned beets."

The pack seemed half Hugo's weight. He stooped as much as the little man had, but stepped into place in the procession. The little man moved ahead of Hugo, glancing back, a sudden spring in his strut.

The two on either side of Hugo, both big fellows, handled their loads well. The one carrying the lantern laid a hand on Hugo's shoulder, and they walked like this for a bit.

CHAPTER 24

MALIK

Yibna
Contested Palestine

Malik waited in the shadows of an alley.

He could not read any of the street signs or the trash at his feet. He trusted that he was at the proper place and time.

The last daylight trickled away. Malik pushed back his cowl to stride into a dirt street of little homes, all mud huts and wood shanties. Nothing of stone stood in the village, nothing ancient, everything poor. Yibna was a colony for fieldhands.

Across the dirt lane sprawled cereal fields, green barley, and bronze wheat. The crops looked to be in fine shape. The Jews might not burn them.

The gravel road behind Malik crunched.

A police car with its headlights off rolled to a stop. Malik spread his hands to show the arriving Jews they were empty.

Two policemen got out. They nodded to Malik, then helped Mrs. Pappel from the rear seat. One policeman held her crutches while the other lent a hand to put her on her foot. Malik hurried forward so Mrs. Pappel would not have to take a step with the crutches. But she did, to show that she could.

The policemen drove off to find shadows of their own.

Malik put both hands to Mrs. Pappel's shoulders to halt her. Her grey braid hung down her front to her belt. Malik had never seen hair like this on any Muslim woman. Mrs. Pappel's beauty was like a mirage, it changed with the distance from which it was viewed. With his hands on her, close to her, her magnificence became something else: wondrous, warmer, even hard.

Mrs. Pappel spread her arms as if she might fly. She let the crutches fall away.

On one foot, she leaned against Malik, a cheek to his chest.

She asked, "How did you manage this?"

Malik produced a sheaf of currency. The bills would flutter away if he let them go and become more trash he could not read.

"These. They are better than a gun."

Mrs. Pappel laughed well. If he let her go she might lose her balance.

"Set me down."

He lowered her to the raw road, then sat as she did, with legs crossed as if by a campfire. Her missing foot was not so plain.

She said, "You have all your rings."

"I have not needed them."

"How did you get this money?"

"Many Arabs are leaving Lydda. They go with nothing because they have been told the war will be short. They believe they will return soon to their homes. Other Arabs come, people who have been touched by the war. They arrive with nothing, and think they will be safe in a city full of Arabs. I stand between them, the coming and the going."

"Do you steal?"

"You wound me, woman. I buy and I sell."

From inside his robes Malik pulled a second packet of currency, thick as his wrist. He pushed it at her. "Take this."

"No."

"I have more."

Gently, Mrs. Pappel took the money. She shook her head as if all this was silliness. She thumbed the bills. "Goodness, Malik, how much is this?"

"I do not know." HeMalik gestured at the hovels of the crop pickers of Yibna. "Use it to buy the best house. For you and Rivkah, and the child."

"And you, Malik?"

"What of me? I can sleep anywhere."

"I trust you will not."

"I will." Malik closed his hand around Mrs. Pappel's. "But on your word, I trust I will not always."

Sitting in the road, they talked a while. Malik knew how far he might ride under a given sun, what distance he could shoot in a wind, but the time with Mrs. Pappel left no track. He asked if she were in pain; she was not. If she needed anything, she should tell him. She had no requests. Had she picked a home yet? No, but soon, in Zichron Ya'akov. When would she get a false foot? Soon, in Tel Aviv.

Full darkness fell. The police car flashed its lights on them. Malik told Mrs. Pappel he would go give the Jews another bribe, to have them wait longer.

She said, "Lift me."

"We are not finished."

"No, we're not. Lift me."

Malik gathered the crutches, then placed Mrs. Pappel between them. She said, "I'll make myself very easy to find in Zichron Ya'akov."

"You know of no one who can find so well as I, Missus Pappel."

She stood with good strength, framed between the wooden sticks.

Mrs. Pappel said, "You've never kissed me."

Malik cocked his head. The police car blinked again.

"No. But I have seen your hair."

He lay a hand softly below Mrs. Pappel's throat.

"And this lion's heart."

He pressed his hand to his own breast and inclined his head to it. Malik kept his wishes to himself, swept his cape around him like a night wind, and departed.

CHAPTER 25

HUGO

Beit Mahsir
Burma Road

Hugo slammed shut the truck bed gate. He slapped it like a man sending away a horse.

"Goodbye."

In the night, the convoy revved all together, a kind of choir for Naftali. The Romanian would not go up to Jerusalem on someone's back or hauled there in a donkey cart. The engineer would ride in a truck, the first truck to go the full distance of the Burma Road. This was fitting, and he would have thought so. Naftali had a brother in Jerusalem who would give him a proper burial.

The supply column grinded upward behind their headlights. Tires slipped but stayed on the narrow road around the first switchback. The valley cupped the rumble of their motors and the clangor of gears. It did sound like a song.

Hugo climbed up on his dozer to watch the procession pass. He had Naftali's flask. The memory of the Burma Road rang in his hand as he took a sip of the engineer's apple brandy.

One truck slowed in front of Hugo. Still moving, the passenger door opened. Vince swung down, closed the door, jogged to a stop, and the vehicle rolled on.

Hugo said, "Ah."

Vince put out a hand. Hugo jumped off the machine to take it. They stepped back, assessing each other in the early evening. A blotch stained Hugo's shirt. Vince looked worn out.

Vince said, "Don't say I look like shit."

"I won't if you won't."

"Good to see you."

"I'm going to guess Pinchus sent you."

"I got a note."

Hugo handed over Naftali's flask. Vince took a swig, Hugo followed suit, then tucked the flask away.

Vince had no bag, only khakis and a white shirt, his old straw hat, and a pencil behind his ear. He was not staying the night. Vince must have a car. Hugo would ride out of here with him.

They walked downhill to the workers' camp. A low quarter moon brightened their way. The road was smooth among easy hills. Vince sent a stone skittering with the toe of his boot.

"This was built in two weeks? This whole road?"

"Ten kilometers."

"Amazing."

"Tomorrow they'll start the water pipeline."

"I suppose this means Jerusalem's saved."

"It means for now Jerusalem is saved."

"Who did the work?"

Hugo shrugged. It made no sense to parse the hundreds.

"Jews."

"Whose blood is that on your shirt?"

"What time is it?"

Vince checked his watch. "Nine o'clock."

"In three hours, the truce will start. The Arabs figured they had to do something to slow us down. At sunset yesterday, they sent snipers down from Latrun. They killed nine. One was a friend. I happened to be standing next to him."

"Hugo. I'm sorry."

"I've been keeping up with your newspaper columns. I read a list. Rivkah's alive. And Red Yakob."

"Yeah."

"You saw her while you were in Amman?"

"Yep."

"And I suppose you tried to get her out."

"I did."

"Stupid."

"Yep."

Hugo asked, "Are you going to write about me again?"

"If I don't, I'll get another visit from Pinchus."

"If you do, I'll get another visit. How is Missus Pappel?"

"Annoyed you haven't come to see her."

"I have other people's crap under my fingernails. I prefer it if she sees me when I'm more settled."

"You think she cares?"

"Of course she cares. I'm her opposite. I'm Irgun."

"Still Irgun? Pinchus got to you."

"No. The Arabs who shot my friend got to me."

At the workers' camp, Vince went off to fetch his car. Hugo took a last cold shower and dried off with Naftali's towel.

On the ride to Tel Aviv, Hugo promised to visit Mrs. Pappel.

When Vince dropped him at his flat, Hugo said, "I'll see you soon."

"What's up?"

Hugo had been in these same clothes for his five days working on the Burma Road. He would cut the bloody shirt into rags to wipe his hands.

He closed the car door and leaned through the window.

"Come, Vince. Do you think Pinchus sent you to write about a little Jew plumber on a bulldozer?"

Hugo patted the car roof to send Vince on his way.

CHAPTER 26

June 12

TEL AVIV
ISRAEL
By Vincent Haas

Herald Tribune News Service

There's a break in the war between new little Israel and five invading Arab nations. Friday night, June 11 at midnight, a truce went into effect. It's supposed to last four weeks.

The ceasefire was brokered by the United Nations, itself a fairly new entity, just three years old. This is the U.N.'s first real test of global clout.

Jews and Arabs alike are glad for the pause. Israel gets the chance to take stock of her army's first war-making. The bogged-down Arabs can keep thumping their chests without losing more blood. The regent of Iraq recently summed up the Arab mindset: "We cannot be beaten by the Jews. We must not be beaten by the Jews. I am ready to go to the front myself with a knife. But if fighting is stopped by the United Nations, that would be a different matter."

The first U.N. observers have begun to appear in the battle areas. They bump over rutted roads in white-painted jeeps, wearing khaki shorts and sky-blue berets. They hail from New York, Paris, Stockholm, and Brussels.

The peacekeepers have been sent by the United Nations Truce Supervision Organization, a grandiose moniker for a group with an almost impossible task. They must enforce the truce not only on the front-lines but at airports and harbors to stop the shipment of war matériel into the conflict. The U.N. must also check the influx of military-aged immigrants into Israel.

The observers are unarmed, though the NYC Police Department has donated fifty pistols. The U.N.'s chief mediator in Palestine, Count Folke Bernadotte of Sweden, nixed the idea of his peace-keepers carrying weapons and sent them back.

Bernadotte himself is a puzzling choice to play lead diplomat between Israeli and Arab. The for-mer head of Sweden's Boy Scouts and Red Cross, a member of the Swedish royal family, Bernadotte is lacking in background with both the cultures and ten-sions of the Middle East. Maybe that's why he was chosen, in hopes he might act without bias. To date, Bernadotte's crowning achievement has been the lib-eration of thousands of Nordic Jews from German war camps. To pull that off, he negotiated with Heinrich Himmler and the Nazis. Not surprisingly, the Israelis view the count with skepticism.

Once the truce started last night, all the war gains and losses between both sides were locked down. The final few days of the fighting produced a frantic scramble for advantage.

Egypt reached Isdud just ten miles south of Tel Aviv and stalled there. In the east, an Egyptian force idles at the southern gates of Jerusalem.

Syria captured Mishmar HaYarden, a moshav in upper Galilee, near Tel Hazor, the greatest of the Bronze Age cities. The Syrians have gained a toehold in Israel but little else.

Lebanon captured, lost, and recaptured a small fort at al-Malkiyya on its border with Israel. Al-Malkiyya is Lebanon's only success of the war. So far, the Lebanese have lost ten men.

Iraq's force occupies a few Arab towns in Samaria, around Jenin and Mt. Gilboa. They've managed to defend their posts but have taken no land that Israel covets.

The Jews have held onto most of the territory ceded to them by the U.N.'s partition plan of 1947. On top of that, they've conquered large swaths that, before the invasion, were located in Arab Palestine. So far, the Palestinians have lost two hundred villages and several large towns. The Israelis have set their sights on more once the truce ends.

Among the Arabs states, only Transjordan has improved its position. King Husseini holds the eastern half of Jerusalem; he has his work cut out for him to get the rest. A hundred thousand Jews remain in the western half, called the Old City, and a thousand Jewish fighters are there, many of them Irgun.

To avoid an out-and-out battle for Jerusalem, Husseini has chosen not so much to conquer the city as to starve it.

With plenty of artillery and three thousand fighters—a third of Transjordan's entire force in Palestine—Husseini's Arab Legion has taken possession of a former British police fort in Latrun, on a hilltop dominating the highway between Tel Aviv and Jerusalem. Israeli convoys can't pass without crippling losses. For the past month, Jerusalem has been choked to a trickle of the food, water, fuel, ammo, and reinforcements it needs to survive.

The rescue of Jerusalem is paramount for the Jews. They say if there is no Jewish Jerusalem, there is no Israel.

The Israeli army has attacked Latrun three times. For the first assault, on May 25, they sent into battle a thousand fighters, among them two hundred immigrants fresh off the ships from Europe. These raw recruits had only trained with sticks and rocks in displaced persons camps; arriving in Israel, they spoke Polish, Hungarian, Russian, Rumanian, some Yiddish, but no Hebrew.

Immediately, the Israeli government mustered the new émigrés into the 72nd Battalion of the 7th Brigade, then sent them as part of a strike force against Latrun. The Jewish attackers had no tanks, and their only artillery was two 65mm cannons on wooden wheels, forged in France in 1906. The immigrants could barely understand the orders shouted at them in Hebrew. The assault force gathered under a full moon across the Valley of Ayalon where Joshua once commanded the moon to stand still.

The legionnaires beat back the Jews' first attack. They beat back the second five days later. The third assault, led by American Army Col. Mickey Marcus, was defeated on Thursday, two days ago. Trying to capture Latrun, Israel has lost seventy-five dead, twice that number wounded. The casualty count may wind up higher; the immigrants were sent into battle so fast they weren't properly listed. There's no official record of how many died at Latrun.

The Arabs have shown they will not surrender the fortress.

The Jews will not surrender Jerusalem.

Instead, the Jews discovered an alternate route into Jerusalem. It turns out there's a second valley running parallel to the one below Latrun, two miles south, behind high ridges that make this other valley invisible to the Arabs' cannons. Until two days ago, it was impassable to all but mules.

Another thousand Israelis, not fighters but engineers, farmers, clerks, plumbers, former Irgunists, men and women together, answered the call for laborers. Over two backbreaking weeks, laboring by sunlight and lantern, they raced the truce deadline with heavy machinery and garden tools, to defeat six miles of granite hills.

It's a rough-hewn path, full of hairpin turns, hugging steep defiles and embankments, but the Jews have successfully carved a new route to Jerusalem. They call it the Burma Road.

I watched a stream of jeeps and trucks climb up and over. Teens drove a herd of cattle. Soldiers bore on their backs bundles of rifles and Sten guns. Hordes of civilians carried tons of everything else precious for Jerusalem.

Things take root in Israel. I've seen orchards flourish where there was only sand, grain where there was stone. A road where there was just a donkey track. I don't know if peace can grow here. Now that the U.N. has planted it, I'm not sure if their man Bernadotte is strong enough to sustain it.

He'll have to be. These warring peoples on both sides will respect, or recognize, nothing but strength.

Reporting from Tel Aviv, Israel.

CHAPTER 27

VINCE

June 13
Tel Aviv

Vince stepped out of the Kaete Dan guesthouse. A *hamsin* wind blew dry and hot from the south, from Sinai.

He took his time along Hayarkon Street, a block off the boardwalk and the sea. Breakers rolled in tall rows, brushed upright by the winds.

Sunday families splashed in the surf. Hundreds more took their leisure on the sand. The Jews in Israel didn't go in for umbrellas and beach chairs like they did on Coney Island. Here, in their own country, they sat on blankets in the sizzling sand.

Vince strolled a mile to the Red House. Ben-Gurion's headquarters was a plain, faded pink stucco building facing Hayarkon, keeping its back to the Mediterranean. Sunburned young men and women in matching tunics and khaki shorts, Sten guns on their backs, manned sandbag roadblocks. Ben-Gurion's headquarters resembled him; it was unadorned and defiant.

Sentries stopped Vince. He showed them Ben-Gurion's note, slipped before dawn under the door of his room at the Kaete Dan. The guards let him pass. Vince entered on Hayarkon, identified himself to another guard, and was directed upstairs to the prime minister's door. Vince knocked, heard a call, then entered.

In his small, cluttered office, Ben-Gurion wore a loose white shirt and sandals, dressed more comfortably than Vince. He stepped from behind his desk.

Ben-Gurion shook, then took a chair. A copy of yesterday's *Palestine Post* lay on his desk. The prime minister stabbed a finger onto the newspaper.

"How does this help?"

Vince didn't wait for an invitation to sit. His breakfast had been two cups of coffee. He'd sweat through his shirt on the walk over. He took the cushioned seat opposite Ben-Gurion and already wanted to leave.

Ben-Gurion said, "You told me you would help."

"No. I said I'd be glad to carry back-channel messages to Husseini. I said I'd bring you any insights I might get about Bernadotte. I said not a damn thing about using my newspaper to help you. Or hurt you."

"Bernadotte. I don't trust that Swede. He's in Cairo right now drafting his proposal. Yes, Cairo."

Again, the prime minster dug a finger into the newsprint.

"You mention Irgunists on the Burma Road."

"They were there."

"You tell the world we sent raw immigrants to Latrun."

"You did."

Ben-Gurion planted an elbow on top of the *Post*.

"Do you know why? We've lost over a thousand soldiers and civilians so far to this *fakakta* war. We sent the immigrants to Latrun because we needed them at Latrun."

"Did you need them that fast?"

"That is not your business. You don't understand how bad it has been in Jerusalem. How do I trust you after this?"

"Same way you trusted me before."

Ben-Gurion waved away his displeasure; it seemed manufactured anyhow.

"I believe you know Major Dayan."

"We've met."

"In a few days, he will call on you. Something I want him to show you."

"Is that why you called me here?"

"No. I have news."

"Good or bad?"

"Both. I have exchanged messages with Husseini."

Vince sat forward as Ben-Gurion pushed back in his chair.

"As you say, the Egyptians are in Hebron and Bethlehem. Even with the truce, they will not allow us to retrieve the bodies at Gush Etzion. One hundred and fifty Jews lie on the open ground until this war is done. It is a *shonda*." A disgrace.

The prime minister said, "Perhaps to make amends, Husseini has granted my second request. He will release the women his forces captured at the Etzion bloc."

Before he knew it, Vince was on his feet.

"When?"

"One-half will return next week. The rest will come later. I made certain your friend's name was on the first list."

Vince flattened palms on Ben-Gurion's desk. The prime minister's chair creaked as he lay a hand across Vince's knuckles.

"I was specific that they put the young lady on a truck, and to make certain they see her off."

Ben-Gurion folded the newspaper, then dumped it in his trashcan. "Perhaps now that the truce is in place, you may find some time for yourself."

"Thank you, Prime Minister."

"I cannot say when this war will end. In one shape or another, it may never end. For now, you must understand. The state of things is Israel versus the Arabs. In all things, Mister Haas. All things. Even your newspaper. Good day."

Vince flew down the stairs. Outside the Red House, he ran into the heat. Rather than hurry the mile to the Kaete Dan for his car, he hailed a taxi on Hayarkon Street.

Jumping into the cab, Vince blurted, "Army Hospital Number Five."

CHAPTER 28

RIVKAH

June 16
Allenby Bridge
Arab-controlled Palestine

Fifteen women filed out of the back of the truck. All jumped off the tailgate except Rivkah. She left the truck last on helping hands.

The Arab driver did not exit the cab nor the guards leave the bed. Once Rivkah stood in the road with the rest of the freed women, the truck belched and rumbled back across the Allenby Bridge, east over the narrow Jordan River, into the desert kingdom.

A second truck awaited the women. At the ends of each bumper flew small sky blue flags. Five UN peacekeepers shook every woman's hand. They said to all, "You're free now."

A separate car waited for Rivkah.

✳ ✳ ✳

The driver lent an arm for Rivkah to step from the jeep. She hugged him goodbye. The peacekeeper was a stocky man from Bruges. In English they'd talked for the three-hour drive from the border through Arab-held lands, west beneath quiet Latrun, north to Zichron Ya'akov. He was a

young father in Belgium. He believed there could be peace between Arab
and Jew and would pray for it.

Flowers and thorns scalloped Mrs. Pappel's doorway. She stood on
her small porch framed in bougainvillea. Rivkah caught her breath to see
Mrs. Pappel on two feet, though the left one could not have been a foot.
Rivkah ran the short distance from the street to her.

Both kissed the other's wet cheeks. Rivkah released her embrace
first. Mrs. Pappel wasn't ready to let go, and whispered, "I'm so happy."

"Me, too."

"How is our child?"

"Impatient."

Mrs. Pappel stepped back, keeping hold of Rivkah's wrists.

Rivkah asked, "How is the foot?"

"Wooden. Come inside. I have a surprise for you. We'll get you
settled, then have tea." Mrs. Pappel linked arms with her.

Rivkah held back to admire the two-story stucco house and peaked
tile roof. Flowerbeds and grass framed the walkway, flowering vines the
porch. On the porch, a pair of cane rockers spoke of the night and nights
to come. The home was the largest on the block.

"It's lovely."

"Needs a little work. But it's roomy."

"How can you afford this?"

"I kept some money of my own. Malik gave me the rest." Mrs.
Pappel wagged a finger. "Not now."

Mrs. Pappel limped inside. In the foyer she took a cane from an
umbrella stand. The entry hall ran past a staircase, to the kitchen at the
rear. The plaster walls were white and bare but the sitting and dining
rooms had furniture. Something rattled in the kitchen.

"That," said Mrs. Pappel, "is your surprise."

She sent Rivkah down the hall. Rivkah trailed a hand against the
wall as she went, making the home real. The noise in the kitchen, metal-
lic, happened again.

Rivkah eased her head through the open doorway.

Two legs in denim overalls extended from beneath the sink. Shadows and the cabinet obscured the rest. A plumber's toolbox lay near his dirty boots.

The man under the sink said, "A month in jail. Pity."

Rivkah covered her mouth. A gasp seeped through her fingers.

"Five months for me. Death row, to be exact."

A small hand reached from the dark of the sink cabinet. Fingers wriggled for the toolbox but did not find it. Each fingernail was grease-stained, slices of black moons.

"Hand me the spanner on top."

Rivkah tiptoed closer, controlling her breaths. She selected the heavy wrench from the box and kneeled.

"This one?"

Hugo snatched it. Rivkah stayed beside him. He made a grunt, then another hard sound with the tool.

"Vince didn't think you'd leave Transjordan."

"I wasn't given a choice."

Hugo dug his heels into the floor to slide himself out. He sat up, full-faced and fine. Before he could speak, there on the floor, Rivkah wrapped him in her arms.

✳ ✳ ✳

Rivkah's room on the second floor had a view of the azure sea two miles away. Mrs. Pappel, standing in the window with her, said that whenever Rivkah missed her mother and father, she might look west and the sea would always be blue for her, beautiful or sad.

Mrs. Pappel had settled into the bedroom at the rear of the upper floor. There she could gaze over vineyards and the foothills of the Carmel Mountains. The small room between her and Rivkah was going to be the nursery.

Hugo proposed a stroll through Zichron Ya'akov. Rivkah was hesitant, not knowing yet how well Mrs. Pappel could walk.

At the kitchen table, Mrs. Pappel rolled up her pants leg. The wooden foot and ankle joint were held in place by straps, rods, and hinges. Hugo examined the workings; he liked machinery.

Mrs. Pappel said, "I'll take Hugo's arm."

Out of the house they turned right along the lane. The homes on this old street had been built four decades ago in the European style, with courtyards and painted window frames. Shops were blended in with the houses, and more cars than pushcarts plied the streets.

Mrs. Pappel's limp didn't worsen as they walked. She leaned on Hugo and used the cane.

Rivkah asked, "What are you going to do here? Teach?"

"I'm done with teaching. With farms. And for that matter, guns. I'm going to buy a little storefront and open a tea shop. All sorts of teas. And we'll have cakes. Big and small ones." She patted Hugo's elbow tucked inside hers. "Hugo will help me."

Rivkah said to him, "I didn't know you liked tea."

"I don't. I like cake."

They ambled past a grocery store, a pub, more well-tended houses. Women watered potted geraniums and herbs, swept walkways, and carried mesh shopping bags. They nodded to pregnant Rivkah. Zichron Ya'akov had few men of Hugo's age or younger, but his overalls and dark nails showed he was no shirker. Strolling, they said nothing more of prison, prosthetics, or the war. No one mentioned Vince, why he was not here. The first hour of Rivkah's return was to be sunny and agreeable.

They halted at the town's northern limit where the road petered out. A wooded slope ran down to a ravine of wildwood and brush. Across the way, on a mirroring hill, a hundred humble homes and a minaret revealed an Arab village. In the emerald east lay hundreds of acres in grain fields and vineyards. Flowers adorned the village windows, Arab boys and old men rode donkeys. A footpath ran down the hill below where Rivkah, Hugo, and Mrs. Pappel stood; the path entered the wooded defile at the bottom, then rose up the opposite slope.

Mrs. Pappel said, "That is why I came here."

Rivkah said, "It's an Arab village."

"El Fureidis. It means little paradise."

"How many live there?"

"Seven hundred."

"How are they still there?"

"What do you mean?"

"I mean why hasn't the army run them off?"

"El Fureidis signed a peace agreement. They won't harbor any outsiders. They've given up all their guns. The people don't want to fight. They just want to stay in their homes. We're trying to convince the army to let them."

Rivkah asked, "Can you do it?"

"We'll have to. The crops and vines will rot without them. There isn't enough manpower in Zichron Ya'akov. These two villages have worked the fields together for fifty years. There's no reason to stop."

Hugo muttered, "Yes, there is."

Mrs. Pappel pulled her arm free from his. "Hush."

"Actually, no. I won't hush."

Hugo addressed only Rivkah.

"Every soldier it takes to keep an eye on that village means one less fighter at the front. That's seven hundred Arabs, right there, half a kilometer away from us. Let them go. A couple hundred thousand have already left."

Rivkah said, "They left because they're afraid of another Deir Yassin."

Mrs. Pappel said, "Both of you. Stop."

Hugo thrust out his hands. "You haven't seen what I've seen."

Gently, Rivkah reached for him. She meant Hugo no scorn. Her heart cracked for him.

"Yes, I have." She pointed to El Fureidis. "But why should they?"

Mrs. Pappel said to Hugo, "Once we were strangers in Egypt. Then we were strangers in Europe, in our own homes. You know this, Hugo. Will you do that to every Arab in Israel? Make their homes an Egypt?"

"Why should we help them? They're not Jews."

"Because we are."

She gave Hugo a little push. "Go home." He held his ground to go another round. Mrs. Pappel nudged him again. "Go on. I'll make you a cake."

"Make it for Rivkah."

He turned away, then stopped himself.

"How is Red Yakob?"

"The boldest man in the camp."

When Hugo was gone, Mrs. Pappel linked her arm in Rivkah's.

"Do you know what frightens me, *liebling*? You're both right."

"Don't defend him."

"I will."

"Why?"

"Who else does that man have?"

Together they gazed over treetops to the Arab village.

Mrs. Pappel said, "You know, Vince arranged your car. With Ben-Gurion himself."

"Where is Vince?"

"He wanted to be here."

"No, he didn't."

"Liebling."

Mrs. Pappel let go of Rivkah. She wobbled but gained her balance with the cane.

"When you didn't come back from Transjordan with him, you hurt him. Rather badly."

"He had no right to ask me that."

"He had every right."

"I've already argued with Hugo. I won't with you. Where is Vince?"

"Running around, seeing secret things. He'll come. He always does."

"Missus Pappel."

"Yes."

"Tell me why you're here."

Mrs. Pappel pointed her cane at El Fureidis.

"That's where Malik will live."

CHAPTER 29

VINCE

June 17
Tel Aviv

Vince leaned in on the Škoda's driver's side. The unmarked black sedan flew no flags or insignia.

"Should you be driving?"

"Of course not. I only have one eye. Get in."

Vince climbed in. Dayan pulled away from the Kaete Dan guesthouse. In civilian clothes, he drove with ease, one hand on the wheel.

They headed north on the coast road in summer eve traffic. The day's heat had faded; a breeze played through the seafront palms. Tel Aviv's citizens spilled onto the boardwalk, plazas and street corners swayed with lingerers, bars droned with neon and young men on leave. Girls went on promenade, too, now that the boys were back for the truce.

Vince asked, "How'd you lose it?"

Dayan answered with a casual ennui he might use to impress a woman.

"Lebanon, in forty-one. Fighting the Vichy Nazis with the British. A French sniper put a bullet into my binoculars. Bastard, but a marvelous shot."

Vince carried no pencil; no written record was allowed tonight. That was one of Ben-Gurion's conditions. The others were no specifics, no locations or names.

Dayan switched hands on the steering wheel to raise a finger.

"Don't say you're sorry for me."

A passing taxi lit Dayan in profile. His good right eye was almond-shaped, almost Asiatic. His was a ruined and memorable face, and he was aware of it.

Vince indicated the traffic. "Eye on the road, Major."

✻ ✻ ✻

Dayan traced the seacoast. A gibbous moon highlighted the Mediterranean in close-set frets. The moon would peak at midnight on the ride back to Tel Aviv.

The road ribboned through lit and lively Jewish towns and empty fishing villages that would lose their Arab names. On the ride, Dayan inquired about Vince's upbringing in New York, his time in the American Marines, his year in the Negev at Massuot Yitzhak.

"And you have a child coming. With the woman from Gush Etzion?"

Sometimes, Vince forgot how public he'd made his own life.

"Yeah."

"Will you stay in Israel, then?"

Salt air thrummed in the windows, cooling Vince under his button-down shirt. Dayan's question was out of step with how little they knew each other. Vince owed him no answer, and for that reason he gave one.

"I'm not sure."

Dayan rested his arm on Vince's shoulder. Like this they rode a while, oddly bridged.

At Hadera, Dayan turned inland. Moonlit fields bracketed the road, and in what seemed like the middle of nowhere, the car came to a military checkpoint. Dayan stopped to show his credentials to an armed pair of sentries. He vouched for Vince and drove on.

A half mile past the outpost, he pulled to the shoulder.

"Come."

Vince got out with Dayan, to slouch with him against the Škoda. They watched the western sky. The moon remained low in the east, so the Mediterranean stars shined briskly. Dayan didn't explain what they were looking for, just crossed his arms, leaned back, and squinted into the twinkling blue-black.

He said, "You should stay."

"Will there be an Israel to stay in?"

Dayan stood off the car. He paused to peer deeper into the western night, then raised an arm at one star sparkling brighter than the rest. Vince found it, focused on it, and the star shimmered more.

Dayan said, "There will be."

Driving off, they were stopped again after another mile. Three guards recognized Dayan and waved the Škoda into Ein Shemer Airfield.

Dayan drove onto an immense concrete pad, poured years ago by the British for their largest RAF airbase in Palestine. He parked beside a half dozen tarp-covered trucks and twenty boys in civilian garb. The boys shared the glowing dots of cigarettes.

Twin points of light descended out of the west. Floodlamps came on to light the runway; a windsock hung limp in the sultry air. The boys smothered their cigarettes under heels just as the transport touched down and smoked its tires.

Dayan motored out with the trucks to meet the taxiing cargo plane.

The big twin-engine aircraft rolled to a paved ramp off the runway; there it shut down. A door opened in the fuselage just as the first lorry backed up to it. Two powerful men inside the plane swung crates down to the lads in the truck bed.

Once the first truck was full and pulled away, Dayan moved in front of it to stop it. With Vince, he walked around to the tailgate.

An armed soldier rode in the truck bed, sitting on the crates. Dayan instructed him to open one. With a crowbar, the boy popped open the crate where he'd sat. He handed down to Dayan a bolt-action rifle. Dayan gave it to Vince.

The gun had been freshly oiled, but it wasn't new. Gouges marred the stock, the butt plate showed some corrosion. Vince ran his thumb over a spread-winged eagle stamped into the steel receiver and a swastika engraved in the barrel.

"Mauser K98."

Dayan said, "Correct."

"It's a Nazi rifle."

"The irony is quite thick."

Vince returned the rifle to the soldier in the back of the truck.

"Where's it from?"

"Czechoslovakia."

"How many did you get?"

"Tonight? Thousands. It doesn't matter. Regardless of the number, we'll buy more."

"What else is on the plane?"

"Tank parts, plane engines, rifles, bullets, pom-pom guns. A lot of it is German. But you Americans left behind a massive amount of weaponry in Europe, as well. We'll buy that, too."

"Who's selling?"

"Mostly the Czechs. We've dealt with quite a few Soviet satellites. We also have thirty Sherman tanks coming in from Italy. From Russia we buy bombsights, chemicals for explosives, radar, bazookas."

"Is this a political thing?"

"Goodness, no. These are simply cash transactions."

"Whose cash?"

"Ah. This will be of interest to you. Mostly American cash. The United Jewish Appeal is a great ally to Israel. Did you know there are more Jews in New York City than in all of Western Europe and Palestine combined?"

"I did."

"Walk with me."

Dayan led Vince off the tarmac, into an unlit field, far enough from the floodlights for the stars to reemerge. Dayan gazed back at the Czech smugglers' plane.

Vince asked, "How are you getting away with this? Where's Bernadotte? Where's the UN?"

"Egypt and Transjordan have made several of their airstrips off-limits to the United Nations. In fairness, Israel has notified the UN that a select few airfields in Israel will also be closed to them. It is often remarkable, Mister Haas, how the Arabs assist us in ways they do not foresee."

Again, Dayan faced the west, dark over the sea. Vince stood to the major's left, on the side of the missing eye. Dayan dug hands in his pockets, thoughtful. Vince could believe Dayan had forgotten he was there.

After minutes, another glimmer swelled.

Dayan bounced on his toes.

The second plane zoomed in and touched down with a screech of rubber. The pilots nosed around to the loading ramp and the waiting trucks.

Dayan said, "There will be a third plane tonight. And a fourth. More tomorrow."

The night pooled in Dayan's black patch.

"The truce will end in three weeks. By then, we will have doubled the size of our army to seventy thousand. We will not be the same force the Arabs fought before."

"So there'll be no peace negotiations."

"With the Arabs? No. We'll simply beat them. You'll see. It will be better."

"For who? Israel?"

"Of course. And for you, Mister Haas."

"Me?"

Stepping towards the car, Dayan patted Vince's back.

"For your Jewish child."

CHAPTER 30

GABBI

June 19
Kerem HaTeimanim
Tel Aviv

In the tight alley, Tarek's father answered the door.

"Come in."

Tarek said, "Let's go for a drink."

His father stepped out and closed the door.

Tarek said, "This is Gabbi."

His father nodded without giving his name. Tarek said it for him, "Ibrahim."

Ibrahim was shorter and thicker than Tarek. Father and son shared the same long, bearded face and shining green eyes. Gabbi walked between them to a little restaurant where they took a table on an empty patio. The sun felt close; the day would be warm. Many Yemenis were already out on the streets for their Saturday shopping.

Ibrahim said to Gabbi: "The Kerem is one of the oldest neighborhoods in Tel Aviv."

He said this to justify their presence here, the dark Jews.

Gabbi said, "Of course."

Ibrahim raised a hand. Quickly, a large bottle of beer, three glasses, and a *malawah* flatbread arrived. Ibrahim was known in this restaurant. Tarek poured.

"Sometimes my father feels the need to explain himself."

Ibrahim tore at the malawah. "Not just sometimes." He asked Gabbi, "You are a soldier?"

"Tarek and I are in the same company."

Ibrahim dipped a shred of bread in a sauce bowl.

"I have not seen my son."

Gabbi said, "I'm so sorry."

She said this not to answer for Tarek's absence in his father's world but to answer what Ibrahim had truly said, that his wife had been killed and his son's absence made the pain even worse.

Tarek's and his father's green gazes did not meet. One or the other looked to Gabbi, to the ground, or into their hands, every moment.

Ibrahim asked, "How are things at the frontline? Tarek does not send me letters."

Gabbi said, "We've been very busy."

"Are you going to win the war?"

"I believe so."

"What do you do?"

"I'm a machine gunner. I ride next to Tarek." Ibrahim stroked his beard trying to imagine this. Gabbi made it simple. "Your son is an extraordinary fighter."

She reached to Tarek's hand, the one holding a beer glass. She could not say to Ibrahim that when his son trembled in the night and called out, she held him. So she touched Tarek's hand to ease the father's heart that his son was not alone.

Tarek pulled away to drink. He drained the beer, poured another, and this was how he spoke to his father.

"Perhaps," said Ibrahim, "you can persuade him to write."

"I will." Gabbi smiled with the lie.

Ibrahim sheared another piece from the wheel of bread. Tarek circled his glass with both arms as if to protect it. In the street a vendor rolled past selling hummus, *kasher* wine, and chocolates.

Ibrahim asked Gabbi again, "How are things at the front?"

He asked Gabbi not because he wanted her to answer but to embarrass his son, to display for Tarek that he did not know how things were at Yad Mordechai, Negba, Nitzanim, Hill 69, and Beit Daras. He was telling Tarek that this young woman will answer me, but you won't.

Gabbi said, "Maybe I should let the two of you talk."

Ibrahim was grieving. He had a role to play, the man wronged by God. And if by God, then by everyone.

Tarek looked up when his father looked down.

"What would I write?"

Ibrahim clearly had no urge to ask his son for kindness.

Tarek pressed. "What would I say? That I'm going to die?"

"No."

"What would you like to read?"

Ibrahim tucked in his chin until his beard folded against his chest.

"About the food? The heat and dust? The fleas? Maybe the arms and legs we gather up. The Arabs we kill. Or the Jews they kill. *Ayin tachat ayin*." An eye for an eye.

Tarek lifted the empty beer bottle and pivoted to shout "Hey" to the waiter. When he turned back, Ibrahim had not raised his own jade eyes.

"What suits you? Maybe you'd like to know how Benny died without a drop of blood on him because his guts had exploded from the inside. Or that I piss red some days from riding in those fucking jeeps, from not enough water, not enough sleep. Maybe when I get back tonight I'll write you how Gabbi and I drove into Tel Aviv this morning and saw five thousand people on the fucking beaches."

Tarek paused for the waiter to bring a fresh beer. Tarek filled only his own glass but took no swallow. He wasn't a drinker; before this morning Gabbi had never seen him with a beer. He and his father breathed hard like boxers.

"I can," said Ibrahim.

"You can what?"

A tremor shook Ibrahim's dark head. He fought with himself, against what he might say next. The words seemed to shame him before they left his mouth. He raised his eyes to Tarek's.

"I can petition the government."

"What?"

"You're an only child."

Tarek shot to his feet to stand above his father.

Ibrahim said up to him, "I'm a widower."

Tarek flung the patio chair onto its back. Gabbi pressed Ibrahim's slumped shoulder before hurrying to catch up with his son.

CHAPTER 31

HUGO

June 20
Kfar Vitkin beach

Hugo dug a shallow bowl in the sand, then nestled down to lounge his back and cross his ankles. He watched the sun douse in the wide water and the stars emerge. The sea slid in and out, whispering like it had secrets.

Hugo knew the names of none of the hundred armed men and women waiting on the secluded, half-mile-wide beach. They were Irgun, too, and like him had hidden themselves for years. Tonight they stayed isolated the way Hugo did beneath a rising full moon, or they chatted softly in twos and threes.

An hour after nightfall, Pinchus walked down the beach into the seafoam; he signaled out to sea with a red-shaded torch, three blinks, a pause, three blinks. Five minutes later, he flashed again. Pinchus kept this up for an hour. Hugo marveled to see Pinchus barefoot. He carried no weapon. Hugo had never seen Pinchus touch a gun. Hugo was unarmed. He was a terrible shot.

At 9:00 p.m., the signals from the beach were answered out of the darkness offshore. Hugo brushed his trousers and walked across the cooling sand, two hundred meters up to the coast road.

Trucks lined the street. Hugo walked two blocks to the one he'd driven to Kfar Vitkin, opened the passenger door, and shook Vince by the shoe to wake him.

✳ ✳ ✳

The *Altalena* bumped into a shallow underwater shelf and had to back away. Fifty meters offshore, the lightless freighter cut engines and idled. From its masthead, the ship flew the new flag of the state of Israel.

Hugo and Vince stood with the Irgunists peering out at the moon-silver ship. Many walked into the water calf-deep just to be closer. The sea lapped at the *Altalena*'s hull and the legs of the silent Irgunists. The ship had come a long way; the Irgunists wanted to cheer her arrival, but the stealth of the night, the lonely beach, and their clandestine nature kept them quiet.

A launch motored away from the ship, puttering through the small surf. Pinchus stepped from the crowd accompanied by another man, also carrying his shoes and socks. Together, they crossed the sand not to greet the launch but in Hugo's direction.

Hugo did not know the man with Pinchus, but some Irgunists called out to him. Begin.

The man's name spread fast on the beach. The Irgunists, even Hugo, wanted to give him hurrahs but could not out of long habit, so the voices remained pent up, and the crowd only whispered "Begin" with the little waves coming and going.

Vince asked Hugo, "Who's Begin?"

"The commander of Irgun."

Pinchus and Begin approached. Hugo had never seen Begin before, but the man's similarity to Pinchus was noteworthy. Both were bland men, Pinchus in slacks and white short-sleeve shirt, Begin in a summer grey suit, jacket over his arm, his tie loosened. Begin's lips were full below round wire-rim glasses, his slender shoulders and spidery fingers made him appear clever. Pinchus smiled to make the introduction.

Pinchus said, "Menachem Begin. This is Vince Haas."

CHAPTER 32

VINCE

Over a handshake, Begin said, "Finally, I meet Vince Haas. Pinchus speaks well of you."

The commander was no older than Vince. An Eastern European accent colored his English. He was small-boned, but his hand felt consequential.

"Would you join me on the *Altalena*?"

"I would."

"You might want to take off your shoes and socks. We'll be there a while and you don't want them wet."

Hugo bent to untie his own shoes.

Pinchus said, "Hugo."

Looking at his own feet, plucking at his laces, Hugo said, "You made me his liaison. I go where Vince goes."

No one spoke until Hugo had stripped away his brogans and socks. Straightening, holding them, he said to Vince, "Tell them."

Vince said, "I suppose he's with me."

Begin pushed up his glasses with one finger, a delicate gesture.

"This is Kharda?" Begin knew Hugo's *nomme de guerre*, the Arabic word for scrap iron.

Pinchus said, "It is."

Begin stepped back, and both slight men holding shoes beheld each other. Begin gave an appraising nod, then turned for the launch bobbing in the froth.

Pinchus walked after Begin. Vince undid his boots and socks and followed Hugo to the launch.

✳ ✳ ✳

A thousand young Jews clapped the instant Begin stepped aboard the *Altalena*. Men and women closed around the commander to touch him and say "thank you" to his face.

They'd been at sea for almost two weeks and looked it: tanned, in khaki shorts, sandals, berets, and ballcaps. Sharp, honed by privation, these immigrant Jews looked ready to plunge wherever they might be pointed.

Hugo left Vince's side to wade into the hurly-burly around Begin. Pinchus stayed back with Vince.

Vince asked, "Irgun recruits?"

"When they reach shore, the army will take them to Netanya and induct them. That is the agreement."

"Are these ones trained, at least?"

"We worked with them for a month in Marseille waiting for the ship to leave port."

"A month."

Pinchus shrugged. Humans were math.

Vince asked, "Where'd you find them?"

"DP camps in Europe. Mostly Italians, Austrians, Germans, Czechs. A few volunteers. Two from America. Fifteen are Cuban."

"What about the embargo?"

"These are Jews, Mister Haas. We make no determination beyond that."

A babel ringed Begin; the young folk raised hands hoping he would look their way. Hugo vanished into the swarm, too.

Vince asked, "Don't you want some of that? You've been living underground for years. Go get a pat on the back."

"I don't want credit, Mister Haas. I don't intend to stay political beyond today."

"What do you want?"

"A lemon tree. Maybe two."

"You've got blood on your hands, Pinchus. A lot of it."

"The lemon is a bitter fruit."

"What about today?"

"Today, I have guns."

"Alright. How many?"

"The *Altalena* has brought three hundred light machine guns. Five hundred PIATs. Five thousand or so rifles. I don't know how many grenades. Anti-aircraft guns. Five tanks. Five million bullets."

Vince whistled. "All this goes to your fighters in Jerusalem?"

"Only one-fifth to Jerusalem. Two-fifths to Irgun battalions inside the Israeli Defense Force. The rest will be given to the government."

"Did Ben-Gurion agree to that?"

"He is aware of everything. We brought the ship to Kfar Vitkin on his suggestion. He knew it would arrive today. He knows we have brought recruits and arms."

"Then what's the disagreement?"

"We haven't settled the distribution of the guns. That is the government's only quarrel. But is it too much to ask that the nine hundred who arrived on this ship be allowed to enlist in the IDF fully armed?"

"Who paid? America?"

"Certainly our American friends contributed. Also Belgium and Sweden. Spanish anarchists. The French government."

"That's quite a list."

"Many in the world do not admire the idea of British influence in the Middle East. They support a free and strong Jewish state as a check on that."

The euphoria over Begin's arrival faded; the departure of the immigrants started. The *Altalena*'s launch and two lifeboats shuttled ten at a time to the beach. In the moonlight, several private watercraft arrived to help the debarking.

To watch the goings-on, Vince climbed the metal steps to the ship's pilot house. Some American crew members passed him sitting there, but Americans weren't Vince's story.

✳ ✳ ✳

By dawn, most of the new arrivals had been ferried ashore and taken away to serve in the IDF. A third of the *Altalena*'s cargo had already been moved to the beach.

Pinchus disappeared in the night. Vince wished for Pinchus that life would treat him fairly but couldn't guess what fairness would look like for a man such as him. Perhaps lemon trees, likely not.

Crates were hoisted out of the *Altalena*'s hold and swung on deck; from there, strong shoulders carried them down the gangway to the motor launch and lifeboats. A few *moshavot* from Kfar Vitkin rowed out in dinghies to spirit away the smaller cartons.

Onshore in the brightening morning, the boxes mounted in the sand. The Irgunists had stopped transferring the crates to their trucks waiting on the Kfar Vitkin road. No one on the *Altalena* knew why. Vince hitched a ride to shore.

He stepped out into the rolling shallows and didn't care if his boots got wet. The morning had dawned hot, there'd be time to dry. Vince tied on his "P" armband so no one would expect him to carry anything. Walking the beach, he scribbled a fast inventory of the weaponry bottlenecked on shore: two million English cartridges, a thousand English rifles, thirty Bren guns, three thousand PIAT shells. The hundred Irgunists stacked the crates neatly on the sand, then stood guard. Across all their backs rode Sten guns and Mauser rifles.

Two miles offshore, a duo of sleek corvettes paced the horizon, Israeli naval ships monitoring the *Altalena*.

To find out why none of the arms were being transferred to vehicles, Vince walked up to the coast road.

Manned barriers blocked the pavement in both directions. Army trucks clogged the road and the weedy shoulder. Two soldiers approached, pistols in hand. They called out in Hebrew.

Vince tapped his press armband but that got him nothing; the soldiers did not holster their sidearms. He tried English, then German, but the pair didn't understand. Vince began to back away when an order in Hebrew was snapped like a whip from behind the guards. The two put away their pistols.

Dayan advanced between them.

"Mister Haas. Why am I not surprised to see you here?"

"Major. You took the words right out of my mouth."

When Dayan turned to walk off, he trailed a hand for Vince to join him.

Vince asked, "On the record?"

"No."

Vince stuffed the pencil back into the band of his straw hat.

He asked, "Why aren't you letting the guns off the beach?"

"The Irgun is flaunting them in the face of the government. In the face of the embargo."

Vince stepped in front of Dayan. He pushed out a hand like a man reaching for a doorknob.

"Hang on. You took me to watch planes come in from Czechoslovakia filled with guns. How's this any different?"

"Those airplanes are being done secretly. Elegantly. At a closed site. If I hadn't taken you there, you wouldn't know about it. This."

Dayan aimed a finger at the beach where the Irgun's guns mounted.

"This a carnival. Begin is thumbing his nose at the United Nations. He's showing the world the Irgun still has powerful friends. It's vulgar. A public defiance of the truce. The fact that you're here should tell you that."

"So what are you doing here?"

"I have six hundred soldiers surrounding the beach. The Irgun will not break out. Those crates will not leave Kfar Vitkin in any trucks but mine."

"What if Begin won't give them up?"

"Then I will take them."

"By force?"

"We will return fire if fired upon. Those are my orders."

"Jew against Jew. You would do that?"

"Mister Haas, understand that we are building a nation. A nation for Jews, yes, but first a nation of laws. If we permit two armed forces in our state, then there is no state. There is no Israel. The Irgun is welcome to play at politics. They are not welcome to have their own army. If Begin tries to give weapons to anyone but the government, he is a traitor to Israel. So, yes. Jew against Jew. If I have to."

"Well, good luck to you."

"Where are you going?"

"Back down to the beach. To do my job. On the record."

Dayan put a hand in Vince's chest.

"I would stay off the beach."

"Why?"

The major unbuttoned a tunic pocket to retrieve a folded page. He handed it to Vince.

"Right about now, Begin is reading this."

CHAPTER 33

HUGO

Aboard the Altalena
Off Kfar Vitkin

The instant the motor launch was secured alongside, a crewman leaped out. He flew up the *Altalena*'s gangway, a sheet of paper clutched in a fist. On deck, he hurried to find Begin, handed over the page, and stepped aside, huffing.

Several of Irgun's leaders surrounded Begin. Hugo drifted in close behind them.

The commander read the message privately. As he read, he grumbled, "I seem to recall the British gave me ultimatums, too."

Begin held out the page for whomever wished to read it next. Someone took it; Begin hurried off, shouting that the offloading of the weapons and munitions must stop. The Irgunist who took the message read it aloud:

> To: M. Begin
>
> By special order from the Chief of the General Staff of the Israel Defense Forces, I am empowered to confiscate the weapons and military materials which have arrived on the Israeli coast, in the name

of the Israel Government. I demand you hand over the weapons for safekeeping and inform you that you should establish contact with the supreme command. You are required to carry out this order immediately.

If you do not agree to carry out this order, I shall use all the means at my disposal to implement the order and to requisition the weapons which have reached shore and transfer them from private possession into the possession of the Israel government.

The entire area is surrounded by fully armed military units and armored cars, and all roads are blocked.

I hold you fully responsible for any consequences in the event of your refusal to carry out this order.

The immigrants—unarmed—will be permitted to travel to the camps in accordance with your arrangements. You have ten minutes to give me your answer.

D. Even
Commander Alexandroni Brigade

Begin stalked back to the group. He snagged the IDF's order, folded it and stuffed it into his trousers.

An Irgunist asked, "Ten minutes. What are you going to do?"

Begin turned his eyes skyward, playing out scenarios. Then he leveled his gaze.

"I'm going ashore."

Hugo said, "I'll go with you."

"Kharda. Of course."

CHAPTER 34

VINCE

Kfar Vitkin beach

The thrum of an airplane coursed across the water.

Out of the south, from Tel Aviv, a little Cessna, white like a dove, flew two hundred feet over the sunny Mediterranean. It descended enough to fly behind the bobbing cargo ship before it zoomed above the beach where Begin's guns piled up. Then the white plane flew parallel to the coast road where Vince stood among Zahal soldiers readied for a fight. Blue letters marked the Cessna as a UN spotter.

Just as the plane banked for another circle over Kfar Vitkin, a motorboat left the *Altalena*. Two men manned the burbling craft. Menachem Begin stood nimbly in the bow; he kept his feet when the boat struck the shallows. Hugo, who could drive anything, sat at the throttle and tiller.

Dayan marched the road with martial flair, hands behind his back. Vince got in behind him and stayed five paces back. Dayan didn't speak but didn't chase Vince off. The armed force Dayan commanded to confront a hundred Irgunists was four times larger than what he'd had to defend the Deganias against the Syrian army. This time, facing Jews, he had mortars, machine guns, even a pair of tanks to clog the road.

The sunlit confrontation hummed and coiled. Trivial waves scrolled ashore. The Irgunists stopped wrangling crates to duck behind them and aim up at their brethren. Overhead, the UN plane droned in wide, observant circles.

Hugo surfed a wave to beach the launch. Together with Begin he dragged the boat onto the sand. Neither he nor Hugo hid behind cover, though Dayan's many guns were in plain sight and pointed at both. Lying in the seagrass and saltweeds, soldiers shouted to each other that someone should just shoot Begin and be done with it.

On the sand, the Irgun commander called to gather his men around him. Warily, keeping an eye on the IDF, the Irgunists left the cover of the crates and flocked to him.

The ten-minute deadline passed. Vince caught up to Dayan.

"Try not to shoot me."

Dayan did a double take. "What?"

Vince stepped off the coast road onto the beach.

CHAPTER 35

HUGO

Kfar Vitkin beach

When Begin beckoned, his Irgunists formed into a hundred-man square, him at the center.

Vince strode down from the boardwalk. Alone, Hugo walked across the sand towards him. Vince blended in with the beach: straw hat, ashen hair and dun complexion, white shirt and faded khakis. Vince trod through heat mirages, one arm raised so he would be seen and not fired on.

Hugo called, "You need to wear a red scarf."

Vince shrugged to show he didn't understand Hugo's jibe.

"What do you need, Vince?"

They stopped at handshake distance but did not reach to each other.

"You remember the time you told me to get out of the King David Hotel? Just before it blew up?"

"Vividly."

"Get off this beach, Hugo."

"Why?"

"Why? Because I just came from the army. There's six hundred soldiers up there. They're not going to let you keep those weapons. They've got orders to take them from you. They'll shoot, Hugo."

"They won't."

"Yes, they fucking will. They've got tanks. Mortars. They've blocked the road. Look offshore, there's two gunships out there."

"Begin is still negotiating."

"He says he is but he's not. It's done, there's no agreement. Ben-Gurion's going to take the *Altalena*. Begin will have to give it up."

"Begin won't."

"Then he's going to get people killed. Listen to me. You don't need to be here. You're not a fighter."

"I beg your pardon."

"Remember, it's me you're talking to. You and I both know the only thing you can do here is get yourself shot or arrested. I'm telling you. As your friend. Get off this beach. No one will say a word, not to you. You're Kharda."

Begin's speech to his followers was too far away to be distinct, muted by waves and cawing gulls, but resentment was plain in his tones.

"Why stay, Hugo? Why? When have you given enough?"

Vince had his back turned to the road, to the army there. He didn't see what was occurring behind him.

A dozen, then twenty Zahal soldiers flowed down from the road. Their rifles were on their backs, not in their hands. They trotted with arms uplifted in greeting.

Hugo let Vince wait for an answer, wait until the deserting soldiers swelled to fifty crossing the hot beach under the gun barrels of the IDF.

When Hugo pointed, Vince turned to see.

Hugo said, "This is not about what I've given. It's about what I've earned. Them, too."

Now he extended a hand. Vince took it. Neither squeezed but only held the grip. To make the handshake firm would be to say goodbye, and they would not. Hugo released Vince.

He jogged off to join the returning Irgunists, to stand with Begin.

CHAPTER 36

VINCE

Kfar Vitkin beach

Vince walked the IDF lines, a half mile from blockade to blockade.

Not a soldier or Irgunist sat or stood in the shade. The midsummer sun beat on them all equally, unstinting, stirring. The uncovered mood of both soldiers and dissidents spoiled in the heat. Two hundred yards separated the two forces. On the sand, the Irgunists milled about, trapped. Behind them the *Altalena* bobbed, awaiting orders. Offshore, the duo of Israeli corvettes stalked the blue rim.

The afternoon simmered on. The Irgun had ignored the army's ten-minute ultimatum for several hours; every soldier felt the slap of that. The Zahal understood what the crates of war matériel would mean for their defense of Israel, and knew, too, there was much more left on the *Altalena*. They wanted to take it all and saw no reason to dither.

The day slouched toward sunset. Vince bummed a full canteen then took a seat on a sand berm. He pulled low his straw hat and gazed at the blue water and paltry waves. He could not spot Hugo on the dazzling beach.

An hour before dusk, one Irgunist under a white flag walked across the sand. Dayan went down to meet him. After a quick consult, Dayan nodded. The Irgunist returned to the beach, waving an all-clear.

Begin and four men came up the beach unarmed. Dayan shouted to his soldiers to let them through unaccosted.

The Irgun commander and his men reached the road, then walked north to the blockade there. Vince followed Begin at a distance. Outside the barbed-wire blockade, a black sedan waited.

No soldier said a word when Begin walked by.

✳ ✳ ✳

The sun hung just above the sea ninety minutes later when Begin returned to Kfar Vitkin. IDF guards stopped Vince from getting close enough to ask him anything. In jacket and tie, the commander fast-walked across the sunset beach. The four Irgunists loped at his sides like hounds.

Vince approached Dayan. "What happened?"

"Begin went to Netanya to speak with the government."

"What did Ben-Gurion say?"

"This."

Dayan handed over another piece of paper: a small, blue onionskin sheet. A short paragraph had been typed in the name of Ben-Gurion and delivered to Dayan as force commander:

Either they accept orders and carry them out, or you shoot. The time for agreements has passed, force must be applied without hesitation.

At the bottom of the page, beneath his name, Ben-Gurion had scribbled, "Immediately."

Vince held the page too long; Dayan plucked it from his hands. He walked off, tucking the paper into his tunic.

Vince didn't go back to his berm but stayed behind the Zahal frontline. Beyond the quiet *Altalena*, the sun leaked gold into the sea.

Once more on the beach, Begin gathered his Irgunists; again they made a square with him in the middle. Begin's words were indecipherable, but his movements inside the rectangle were those of a tired man.

On the sand, Begin raised an arm, then chopped it down. That one gesture by Begin, for some anonymous soldier, was enough.

An IDF machine gun opened up.

Jew against Jew.

CHAPTER 37

HUGO

Kfar Vitkin beach

Hugo and others ran towards Begin. Someone threw the commander down; Hugo lunged into the sand to put himself between Begin and the Zahal's guns.

Up and down the beach, the sudden wounded were dragged behind crates. Bullets winged on all sides of the Irgunists, zipped overhead and plumed in the sand. A volley raked close to Hugo. One of the Irgunists surrounding Begin shouted, "Get him off the beach!"

The rest of the hundred dissidents returned the army's fire. In seconds, Kfar Vitkin became a battle zone. With a thump, a mortar round blew in the sand. Furiously the Irgun and IDF traded bullets. A breeze shunted the gun smoke over the water.

A wounded Irgunist cried out at the soldiers, "What are you doing?"

Begin squirmed under the men lying on him. "Let me up!"

The Irgunists rolled off Begin. Sand stuck to his cheek, his glasses were askew. He glared at Hugo beside him.

"No," he said, as if giving Hugo an instruction.

Begin clambered to his feet, spilling sand off his coat and tie. Hugo and the others tightened ranks around him. Bullets stitched the beach; the soldiers knew which man was Begin. One of the Irgunists tugged the commander's arm. Begin yanked free.

He shook both fists at his Irgunists. He screamed, "Do not shoot back!"

If the Irgunists heard him, they didn't heed.

Before Begin could shout again or take a bullet, he was bundled away to the water's edge. Hugo and the others stayed close around him. Before Begin climbed into a waiting rowboat, he cast a heartbroken look through the cordite haze. He rubbed his lips with a trembling hand, then climbed over the side.

Hugo expected one of the bigger fellows to jump in. But the largest one shouted at him, "Can you row?"

"I can do it."

"Get in."

Hugo bounded into the rowboat. He faced Begin and took up the oars. Four Irgunists shoved the rowboat off the sand until it floated. Knee-deep in foam, they shrugged their weapons into their hands then sprinted back to the gunfight.

Leaning into the oars, Hugo pulled through the swells, rowing hard. Begin didn't look back at the receding beach. The violence didn't stop. Begin clutched the wooden bench under him with pallid knuckles.

"Kharda."

"Yes."

"Why did they do it?"

"Have you never been shot at before?"

"No. I was tortured once."

Hugo stroked, too busy with the oars and breathing to engage. What could he tell Begin? That Jews were never cruel, mindless, or jealous of power? That Jews would not fear other Jews? Begin knew the truth, of course, about Jews and every man. But Begin was wretched and forgot.

Out on the sea, machine guns chattered. The two Israeli navy ships charged in, firing all the way. Though the warships were a mile off, Begin raised imploring hands at them.

Hugo could not row so fast that he and Begin might reach the *Altalena* before the corvettes came in lethal range. Hugo poured his depleting muscles into the oars while Begin sat on the wooden bench, arms out, palms up, begging *why?* In the dusk, Begin seemed magnificently small.

Over the slapping oars and Hugo's laboring lungs, the engines of the *Altalena* revved. He risked another glance over his shoulder.

The freighter was maneuvering broadside to the Kfar Vitkin beach, to make itself a shield between the rowboat and the onrushing corvettes. Begin dropped his arms, safe for the moment. Hugo waned but still rowed with such force that Begin had to say "stop" when they neared the freighter.

Hugo's shoulders and knees ached. Begin helped him out of the boat onto the *Altalena*'s lowered platform.

Begin left it to others to get Hugo up the gangway. The crew didn't waste time with the rowboat but left it floating behind when their ship churned away from Kfar Vitkin.

Staggering onto the deck, Hugo peered at shore through the last of twilight. The pops of rifles and the burr of submachine guns did not fade with the onset of the stars and Begin's escape. The civil war for the crates was not over; the Zahal and Irgun continued to slug at each other across the beach.

On deck, Begin's cohort gathered around him. Hugo limped close enough to listen.

Begin said, "We'll head south."

The American captain asked, "Where?"

"We'll run aground in Tel Aviv. Off the beachfront."

"Why?"

"Whatever Ben-Gurion is brewing up, he can't do it in front of ten thousand people. The Yishuv will be on our side. UN observers will be there, and the press. In Tel Aviv, Ben-Gurion will have to talk directly to me."

Begin addressed the radioman with a headset around his neck.

"How many have we lost?

"Six killed. Eighteen wounded."

Begin lifted both hands behind his head, a pose of surrender. Stricken like this, he turned away. He faced Hugo, the only one on board who'd been on the beach with Begin.

Hugo said, "Put your arms down."

Begin nodded and lowered them. He walked aft. No one but Hugo walked with him.

At the stern rail, they looked beyond the freighter's roiling wake. Two hundred meters back on the dark sea, the two corvettes shadowed the *Altalena*.

CHAPTER 38

VINCE

Kfar Vitkin beach

Vince ran behind the Zahal's positions. He couldn't find Dayan to tell him to stop the shooting.

Irgun bullets whizzed above his head. When Vince was done running, he propped his hands on his knees to catch his breath. He waited for his heartbeat to drop, then walked the coast road.

Hundreds of soldiers swapped rounds with the Irgunists on the sand or took long-distance potshots at the rowboat stealing Begin back to the *Altalena*. Many of the Zahal refused to fire; they laid down their guns or pretended their weapons were jammed. Their officers yelled but that was all. Medics tended to several wounded. Two soldiers lay dead.

The Mediterranean stayed calm. Nothing the Jews did to each other across the sand of Kfar Vitkin whipped up the waters or the wind, and the evening fell lush and still. The fleeing *Altalena*'s steaming lights melted south towards Tel Aviv, hounded by the two warships.

Vince put away his pencil and found a palm to sit against. On the warm ground, he pulled down the brim of his tattered hat. He should get a new straw fedora. When he crossed his legs he thought the same of his boots and khakis. He'd bought the hat and clothes in a Brooklyn haberdashery three years ago. His pencil was new, from the boarding house in Tel Aviv.

***

Vince dozed through gunfire. When the reports dwindled and quit, he lifted his chin.

He checked his watch by the low, seaward moon: 5:00 a.m.

With a rattle of arms, six hundred soldiers left the road to flow onto the beach. They covered the area like animals returning to the sea. They shouted for the Irgunists to drop their weapons. The pair of tanks rumbled forward, dawn sentries over the Irgun's surrender.

Stiff from sleeping upright, Vince joined the uniformed boys flooding the beach.

The Irgunists were disarmed and arrested, the IDF deserters, too, all put in a line and marched away. Soldiers bore the crates off on their shoulders, to their own trucks on the coast road.

The moon painted a silver key on the sea. Vince asked soldiers and dissidents alike for news of Hugo.

CHAPTER 39

HUGO

June 21
On board the Altalena
Tel Aviv

The crew of the *Altalena* was a game bunch. When the corvettes fired a stream of white tracers across the bow, none of them flinched. The sailors were all former US Navy; they'd survived live fire before. Hugo had seen tracers at Deir Yassin. Begin, his Irgunists and the several dozen immigrants who'd stayed on board seemed the most rattled.

At midnight, with the lights of Tel Aviv in the offing, the captain angled towards land. One of the warships pitched ahead to cut the *Altalena* off from shore. The freighter's Yank skipper gave no quarter and held to his course at top speed; the cargo ship and one corvette bumped hulls. It seemed a needless and bellicose move from the navy. The immigrants sprang to the rail to shout a mash of languages at the Israeli seamen. Stop, they shouted, stop.

Over the loudspeaker, the *Altalena*'s captain announced, "Everyone. Brace yourselves."

The corvette peeled away from the freighter. Hugo held tight to a stairway rail and barely kept his feet when the ship scraped bottom. Every rivet groaned, her steel stretched; the *Altalena* scratched deep into the sand, then ground to a halt.

The captain shut down the engines. The *Altalena* shuddered a last time, steaming and panting from the final leg of her race. In the sudden quiet, Hugo and all aboard gathered at the bow to see where they'd ended up.

Begin, still in jacket and tie, pointed to shore one hundred fifty meters away across calm water.

"There's the Ritz Hotel on Frishman Street. The Palmach keep their headquarters there. Good. They won't have far to walk."

Begin, his bravado regained, commanded everyone to rest.

"In the morning," he said, "Ben-Gurion and I will end this."

Hugo found a cargo net spilled on the deck. The ropes were soft enough to be pushed about to make a sort of bed. He loosened his suspenders and lay in the netting. The *Altalena* cut off her deck lights. Hugo closed his eyes as the immigrants sang softly to themselves of comfort and prayer, songs Hugo recalled from the camps.

CHAPTER 40

VINCE

Tel Aviv

At the Kaete Dan, Vince grabbed an hour of sleep, a shower, and a change of clothes.

Sunrise found him sipping coffee on the hotel terrace with twenty other journalists. Together they watched Tel Aviv's Home Guard clear the beachfront of civilians while hundreds of Zahal troops unloaded from army trucks. The soldiers stacked sandbags and commandeered the boardwalk wherever they had a clear view of the sea.

The silent *Altalena* lay off the beach in glassy water like a ship-wrecked giant who'd crawled ashore in the night.

Last night at midnight, the jangle of far-off machine guns had drawn the newsmen out onto the Kaete Dan terrace. The white dashes of tracers at sea sent them all rushing down to the beach. Right in front of them, the *Altalena* rammed into the sand. The leviathan groaned but nothing more happened; after a while, the press returned to the hotel.

None but Vince had been at the battle of Kfar Vitkin. The others had nothing to go on but government pronouncements and rumors.

As the sun crested the buildings of Tel Aviv, the reporters interviewed each other over coffee and yesterday's pastries, to see who knew what. On the veranda, a reporter from *Die Welt* approached Vince.

"*Morgen.*"

"Morgen."

"What do you hear?"

"Same as you."

"No, Vincenz Haas. Not the same. What do you hear?"

"I'm pretty sure Begin's on that ship."

"*Ja?*" The German looked around as if Vince had given him gold. The man was thin with a prominent Adam's apple and a missing lower tooth. He slurped his coffee to appear nonchalant. "*Was noch?*"

"Ben-Gurion's done talking. There won't be any more negotiations."

"You say Ben-Gurion will take the Irgun ship?"

"*Ja.*"

"*Wie?*"

"Any way he has to."

"By guns?"

"Any way he has to."

"You are sure?"

"*Ich bin mir sicher.* What do you hear?"

"Gossip. I hear gossip."

"Like?"

"The usual breathlessness. Menachem Begin is a fascist. He will bring his guns onto the beach and take over Tel Aviv. He will declare his own Irgun state."

"*Nein.*"

"Yes, I understand. *Nein.* Gossip. But this is what is being said. By the government. By the soldiers with weapons pointed at *das boot.*"

"Begin thought he could bargain with Ben-Gurion. He miscalculated."

"Will there be more shooting today?"

"Maybe." Then Vince said, "Yeah."

"*Ach. Die Juden.*"

This sounded wrong coming from a German. Vince patted the reporter's scrawny arm and left him to grab another coffee.

✳ ✳ ✳

A hundred foreign newsmen filled the chairs in the Ritz ballroom. Vince stood at the back, one dirty boot against the fancy wall. He figured he'd hear nothing this morning he didn't already know. If he chose to leave, he could slip out without a fuss.

The crowd of journalists all were working on high alert, caffeine, and nicotine. They quizzed each other, leaning left and right; because their chairs were arranged on a dance floor and a mirrored ball dangled over their heads, the press corps, even sitting, appeared to dance.

Israel's foreign minister entered the ballroom with an echoing stride. The reporters hushed when he tapped a few pages on the lectern before them. The minister needed no microphone; the big room had marvelous acoustics.

The minister had a doe-eyed composure and a bristly head of hair. His moustache was very thick. He did not start with a greeting of the journalists. In Russian-tinged English, he read a statement:

"The government is resolved to maintain its sovereignty. We will not permit political and military anarchy from rebellious dissidents. The Jewish people are badly in need of arms, but it is better to see them go up in flames than into the hands of those who will turn them against the state. The *Altalena* must be turned over to the government immediately, and unconditionally."

Vince lowered his boot from the wall. This was, indeed, nothing new.

Then the minister lied.

"The Irgun has broken all agreements it made with the government. They did not inform us of the date of the boat's arrival nor where it was going to anchor."

Pinchus had told Vince the exact opposite. Also, the pair of Israeli navy warships prowling around the *Altalena* demonstrated that Ben-Gurion had known precisely when and where the Irgun ship would arrive in Israel's waters. Added to that was Dayan's prompt appearance with six hundred armed troops and twenty empty trucks.

The minister read more:

"Early this morning, at Kfar Vitkin, one hundred and fifty Irgun rebels surrendered to an overwhelming IDF force. The Irgunists have been retained for questioning. The weapons and munitions the dissidents loaded illegally onto the beach have been recovered."

A French reporter asked: "How much did you get?"

The minister shuffled for the proper page. "Two million English cartridges. Fifteen hundred English rifles. Forty Bren guns, five PIATS, and three thousand PIAT shells. Sixty more crates have yet to be opened."

According to Pinchus, the *Altalena* had almost three times that arsenal still belowdecks. Ben-Gurion would sink it or blow it all up before he'd let Begin keep a single bullet.

A question came from the German reporter. "To take the ship, will the government use force?"

The foreign minister tapped his papers again on the podium to show this was the last answer he'd give.

"The State of Israel is engaged in a civil war. If we are given no choice, then we will resort to force, as would any other nation."

"What if you do not take the ship?"

"Then we must disband our own army. Israel cannot have two separate militaries."

The minister walked across the long ballroom floor to the door. The reporters, whether out of respect or fascination, waited out the official's clicking exit. Before they could stampede out of the Ritz, Vince got a head start.

✳ ✳ ✳

He didn't rush back to the Kaete Dan terrace with the rest of the journalists. As he had at Kfar Vitkin, Vince walked the IDF's lines. No one told him to leave, maybe because he'd been seen yesterday with Dayan. This morning in Tel Aviv, Dayan wasn't in charge and was nowhere to be seen.

The beach stayed empty. On board the *Altalena*, Begin and his men kept out of sight. Vince caught no sight of Hugo.

Palmach troops arrived in droves. By the dozen, they jumped off the gates of hurried trucks to spread out along the beachfront. They set up sandbagged machine-gun nests, snipers took perches on roofs.

Ten thousand citizens of Tel Aviv thronged beachfront patios and sidewalks. Even hundreds of yards away, they were in range of the weapons of the IDF and the *Altalena*.

More trucks rumbled up on the coast road, disgorging troops. The firepower facing the quiet cargo ship was immense. This was no bluff by Ben-Gurion.

Into the midmorning, the *Altalena* stayed buttoned up. Tel Aviv was hotter than Kfar Vitkin; tall buildings blocked the breezes, and miles of concrete beamed heat. Vince walked in the sun where the soldiers were.

Gradually, the stillness of the standoff began to dissolve. A zephyr off the sea crashed growing waves onto the beach with chesty rumbles. The stranded *Altalena* began to bob in the shallows as the tide came in. The heat took on an audible sizzle, insects in the seafront trees ticked.

At noon, Vince cupped a hand above his straw brim to look out to the *Altalena*. Out from behind the ship's hull puttered a small motor launch. Soldiers onshore leveled hundreds of guns at the twelve men in the little craft.

No one fired. The Irgunists were allowed to hop out into the froth and drag their boat onto the beach. They dispersed quickly. Each carried a weapon, two on his back. The Irgunists dug into the sand just thirty yards from the soldiers. From there, the Jews pointed guns at each other.

A second launch swung around the bow of the *Altalena*. A dozen more Irgunists and their weapons headed for shore.

Near Vince on the warm sidewalk, two soldiers crouched behind a Spandau machine gun. One manned the trigger, the other the ammo belt. A lieutenant arrived behind them.

"Do not let that boat reach shore."

Without hesitating, the gunner pulled his hands off the grips, the ammo man let go of the bullet belt. Both stood to face their officer.

The gunner said, "I will not."

The ammo man said, "No."

Every soldier within earshot froze. A wave thumped in the shallows while the second Irgun boat motored in.

The lieutenant did not turn from the Spandau crew. Nearby, two more soldiers manned a Bren gun. The lieutenant issued the same command to them. These gunners, too, stood away from their weapon, against the order. The officer drew his sidearm but did not lift it, as though the pistol had broken his arm.

The second Irgun launch had motored halfway to shore. On the boardwalk, another officer, a captain, stamped up to the Spandau and Bren crews. His jaw muscles worked. He was a trim man, chiseled down to bulging veins and eyes.

The lieutenant had not raised his pistol. The captain gestured at the Spandau crew.

"These men defied a direct order."

"Yes."

"You soldiers. Open fire on that launch. Now."

The Spandau and Bren crews all shook their heads.

The Spandau gunner said, "I'd rather hang."

The captain shot a glance at Vince. He seemed to want to do this in front of a reporter. He motioned to the younger lieutenant, then the Spandau crew.

"Shoot them."

The lieutenant holstered his sidearm.

"Not that."

The captain pointed at the *Altalena* and the launch.

"If that second boat lands, there will be a third and a fourth. We will have a battle with the Irgun in the middle of Tel Aviv. More Jews than these two will die today. Shoot them or I will shoot you."

Vince took a step forward. He couldn't speak or act; he'd be arrested. But he couldn't stand and watch.

One of the Irgunists in the sand lay close enough to hear. He shouted, "Kill your own people, will you? Is this what you want?"

The captain reached for his own pistol in a black holster at his hip. He drew the sidearm.

Vince took a second step.

The captain hesitated, eyes on Vince now. He'd not anticipated a reporter who might act.

"Step back, Mister Haas."

Vince said, "No."

"You're not a Jew. This is not your concern."

"I know."

Then, the same way it happened at Kfar Vitkin, someone on the IDF's line, some unknown soldier, fired.

CHAPTER 41

HUGO

On board the Altalena
Tel Aviv

The Zahal opened up on the Irgunists. Those lying on the beach burrowed deeper into the sand; the dozen men in the motorboat plowed through water skewered with bullets all around them. In the shallows, the launch turned sharply and sped back to the *Altalena*.

None of the Irgunists returned fire.

Hugo watched with Begin from the *Altalena*'s bow. He demanded, "Why aren't they shooting back?"

Begin said, "I told them no. There will be no *milchemet achim*." No war of brothers.

Hugo slapped the rail as if to wake Begin. The commander walked away.

Quickly, the dozen fighters on the beach were overwhelmed. The Zahal flanked them; the Irgunists could not escape by sea or land, so they surrendered. When the shooting stopped, only three of the Irgun rose to their feet; four were wounded and needed help off the sand. Soldiers carried away the five Irgunists killed.

Hugo stayed at the ship's bow. On the *Altalena* the Irgun had enough machine guns and PIATS and fighters to hit back hard at the Zahal and force them to deal. Begin had said he and Ben-Gurion would negotiate. The bodies of Irgunists were Ben-Gurion's opening bid. Where was Begin's counter?

None of the Irgunists in the second launch had been wounded, though many holes splintered the little boat's side. The men ran up the gangway while more rounds pinged off the *Altalena*'s bow.

Hugo dove for the deck. Automatic rounds raked the superstructure and drubbed on the hollow-sounding hull. On all fours, Hugo crawled fast to find Begin.

The commander kneeled at midship beside a crewman. The sailor, an American, had been struck in the chest by a ricochet. Men shouted for medical help while Begin held the young Yank's hand. He leaned over close to speak in heavy, quiet English. Begin's tie dipped into the blood of the American's wound.

The dozen fighters from the launch straggled onto the deck from the gangway. Instantly, one crumpled, struck in the leg.

Hugo slithered to Begin until his ribs were against the commander. He stayed tight to Begin while the hurt crewman and Irgunist were dragged off.

CHAPTER 42

VINCE

Tel Aviv

Many soldiers fired at the *Altalena*, many would not. Officers tramped behind them shouting that they must shoot or go to jail. A few put down their guns and walked away into Tel Aviv. Others stood to be arrested. Most aimed high above the ship or bounced rounds off her steel hull to keep the officers off their backs.

This nibbling went on until noon. No one on the *Altalena* shot back at them. The heat made the day drag; the Zahal's shots became sporadic. Vince considered returning to the Kaete Dan for lunch but worried that if he left the IDF's position he might not be allowed back in past the barricades. Dayan wasn't here. Probably, even wisely, he'd picked today to take the Jerusalem job.

With the sun peaking, the white sand made everyone wince. After noon, the shooting stopped altogether. A government negotiator with a bullhorn padded out onto the beach. He rolled up his white shirtsleeves but not his pants and did not take off his shoes to wade into the water.

"*Altalena*." The bullhorn made the man's voice tinny.

A loudspeaker crackled on the ship. Begin replied, "Yes."

"A representative of the government will board your ship and arrange to have the wounded taken off. We will also arrange the unloading of your cargo."

Begin mulled this for moments, then said, "We do not want war with our brothers."

"Nor do we."

"We wish to have our wounded treated."

"We will come aboard and help."

The loudspeaker clicked once, as though Begin had started to speak but caught himself—or was interrupted.

"We want to negotiate."

The government man stood firm against a small wave that soaked his shirtfront and tie.

"No."

The conversation, amplified by the bullhorn and the ship's loud-speaker, carried to every soldier on the coast road, and every one of ten thousand Israeli citizens watching from the boardwalk, beachfront shops, and rooftops.

Begin pleaded, "Please send help for the wounded. Also, we have dead."

The bullhorn said, "First, you must surrender your ship and cargo without condition."

"Is requesting help for the hurt and the dead a condition?"

The government man hesitated over this.

"Yes."

The government man waited for Begin's reply. He lowered the bull-horn and stood a long while in the surf.

✳ ✳ ✳

The *Altalena* hunkered, silent and stagnant, long into the afternoon. The waves lessened and the ship no longer rocked on them.

The Zahal brooded, as well. Vince talked with the soldiers. He sat between two brothers in steel helmets manning a mortar.

"What do you think?"

"The Irgun wants to split Israel in two."

The second brother added, "We've got to stop them."

Vince said, "But aren't they like you? Jews who just want to fight for Israel."

"The state matters more."

"More than anything?"

"Than anything."

"How about those soldiers who didn't shoot?"

"We know who they are."

"And the ones who walked away?"

"They'll answer."

Officers roamed among the boys and girls they commanded. The officers didn't shout anymore but spoke plainly. They said, "Begin's a criminal. So are the Irgun. They'll destroy Israel for their own power. Only you stand in their way. Remember to follow orders. No matter how hard."

At three o'clock, hungry and sweat-soaked, Vince headed across the coast road to the Kaete Dan for a meal, coffee, and a fresh shirt.

He tipped his straw hat up to the reporters on the veranda. Before he entered the guesthouse, a truck headed his way on Hayarkon, popping as if backfiring. Vince stayed beside the road while the truck, weaving across both lanes, rushed closer. The pops were not the engine backfiring, but gunfire. Vince hustled into the hotel.

He ran up a stairwell to the veranda. There, with twenty ducking journalists, Vince peeked down at an army lorry barreling past. In the truck's bed, ten soldiers fired Stens and rifles at the backs of the IDF soldiers arrayed along the seafront. The truck smashed through a striped-pole barrier, then careened around a corner.

A second military truck rumbled in from the opposite direction. Again, the soldiers riding in the bed took shots at soldiers on the boardwalk.

When both trucks had gone, Vince and the others got to their feet with caution. A few had not put down their afternoon gins. One was a UN truce observer, a middle-aged Parisian with a hand-rolled cigarette stuck on his lower lip. His drink was anisette.

The Frenchman pinched the cigarette off his lip. He whirled it beside his head as he asked Vince, "What was that?"

"Irgun."

"But they were soldiers. In uniforms."

"They're probably from Jerusalem."

"They abandon Jerusalem? To come here and shoot at other Jews?"

"You saw what I saw."

"They fight for the ship of guns."

"No. It's for the dead Irgunists at Kfar Vitkin. And here."

Vince, the UN observer, and six other journalists climbed three stories to the Kaete Dan's roof. The view of the *Altalena*, the beachfront, and the city was good enough, and the risk was a lot less. Vince had pushed his luck plenty over the last two days.

The roof had no shade, and Vince didn't know how long he could take it under his straw hat. Irgun sympathizers careened the avenues in stolen army trucks, entreating supporters through loudspeakers to bear witness to the government's crimes against the *Altalena*, Ben-Gurion's civil war. Tel Aviv's civilians rushed from one block to another running from the sounds of gunfire or, curious, to it.

At the Armon Hotel a block away a gunfight broke out. The shooting sounded insistent, the noises of men trying to kill each other. Sporadic barks of sniper fire issued from a park on Ben Yehuda Street and from Allenby in the business district. On Hayarkon, truckloads of soldiers raced back and forth, loaded with angry boys from both sides. Twice an IDF lorry passed a truck filled with Irgunists; they zoomed by each other, then traded rounds as afterthoughts because all the fighters wore the same uniform.

Along the boardwalk, in cafés, hotels, and homes, Irgunists and Zahal took up positions. The clashes were short-lived but fierce. A woman with yellow hair stumbled past the Kaete Dan, blood trickling off her arm. A screaming soldier dragged his wounded buddy out of the park. An Irgunist lost the top of his head to a sniper bullet; he jogged in small circles for strange moments until he fell in the middle of Hayarkon.

Skirmishes flared in the south and center of the city. On the smooth sea, the *Altalena*'s shadow reached for shore. She was the prize and the cause. The government man with the bullhorn, who'd stood in the surf in his shoes, never reappeared.

The day grew late, stewing in violence. Vince wanted to get out of the sun but couldn't, not with the running combat swirling around the Kaete Dan. As he sketched the *Altalena* in his notebook, a jagged whistle high overhead stopped his pencil. Out on the water, a hundred yards behind the *Altalena*, a white pillar spouted.

Vince muttered to no one, "No."

Another shell overflew the ship, exploding closer, fifty yards away from the hull.

The French peacekeeper asked Vince, "These are warning shots, yes?"

Vince said, "I don't know."

A third shell landed close enough to spray the *Altalena*.

Instantly, the ship's Star of David flag was lowered. In its stead, a white banner was run up; the surrender banner whipped in the wind. Along the beachfront, on Hayarkon and in the park, the gunfight between Irgun and Zahal paused.

Vince had not heard the cannons that fired the first three shells at the *Altalena*. Nor did he hear the fourth.

CHAPTER 43

HUGO

On board the Altalena
Tel Aviv

Hugo ran without knowing where. The three falling artillery shells had simply set him running.

He stopped sprinting at the bow, facing land and the guns there, arms at his sides, shoulders square. He hadn't died in Germany. Would Jews kill him in Israel?

The next shell slammed into the *Altalena*. Hugo was rocked off his feet. He scrambled upright and shrieked at the shore.

Within moments, smoke coursed from the ship's midsection; the cargo hold had caught fire from the blast. Irgunists shouted and pointed up at the white flag. Others took up weapons to fight back.

Already aground, the ship could not sink. But it could blow up. Hugo went looking for Begin to throw him overboard if he had to.

Begin appeared, flashing down the stairs from the superstructure. He sprinted along the ship's starboard rail, tie and coattails flying; shouting for his men to stop firing. Begin pushed down on gun barrels. "They're your brothers! Do not shoot!" Every Irgunist he accosted lowered his gun. After Begin ran past, some took up firing again.

Hugo stepped into his path. Begin stopped and beheld Hugo with a tight nod to show he was glad Hugo was alive still.

Begin said, "I need you."

"We've got to abandon ship."

"You're a plumber. Go below with some of the crew. Open the pipes, put out the fire. Save the guns."

"It's too late."

Begin brushed past and said no more to Hugo.

He started to call after Begin, but a big Irgunist yanked Hugo by the arm.

"You heard him."

✳ ✳ ✳

Munitions cooking off belowdecks shook the freighter's ribs. Hugo hurried down the steel stairwell along with six Yank crewmen.

The engine room was a miasma of turbines, tubes, pistons, and gauges. In the mint-painted enclosure, Hugo and the Americans opened every valve that might fight the blaze. Nothing pressurized. They didn't have enough time to build up steam in the boiler of a ship that had been dormant for eighteen hours. They might flood the hold with seawater, but those valves were elsewhere, deeper and towards the blaze. When Hugo and the seamen left the engine room to head there, smoke filled the passageways, heat coursed in the walls.

One American said, "Nope."

Instead of going down, the American leaped up the stairwell two treads at a time. The other Yanks followed, Hugo in the rear.

On deck, they reported to Begin. The ship was on fire, and nothing could stop it. Begin looked to Hugo for the final word. Hugo nodded.

Begin said, "Everyone overboard."

The crewmen hustled away to spread the word: the ship was lost. Begin put his back to the smoke coursing from the burning gash in the *Altalena*. He faced shore, perhaps wondering, like Hugo, if Jews would kill him today.

Without facing him, Begin said, "Go, Kharda."

"I'll stay with you."

"Are you still Irgun?"

Hugo moved in front of Begin to give his answer.

"Yes."

"Then do as I say."

"Thank you, Commander."

Begin walked away.

He seemed unhurried; he could no longer affect events. On all sides, men plummeted off the ship. The deck trembled from another detonation, the hull pinged from striking bullets. Even with the *Altalena* mortally hurt, the Zahal on shore opened fire again.

Hugo hurried after Begin. Once more, he put himself in Begin's path.

Hugo said, "Thank me."

"For what?"

"You know who I am. What I've done."

"I do."

"Then fucking thank me."

Gunshots and ricochets swirled around them; the timpani of more blasts tolled inside the *Altalena*.

Begin said, "No."

The big Irgunist who'd sent Hugo down to the engine room swept in. He drove one broad shoulder into Hugo's chest and lifted him with little effort. Hugo was kicking when the man threw him feet-first over the starboard rail.

Hugo waved his arms and legs on the long drop and shouted nothing intelligible. His shoes stuck the water hard; he plunged to the sand where his toes touched.

He exhaled to stay underwater. Hugo stood beside the great hull wedged into the sandbar. Sunlight wavered around him in strips, like wings without birds. He closed his eyes, crossed his arms, and rested.

The water muffled the violence up in the dry world. The sea cooled Hugo and swaddled him. He was made light. He thought of nothing and paused his memory. His arms floated off his chest. Hugo wished only to stay longer.

He pushed off the sand, surfaced, and drew a gasp. Men splashed around him and bullets fizzed. Water flooded into Hugo's open mouth. The sea was salty off Israel; it tasted like blood.

CHAPTER 44

VINCE

Tel Aviv

Vince charged down the steps of the Kaete Dan. He burst into the street then across open ground. Soldiers ordered him to stop, but no one raised a gun. He didn't break stride.

On the boardwalk, Vince hopped the rail to the beach. Many others were on the sand, too, brave residents of Tel Aviv trying to get in between the Irgunists and the soldiers, trying to do something, anything, to stop the fighting between Jews. Vince joined them at the lapping edge of the water 150 yards from the flaming, booming *Altalena*.

Bullets whizzed above their heads. Snipers in the Ritz Hotel and nearby houses kept targeting Irgunists leaping off the ship or swimming ashore and those citizens swimming out to help. The people of the city shouted at the Zahal, "They are your people, what are you doing?"

The *Altalena* burned terribly. A wind from the east blew the smoke out to sea; the fire climbed high enough to lick above the deck. The wounded were lowered by ropes to kayaks rowed out by civilians. The snipers targeted even them.

The first survivors from the ship straggled into the shallows. The people of Tel Aviv pushed through the waves to reach them. Irgunists and immigrants landed on the sand exhausted; they collapsed on their backs or sat with sopping heads between their knees.

Vince asked many of them, "Do you know Hugo Ungar? Kharda? Did you see him?"

No one knew Hugo. In the chaos, Vince had no more time to inquire; the IDF arrived to take the soaked Irgunists into custody. The men and women of Tel Aviv jeered at the soldiers.

Vince tore off his shirt and straw hat, then ran into the waves until he dove. He swam his fastest.

A small fleet of rowboats and canoes arrived around him at the *Altalena*. More Irgunists fell, surfaced, and clambered into the dozens of crafts to be spirited away. They were not taken to shore where the IDF would arrest them, but south so they might escape.

Vince swam close enough to the hull to hear the steel flex from the heat. More explosions pounded below the waterline; the blaze was touching off antiaircraft shells and the millions of bullets. Three more Irgunists splashed down. The first to pop up was Begin in jacket and tie. The others were American crewmen. Lifeguards paddled in close to pull all three onto large surfboards. Begin and the Americans were rowed away south, too.

No one else jumped off the dying ship. The shooting from shore stopped. Vince backpaddled, took a last look, then stroked for shore. Behind him, a series of detonations finished the *Altalena* in pulses that shook the water.

In the shallows, Vince dragged out of the sea. He reclaimed his shirt and straw hat. Bare-chested, dripping, he trudged to a row of six soaked corpses in the sand. They lay face up, glistening in the sun.

Someone else had found Hugo.

CHAPTER 45
June 22

TEL AVIV
ISRAEL
By Vincent Haas

Herald Tribune News Service

The Jewish civil war is over.

It flared over the *Altalena*, a ship of guns. On one side stood the Israeli government, on the other the Irgun, the dissident group who along with the Stern Gang chose violence as the tool to drive the British out of Palestine.

Menachem Begin commands the Irgun. David Ben-Gurion runs the government. The two despise each other.

Soon after the creation of the Israeli state in May, Irgun's Begin found $3 million to buy a freighter stuffed with weapons and ammo. Eleven days ago that ship, the *Altalena*, sailed from France carrying war matériel and 940 Irgun recruits from the displaced persons camps of Europe. The Royal Navy trailed the *Altalena* all the way across the Mediterranean. The guns were intended to arm Irgunists defending the Old City of Jerusalem. The rest of the arsenal was ticketed for the Israeli Defense Force, called the Zahal.

Begin claims the government knew about the ship, the cargo, the plan, the landing site, everything. Ben-Gurion says he was shocked to learn the Irgun had been importing weapons in violation of the embargo. The truth is that the *Altalena* arrived in darkness at a site picked by the government, an out-of-the-way spot at Kfar Vitkin, to avoid scrutiny from the U.N.'s peacekeepers.

Then, at the eleventh hour, Ben-Gurion refused to let the Irgun keep any of the guns. He demanded they turn over the ship and its cargo, though every weapon on the *Altalena* would've been trained by the Irgun at the invading Arabs in Jerusalem and across the frontlines.

Ben-Gurion accused Begin and the Irgun of attempting a *putsch*. He said Begin intended to set up his own government in Israel, arm his own military, then challenge Ben-Gurion's authority.

Begin says this is horse feathers.

So a civil war flared up. Ben-Gurion and Begin. Zahal against Irgun. Jew against Jew.

They squared off first at Kfar Vitkin, a remote beach north of Tel Aviv. There the *Altalena*'s crew managed to ferry a third of the cargo onto the beach. The Zahal arrived to confiscate it. A one-sided battle broke out; Begin commanded that his Irgunists not return fire.

The *Altalena* retreated out to sea. Hours later, at midnight, Begin ordered her run aground in the shallows off the beach in Tel Aviv. She came to rest 150 yards offshore. That afternoon, another battle broke out when hundreds of Irgunists from around Israel rushed to Tel Aviv to defend their mates and the

Altalena. Ten thousand horrified Israeli citizens witnessed six hundred Jewish soldiers fight the Irgunists in the streets and across the simmering sands. Many Zahal soldiers laid down their guns, some walked away, rather than fire on their brethren.

At four in the afternoon, Ben-Gurion sent word; he wanted the matter finished. With the sun high and hot, a Zahal artillery shell struck the *Altalena* in her port beam just above the waterline. She burst into flame. Dozens of precious tanks and anti-aircraft guns tumbled into the sea, thousands of rifles warped in the blaze, millions of bullets cooked off. Irgunists jumped off the blazing ship. Zahal snipers continued to fire at them swimming ashore, fired even as the wounded were lowered into small boats rowed out by the people of Tel Aviv.

In the internecine battles of Kfar Vitkin and Tel Aviv, sixteen Irgunists died, one IDF soldier. Scores on both sides were wounded.

One of the Irgunists was my friend. I have written about him many times. His name was Hugo. He jumped off the *Altalena,* came up for air, and took a sniper's bullet to the brain.

By destroying the ship, Ben-Gurion's army will receive none of the cache of weapons and munitions still onboard. Ben-Gurion preferred to wreck it all, risk the defense of Jerusalem, and kill or maim Irgun fighters and new immigrants before he'd tolerate a perceived challenge to his authority.

Moments before the *Altalena* exploded, Menachem Begin leaped overboard. Citizens plucked him from the water; he was whisked away on a surfboard.

After dark, Begin broadcast from Irgun headquarters in Manshieh, south of the city. His Irgun loyalists still controlled part of Tel Aviv's waterfront and the Manshieh area. He instructed them to halt all resistance. The Irgunists complied. Begin disappeared from his headquarters moments before an armored column pulled up to the gates.

The following day, Ben-Gurion secured his victory. He clapped two hundred Irgunists in jail. Every Zahal soldier who would not shoot was arrested. Eight who deserted the battle will be court-martialed. The Irgun has been gutted and disbanded.

Ben-Gurion suffered only minor protests in his government for choosing to shell the *Altalena* rather than negotiate with Begin. Two cabinet members resigned. His supporters tout that Ben-Gurion accepted a localized civil conflict in order to avoid a larger constitutional crisis: the division of Israel into halves, both with their own armed force.

Ben-Gurion won the day. If he was right to act as he did, he can be held innocent of the bloodletting between Jews.

And he was likely right.

He may still be guilty. Of what?

It's possible Ben-Gurion saw the opportunity to silence the Irgun, a powerful and dissenting group. By destroying the *Altalena*, he declawed the Irgun and, more importantly, his nemesis Menachem Begin.

And what of Begin? He may be accused of pursuing his own agendas, political and military, and guilty of acting independently of the government.

Due to their ambitions and personal enmity, these two men brought their young nation to a brink. His back to the cliff, Begin wanted a compromise. Ben-Gurion had law and power on his side, so he pushed. Why compromise?

Because that's what democracies do. They allow for opposing voices. Israel's government is only a few weeks old; how does it alone know the best way forward?

This is Israel today. Brash and cacophonous, fighting in every quarter, swinging so hard they sometimes hit themselves.

Three weeks are left in the truce. When the war resumes, Israel will probably win. Then what? Will the Jews go on like this, battling each other when they're not fighting the Arabs? Can Israel win a fight against Israel? A war between brothers?

Of course they can't.

They must learn to love themselves a lot more, because much of the world is going to hate them.

They'll need to see that the path ahead must be lit not by a few, but many candles.

Reporting from Tel Aviv.

CHAPTER 46

RIVKAH

June 23
Zichron Ya'akov

Mrs. Pappel sat on a cask in the afternoon shade of a grape arbor, swinging her heels. She evidently enjoyed the different sound her wooden foot made, even in a shoe, against the barrel.

She drank red wine from a skin given her by one of the vintners. Perhaps the skin was meant for Rivkah, since Rivkah was the one working. Rivkah, careful for the child, drank only water when the bucket and ladle came around.

Mrs. Pappel got herself tipsy. She prattled while Rivkah pulled weeds. The work was important; the weeds needed to come up so the vines wouldn't have to compete for nutrients. Rivkah worked on folded legs, belly resting on her thighs. The child felt comfortable there, and all through the morning she imagined the child working alongside her.

Rivkah threw the weeds onto a tarpaulin. In a neighboring row of vines, two more volunteers from Zichron worked: a boy and a girl, neither of them old enough to be away in the military. At sundown, when the labor stopped, the tarp would be dragged to the burn pit.

The vines were flowering at a rapid pace. Winemakers were already refitting the grape presses for the September harvest, preparing the tractors and machinery, labeling the warehouse casks.

Mrs. Pappel swigged from the skin. She said, "This is a good red."

"I'm glad you're enjoying it."

"I've never asked you before. I've seen you drink both. Do you like red or white?"

"I drink both. But red, I suppose."

"This is red."

"I know."

"Maury liked white, though he didn't eat fruit. He ate steak, a food for red wine. In London, you see, he'd order a steak and white wine. You could see, the English were thinking, 'Jew.' Maury wouldn't like it here. He would never have come here. He made deals, and that was London. A bomb killed him."

"I know. I'm sure he was a good man."

"Not necessarily. Maury made deals. Do you think?"

Rivkah sat back on her haunches. "Do I think what?"

"Do you think Malik is *tov*?" It was the Hebrew word for okay.

"He's Malik. He can only be tov."

Rivkah tugged off the gloves to untie the bandana from her neck and wipe her face with it. Mrs. Pappel tossed the wineskin at Rivkah's knees. She took a gulp; the red wine was warm.

She tossed the skin to the boy and girl in the next row. "One swallow each."

Mrs. Pappel said, "You'll be tov, *liebling*."

The grapes did not need bees or insects to pollinate but spread their powder by the wind. Such a breeze spun coolly though the vines and rustled the buds and leaves twirling off the arbors.

Mrs. Pappel slurred a little. "You know that, right?"

The two children drew arms across their lips then flipped the wine-skin back. Rivkah left it in the dirt and stretched out beside it. The baby weighed on her pleasantly. The shade from the grape leaves sparkled as though the vines were jewels.

✳ ✳ ✳

The weather stayed sublime through dusk. The day's work pleased the winemakers; the owners asked the thirty volunteers from Zichron and the thirty Arabs from El Fureidis to stay a while. The great pile of weeds was kindled with gasoline, then logs were tossed in the pit to make a bonfire. Two weeks ago, a late, strange frost had dripped down from the Carmel Mountains. For three nights, all the vineyards lit bonfires to keep the mists at bay. From their windows Mrs. Pappel and Rivkah watched the valley flicker. For those three nights, even during the truce, They talked of the war and wondered when Vince would come, as if he might walk out of those fires.

The vineyard owners hammered spigots into two casks of last season's red vintage. Anyone with a cup or a skin could have their fill. The volunteers and Arabs let their children sip. Jews shared blankets with Arabs.

Mrs. Pappel laid her head on Rivkah's shoulder.

"Can't you see Malik right now? He'd walk to the middle, so dark the fire would barely light him. He'd recite a poem about the wine and the fire and would say he'd just made it up."

Mrs. Pappel folded her whole leg under her and left the part-wooden one extended. She looked to be taking a hurdle.

Around the bonfire, the drinking was tame and the talk temperate. No young Jewish or Arab men were around to sing or compete or climb trees, for the war had laid claim to them. The volunteers from Zichron were tired, and the fire lulled the children. The Arab fieldhands had worked the vines for years; they were not so tuckered.

The mothers told each other how they prayed their Jewish and Arab sons and daughters would not see each other in any battle. How terrible to consider. To the crackle of oak logs, the seated women took each other's hands.

The vineyard owners brought out baskets of bread, cheese, and stuffed grape leaves. In the barn, the mules brayed to be fed, too. The daylight purpled, then greyed. The bonfire tinted the ring of people ocher, and all their different shadows mingled.

After dark fell and the food was gone, the Arabs rose to say their farewells.

Four Zahal soldiers walked out of the starlight, into the firelight.

A tall officer said, "Everyone stay where you are." The Arabs held their ground but did not sit.

Disobeying, the two brothers who owned the vineyard got to their feet. Both wore khaki shorts, knee socks, and white Oxford shirts. A silver-haired Arab gestured for the other Arabs to take their seats. He strode forward in loose black trousers and a long jacket, a knit kufi on his head. Two Zichron women in headscarves came forth.

Mrs. Pappel said, "Help me up."

Rivkah hesitated; Mrs. Pappel started rising without her. Rivkah could not hold her back, so popped to her feet and pulled Mrs. Pappel up.

"Come on." Mrs. Pappel tucked an arm inside Rivkah's elbow. The townsfolk and the brothers nodded at Mrs. Pappel's approach.

The IDF officer gestured the seven to go back to where they'd been seated. None complied.

The brothers introduced themselves as the vineyard owners. No handshakes were shared.

The tall soldier said, "I'm Major Keisch."

He looked ready to make some pronouncement. Mrs. Pappel beat him to it.

"Missus Pappel." She dipped her head to her left to say, "Rivkah."

The two townswomen, sisters, gave their names, Martha and Marcia.

Inclining his head in the firelight, the old Arab said, "I am Fahad. Of El Fureidis."

Keisch directed himself to the brothers.

"I'm with the Alexandroni Brigade."

"You're welcome here. What can we do for you?"

"I require you to tell the Arabs to return to their village. They must stay there."

In tandem, the brothers asked, "Why?"

The major swum his hands, a small move like a dogpaddle.

"We can't have them moving around like this."

Mrs. Pappel asked, "Like what?"

Keisch ogled her. She tapped her own breast to remind him. "Missus Pappel."

The major took a moment, then said, "El Fureidis is one of the last Arab-held villages in this region. It's been determined that the village is a security risk."

Mrs. Pappel asked, "Who determined this?"

"The Alexandroni Brigade."

"So you?"

"Yes, madam. Me."

"They don't move freely," said one brother. "They work in the vineyards. Then they go home."

"There are five hundred Arabs in El Fureidis. We don't have the manpower to monitor their movements."

The second brother said, "A third of that five hundred work in the fields, ours and others. We pay them wages. If they don't work, they'll be impoverished. Who's going to feed them? You?"

"We're considering moving them to a camp."

Mrs. Pappel let go of Rivkah's elbow.

"A camp?"

Sister Marcia took one step towards the major, palms together.

"Major, please understand. There's no need for this. When the war started the people of El Fureidis wanted to leave. No one would have blamed them. But we asked them to stay. We told them how much Zichron Ya'akov needed their help and they need ours. We promised we'd protect them in their homes. El Fureidis is not a threat. They've surrendered without a fight."

Fahad underscored this. He did not press his hands together but spread them. He told the Jewish major that the people of El Fureidis could have fought, could have taken up guns like other Arab villages, but chose not to.

Martha said, "If you drive the people of El Fureidis from their homes, we'll be liars."

Old Fahad said, "That would be so."

The major spoke to Fahad. "There's been sniping from your village on the main road."

One brother asked the Arab, "Truly?"

"It was the work of outsiders. We put a stop to it."

The second brother asked, "Major, would you consider an option? What if we put a curfew in place? The Arabs can work the fields then be back in El Fureidis before sundown."

His brother continued; this was something they'd discussed before.

"We'll give them identification cards. Any fellah out after curfew will have to produce the card."

Keisch shook his head. "The risk is still too great."

Mrs. Pappel kicked him. Her wooden foot was unforgiving. The major hopped backwards into the arms of his men.

"Are you out of your mind?"

Free of Rivkah, Mrs. Pappel tottered from the red wine and the falseness of her foot. Rolling up her trousers, she showed the prosthesis and the shoe tied at the end of it.

"Would you like to tell me about risk, Major?"

"Madam."

"This was taken off me at Gush Etzion. This girl here was almost raped there. She was rescued seconds before she was murdered. Rescued by an Arab. A hundred of our friends were gunned down. If we tell you the people of El Fureidis are under our protection, under our trust, then I suggest you believe that is something neither I, this girl, nor these people grant lightly."

Keisch remained out of range.

"I'm sorry for your losses. I am. But if you kick me again, or anything vaguely similar, you and I will leave this place together. You understand?"

"Of course. Now, what will you do?"

"I don't know what I can do."

"You determined. You can un-determine."

"It's not so easy."

"I don't suggest it is, Major. I gave my foot for Israel. I've asked nothing in return until now. I'm asking for something difficult. Should I be told no?"

Keisch considered. He peered down at Mrs. Pappel's wooden foot, not in fear of it this time but with a seed of sympathy.

"I'll speak to my superiors. But for now. If you please."

Mrs. Pappel smiled again, fake as her foot.

The young major said, "Send the Arabs home. They'll stay there until further notice."

One of the brothers asked, "What about the vines tomorrow?"

Keisch turned from the firelight. With a darkened face over his shoulder, he said, "I think there's been enough wine for a while."

＊＊＊

At the kitchen table, Mrs. Pappel put down her elbows and propped her eye sockets on her palms. Rivkah set the kettle on the hot plate. Speaking between her forearms, Mrs. Pappel complained that she'd done it backwards; one should never sober up after dark.

When the kettle whistled, Rivkah poured two cups, then headed out of the kitchen. "Come along."

They settled into the cane rockers on the evening porch. Rivkah handed Mrs. Pappel a china cup, then rocked back in the scent of blooming bougainvillea. The sea two miles away made the night smell like clean skin.

Rivkah said, "I miss my mother."

"I'm sorry, child."

"I didn't mean you to be sorry. You're as much a mother to me as anyone could be."

Rivkah rested a hand on her belly, amazed always what grew there. In the Negev she'd prised rocks from the ground, turned salt into soil. The planting became the harvest, and the harvest became life shared by all. This harvest, this life under her hand, belonged only to her—and Vince.

"She was a good mother. I wish she could show me how."

"What of your father?"

"He was a hardhead. The child will need no help with that."

A horse and cart jangled past with empty bottles for the sunrise milk delivery. Bats chased through streetlights that beamed down on no boys malingering, no girls arm-in-arm. A car grumbled by. An old couple made their way without a word or touch of each other.

Mrs. Pappel's tea cooled. She set the cup and saucer on the porch floor.

She pulled up her pants leg to undo the prosthetic's straps and rods. She freed her pink stump and let the prosthesis fall aside. Mrs. Pappel rocked on pushes of her good leg.

Rivkah asked, "What will you do if the army expels El Fureidis? What will happen to Malik?"

Mrs. Pappel stroked her grey braid, hand-over-hand as if climbing it. She nodded towards the street. Rivkah waited for a reply. Mrs. Pappel seemed to be waiting, too.

Mrs. Pappel stopped rocking.

"I don't know. Maybe Vince will."

Rivkah asked, "What?"

Vince's boots didn't announce him. The road brought no car; he carried no bag. He came out of the night looking too tired and slender to make any sound. Mrs. Pappel didn't react, as though she'd summoned him and was expecting him.

Rivkah put her teacup in Mrs. Pappel's lap to free her hands.

CHAPTER 47

VINCE

He hadn't expected her to be waiting on the porch. He'd never before been in Zichron Ya'akov and had only that moment found the right address, when there she was.

Vince didn't enter the property but stayed on the sidewalk. He wanted to walk to Rivkah but couldn't figure out why he wouldn't step past the shrubs. He stood in front of Mrs. Pappel's house in the bouquet of bougainvillea. Mrs. Pappel sat on her porch without one foot. Vince waved first to her, then raised his arms to Rivkah.

He didn't lift them high enough, not above his waist. They were the arms of his weariness. He raised them higher, and she came off the porch.

Rivkah quickened. The excitement in her approach gave way to tenderness. She eased into his arms.

Vince didn't know what to absorb of her first. Her arms circled his neck, her hair curtained his face, her smell blended toil and blossoms. Her cheek against his stubble closed his eyes as if she'd blindfolded him. Her breasts lay against his ribs. Vince straightened his spine to raise Rivkah, wrapped around him now, to her toes.

The child had grown in four weeks, since Transjordan. Vince didn't know how careful to be so didn't embrace her hard. They kissed; their lips reached across the child between them.

She stepped back, keeping hold of Vince's hands. They stood like a couple waiting to begin a folk dance.

Vince said, "It's really good to see you."

She blinked and almost frowned. He regretted that he'd said so little with his first words. Then Rivkah smiled and nodded. She had a lot to say, too.

"Come up on the porch."

Backpedaling, she towed him up the steps to the rocker she'd vacated. Mrs. Pappel reached for his hand. Ensconced in these women and his child, Vince could not dam himself up. The tears that released down his cheek caught in the straw stubble of his chin, then fell.

Before this, Vince hadn't cried, but the news he brought to Zichron Ya'akov broke him open. Or was it his relief to be with these two women? Vince couldn't separate one sensation, his sadness, his joy, from the other. Like the tears, together they were too heavy for him.

Mrs. Pappel pressed his hand, Rivkah the nape of his neck. Mrs. Pappel's prosthesis lay beside her rocker. She nudged it with her proper foot.

"It's not so bad."

Vince struggled to say something. He turned from Mrs. Pappel to hide another course of tears. The child was at his eye level. Vince spread a hand over Rivkah's bulging navel. He took a mental image, his hand over her belly, to keep the moment as a memento.

"Hugo's dead."

Rivkah and Mrs. Pappel recoiled, but Vince held onto them both; he balled Rivkah's shirt in his fist and closed his other hand around Mrs. Pappel's wrist. He was selfish to do this, when they were happy to see him. But he'd not come to give anything.

CHAPTER 48

GABBI

June 24
Gevim
Israel

Gabbi muscled her machine gun onto the front swivel. Abner, the new rear gunner, arrived wearing a sock cap, his big weapon over his shoulder like a fleece. He was one of the South African Jews, a meaty man with a weak chin and buggy eyes. He climbed onto the jeep's tail; the suspension tilted under his size. Abner flipped the MG 34 onto the rear tripod then left to fetch more ammo canisters.

Jonny emerged from the barn; the breakfast briefing was over. He shielded his eyes against the early sun and carried a radio.

He walked straight to Gabbi. Jonny held out the radio, a wooden box the size of an egg crate, crammed with tubes, dials, battery, and antenna.

She pushed it back at him. Jonny goaded it into her ribs so she had to take it in her hands or be shoved backwards.

"I don't want it."

"I don't care."

"I'm a gunner."

"You're on radio today."

Gabbi indicated the boys preparing the other three jeeps. They lugged fuel jerry cans, ammo belts, sandbags, and machine guns.

"Give it to one of them."

"It's your turn."

"I've been here longer than most of them."

"So it's your turn."

Tarek came out of the barn with three drivers. Jonny patted the radio like a mutt he was leaving in good hands. He and Tarek passed each other without swapping glances.

Seeing the radio, Tarek cupped a warm hand under the curve of Gabbi's jaw. His dark thumb caressed her temple and the cockle of her ear. A smile shined from the depth of his beard.

"Stuck with the radio, I see."

"Apparently."

"It's your turn." Tarek climbed behind the wheel. "Try to hang on."

The road to al-Faluja replenished its dust every day. No goggles had been delivered to the company; Gabbi and Tarek covered their noses and mouths with bandanas. In the rear, Abner stood tall, his mouth above the cloud.

Tarek took the lead. At a hundred kilometers per hour, the road to Gvar'am lasted ten minutes. Gabbi clutched the radio; she didn't ask Tarek to slow down, knowing he wouldn't.

At Gvar'am, the road turned east. Tarek crossed the shoulder in the same spot as yesterday. He led the platoon into the raw field, following his own tracks into the weeds and dirt.

The truce boundary lay two kilometers ahead. Tarek drove with one hand; the other he sluiced through mustard weed pollen and blue lupin. The radio in Gabbi's lap chirped.

"Absalom One, Absalom Two."

She answered. "Absalom Two, go."

"Your location, Absalom Two?"

"Approaching the dead bridge. Over."

"You're five by five. Keep the channel clear. Over."

Gabbi clicked the mic twice to tell Jonny "Out."

The four jeeps barreled in a line abreast. The run to the wadi and its ruined bridge was short, and on the way they crushed brown thistles and red-veined sorrel, knocked down sumac sprigs that flung auburn berries over their heads. In one skyward burst, Abner cleared his MG 34. Gabbi set the radio between her boots to do the same. The other commando gunners followed suit. They were not here to be secretive.

✳ ✳ ✳

The three-mile-long wadi was steep but not wide. Going around it north or south would definitely take the jeeps into Arab-controlled lands.

One army or the other had blown up a mule bridge across the wadi. For the second day in a row, the four jeeps idled at the western lip of the depression. Tarek and Abner passed binoculars between them to glass al-Faluja three kilometers east. Behind the village rose the Judean foothills and, somewhere ahead, the ceasefire line.

Five thousand Palestinians resided in al-Faluja behind the Egyptian army's lines. The four jeeps had come close enough to spot the village's minarets, dyed cloths strung up in a *souk*, palm trees nodding above stone homes, and farm trucks in the dirt lanes. Wheat and sorghum wavered in the bordering fields.

Tarek handed Gabbi the spyglasses.

In the sunny panorama of a stalled war, rows of military tents hunkered among the uncut crops. Gabbi had not spotted them with her naked eye.

She said, "They weren't there yesterday."

Tarek said, "No."

"How many tents, do you think?"

"Fifty."

"Looks like we found them. How many Egyptians?"

"I can't guess."

She said, "Me, neither. Jonny's going to want a number."

Tarek said, "One way to find out."

✳ ✳ ✳

Tarek inched the jeep onto the downslope. The incline was so sharp he and Gabbi lay back in their front seats; Abner sat on his haunches.

Tarek wrestled the jeep to keep it from skidding sideways and rolling over on them. The motor whined; the brakes smelled hot.

Tarek muttered, "Whoa, whoa," talking the jeep down the twenty-meter incline like a horse. Reaching the bottom, Gabbi flexed the strain out of her hands and swore she would throw the radio away. Leading the others, Tarek cut a swath through wildflowers on the wadi floor to the opposite bank.

He took the company up an eastern wall that was less steep. Reaching the crest, Tarek tapped the radio in Gabbi's lap.

"Tell Jonny what we're doing."

She clicked the mic's press-to-talk. "Absalom Two, Absalom One."

"Go, Absalom Two."

"Two kilometers west of al-Faluja. We crossed the wadi. Possible enemy troops. Over."

"Absalom Two, go take a look. Tell me how many. Over."

"Roger. Out."

The four jeeps crept forward, almost rubbing fenders in the wild meadow. Tarek traced his fingers across a map strapped to his thigh. Gabbi set down the radio to take the machine gun grips in hand.

Tarek stopped a kilometer west of the tents.

With a war cry, Egyptian soldiers streamed out by the dozen. A trumpet blared while some Arab banged on a pot. Arab soldiers flattened the grain, coursing into the field. Caught unawares, they tugged on tunics. With whoops and racket, two hundred Arabs, then twice that many, galloped shouting at the four Israeli jeeps.

Gabbi asked, "Where's the ceasefire line?"

Tarek swatted the air. "Around here."

Gabbi and the gunners leveled their machine guns.

A hundred meters away, the Egyptian troop bunched into a picket line, like at the edge of a precipice. They hushed in the field, rifles in hand, gawping at the jeeps, as unsure of the peacekeeping border as Tarek. The early sun made the scene acute, a clarity of kelly grass, red poppies, umber Arabs.

Tarek said, "Tell Jonny."

Gabbi reported a full Egyptian battalion in al-Faluja.

Jonny asked, "Are there more?"

"I don't know. Over."

"Find out."

Gabbi asked, "What the hell?" but Jonny had signed off.

Tarek said, "Okay." He got out of the jeep.

Gabbi said, "Wait."

Tarek stepped on the front bumper, then the hood. Hands cupped over his mouth, he yelled something in Arabic. The Egyptians replied in loud Hebrew:

"Mister Mizrachi! Come over here."

"Mister Mizrachi, how are you today? Shall we slit your throat?"

"Mister Mizrachi, good morning!"

Tarek climbed back behind the wheel.

"Fire over their heads."

Gabbi said, "What? No. What about the ceasefire?"

"Honestly, I think the line's behind us. Abner."

The big South African loosed a burst until Tarek waved him off the trigger. Blackbirds spooked out of the grasses and flew off in a dark clot.

Tarek said, "Both of you hold on."

He revved the engine; the other three jeeps did, too. Gabbi latched onto the radio and the gun mount just as Tarek peeled out.

The four jeeps raced single file across the grassland parallel to the wadi. Quickly they left the Arab battalion behind. Wildflowers and pollen splashed against the speeding jeeps' grilles. Gabbi blinked through emerald and golden debris.

A chorus of trumpets sounded in al-Faluja. Tarek yanked the jeep around to have a look. They were surely on the wrong side of the peace-keeping line now.

Out front lay a cornfield, thick enough that the jeeps could not enter. Ten meters from the green palisade, Tarek skidded to a stop.

Abner called down, "We need to get out of here. Now."

Gabbi jumped on her seat to see what Abner was looking at above the tassels. Two hundred meters off, two dun-colored tanks rolled out of a barn where they'd been rivetted. Both cannons were depressed to fire through the corn.

Gabbi plopped fast into her seat.

"We should go."

Behind them, fifty Egyptians blocked their path along the rim of the wadi. The jeeps could not retreat that way.

A bullet snipped the stalks and ripped past the jeeps. Tarek dipped his forehead, his sea green eyes narrowed. He was about to do something.

He cranked the wheel, hard, shifted, then popped the clutch; the tires spun on the slick grass. The jeep bucked as it pivoted on its center, a sensational piece of driving. More bullets pierced the corn. Tarek's bolt straight for the wadi made Gabbi's head snap back.

The jeep crashed through wildflowers, over saplings and a hedge of thorny shrubs. More blackbirds winged out of the way. To get away, Tarek dodged nothing.

The Egyptians fired volleys after them. The jeeps fled through bushes that switched Gabbi's bare arms and neck. Arabs ran after them, firing wildly, but a lucky shot or a tank shell remained a threat.

Gabbi shouted, "Slow down."

Tarek did not. He drove maniacally. She had no free hand to shake him out of it. She could only shout one more time before the jeep's wheels left the ground.

Free of gravity, the radio and Gabbi's left arm floated on their own. Her butt rose off the seat, her boots drifted from the floorboard. Only her grasp on the gun mount with her right hand kept her above the jeep, which fell away from her.

The front axle struck. Gabbi crashed down, her neck whiplashed, she lost the radio. The rear tires smacked down and Gabbi catapulted out. The sky and the ground flipped.

She awoke on her back with a sharp, surfacing breath. Her ribcage ached. Her head rang. Blood tanged her tongue.

Abner's face blocked the sun. "Can you get up?"

The big South African helped her to her feet and back into the jeep. The radio lay in pieces. Tarek stanched his bleeding nose; he'd banged it on the steering wheel.

The other three jeeps arrived unhurt; they'd not taken flight off the lip of the wadi. The platoon had no time to take stock, the Egyptians might run to the edge and shoot down on them. No one knew where the peace-keeping line was. The jeeps took off without Tarek, annoyed with him.

He said to Abner and Gabbi, "I'm sorry."

She said, "Drive."

Abner said, "I need a drink."

✳ ✳ ✳

Rehovot

Tarek explained to the boys that the radio was broken so why not take the rest of the morning? For that, they let him stay platoon leader.

On the road to Tel Aviv, Gabbi's tailbone hurt. Near Rehovot, among citrus groves and warehouses, a hand-painted sign advertised beer and felafel for just four mil. Tarek pulled over; the other jeeps followed.

The eatery was no more than a kitchen and smokestack under a lean-to roof and tables and chairs on grass in the shadow of a great elm.

Gabbi asked the rest of the platoon to leave her alone at a table with Tarek. She and all the boys were dusty white as bakers. The other commandos took nearby tables under the tree.

A young waiter brought beers, bread, and hummus. His left hand and arm were missing below the elbow; gauze covered the fresh stump. When Gabbi asked, he said he'd lost the arm in May, fighting Syrians in the Galilee. He unwrapped the dressing to show how well he was healing. An older man, maybe the boy's father, worked in the kitchen over a deep fryer.

Gabbi tore the loaf; she dipped a shred of bread in the hummus. The elm's shade daubed their table in a lively way. Tarek's attention was skittish, flitting to her, to the wounded waiter, to the others, to her.

Gabbi asked, "What do you want to say?"

"About?"

"Then never mind."

He pulled apart his hands then brought them together, to show he would do what she asked if only she would tell him what it was.

Gabbi said, "At the wadi. You almost broke my back."

"I told you I was sorry."

"Then tell me the rest. What's going on?"

"Nothing."

Gabbi chewed and nodded, and together this made her stare very active.

Tarek said, "It's not easy to talk about."

"Then don't."

"You're mad."

Gabbi said, "Tell me or don't."

"I've been thinking."

"About?"

"What my father said."

"That you're an only son."

"He can apply to the government."

"To get you out of the war."

The waiter set a tray of felafel on the table. He paused; he seemed to want to talk. Gabbi ignored the boy, but she was tempted to use him as an example of what Israel demanded. The waiter walked away swinging his one complete arm.

Gabbi said, "We've all got limits."

"You don't."

On the table were beer bottles, a basket of felafel balls, hummus, and torn bread. Tarek touched none of it as Gabbi ate. He kept hands in his lap while she dipped and drank and eyed him.

She said, "I know you want me to be kind right now."

Tarek shrugged, giving himself over.

She said, "We'd either have to replace you, or divide your job among the rest of us."

Gabbi licked grease off her fingers. The commandos ordered more beers, Abner called for hummus. The jeep boys made the one-armed waiter laugh. Tarek gazed up into the elm where a lone bird twittered.

To leave some food, to let him rejoin her in the meal and the war, Gabbi slowed her eating.

Before long, Tarek's eyes fell from the tree. He popped a falafel ball into his mouth and pronounced it good. He made no more mention of his father.

CHAPTER 49

RIVKAH

June 24
Zichron Ya'akov
Israel

Vince bent over to wash Hugo. Everything about Vince stooped, his shoulders, jaw, eyes; Rivkah had never seen him so small. Vince passed a wet cloth across the quiet pale of Hugo's leg.

From her chair, Mrs. Pappel said, "Now cover the leg."

Vince swept the linen down.

"Do the other leg."

Vince reached across Hugo to pull back the sheet.

"No. Don't reach across the body. Walk around the table."

Vince shuffled past the covered mounds of Hugo's feet. Rivkah followed with the water bucket; Vince dipped and wrung the cloth. He said, "Thank you," when all Rivkah had done was hold the bucket.

Next, Vince used a kitchen knife to clean the dark quarter moons of Hugo's fingernails. He did this without hurry.

Vince washed Hugo's chest and waist, then between his legs. When it came time to clean Hugo's back, Rivkah helped roll him onto his side so Hugo would not be turned face down during the purity ritual. Vince swiped the cloth down the length of Hugo's spine. Hugo had small shoulder blades, like a child's hands pressing to be let out. Blood had pooled cobalt blue in his buttocks, calves, and ribcage.

Rivkah and Vince eased Hugo down, supine on the table. Mrs. Pappel approached to cross Hugo's hands over his chest. Vince stepped back, Rivkah beside him.

Mrs. Pappel beckoned them both to the table, to stand at the corners on either side of Hugo's head.

"Come, you two."

She stood between them.

"Vince, a year and a half ago, you brought this man to us. He became *mishpocheh*, family, like you did. We were all Hugo had left. Everyone, everything had been taken from him. You did the right thing to return him to us. I know you loved him. I know he loved you. But you must know Hugo didn't live for you. He lived for Rivkah and me, for the child, and for Israel. He died for us."

Mrs. Pappel laid both hands against Hugo's temples.

His lips were taut. He winced, as if caught in the moment of being stung. A hole the width of a finger dotted his right brow, a neat puncture. The smoothness of the entry wound implied the neatness of Hugo's killing.

Rivkah rinsed the cloth in the bucket. She drew it across the small expanse of Hugo's forehead. She felt the rim of the hole in his skull, traced the dips into his sockets and the sharp rise of his nose. His brown hair smelled of seawater. Hugo's flesh was still supple enough to stretch under her fingers; by accident with the cloth she made him grin. She lifted the cloth away, but the rictus stuck.

Mrs. Pappel lifted Hugo's head so Rivkah might clean the back of his neck. Light entered the tunnel through his head. Rivkah put down the cloth and retreated against the dining room wall, hands over her belly to hide unborn eyes.

Vince took up the cloth. He finished cleaning the rear of Hugo's head. He rinsed the cloth many times and the water turned wine dark.

Mrs. Pappel lay down Hugo's head.

"Now we pray."

Vince asked, "For what?"

"We ask the dead for forgiveness. I'm going to tell him I'm sorry it was the Jews who finally killed him."

Mrs. Pappel muttered in Hebrew.

When she was done, Vince said, "I don't know what to say."

"Be humble."

He stood hands to hips, tall once more. He seemed offended.

Then he approached haltingly, as if Hugo were asleep and Vince had to wake him to tell him something.

CHAPTER 50

VINCE

Vince carried two teacups out to the porch, one for Rivkah. Hugo's trousers lay across her lap. She was busy stitching shut the pockets.

Vince folded into the open rocker. Rivkah reached for one of the teas; Vince handed it over.

"Why are you sewing up his pockets?"

Rivkah said, "We enter the world with nothing. We take nothing with us."

"This is some ritual."

"What did you tell him you were sorry for?"

"Am I allowed to say it out loud?"

"Hugo's not a birthday cake. You didn't make a wish."

"Maybe it was me that got him killed."

"How on earth?"

Vince sipped. The cup was warmer than the tea, as if it remembered the life of the tea. He set the cup on the porch so he could gesture.

"Right from the start. In Buchenwald, I picked him up out of a barrack. I carried him out in the sun and set him down in the middle of the camp. He looked awful. There were thousands just like him, thin as a rail, a day or two from dying, maybe less. I got him condensed milk, got him a chair. Then I interviewed him. Right then and there. That's what I did. I asked Hugo to show me around. The terrible stuff. A guy who was hours from being dead. I asked him to do that."

"It was your job."

"No one's job is that."

Rivkah rested the teacup on the ledge of her belly. She ran a finger around the rim of the cup and looked down into it. She seemed to be granting Vince privacy.

"Go on."

"I followed him to Palestine. A hundred yards from shore he jumped overboard before the British could catch him. I lost track of him and went home to New York. Hugo sent me a telegram. The story's here, he said. The story is me. By that time he was Irgun. So I followed him again. Followed him to bombed buildings, hangings, whippings. Death row. He took a bullet, I took a bullet. We both killed men. I lost track of him again. But when I needed him I went and found him on the Burma Road. Then I followed him to the *Altalena*. Then here."

"You think Hugo did all that for you? Because you were writing about him?"

"Yeah, I do."

"What should you have done differently?"

"I should have left him in the sun at Buchenwald."

Vince rose from the rocker. She reached up for his help standing. Rivkah tossed Hugo's pants over her shoulder.

"You'll stay tonight."

"Okay. With you?"

"With Hugo."

CHAPTER 51

RIVKAH

Vince left the porch to go dress Hugo in his pocketless pants. Mrs. Pappel came outside to sit with Rivkah.

Zichron Ya'akov's midday did not bustle; the sun mired everything. As she did often when rocking on the porch, Mrs. Pappel took off her false foot; passersby might have thought it a pale cat curled beside her rocker. Framed in bougainvillea, she and Rivkah greeted neighbors made torpid in the heat.

Mrs. Pappel said, "I'm going to call my shop 'Hugo's Tea and Treats.'"

"He'd like that."

"He absolutely would not."

Mrs. Pappel wound her grey ponytail around a finger.

"Liebling. What did you hope would happen when Vince came back?"

"I don't know."

Mrs. Pappel threw the ponytail over her shoulder as if it were salt.

"I so tire of that answer. I didn't ask what you know, I asked what you hoped. You've got a child growing inside her body. Of course you have hopes. I suspect you have little else. Now what did you hope would happen? Vince would step out of the war, back into your arms?"

Rivkah stiffened her grip on the rocker's arms to push herself out of it.

She said, "You can be very annoying."

Mrs. Pappel reached across to stop Rivkah from leaving.

"Do you believe that I care for an instant if I'm annoying? Sit."

Rivkah collapsed into the rocker; her momentum carried her backwards. Mrs. Pappel reeled in her arm.

"Now tell me. What are you going to do?"

"Have this child."

"Vince's child."

"Of course."

"Don't get snippy. Do you still love him?"

"I do."

Rivkah pivoted in the rocker to look behind her, through the front windows into the candlelit dining room, to the big table where Vince tugged a pair of pants over Hugo's short, dead, heavy legs.

"I should tell him."

Mrs. Pappel rattled a finger beside her ear like the clapper of a bell.

"Let me say something about Morrie."

"Are these stories true?"

"*Sha*. He liked deals. Only deals. Call me when you're ready, that's what he'd say. Not when someone wanted to have lunch or a highball. Morrie didn't play golf or poker or roll those bocce balls. He didn't appreciate small gestures. Not even from me."

Mrs. Pappel waved a hand across sleepy Zichron Ya'akov.

"No one in this town has seen more fighting than you. Not even me and my one goddam foot."

She jabbed a finger behind her.

"Except that man. He sees everything. He's in there right now preparing his friend to be buried, his Jewish friend who has no other family in the world. He's doing it, a Gentile. Vince Haas walks away from nothing. So you have to understand how he's being torn in half. He's an American, not an Israeli. And not a Jew. He is fully aware that he never will be. But there you are, an Israeli Jew with his Jewish baby."

"I know."

"The point I'm making, liebling, is that Vince knows."

"What should I do?"

"That's completely for you to decide."

Mrs. Pappel reached back to tug her ponytail over her shoulder, down her bosom, so long the braid curled in her lap. She toyed with it. Gazing off, her lower lip poked out. Mrs. Pappel nodded as if she'd heard some whisper and agreed.

"Like Morrie would say. Call when you're ready."

CHAPTER 52

VINCE

Vince buttoned up Hugo's white shirt, a collarless farmer's tunic. He tugged a white linen sheet up to Hugo's armpits, then made a marine fold. He crossed Hugo's waxy hands on top of the sheet the way he imagined an undertaker might. He left Hugo's grin uncovered.

Vince took a chair, hungry. The Jews had so many rules. He didn't know if he could eat. He couldn't tell if he ought to sit or go out to the porch to tell Mrs. Pappel and Rivkah that Hugo was dressed. Vince lit a cigarette, certain Mrs. Pappel would be displeased.

She came in, fanning her face to display her thoughts on Vince's cigarette.

She said, "I'll make a snack. Then you go upstairs for a nap."

Rivkah entered. In the doorway, she stopped. Vince's grey smoke purled above Hugo.

She asked, "Tonight?"

"Yeah?"

"May I sit with you?"

"I'd like that."

Mrs. Pappel explained to Vince that he was Hugo's *shomer*, his guardian, so Hugo's spirit wouldn't be alone the eve before burial. Then she carried a lantern and book out to the porch, to leave Vince and Rivkah in the dining room with Hugo.

Zichron's humidity clung well past sundown. The candles beside Hugo's upturned face drained his color past death. By the little flames, Rivkah read aloud from the Old Testament. She read Psalms. The passages were all in praise of God, nothing about mortality or grief, as though God had lost Hugo, too, and needed to be cheered up. Vince listened with half an ear.

Vince leaned his chair back against the wall. He lost track of time. At some point Mrs. Pappel entered the house and without a word went off to bed. Somewhere in the night Rivkah stopped reading. She folded shut her Old Testament and left it between the shortened candles by Hugo's ear. She touched Vince's neck then hung back a moment, perhaps for him to thank her. He didn't and she left the deathwatch.

The air was close, the candles lulling, but Vince never grew sleepy. He folded his arms against the slow march of hours and listened to the crickets, owls in the vineyards, the squeak of a delivery truck. He heard these more attentively than Rivkah's readings.

The candles melted slowly like the hands of a clock, at a pace Vince could not catch. Moonlight sifted through the windows until the moon went all the way down.

When dawn came, Vince had yet to grieve. He eased the legs of his chair down to the floor.

"Okay."

He dragged the chair beside Hugo's head.

"Well, pal. You're done."

Vince blew out both candles. Smoke twisted off the wicks. He patted Hugo's shoulder. The stiffness recalled Buchenwald, that brittleness when Vince picked him up.

He touched Hugo's cool knuckles. Vince had never seen Hugo's hands so clean.

"Funny. In the end, you know, you got yourself killed by the Jews."

Vince stood quickly, unsettling the mist.

"I never killed anyone 'til I met you."

He climbed the stairs to Rivkah's room. From her bed without lifting her head, Rivkah watched Vince remove his clothes.

"Throw them in the hall. Mrs. Pappel will wash them before the funeral."

Naked, Vince went to the window's view of the grey-skinned sea.

She said, "Come lie down."

Vince jackknifed to fit in Rivkah's short bed.

She wore a cotton smock; her round belly looked like a birdcage covered for the night. Vince tugged up her night dress. A knurled little wad filled her bellybutton. He ran the same hand over his child that he'd lain on Hugo's shoulder, and everything of death that he'd brought upstairs in that hand dissolved.

CHAPTER 53

RIVKAH

Curled away from her, Vince fell asleep. The soles of his feet lay against Rivkah's shins. She ran a finger down the knobs of his spine. Vince woke briefly to ask her gently to stop.

By midmorning, she could sleep no more. Troop carriers rumbled outside her bright window, and horse-drawn carts clopped.

Mrs. Pappel didn't knock to bring in Vince's ironed clothes. She set them on the chest at the foot of Rivkah's bed.

Mrs. Pappel looked down on naked Vince who slept with no sheet over him. She shook her head at Rivkah like a mother at a child who cannot keep the bird, the animal, she has brought in from outdoors to her room.

"The funeral's in two hours." Then Mrs. Pappel left.

Five old men from the synagogue came for Hugo. The plain pine coffin they brought would decay well in the earth. They needed Rivkah's help to lift Hugo into the box.

When Vince descended bathed and dressed, Hugo was gone. Vince sat with Rivkah and Mrs. Pappel for eggs, bread, figs, and tea.

Rivkah and Mrs. Pappel both wore black to the cemetery, hems to their ankles. Mrs. Pappel took Vince's arm. He had only the clothes he'd arrived in: khaki slacks, rough boots, and white cotton shirt rolled to the elbows.

At the cemetery entrance, Hugo's casket waited in the back of a pickup. The five old men were nowhere to be seen. Vince rested a hand on the coffin.

Mrs. Pappel saw Pinchus in the sunny street. She clasped Rivkah's hand and together they walked to him.

Pinchus said, "I told Hugo he'd be remembered. He didn't believe me."

Pinchus held Mrs. Pappel at arm's length to survey her. In a brown suit, vest, and pocket watch, he might have been a clerk.

Through the cemetery gate walked six dark young sabras.

Pinchus said, "I didn't feel that old men who never knew Hugo should carry him to his grave. These men didn't know him either. But they were Irgun."

Pinchus drew a penknife from a pocket. He took hold of Vince's collar.

"Jacob's sons came to him with a lie, that his favorite, Joseph, was dead. Hearing this, Jacob rent his clothing. I make this cut on the right, Vince, away from the heart. Only parents of the dead wear a tear on the left."

Pinchus made a small slice.

Vince asked to be a pallbearer.

Pinchus said, "In Judaism, mourners do not take the dead to the grave."

"Why not?"

"I believe, in our history, mourners were usually off somewhere tracking down the ones who'd killed the deceased. That may be just another lie. But I do like the notion."

Pinchus asked Mrs. Pappel, "After the service, may I bring these boys and a few others to your house? We'll make a *minyan* and sit *shiva*."

"Of course."

Pinchus moved to the front to join the Irgunists hoisting Hugo's coffin onto their shoulders.

Vince took a stride toward the graveyard gate. Mrs. Pappel held him back.

"You walk behind the dead."

In lockstep, Pinchus led the pallbearers through the gate. Vince followed. Sniffling back tears, Mrs. Pappel tucked her arm inside Rivkah's.

Entering the grounds, the Irgunists stopped. Pinchus turned to Vince.

"We will pause seven times. This allows us to consider how precious our own lives are."

The stone garden of the cemetery held neither grass nor shade. Granite and marble markers consumed every meter, making the place saw-toothed and hard. The plot Mrs. Pappel had purchased waited in a far corner.

Three more times, the procession halted. Rivkah needed to sit soon but every place that might make a bench was a headstone. At the fourth stop, the child kicked. Mrs. Pappel called ahead for Pinchus to move things along. Pinchus shortened each pause.

Vince walked somberly in his faded clothes and pale complexion. He seemed another gravestone. At Hugo's site, the Irgunists set the casket beside a hole where no rabbi waited.

Vince sat in the lone chair. Rivkah and Mrs. Pappel stood behind him, each with a hand on his shoulder. Two pallbearers secured ropes to the coffin.

The Irgunists lowered the coffin. Hugo dropped from sight.

Pinchus presided.

"It has been said that the meaning of life is that it ends. Now that Hugo Unger's life has ended, we may better hope to know the meaning of it. Let us ask God to grant us that understanding, and to allow Hugo peace. I will recite the prayer for peace, *El Maleh Rachamim*, in English for Vince."

Pinchus turned up his hands and eyes as though God might drop something and Pinchus would catch it.

"Compassionate God, grant true rest upon the wings of the Divine Presence, in the exalted spheres of the holy and pure. Shelter Hugo with the cover of your wings, for the Lord is his heritage. May he rest in his resting-place, in peace."

Pinchus addressed Vince, Mrs. Pappel, and Rivkah.

"I won't claim to have known Hugo like you three. I knew him only as a fighter. I suspect there was something of the fighter in everything he did. In fact, I can't imagine how he might have survived if he were not. Hugo has earned from all of Israel, honor. From me, gratitude. From you, love. He is at rest now. His fight is done. But for those of us who stay behind…"

Pinchus gestured to pregnant Rivkah.

"…and for those to come, the fight for Israel will continue."

Mrs. Pappel said, "That's enough, Pinchus. This is not the time or place."

Pinchus put a hand on his vested chest. He smiled into the grave.

"I'm sorry Hugo missed that exchange, Missus Pappel. He would've had a great deal to say. But I will say now Amen."

A shovel handle protruded from the mound beside the grave. Pinchus tugged out the shovel and extended it to Vince who rose, took it, and tossed the first dirt over the box. Sod thudded on the pine. Vince threw in more. Pinchus took back the shovel and nudged Vince onward.

After Pinchus, Rivkah tossed in a small shovelful. The dirt landed in hollow pats.

CHAPTER 54

VINCE

Mrs. Pappel covered all the mirrors in the house. She explained to Vince that no one in mourning must be distracted by their own appearance. She set him on a low stool in the dining room and told him to contemplate from this low perch Hugo's return to the soil. Then she kept Rivkah busy in the kitchen.

Vince sat with his collar torn and his knees higher than his hips. Pinchus arrived with the six pallbearers and five other Irgunists, a hardened bunch of trim beards and raven eyes. None knew Vince but he was the one on the stool. Each patted his shoulder and said, "Sorry."

Then they ignored him. Pinchus and the Irgunists donned skullcaps and white-fringed shawls for Pinchus to lead them in murmured prayers. The Irgunists knew the words and tapped knuckles over their swaying hearts.

Before Pinchus and the Irgunists finished, Vince got up from the little stool. He left the dining room to no one's notice. On the front porch he sat in the scent and broken shade of bougainvillea. Mrs. Pappel came out.

"Does any of this help?"

"Not really."

"What would?"

"I'm a New Yorker. We talk to bartenders."

"Would doing a good deed help?"

"Sometimes."

"Take a walk with me."

Vince offered his arm. Mrs. Pappel accepted it and turned them north on the sidewalk.

She wore her funeral dress, her long ponytail spooled into a silver bun. Zichron Ya'akov buzzed; the day had grown later than he'd noticed. Vince felt like he'd just arrived.

Mrs. Pappel said, "For Jews, you know, there's no afterlife. The way we see it, this is all we get."

"What about a soul? I sat up all night to keep Hugo company."

"Pish. To be honest, all that's for the living. It helps us say goodbye, gives us some quiet time with the dead. Either way, Jews have no great reward, no heaven. If we live forever, it's because we've inspired some-one else, and so on. Death for a Jew is life in another."

Mrs. Pappel led him down the main avenue, past the last houses and shops. The street ended at a downward slope. At the bottom ran a slim valley of trees and brush. A path had been worn through the greenery then ran up the side of a matching hill to a village of stone homes and winding streets. A minaret presided over it all.

Mrs. Pappel said, "I haven't heard from Malik."

"Is he still in Lydda?"

"I don't know. I assume so."

"It's got to be hard for him to get word out. Don't worry too much."

"I do worry. He's in the way of the war."

"You all are, Missus Pappel."

"Not like Malik. I want you to go find him."

"In Lydda? I can't go there."

"You went to Jordan for Rivkah. You can go to Lydda for me."

"There's forty thousand Arabs there."

"There's one Malik."

"How am I supposed to do that?" She began to lift a hand, but Vince pushed it down. "No, don't do that. Don't say I'm Vince Haas."

"But you are."

"Mrs. Pappel, come on. Lydda."

She found no reason to say more.

"Okay. I'll do what I can."

"You'll go."

"I'll do what I can."

"Who else should I ask?"

"Alright, stop."

"Find him, Vince."

"Look, I'm not going to say I can find Malik. But if I do, what do you want me to tell him?"

"I want him safe." Mrs. Pappel pointed at the village. "I want him there. In El Fureidis. He'll be safe."

"Listen to me. I've seen a hundred places like that. The IDF is going to run those Arabs out. They're not going to let them stay there."

"The villagers will stay."

"How do you know that?"

"Because you're going to tell Ben-Gurion."

"Am I?"

"Yes, you are."

"Is this before or after I find Malik?"

"I'll leave that up to you. Probably better if before."

"When did you get this idea?"

"When Hugo got shot through the head and brought you back to us. There's nothing else good that can come of it."

She pivoted Vince away from El Fureidis.

"Let's go back to the house."

"I'm not sitting on that stool."

"We'll sit on the porch. I've got some schnapps hidden away. I'll pour some in a teacup for you. Let the Jews pray for Hugo. You can talk to me."

CHAPTER 55

MALIK

July 1
Lydda
Arab-controlled Palestine

Three legionnaires marched Malik at the ends of their rifles.

They herded him across a blinding bright courtyard. Malik ran a hand along the flank of a parked armored car; the steel had soaked up many days of heat. Never had Malik been so hot on a camel as a man would be inside this machine.

No soldiers manned the ramparts of the thick walls. Dozens of them in red keffiyehs stayed out of the sun, lounging in the steamy shadows of the former British fort.

The three legionnaires brought Malik to a metal door off the courtyard. The door was ajar, bars in the one window. The soldiers gestured him inside.

Malik stepped out of the sharp light into a cramped office. The room was choked for air; a perspiring little man behind a desk looked to have been stewed in a pot.

No chair waited for Malik. The officer did not stand. He wore the same uniform as his men, adding a belt across his chest and a pistol in a hip holster. Bareheaded, balding, he looked close in age to Malik. A moustache masked his upper lip; his eyebrows and ears needed to be plucked.

Malik dipped his head. "*Effendi.*"

The officer moved the slightest bit.

"I am told you are stealing rifles."

Malik revealed his hands from his sleeves.

"Effendi, this is an untruth."

"Then explain how you claim to have so many guns."

"The weapons I have are not from your soldiers. You are the Arab Legion. Your men are excellent, Effendi."

"What is your name?"

"I am Malik Mahmoud Akbar al Saneá of the Tarabin."

"Where do you get the guns?"

"There are three hundred legionnaires in Lydda. You rarely leave this fort. In the city there are more than a thousand Palestinians with guns. They are not Legion like you. They are militia and fellahin. All of them are refugees and tribesmen. They are more careless."

"You speak like a spy, Malik of the Tarabin."

"Like a merchant, Effendi."

"You tell me you simply find these weapons."

"No, Effendi. They are stolen."

The officer shifted again. "Be careful what you say next."

"Effendi, I have no hand in this. When the simple fellah falls asleep in an alley. When the militiaman relieves himself in a bush. When he plays *tavla* beside a bottle of *raki*. His gun is stolen then. By thieves, Effendi, not me."

"And you know these thieves."

"It is an unfortunate acquaintance. But all are children of the prophet."

"You purchase the rifles from the thieves."

"Yes, Effendi."

"But you say they are not your thieves."

The Quran permitted a man to lie in three instances. When he spoke to please his wife, to reconcile between people, and in war.

"No, Effendi."

"You play a dangerous game, Malik of the Tarabin."

"In my life I have never played a game, Effendi."

"How many rifles do you have?"

"Seventy-two. I ask only a small commission."

"Where are they?"

"Where money will find them."

The officer pushed back his chair. "Whatever figure you have in mind, cut it in half."

"Yes, Effendi."

"I warn you to stop dealing with thieves."

"Yes, Effendi."

The officer indicated Malik's jeweled fingers. "You wear your wealth on your hands."

"Some of it."

"I think you are getting quite rich for a Bedu."

"Wealth for a Bedu is water beneath the sand."

"The Jews will come to Lydda. When they do, how will money serve you? Those rings will be taken from you."

"I have love in my heart, Effendi. Neither money nor the sand may touch it."

Malik gave the officer his price, slightly more than he had had in mind. The officer handed him a chit for the funds. Malik turned to leave.

Behind him the officer said, "Return only seventy-one rifles. You are a clever man. Keep one for yourself."

"Why, Effendi?"

"To help us kill the Jews."

Malik inclined his head, palm to his breast. "I shall bring you seventy-three rifles."

He returned into the sun.

CHAPTER 56

VINCE

July 2
Grand Hotel of Roses
Rhodes
Greece

Vince ducked behind a white oleander bush, figuring it would hide his pale shirt better than the red blooms across the courtyard.

A tune from a poor violinist scratched through the courtyard, emanating from the casino behind Vince. The garden needed a clip; the shrubs had grown out of square. Vince kept watch through the flowers. In the scented Aegean air, he wished not to be found for a while.

A teenage boy's laugh bounced off the hotel's walls. Another boy wailed, younger, caught.

Shoes scraped on the garden flagstones. Vince raised his head to see Count Bernadotte poking about the shrubs on the other side of the garden.

"Mister Haas. Seriously. Do come out."

Vince stood from the bushes.

"Count."

"Ah. There you are. A committed player of hide-and-seek, I see."

"Your kids asked me."

"I apologize."

"No need."

"Last week, you know, they and my secretary played so thoroughly that all three were missing past lunch. My wife called the island police. They returned at dusk. Imagine. Shall we?"

Trailing a hand through the blooms, Vince stepped around the hedge.

Bernadotte motioned Vince to walk alongside him. The negotiator's eyes were blue to pastel, his nose upturned, black socks tugged to his knobby knees. His voice was buttery. This was a nobleman, and the Jews did not trust nobility.

"I had thought we might speak on my veranda. There is a capital view of Turkey on the horizon. But if my boys get their hands on you again, I fear I will have to shoo them off. Lately, I see too little of them to be firm. A stroll on the beach, then?"

Vince and Bernadotte moved through the unkempt garden, past dusty lawn chairs and rusted rails to the waterfront. The Rose Hotel was not as grand as it once was; Rhodes had gotten worn down during the two-and-a-half-year German army occupation. Few guests were on the register, so Bernadotte's children had the run of the place.

"I'm glad to have my family with me right now. I went for a swim in the sea. This morning I threw a ball to my sons. My wife and I dined to that terrible violinist. My family is an immense help to me. You see, I cannot bear waiting."

The turquoise water lay flat and shiny as mercury. Bernadotte ambled along its edge. He pointed to the northern tip of Rhodes a quarter mile off.

"There once stood the great colossus. A hundred fifty feet high. It could be seen from a great distance."

"One of the seven wonders of the world."

"Did you know, the colossus stood for only fifty years? It fell to an earthquake in 226 BC."

"I didn't."

"I find it inspiring that something which lasted for such a short time, so long ago, should remain a marvel throughout history."

"You figure that's what you're doing?"

Bernadotte said, "If we could establish peace in Palestine. Even for fifty years."

"You've turned in your plan?"

"Yes. I wish to be clear. It is a first proposal only. A draft, intended to spur dialogue and gain time."

"What did it say?"

Walking slowly, the count outlined his proposal.

First, Israel would keep its own state and the Palestinians would gain one. The two would form a Union; the Arab area would become part of Transjordan, the Jews were to remain as Israel.

The Union would function like any other, coordinating issues like foreign policy, economies and common defense. Their national boundaries would be created in consultation with Bernadotte as mediator.

While each state controlled its own immigration, the other would have the right every two years to review the Union's settlement policies. Holy sites were to be protected and shared. The Negev fell to the Arabs, the Western Galilee to the Jews.

Palestinian refugees would be allowed to return to their homes. Jerusalem would become Arab territory.

Vince and Bernadotte reached the tip of the island.

"Thoughts, Mister Haas?"

"I can tell you Husseini's going to be pleased. He'll get everything he wants, especially Jerusalem for his capitol. The rest of the Arabs won't be happy to see Transjordan get bigger while they get nothing. And they aren't going to be thrilled for the Jews to keep a homeland."

"What of Israel?"

"You're asking them to give up some sovereignty. A lot of land. And Jerusalem."

"For peace, Mister Haas."

The count pivoted to walk the beach back to the Rose Hotel. He kept a light clasp on Vince's forearm, conspiratorial while they strolled south.

"The UN has signaled its unofficial endorsement. America, too. England is unsure about handing Jerusalem to the Arabs. Certainly, I understand. The British have had enough of making the Jews angry. I, however, am on my first go-round."

"What've you heard so far from Israel?"

Bernadotte hugged Vince's arm.

"It's promising. I received a coded message yesterday from Tel Aviv. The foreign minister has offered to come to Rhodes to negotiate. This is actually wonderful news. It means the Jews have accepted my plan as a basis for talks. The proviso, of course, is that the Arabs must accept a similar invitation."

"That was my next question."

"The Arabs have been silent. But the time is young. We shall see."

The count released Vince's arm to sit in the sand. He unlaced his shoes and peeled away the tall socks. In bare feet, Bernadotte walked the blue sea's skim, kicking in a boyish way.

CHAPTER 57

GABBI

July 5
Gevim
Israel

Tarek leaned against the barn out of the sun. Gabbi sat cross-legged under a spindly tree. Tarek kept his distance while she cried.

When he could not stay back any longer, Tarek marched the short distance to sit with her in the speckly shade. Gabbi dried her eyes, then lowered the letter she'd read twice. It was the first letter to find her in the war.

She handed him the pages written in German, not a good language for Tarek. He flipped through them to show interest.

"What's wrong? What does she say?"

"She's in Zichron Ya'akov. Living with Missus Pappel. They have a house, it looks over a vineyard. She's due next month."

"That's good, yes?"

"Missus Pappel has a wooden foot. Rivkah says it makes her act even more like a pirate."

Gabbi wasn't ready to laugh.

She said, "Hugo's dead."

"He's the Irgunist."

"He was almost famous. They never managed to hang him."

"How did he die?"

"He was on the *Altalena*. The Zahal shot him."

"I'm sorry."

"He was a funny little man."

"I'm sure."

"Vince was at the *Altalena*, too. He brought Hugo's body to Zichron to be buried. Hugo has no family so Vince was his mourner. Missus Pappel and Rivkah showed him how."

"Vince sounds like a good man."

"He is."

"I'd like to meet him sometime."

Tarek stood, then offered his hand to lift her. Tarek's eyes were the color of the young tree's leaves.

She said, "You'll have a lot in common."

"Will we?"

Gabbi threw her arms about Tarek's neck.

CHAPTER 58

VINCE

July 6
Israeli Foreign Ministry
Sarona
Tel Aviv

Bernadotte let himself out of the Foreign Ministry building. He stepped into the sun wearing a summer pinstripe suit and clutched tight a manilla folder. No one from the ministry accompanied him.

Beside the walkway, forty reporters and photographers jockeyed for position. None gave deference to Vince or any other; even the younger journalists came from old cities.

The press shouted in English, German, Swedish, and Hebrew. Bernadotte never cut his eyes at the press but made a beeline for his UN car. His gait was self-possessed but pacey, he swung only one arm with his long strides.

He spotted Vince, taller than the rest. Bernadotte halted, tugged his suitcoat hem, and shot his sleeves for the whirring cameras.

"My boys send their regards, Mister Haas."

"Tell them I'm still hiding."

"I won't. They will believe me."

Bernadotte's UN driver held open the limo's rear door. As the count crouched to enter the car headfirst, he unbuttoned his coat. He tossed the folder onto the seat ahead of him.

✳ ✳ ✳

The Red House
Tel Aviv

In the afternoon, a cold front slipped in from the Mediterranean. Clouds stacked up in grey scaffolds hinting at rain. At dusk, boardwalk strollers carried closed umbrellas. Vince hoped for a drizzle tonight to cool the city. On his covered porch at the Kaete Dan he might listen to the rainfall.

Ben-Gurion answered Vince's knock by opening the door himself.

The prime minister didn't retreat behind his desk but took the leather chair opposite Vince. In a loose linen shirt, a floor-to-ceiling bookcase for his backdrop, Ben-Gurion plattered a hand for Vince to begin. He appeared to know what Vince would ask.

"What did you put in your answer to Bernadotte?"

The prime minister raised his bulldog chin.

"Oh ho. That Swede. Why? What do you know?"

"He left the Foreign Ministry this afternoon looking like he'd been jilted. No one from the ministry came out with him. He didn't talk to the press."

Ben-Gurion leaned in, elbows to his knees.

"Nobody who has the slightest inkling of three millennia of Jewish history would ever submit such a proposal as Bernadotte did."

Ben-Gurion sat back. Just the tips of his shoes touched the floor.

Vince asked, "Then why did you send him the message that you were willing to negotiate?"

"I wasn't interested in being the first to reject it."

"Was that fair?"

"Fair?"

Ben-Gurion cocked his hands on the chair arms but did not rise.

"There is only one recognized plan for the question of Palestine. The 1947 UN proposal. Bernadotte's *dreck* ignored it. Hand the Negev to the Arabs? Give Arab Palestine to Husseini, that little *pischer*?"

Ben-Gurion scooted forward. He looked as if he might jump from the chair.

"Limits on our immigration? Tell Israel we must get permission from the Arabs before we can grant citizenship? Is this what a sovereign nation does? No Jew will be refused entrance into Israel. Not one."

Ben-Gurion collapsed into the chair's cushions. He had more disappointments to name.

"Jerusalem to the Arabs? A city that was two-thirds Jewish before the invasion must now become Arab? Write this in your newspaper, Mister Haas. Every Jew of every generation now and for a thousand years will resist this. The Swede is insane."

"He's not."

"Oh, he isn't? What is he, then?"

"He says he's neutral."

"Of course. The famous Swedish dispassion. Do you think he's neutral?"

"I do."

"Then let me tell you what his neutrality has done. It led him to become friends with the Nazis. Yes, yes, he got the release of many Jews, let's not forget. But to do that, he sat with the Devil. Here's a man who speaks with the Jews, then speaks with the Arabs. He is conciliatory, a bargainer. But I think, here is a *gonif* who sat with fucking Himmler and used the same persuasive tones."

"What do you guess the Arabs will say?"

"Husseini's pissing himself, he's so happy. He sent me a message that he doesn't want to fight any more and we shouldn't touch him. Lydda and Ramle are still in Transjordan's hands, so I could not accept."

"What about the rest of the Arabs?"

"They'll shit on Bernadotte's plan."

"Why?"

"Because, Mister Haas, use your eyes. Even with this terrible proposal, there will still be an Israel. And the Arabs find that intolerable."

"The count says it's just a draft. To get the conversation started."

Ben-Gurion rose to his feet, hinging from the chair unhurried.

"Then he should be congratulated. It has done that. I'll see you out."

Vince kept his seat.

Ben-Gurion asked, "What?"

"I need a favor. Two."

"Two favors?"

"Yes."

"Let's start with the first."

"I need to get into Lydda."

"This is not like asking me for a bus ticket."

"I know."

"Lydda is a key to our entire military strategy."

"I understand."

"Then understand that in four days, Lydda will fall under a major attack. You will keep this private, of course."

"Of course."

"Why on earth would you want to go into Lydda?"

"I have a friend there."

"A friend? An Arab?"

"Yes."

"You want to get this Arab out? Don't answer. But you understand, rescuing Arabs is not the point of attacking Lydda."

"He's my friend."

"You've said."

"I'll go in with the army."

"And if I tell you no?" Ben-Gurion put forth a hand. "Again, don't answer. I know. You'll go in with the army anyway. Look, I don't want you bothering my officers. Have my secretary draft something. If you get killed trying to save this Arab, I will not be pleased. I don't like the press. And very few Americans. You, I can stand."

"I feel the same about you, Prime Minister."

"What's your second favor?"

"It's not for me."

"For who? Ah, the girl. The kibbutznik. How is she?"

"Pregnant."

"Mister Haas." Ben-Gurion uncrossed his arms to sit again. "A pregnant Jew gets my attention. Ask."

CHAPTER 59

RIVKAH

July 8
Zichron Ya'akov

Mrs. Pappel tapped her cane against one wall. "We can knock this down."

Rivkah wandered to the rear of the first-floor apartment. Returning, she said, "There's room for two ovens."

Together they envisioned the shop: seating for five bistro tables here, display space there, over here shelves and a counter. The flat, three blocks from Mrs. Pappel's home on Zichron's main street, would be ideal after some hammering to convert it to a store.

Mrs. Pappel turned a slow circle on her cane.

Out on the sidewalk an old man, then another, hurried past the open door. Rivkah stepped outside. Mrs. Pappel came behind.

A farmer, a big fellow in overalls and flattop hair, ran towards them. This was Thalhimer, one of the elected leaders of the town. Mrs. Pappel put her cane in his path to slow him, but with no need; he'd come to find her.

"The army's here. In the town hall."

Mrs. Pappel patted Thalhimer's rear with the cane as he jogged on.

Rivkah asked, "What do you think this is about?"

"The truce ends tonight."

Mrs. Pappel closed the apartment door tenderly.

The five-block walk to the town hall made the two of them the last to arrive. The hall was a windowed square that could be bunted or blank depending on the occasion, for weddings or meetings. Twenty of Zichron's council and business notables sat at tables; a dozen farmers and vintners stood cross-armed against the undecorated walls.

Again, tall Major Keisch had arrived as the Alexandroni Brigade's liaison; he appeared before the locals with a sidearm on his hip. Behind him, three soldier boys in sock hats slouched as if the war had already resumed. No Arabs were present.

Keisch nodded at Mrs. Pappel's and pregnant Rivkah's entrance as if he'd been waiting for them. He had not; Thalhimer had prevented the meeting from starting until Mrs. Pappel and Rivkah took chairs offered by council members.

Thalhimer told Keisch, "Go ahead now."

Keisch was slim like Vince with a long neck and prominent Adam's apple. Keisch seemed sincere, too, but when he spoke he was a different man than Vince. Keisch was certain.

"I have news."

Someone said, "Good," in an impatient tone.

"I won't waste your time. You know the fighting will start again tomorrow. This morning I was given orders to inform you that the Alexandroni Brigade was going to transfer the population of El Fureidis to a prisoner-of-war camp."

A few councilmembers sprang from their seats, calmer hands tugged them down. Keisch's soldiers shuffled behind him. In the hall, one of the sisters, Martha, spoke up:

"You said '*was* going to transfer.' Are you?"

"Be aware. The Iraqis are only thirty kilometers to the east in Samaria. If they make a move towards the sea, they'll have no choice but to come past your town. If the enemy reaches the coast, the Galilee will be cut off from the rest of Israel. Haifa will be threatened. We can't allow any Arab villages in the Iraqis' path who might help them. This may be hard for you to accept. But it cannot be hard to understand."

Mrs. Pappel asked, "But?"

"Missus Pappel. Why is it you do not surprise me?"

"We're both very suspicious people."

"I suspect you more so than I."

"Give it time, Major."

"Yes. Well, madam, as you say. But. This morning, it seems the prime minister has intervened personally in the affairs of El Fureidis."

Rivkah reached to squeeze Mrs. Pappel's wrist. Keisch noted this and cocked his head but pressed on.

"Any action by the Zahal to uproot the inhabitants of El Fureidis has now been delayed for four weeks."

Keisch was not pleased when Zichron's businesspeople and officials cheered.

When the clapping faded, Mrs. Pappel asked, "There's another 'but,' isn't there, major?"

"Unerring, Missus Pappel."

"High praise, Major."

"Yes. There is. *But*. Ben-Gurion has stopped us only from removing the residents of El Fureidis. He was silent on other matters."

"What does that mean, exactly?"

"There's still too much free movement between El Fureidis and nearby Arab villages. It would be a simple matter for Iraqis or other hostiles to infiltrate. Please, you must see that."

Mrs. Pappel asked, "What if we do?"

"The Zahal is going to issue identification cards to every Arab adult of El Fureidis. The cards must be produced on demand. We are going to install a police station inside the village. The Arab residents will be subjected to a round-the-clock curfew."

"A curfew?"

"Yes, madam."

"You're going to lock the workers of El Fureidis out of the fields?"

"That would be one impact of the curfew, yes."

Vineyard owners and farmers erupted, red-faced. Who was going to pick? Who would weed, water, drive the mules, crush the grapes? Who would harvest the olives, then the oranges? Zichron lacked enough volunteers to do but a fraction of that work.

Behind Keisch, his three soldiers continued to slouch.

Mrs. Pappel struggled to stand. When she was upright, the protests muted.

"Major Keisch."

"Madam."

"You didn't come to tell us this. You don't need Zichron's approval to do any of that."

"No, madam, I do not."

"Tell us the rest."

"I was about to. If everyone will keep their seats."

"We'll see. Go on."

"Arab workers will be subject to curfew, unless Zichron Ya'akov will pay to the Zahal eight hundred and fifty Palestinian mil per worker, per day."

Arguments swelled again across the room, but no one took to their feet. Keisch spoke over the clamor.

"Five hundred mil will go to the Arab laborer. Three hundred and fifty to the army for expenses."

Mrs. Pappel lifted her cane for quiet. When she had it, she said, "That's almost a pound sterling each."

"Yes, madam."

The townsfolk groused that this was more than twice the pay they'd previously given the Arabs. They accused Keisch of using this scheme to break Zichron's support for El Fureidis. The curfew, these payments, were simply the army's opening gambits before emptying the village.

In the rear of the hall, a vintner asked, "Can the army wait?"

"What would we wait for?"

"Autumn."

"Why autumn?"

"The end of the harvest."

"And then?"

The vintner lifted his hands to Keisch. The gesture said, Do what you will.

Mrs. Pappel stamped her wooden foot as she rose. She turned on all.

"Listen to me. The Arabs of El Fureidis will not lose their homes. Not to the army. And not after you've finished your goddam harvest. We gave them our word. We will keep it."

In the hushed hall, Keisch's loafing troopers giggled. Mrs. Pappel and Rivkah left the room to the taps of Mrs. Pappel's cane and her unrhythmic steps.

CHAPTER 60

GABBI

Gevim

Under an oak, Gabbi elbowed Tarek to wake him.

He sat upright. "What?"

Abner leaned down, shaking a letter in Tarek's face.

"I just got this from a friend."

Tarek wanted to lie back down. Gabbi grabbed his collar to stop him.

Tarek grumbled, "Alright. You have a friend."

"His name is Zev. He volunteered for an assault unit. They're commandos like us. Jeeps and halftracks."

Gabbi asked, "Where is he?"

"Tel Hashomer. When the fighting starts tomorrow, they're going up against the Legion."

Tarek lay back despite Gabbi's tug to keep him upright.

Abner said, "He wants me to come join him. He says the company is almost all South Africans."

From his back, Tarek said, "Take Jonny with you."

"I'm going to go ask him."

Gabbi asked, "Who's the commanding officer?"

"Some one-eyed major named Dayan."

Tarek said, "Haven't heard of him."

Gabbi said, "We'll miss you."

Tarek said, "Go."

Abner strode off.

The jeep company had finished its maintenance. They'd reloaded every ammo belt, refueled, checked tires, cleaned and oiled the guns. Now they lolled in the shade, sensing the silent ticking of the expiring truce.

Abner returned at a run. Gabbi sat up, Tarek did not.

She asked, "What did Jonny say?"

"He said it's okay."

"Good for you."

"Not just me."

Like a sprung trap, Tarek came up.

"What?"

Abner kneeled to again offer Tarek his friend's letter. Tarek pushed it away.

Gabbi asked, "What did Jonny say?"

"He said take the jeep. And Tarek."

"Can I come, too?"

With little effort, Abner swept Gabbi to her feet.

She reached down for Tarek. "You've been wanting to get away from Jonny. Here's your chance."

Tarek didn't move until Gabbi snapped her fingers. He blew out his cheeks and sat up.

"Screw it." Tarek took her hand. "A one-eyed major. How bad can it be?"

CHAPTER 61

July 9

KFAR SYRKIN
ISRAEL
By Vincent Haas

Herald Tribune News Service

The ceasefire between Israel and five Arab nations ended at 10 a.m. this morning.

The truce lasted twenty-eight days. Israel offered to extend the peace for another month, and certainly would have used the time to import more weapons and fighters under the leaky gaze of the UN.

King Husseini of Transjordan would've been happy to maintain the truce, too. The war's been good to him; he's taken a firm grip on the eastern half of Jerusalem, plus a large swath of Palestinian land west of the Jordan River.

Husseini's Arab allies—Iraq, Egypt, Lebanon, and Syria—spent the truce quarreling over the spoils and shouting to their citizens false news of their inevitable victory. The Arab street has grown far too angry at Israel's mere existence to accept any olive branches. Their leaders have left themselves no choice but to rekindle the war.

So, last night at midnight on the Egyptian front, at kibbutz Negba on the northern rim of the Negev, the Israelis and Arabs violated the truce together in the dark, too eager to fight to wait for breakfast.

I spent last night at a former British air base south of Haifa, awaiting the arrival of Maj. Moshe Dayan, the officer in charge of a new mechanized assault unit, the 89th Commando Battalion. For the past week, Dayan had been in the U.S. accompanying the body of Col. Mickey Marcus, an American hero of World War II and a volunteer in the Israeli army. On June 10th, hours before the truce went into effect, a young IDF guard shot Marcus to death when he failed to respond with a password. The Israeli government chose Dayan to represent their gratitude to America for Mickey Marcus.

Seven years ago, Dayan lost his left eye fighting alongside the British. Today he wears a black silk patch. He claims the diminution in his sight is no handicap; instead, it has aided his hearing. Now he can tell where a shell or bomb will land and no longer fears them.

Dayan's plane landed at sunup. Arab villages fired on it but the shooting was amateurish. We got in his waiting car—cyclopic Dayan does not hesitate to drive—and motored east to find his new battalion. On the road, he told me about his commandos.

Dayan's recruitment of 360 fighters for his 89th raised complaints among other army commanders; most of the troops sought permission to transfer from their former units, but quite a few came without their commander's okay. Dayan's raiders have been known to swipe the occasional unguarded jeep, repaint it, and mount it with machine guns. The commandos have adopted the same devil-may-care panache as their one-eyed leader.

Each of Dayan's four companies has a distinct makeup. Young kibbutz and moshav farmers comprise one company. Another is volunteers from Tel Aviv. Former members of the Stern Gang, a dissident group, form a third. The fourth consists of international volunteers, mostly tough veterans of South Africa's wars.

While in New York for Marcus' funeral, Dayan had a chance meeting that influenced his tactical thinking. In the cocktail lounge of his hotel, he encountered Abe Baum, one of the most daring U.S. soldiers of World War II.

Baum was the operations officer of an armored infantry battalion given a special mission by General Patton himself: to liberate 1,200 American POWs—including Patton's son-in-law—from a German camp sixty miles behind enemy lines. Baum's task force was roughly the same size as Dayan's 89th. Over drinks, Baum shared his theories of mechanized warfare.

He'd forged his small force into a spear, a fast-moving column of firepower to race across the front lines into German-held territory. They'd stop for nothing. Within thirty minutes of crossing into German territory, Baum lost half his men and machines. Still, the column rammed its way into the POW camp, but without enough vehicles to carry all the prisoners out or the guns to have any chance. They saddled up what POWs they could, then fought like crazy to get home. Task Force Baum got no farther than halfway to Allied lines before they were wiped out. Many GIs were killed, most of the rest were wounded, including Baum. The survivors were taken prisoner.

Tomorrow, Operation Dani begins, the largest IDF action in the war so far. The mission's objectives will be to shove the Arab League eastward away from Tel Aviv, capture the Palestinian sister cities of Lydda and Ramle, and open another route into Jerusalem. Dayan tells me he'll wait for the chance to put Baum's theories into action. Unlike Baum, he claims, he will bring his force all the way back.

After his long flight from the States, Dayan needed sleep. I kept him talking and offered to drive but this is a man with his hands on the wheel in all things. We arrived at Tel Hashomer, the base where Dayan expected his commandos to be waiting for him. As we rolled up, the column roared out through the gates, headed for the base at Kfar Syrkin, the jump-off point at dawn.

Dayan stopped the jeep. He leaped out like a man who'd just had a good eight hours.

At 10 a.m., the moment of the close of the UN's truce, Moshe Dayan ran towards a halftrack at the head of his new commando force. Before he disappeared inside the steel vehicle, he motioned me to one of his jeeps. He shouted, *"Ag'u el-Yahud."*

The Jew has come.

Reporting from Kfar Syrkin, with the 89th Commando Battalion.

CHAPTER 62

GABBI

Tel Hashomer

Tarek skidded the jeep to a stop. Gabbi hopped out to jump on Vince's back. Arms around his neck, she squealed, "Oh my God."

He bent under the surprise. She let him loose, dropped to her boots, then lunged into his long, spread arms.

Vince rested his chin on her sock hat. Neither moved their feet in their embrace. She spoke without letting him go.

"Tarek, Abner. This is Vince the American."

Still with one arm around her waist, Vince shook hands with the boys. Abner said, "Vince." Tarek said, "Ah."

She stepped back to push palms into his chest, patting him like a child for presents.

"What are you doing here?"

The column dusted past; some drivers called for Tarek to get back in line. Tarek said to Vince, "Climb in."

Abner settled in the jeep's tail among sandbags, jerry cans, ammo, and his mounted machine gun. Gabbi offered Vince her seat in front behind the MG 34, but Vince demurred.

"I'll be fine. Abner, excuse me."

Vince was taller than Abner but nothing like his bulk; he wedged into the tight space, legs tucked to his chest, blue eyes peeking above them.

Gabbi jumped into the jeep. A lanyard tipped up the barrel of her MG 34. The ammo belt playing from the tin box on the floorboard was locked in the breech.

Tarek rejoined the convoy of halftracks, scout cars, and jeeps. Gabbi turned to Vince but didn't talk over the noise of the column. She nodded, not to welcome him to the war, for the war was no one's to give to Vince Haas, but to tell him there was much to say and hear. While nodding, Gabbi patted Tarek's shoulder, signaling to Vince, "Yes, this one."

Kfar Syrkin

The Eighty-Ninth powered past abandoned Arab villages and untilled land. Reaching the Zahal base at Kfar Syrkin, the convoy parked in the moshav's pasture alongside grey-muzzled horses. Vince went off to write his column and wire it to New York. He shook Abner's and Tarek's hands again, hugged Gabbi as if saying goodbye for longer than he would be gone, and wandered off in search of a typewriter.

The arrival of a mechanized battalion seemed to go unnoticed by the moshavot. The odors of their livestock and hens drifted to the base on a warm wind. Hammers rapped in the settlers' workshops, their mules were swaybacked, their generators grumbled, the soil looked hard and unbroken. A hundred farmers bore rifles across their backs, tools in hand. The moshav was close to the front lines, and its people appeared weary.

Vince found Gabbi sitting with Abner beside her jeep, sliding 7.62 Mauser cartridges into fifty-round ammo belts. An hour ago, at noon, Tarek had walked off to the moshav to see if he might buy or cozen some motor oil. The rest of the jeep crews played cards and dice, wrote letters, snoozed, or read paperbacks from America.

Abner got to his feet. Vince cupped the boy's elbow to thank him for the time alone with Gabbi.

He sat in Abner's spot against the rear passenger-side tire. Vince wore the same shabby straw hat as the last time Gabbi had seen him, four months ago at Massuot Yitzhak. As always, a pencil was stuck behind his ear. He was scruffy and gangly, like the old horses.

Vince snatched a bullet from a carton to shove it into the sleeve of an ammo belt.

Gabbi said, "I'm sorry about Hugo."

"Me, too."

"What happened?"

Vince picked another round out of the ammo crate. He pressed the point into the center of his forehead.

She said, "I'm glad it was quick."

He threw the round back into the box, not wanting to handle that one now.

Gabbi touched his wrist. "That was wrong to say."

"It's okay. I get it."

Together they pushed bullets into the belts. In the grazing field, summer insects chirruped. Heat crackled in the steel convoy. She asked about the Eighty-Ninth's one-eyed commander. What was he like, where was he from?

Vince related what he knew of Dayan, then asked how she and Tarek were fitting into the new battalion. What had it been like on the Egyptian front?

She said, "I'm pregnant."

Vince rapped her leg with the back of his hand. It seemed an American gesture.

She said, "I haven't told Tarek."

"Why not?"

"He's like you."

"Okay. How, exactly?"

"He'll want me to go somewhere safe. Leave the army. He might even join me. He's an only son."

"I don't see why that's such a bad idea."

"There's no safe place in Israel, not until we make it safe."

"We're not talking about everyone. Just you and the baby. And Tarek."

"There's only everyone."

"That's good. Can I quote you?"

"Yes."

"Your sister said the same thing to me in the POW camp in Transjordan. I had a letter from Husseini to get her out. She wouldn't take it."

"You should quote Rivkah instead. It'll make her happy."

Vince lifted the ammo belt off his lap. "I'm not sure I know how to do that."

"Do you love her?"

"Yeah."

"Just try to love what she loves."

"I can love the kid."

"How about Israel?"

Vince broke eye contact. He chuckled at his lap.

"You guys are all crazy."

He looked up, ready to make an apology. Gabbi stopped him.

"I get it."

She brought Vince close for a kiss on his prickly cheek.

"Be careful out there."

Vince squeezed her hand. He stood, wished her the same, and left.

CHAPTER 63

MALIK

July 10
Lydda

"Who was he?"

No one on the train platform answered Malik.

He asked the crowd again, "Does anyone know who this was?"

Someone said, "A Jew."

"What was he doing here?"

"Waiting for a train?"

An old woman piped up to say the trains had not run in a week. Why would a Jew be waiting for a train?

Many in the crowd said they did not know. The old woman shrugged to say, See? There is a mystery.

"Why was a Jew still in Lydda? Who was he?"

Heads shook. They did not know or they would not say. Among them, a small boy clutched his mother's hand.

A beardless young man held out an arm to Malik. He was a well-kept sort, perhaps from one of Lydda's good families.

"Why do you want to know his name?"

"To give him a proper burial."

The crowd approved. A man, the one who'd come to find Malik, bragged that this was the reason he'd brought the big Bedu with a cart to the train station.

Another old woman asked, "Will you do it soon?"

"I will."

She said, "Thank you." A younger woman, perhaps her daughter, comforted her.

No one would say why the Jew had remained. His reason for being at Lydda's train station, like his name, had died with him.

A leaflet blew across the platform. Jewish airplanes had dropped them last night, warning Lydda's women and children to leave. Malik could not read it; he handed it to the woman holding the hand of the small boy. She read aloud for him:

"You have no chance of receiving help. We intend to conquer the town. We have no intention of harming persons or property. But whoever attempts to oppose us will die. He who prefers to live must surrender."

Malik asked, "Mother, why are you still in Lydda with this child?"

"The Legion has set up roadblocks. They keep us here."

"Why?"

"If the women and children go, too many men will follow. The Legion has decided we will all be defenders of Lydda."

More than one on the platform had killed the Jew. The work was of several knives. The Jew's throat was slit, face mutilated, hands and feet hacked off. His murderers were in this crowd, blood washed off, watching to see if someone might betray them.

No Arab in the city would care that a Jew was murdered. But the Israelis were coming. And they would. That was why the old woman asked that the Jew be buried fast.

Malik approached the clean young man who smelled like pillows.

"Pick four others. Put the Jew in my wagon. We will bury him."

"What if I say no?"

Malik leaned in closer, only slightly. "Yes. What if?"

"You," the young man said, shifting away from Malik. "And you three."

CHAPTER 64

VINCE

Kfar Syrkin

Vince carried a paper cup of coffee into the pasture. He slumped in the passenger seat of Dayan's scout car.

In the predawn quiet, the crickets and lightning bugs had retired an hour ago with the crescent moon. The old horses lay on their ribs in the grass. When the sun peeked above the horizon and yellow tendrils of light splayed across the camp and fields, hundreds of commandos left their tents.

Dayan's driver and two gunners arrived. They recognized Vince as the American reporter and told him their names and homes; all three hailed from Tel Aviv. They were nineteen and childhood friends. Today would be their first day of battle.

Vince left the front seat when Dayan arrived, to stand in the grass to meet him. Dayan twirled a finger above his head. His Eighty-Ninth cranked its eighty engines.

"Why are you here, Mister Haas?"

"You ducked me yesterday."

Vince handed Dayan the written request from Ben-Gurion that allowed him to embed.

"For the next few days, I'm going to stick by you."

"Will you now?"

"I need to get into Lydda."

"Why would you need to go there?"

"To find a friend."

"An Arab, this friend?"

"Yes."

"I have some of those. I am not going to rescue them."

"I made a promise."

"Then you should keep it. But we don't have orders to go to Lydda."

"You'll get me close."

"I will certainly try to do that."

Dayan's single eye was merry when he jumped into the passenger seat. He didn't check to see if Vince was in the backseat before he pointed his driver forward.

✳ ✳ ✳

Qula
Arab-controlled Palestine

Dayan's convoy was a mile long leaving Kfar Syrkin. After six minutes, the first of the eighty vehicles crossed into enemy territory. Dayan ordered the column off the paved paths, to roll his war machines through the crop fields of the Arabs.

He kept a finger pressed on a map and said nothing to Vince riding behind him. After five more rattling miles, on a raw plain of cactus, thistles, and mulberry, a mortar round exploded a hundred yards in front of his scout car. Dayan radioed the column to halt.

He stood tall in the front seat, hands on the windshield. Vince and the rear gunner stood, too.

The village of Qula lay a half mile ahead, on the other side of an olive grove. On three separate hills, the village was once home to a thousand Arabs. Qula was ancient and stone built; a Crusader watchtower rose beside a minaret. Nothing stirred in the streets. Qula had been abandoned by its thousand so the Legion could make it a battlefront.

A second mortar shell blew, closer.

From the rear of the idling Eighty-Ninth, two halftracks growled forward. Within minutes, both were swapping artillery shells with Qula.

Slowly, the Arab artillerymen got the Eighty-Ninth's range. After several salvos, the halftracks reversed, searching for cover. Dayan instructed the rear gunner of his scout car to "keep the reporter in his seat."

Dayan jumped out. The gunner pressed a hand on Vince's shoulder.

Through heavy cordite haze, Dayan stamped over to the halftracks. A short officer emerged to meet him. As Dayan spoke, he smacked the back of one hand against the palm of the other, then whirled on his heels. When he returned to the scout car, Dayan's cheeks glowed red.

He didn't wait for Vince to query him.

"I've reminded my deputy that we are commandos. Trading shells from a standstill is not how we fight."

"So what're you going to do?"

"We are going to take off the kid gloves."

❋ ❋ ❋

Dayan split his battalion into two groups. He took with him just one company, Gabbi's South African bunch, and left his deputy commander, Pelz, with the Sternists, the farmers, and the Tel Aviv lads. Dayan ordered Pelz to use that force to break into Qula without delay.

With Vince bouncing in the back, Dayan's scout car led the smaller force overland two miles south towards the morning's second target, Tira.

Like its neighbor Qula, Tira was an abandoned village on a sere stretch of hills that had been fortified by the Legion.

Dayan radioed the jeep company at the rear of his column.

"Move into the lead. Don't stop. Repeat, do not stop. Enter the village and open fire."

Eight jeeps dashed to the front. As she zoomed past Dayan's car, Gabbi shot Vince a salute.

Suddenly her dark driver, Tarek, catapulted out of the jeep company's formation, accelerating to be first into the village. All eight jeeps flew right into the teeth of the Arabs' sandbags and shallow trenchworks. Gabbi and the big gunner, Abner, opened up; the seven other jeeps raced in behind them, blasting away too. Quickly, the Legion's forward defenses buckled; the Arabs died or ran. In Tarek's dust, the jeeps broke into Tira, firing their machine guns in every direction. Close behind them, the rest of Dayan's column charged into the village.

The suddenness of the commando assault scrambled the Arab defenders of Tira. The Israelis were behind them before they could adjust. Legionnaires bolted from their positions to duck inside the small homes. From there, they could only snipe, and every round they fired brought the attention of the column's swift machine guns.

Dayan's boys shot at every moving thing. They tore up Tira, speeding through it so fast they popped out the other side. Tarek, still in the lead, wheeled the convoy around to ram into Tira again, as if slapping the village forehand and back.

For the next hour, Dayan and his commandos slashed at the village like this. Finally, the legionnaires came out from cover, hands up, weapons in the dirt. A hundred fifty Arab fighters were placed under guard in the village marketplace. Twenty lay dead, twice that number wounded.

Dayan ordered the jeep that had rushed to the front of the assault and stayed there to report to him. Tarek drove up; Dayan got out of his scout car to shake their hands. Vince and Gabbi said nothing to display they knew each other. Tarek and Abner didn't seem to care one way or the other.

A messenger from Deputy Commander Pelz arrived to say that Qula had fallen. Between the two villages, the Eighty-Ninth had suffered just five wounded.

A small holding force was left behind in Tira. Dayan led the South African company a mile south to link up with the rest of the battalion.

Vince asked Dayan, "What's next?"

"Now I have to go to Tel Aviv. Ben-Gurion ordered me to come see him as soon as I got back from America. I've been avoiding him."

"What's he want?"

"I'll find out."

Pelz himself approached with a report: the big airport north of Lydda had been captured that morning. Dayan put Pelz in charge of the whole Eighty-Ninth until his return from Tel Aviv later that night.

Pelz asked, "Orders?"

"Deir Tarif is next. Take it if you can."

"We can."

"Then I'll see you there."

Dayan climbed into a jeep beside a driver. He gazed ahead as if the vehicle were already in motion. Without a sideways glance, he asked, "Mister Haas, are you coming?"

CHAPTER 65

MALIK

Lydda

In a courtyard surrounded by old limestone walls and keyhole arches, Malik met with his thieves.

The ten fellahin sat in a semicircle; Malik stood at the center. From a tenement nearby, people watched in windows. A woman on a veranda cradled a naked infant, wordlessly asking the thieves, anyone, for help.

A crate served as a table. On it were three warm teakettles; Malik had brewed them in an empty flat. He offered each thief a brass cup and poured. Malik raised his cup in toast and drank.

He heaved the cup against a wall. The thieves did the same; the brass rang the end of their business. He'd kept his word to Mrs. Pappel. He did not steal the guns. Others did. He did not buy them, for the thieves did not own them; Malik only rewarded them for bringing the weapons to him, then he put them in the hands of the Arab Legion. For a fee.

Malik handed each fellah five hundred mil, twice what the weapons in their laps were worth. He told them to keep the guns.

None of the thieves were Bedu, and none from Lydda. All were refugees out of Jaffa, Haifa, Safed, Baysan, and the seacoast, men who'd left their homes when the invading Egyptians told them to leave. The Jews, for their part, did not force them out of their villages. Arabs were welcome to go, or welcome to stay in their homes and die.

Malik smoothed his long black robes. The thieves were clad in mismatched garb lifted from empty houses; they wore mashups of khaki trousers and cotton blouses, vests, suspenders, and fezzes, all mis-sized.

Malik said, "I have a poem."

The youngest one, an urchin, asked, "What is a poem?"

"The words to a song without the music."

All ten thieves had Malik's coins in their pockets, so none objected to a poem.

Malik turned slowly as he recited, to wish all his thieves a good death:

> "I do not know the stars.
> I do not understand what they know of me.
> They have been there as long as I have been here.
> Only that matters.
> Why should the stars be so far? So little known?
> It may be that we can go to them on death.
> What if to have lived well is to go to the stars?
> What if to die well is to become a star?"

The urchin said, "The Jews are coming." So he had understood the poem.

Malik answered, "Tomorrow."

"What should we do?"

"Fight if you feel you must defend a city that is not yours."

"Lydda is Arab."

"Then fight."

The boy asked, "Why will the Jews attack Lydda?"

From a sleeve Malik slid a short blade with an ivory haft, a knife the youth himself had stolen and gifted to him. Malik lay the knife at the boy's crossed ankles.

"Do you think you can stab me?"

"I don't think so."

"Why not?"

"You're big. You have weapons."

Malik turned away from the boy.

"Now? Could you stab my back?"

The boy said, "I suppose."

Malik faced him.

"The Jews cannot leave forty thousand Arabs at their backs and be stabbed."

The urchin snatched the knife off the ground. Malik let him keep it, too.

Another thief asked, "What will you do?"

"Tell me what you think I should do?"

The thief said, "Go away."

"Why?"

"You're Bedu."

"May I not have a home?"

"Lydda is not it."

"Nor is it yours."

"I will return to Jaffa soon."

"What if you do not?"

"It will always be my home."

"I understand."

"The desert is yours."

"No more, cousin."

"With those rings, you can bribe your way past any guard."

Another asked, "So are you going to leave?"

"No."

"Why not?"

"I have not yet been summoned."

Malik made a bow to all the thieves and to their fates. Then he stepped out of the ring, into Lydda.

CHAPTER 66

VINCE

Tel Aviv

Dayan knocked dust off his pants before he rapped on Ben-Gurion's door.

Inside, Ben-Gurion shouted, "Come in."

Vince hung back. Dayan opened and entered. He said, "Prime Minister."

Behind Dayan, Vince poked his head into the office.

"Prime Minister."

At his desk, Ben-Gurion rubbed his thumb and fingertips like a man counting worry beads.

"What are you doing here, Mister Haas?"

"Following him." Vince stepped in beside Dayan.

"You followed him into my office. Without an invitation. What do you want this time?"

"Just doing my job."

"If you want to stay, you'll publish not a word about this meeting until my office clears it."

"Understood."

"You're as dirty as he is."

"The major is a fast driver."

"Sit down, Mister Haas. Dayan, sit."

Ben-Gurion was as agitated as when Vince had last seen him four days ago. The prime minister fidgeted, tapped his desk, and waved a pen while he ignored Vince and addressed Dayan.

"Next time I call you to my office, Major, you come."

"I've been with my troops. In combat."

"That excuse will not work with me again. Now that you're here, I'll tell you. I'm not happy with Jerusalem. The Arabs have got too much of it. I want the Old City back. You'll take over the Jerusalem command."

"Why me?"

"The current commander isn't aggressive enough. You lack a few things, Dayan." Ben-Gurion aimed the tip of the pen at him. "An eye is one of them. Experience is another. But you don't lack for aggression. You're stubborn. I saw what you did at the Deganias. So did Mister Haas."

"Prime Minister."

"You have a reporter in tow, Dayan. That tells me something. You don't mind others knowing your name. So be it, I don't care. I'll make you a lieutenant colonel. Go protect Jewish Jerusalem. You'll be known well enough."

Dayan sat in profile to Vince; the patch revealed nothing. Then he pivoted to face Vince and stayed like that, oddly contemplating, seeming to compose his answer.

He smiled once, deadpan as he often was. Then Dayan faced Ben-Gurion.

"I respectfully decline."

Ben-Gurion's fingers stopped their plucking.

"You're saying no to me?"

"I understand the gravity of the situation in Jerusalem. But I've just taken command of a new battalion. This morning we went into battle for the first time. I can't abandon my soldiers right now. I intend to lead them. I promised."

"On that point, how did it go at Qula and Tira?"

"Casualties were light. We'll move south tonight or tomorrow on Deir Tarif."

Like Dayan, Ben-Gurion regarded Vince before replying. Both men seemed to use him as a touchstone, as if Vince's presence made the two aware of their own history-making.

"So no?"

"For now, Prime Minister."

"I'm not happy, but that doesn't seem a concern of yours. Okay, we'll take this up later. Go back to your unit. Take Mister Haas with you."

Dayan stood. "Prime Minister."

"Mister Haas, stay behind a moment."

As he exited, Dayan patted Vince's shoulder, sympathy that Vince would be left alone with Ben-Gurion.

With the door closed, Vince said, "Thank you for what you did in Fureidis."

"Four weeks was all I could give them."

"I understand."

"You should know, Mister Haas, the position of this government is to leave these determinations in the hands of local IDF forces. If a commander decides an Arab community can stay in place, if he trusts they won't harbor his enemies or turn on him, that's his authority. The reverse is equally true if he decides they must go. I can't override the orders of the army for long. In the end, it will not be up to me."

"I'll pass that along."

"There is a great refugee problem among the Palestinians. They run from the fighting. Alright, this is not the first war to create refugees. They run from fear of us, and this I understand. There have been excesses I will not discuss with you, but they are more than you know. History will judge. And they run from their homes when the invaders tell them to get out of the way."

"How many have gone so far?"

"Half a million. One-third of the Palestinian people have left their homes."

"That's a lot."

"We didn't start the war, so I argue we did not cause the problem. Even so, I fear it will haunt us a long time. I don't know how to stop it. I don't even know if I should stop it. I will say only there must be a majority-Jewish Israel. And there must always be a Jewish Jerusalem."

"I know that's your position."

"Is there another one?"

"Bernadotte thinks there is."

"Bernadotte was a bootlick to the Nazis. He's an errand boy. And the UN is toothless."

"Can I quote you?"

"If you prefer prison food. Are you losing your ardor for Israel, Mister Haas? I don't hear you cheering for us anymore."

"That's the good news, Prime Minister. You don't need me to cheer anymore."

"Israel will love you without your love in return. You have done us great service. What do you make of Dayan?"

"You nailed him."

"Okay. Watch yourself. Don't stay so close to him. I think the man is too brave by half. Now get out."

Ben-Gurion was not displeased when he rose to shake hands, something he had not done when he dismissed Dayan.

CHAPTER 67

GABBI

Deir Tarif
Arab-controlled Palestine

Under the late sun, the rumps of five IDF tanks disappeared north. Tarek waved them off, calling after them, "Go ahead. Go."

He leaned on the hood of his jeep, complaining more. The rest of the company, twenty jeeps, were arrayed left and right. A kilometer east, on high ground behind a row of easy hills, waited the Arab stronghold of Deir Tarif.

Tarek littered the ground with butts as he smoked through a pack and carped out loud. He asked anyone passing why a jeep company had been picked to replace a tank battalion at Deir Tarif? How many Arabs were defending the damn village? What if the Legion decided to attack over those hills? Where was the rest of the Eighty-Ninth?

Gabbi relaxed in the jeep. None of the South Africans told Tarek to quiet down. They took his rants for the normal gripes of an unhappy commando. Besides, Tarek was the crazy driver who'd led the charge into Tira then shaken Dayan's hand. The South Africans were a friendly bunch; they gave Tarek good-natured chaffing whenever they walked by. They said, "You tell 'em, mate."

Nothing dire happened. The Arabs did not descend out of Deir Tarif onto the jeeps. Tarek ran out of cigarettes. The sun crept west and down, a mild breeze carried over the jeeps the tartness of an orange grove. Gabbi was the first to grab a shovel. No word had come that the company would be relieved by nightfall. The jeeps were going to hold their place overnight.

Tarek's mood veered as if he'd snapped out of something. He told Gabbi he was sorry. She saw nothing to gain by throwing his odd distemper in his face, so asked, "For what?"

He relieved her of the shovel. Tarek dug a hole big enough for them both.

CHAPTER 68

VINCE

Southeast of Petah Tikvah
Israel

Dayan pulled off the dirt road, just a path used by the locals to connect the fields. He said, "It's getting dark."

He stepped out of the jeep to inspect the earth under his headlight beams. Bristles of pearly millet bracketed the lane.

"I'm going to assume the Arabs have mined this road. I would if I were them."

Vince asked, "How much further?"

"A few miles. We'll go at first light when we can see better."

"Where do we sleep?"

"I haven't slept on something that wasn't moving in four days."

Dayan shut down the jeep, then waded into the millet field.

July 11

Vince sat up off the pillow he'd made of grain stalks. Dayan, already on his feet, stretched his back. In leaden morning light, they asked how the other had slept.

In the mild air the tips of the crops did not waver. The war felt far off, the countryside seemed a mural of dawn. Dayan and Vince pushed through the grain and returned to the road.

Before starting the jeep, Dayan walked a hundred yards ahead on the road. When he returned, he said, "There are tracks up there."

They climbed in the jeep. Dayan crept forward, keeping his tires in the visible ruts of the other vehicles.

After a kilometer in low gear, the track arrived at a paved surface. Dayan turned right onto the pavement, upshifted, and barreled south towards the frontlines.

The traces of combat were everywhere in the land; the tracks of armored cars ribbed the soil, brass casings spangled the ground. The fighting had left two villages, Wilhelma and Rentiya, with no standing structures, just the skeletons of foundations and chimneys. After wrecking both villages, the war moved on. The Arabs retrieved their dead, the Jews took away prisoners, then both headed off to other battles.

After five minutes on the paved road, with the sun clearing the mountains, Dayan drove into the ruins of Tira where he found his Eighty-Ninth. He inquired for the whereabouts of Pelz. A commando directed Dayan to an olive grove.

Dayan found his deputy lying under a blanket beneath a sloping fruit tree. He bent to give Pelz a prod, then another.

"Wake up, Pelz. Wake up."

The deputy's eyes fluttered, so tired he almost swooned back to sleep. He struggled up to his elbows.

Dayan asked, "What happened while I was gone?"

Pelz muttered a groggy answer. Yesterday afternoon, the Eighty-Second Tank Battalion had failed to take Deir Tarif. They pulled back. The Eighty-Ninth replaced them.

"Replaced them with who? Who's in Deir Tarif?"

"The jeep company."

"Just them?"

"Yes. Now, if you don't mind, Moshe, I have one hour left of sleep."

Dayan left Pelz to snooze. He stomped out of the olive grove, making Vince keep up.

He gathered his four company commanders.

"I'm going to say this one more time. We are commandos. We move and we spit fire. Understood?" Dayan ordered them all to head immediately for Deir Tarif.

He added, "Pelz needs his rest. No one bothers him."

Dayan was livid when he climbed into the jeep beside Vince. He shot to the lead of the convoy leaving the village. He clapped the steering wheel.

Vince asked, "Did you really just leave Pelz?"

"When he wakes up, he'll be the only man in Tira."

CHAPTER 69

VINCE

Deir Tarif
Arab-controlled Palestine

The drive to Deir Tarif lasted ten dust-eating minutes. The Eighty-Ninth had fifty-five commando vehicles left to it, and all plowed overland, staying off the roads to avoid mines.

Vince took no notes and hadn't for days. His memory for the war had become acute, recorded in his senses. He needed no paper and pencil to recall the grinding machines, the smells of grimy soldiers, ruined villages, Arab and Israeli dead, the sight of refugees clogging the roads, the pop and pounding of guns, the chalky taste of dust. His recall was like anything else the war scorched: it became deep and maybe permanent.

Vince rode beside Dayan at the head of the convoy. They arrived at the western skirt of Deir Tarif. Immediately Dayan raced his jeep along the foothills, arranging his battalion into assault positions.

Within thirty minutes, the commandos controlled the western and northern slopes while the Arab Legion held the eastern approaches. Behind the Legion's forward defenses ran a small valley, then another hill; atop it stood Deir Tarif.

Dayan sent one of his halftrack companies to probe the Arab force in the valley between hills. Then he drove to locate his machine-gun jeeps. He found them parked tightly in a hedgehog formation, guns like spines facing outward; they'd spent the night in Deir Tarif exposed and outmatched. Dayan told Vince to stay with the car, then he walked off. He returned with Tarek.

Dayan said, "I like the way this young man drives."

Tarek said, "Vince."

"You two know each other?"

Vince said, "We've met."

Dayan said, "He's going to drive me to the top of the hill. I think you should get out."

"Why?"

"There are snipers."

"Why are you going?"

"I can't see Deir Tarif from down here."

Vince left the front passenger seat.

"Ben-Gurion's office was probably worse." He climbed into the back.

Without objection, Dayan took the vacated passenger seat, Tarek took the wheel.

✳ ✳ ✳

The dark boy drove crazily up the hill. He zigzagged along a twisting goat trail, barely missing boulders except for the two he clipped. Dayan got so bounced around he had to tug his eyepatch back in place; Vince hung on tight. In dervish swoops Tarek sped to the top where he parked behind a pair of great white rocks.

Dayan gave the boy a wondrous look before bounding out of the jeep. Vince had skinned his shins buffeting about in the back.

Vince told Tarek, "I used to know a guy who could drive like that."

Nimbly, Dayan serpentined over the rock-strewn incline, twenty yards up to the peak. He kept his head down; he'd already lost one eye to a sniper. Vince trailed, not so adept, but drew no fire sidling up beside Dayan behind an outcropping.

They peered together over the big rock. Eighty yards below, two of Dayan's halftracks littered the downslope, both disabled by mortar fire. The vehicles showed dents where Arab snipers had sent the crews scrambling.

Between them on the gravelly ground lay a Marmon-Herrington armored car, tilted on its side in a ditch, two tires down in the rut, two free in the air. The Arab vehicle mounted a turreted two-pounder cannon. It had been abandoned but looked to be in serviceable shape.

Dayan's single eye gathered in the rough landscape.

Deir Tarif rose on its hilltop a quarter mile east. The Legion had fortified the town with artillery and mortars, sandbag redoubts, dugouts and trenches. Likely, the Legion had more armored cars, anti-tank guns, even tanks harbored there. The Arabs intended Deir Tarif to be their last citadel on the road to Lydda.

To take the village, Dayan's commandos would have to clamber up and over this rocky hill, battle through the valley below, then climb another hill under an uncounted number of guns big and small.

There'd be no surprise moves for the Eighty-Ninth at Deir Tarif, no commando lightning strikes, not on this terrain. Dayan studied the hills where his soldiers would have to fight. It would be a slogging kind of brawl. Dayan said what Vince was thinking.

"No."

Dayan slid down and put his back against the boulder. Vince joined him.

Dayan rubbed his chin. Vince was on the wrong side; Dayan's black eyepatch made him difficult to read.

Dayan pushed away from the rock. Vince followed downhill to the waiting jeep. Dayan strolled to Tarek on the driver's side.

"Do you think you can drive an armored car?"

"I suppose."

Vince tugged Dayan's arm. "Major, a word, please."

He walked away. Dayan followed uneagerly. In a lowered voice, Vince asked, "What are you thinking about doing?"

"I want that armored car."

"You're going to try to recover it?"

"I am. And I'm going to put your young friend behind the wheel."

"Major, I need you to ask someone else."

"I assume you will tell me why."

"That boy. He's going to be a father."

"Good for him."

"The young woman in the jeep, his front seat gunner. It's her."

"Good for her."

"She's Rivkah's sister."

"Yes. The mother of your child."

"Yeah."

"I see. Is there anything else?"

"She hasn't told him she's pregnant."

"You want to protect this boy and girl. And child."

"That's right."

"Mister Haas, this is a quirk of Israel. There are so few Jews here, or left in the world for that matter, that we value each of us more than perhaps any people on earth. Still, we cannot weigh every tragedy one at a time. We leave that for God."

"I know."

"You don't seem to." As Dayan walked back to the jeep, he spoke over his shoulder. "We're going to Lydda."

CHAPTER 70

VINCE

Dayan returned with a boy, a lean, baby-faced mechanic named Rabinowitz.

"He's from a farm." Dayan presented Rabinowitz to show Vince how handsome the lad was, how there must be a nice family on a kibbutz somewhere waiting for him to come home alive, yet here he was. Vince shook the polite boy's hand.

Dayan gestured the mechanic and Tarek to a waiting halftrack.

"Coming, Mister Haas?"

"You're going yourself?"

"Pelz has awakened and made his way back to us. I can be spared for a bit."

Dayan walked closer to emphasize what he had to say.

"I have something for these boys to do. They'll do it best if they follow me. You'll see. Come along."

✳ ✳ ✳

Dayan's halftrack took the goat path uphill. Sitting in the cab, Vince rollicked between the steel walls, opposite Rabinowitz and Tarek. A coil of steel cable looped over the mechanic's shoulder. Dayan rode in the front peering out a steel slit that cut down his view.

Broaching the hillcrest, the halftrack picked up speed down the slope. Rabinowitz bounced into Tarek's lap; Tarek shoved him away.

Dayan turned to shout above the squalling tracks. "The Arabs have seen us by now. You've got to be quick."

Tarek and the mechanic nodded.

"Get ready."

To make Dayan's point, a sniper's bullet pranged off the halftrack's flank. Dayan eyed the machine gun over his head, thinking of answering. Then the halftrack braked, the squeal of the tracks faded, and the vehicle stopped.

"Now!" Dayan made an underhand motion as if casting the boys out the rear door of the compartment.

The steel towline on his shoulder, Rabinowitz pushed open the metal door to scramble out. He tossed the cable to the ground; Tarek sprang out next. Dust and exhaust roiled in the open door.

The young mechanic hooked one end of the cable to the halftrack's hitch. Tarek lit out across twenty yards of bare ground for the ditch and the upended armored car. Rabinowitz finished securing the cable to Dayan's halftrack then took off after Tarek. The cable unspooled behind him.

A second sniper rifle barked from the far side of the valley. Tarek leaped beneath the armored car. He yanked open the passenger door, then collapsed backward. The corpse of an Arab plummeted at his feet.

Dayan readied to shout at Tarek to get moving, but Tarek recovered and scaled into the driver's compartment. Rabinowitz dove into the ditch, disappearing under the armored car's grille. Another bullet plinked off the halftrack's armor.

Dayan said to Vince, "Good lads."

In the listing driver's seat, Tarek tried to start the Marmon-Herrington. The ignition turned over but wouldn't catch. Beneath the armored car, Rabinowitz reeled in all the slack of the cable, made the line taut, then emerged. He froze, staring down at the dead Arab in the ditch. Rabinowitz shouted up at Tarek through the dangling open door.

Dayan asked Vince, "What is he doing?"

"He doesn't want to get in."

Dayan shouted at the mechanic, "Get in the armored car!"

Rabinowitz ignored Dayan. He leaped out of the ditch onto open ground. The boy took three running strides before the snipers found him.

The first round spun him, the second staggered him. Rabinowitz took a teetering step; he pressed a hand to his waist, then showed his crimson palm to himself. He buckled to a knee and keeled over. The boy lay curled in the open, cheek on the stones, blood oozing through his fingers.

Tarek clambered out through the passenger door to land in the ditch.

Dayan yelled, "Go back!"

Tarek gestured at the downed boy.

Dayan bellowed again, "Get back in!"

Tarek vanished from the ditch, climbing back into the armored car. The driver of the halftrack asked Dayan, "What do you want me to do?"

Dayan crouched. Vince put a hand in his chest.

"I'll go."

Dayan urged forward. "He's not yours."

Vince pushed enough to settle Dayan back in the front seat. He handed Dayan his old straw hat.

"The world's got plenty of Americans."

With long strides, Vince left the halftrack and dashed for the mechanic. The snipers would bait for a second target with the body of the first. Vince didn't slow to scoop the bleeding boy off the ground; that would get them both killed. He grabbed Rabinowitz by the collar to haul the boy howling behind him.

A bullet zipped past Vince's ear, another sailed high. He dragged the mechanic into the ditch and heaved him onto the dead Arab for a cushion, then jumped down.

Vince called up to Tarek, "Give me a hand!"

Together they hoisted Rabinowitz into the armored car. At Vince's feet lay the dead legionnaire, probably the driver of the armored car. He'd taken a bullet in the throat, an unlucky man. The Arab wore his blood on his chest like a bib.

Tarek clutched the screaming mechanic to hold him on the slanted seat while Vince climbed up. The tilt of the armored car was so great they might have tumbled out into the ditch if Vince hadn't fought shut the passenger door. The dead driver had sprayed his blood all around the cab before he died, on the bench seat, windshield, and gauges. The mechanic had seen all this, and it was why he hadn't gotten in.

Tarek honked at Dayan's halftrack to signal he was ready. He shifted the armored car into neutral then cranked the steering wheel left to guide the front tires out of the rut.

The towing cable tightened and rose off the dirt. Vince, the mechanic, and Tarek jounced as the halftrack hauled the armored car through the ditch. Rabinowitz screeched at every jolt until suddenly the tires caught purchase. The armored car jerked hard, then popped out, level onto all four tires. Tarek steered to keep in line behind the halftrack.

Rabinowitz whimpered, frightened at how much of his own blood he was catching. Vince pushed him forward to look for a hole in his back. The boy was lucky; the sniper bullet had drilled clean through. He wouldn't die from that, and Vince told him so.

※ ※ ※

The halftrack towed the armored car to the bottom of the hill into the midst of a hundred waiting, cheering Jews.

When Vince climbed out, Gabbi ran to him; she halted at the sight of blood on his white shirt, fearing it was Tarek's. Vince said, "He's fine," and gestured with his chin for her to go around to the driver's side. She skipped over the towline into Tarek's arms without hesitation that the other commandos would see them. Playfully she slapped Tarek's bearded face to say he'd worried her.

Vince's hands shivered from the withdrawal of so much adrenaline. He'd taken a battering inside the swaying armored car, holding the mechanic in his arms.

Medics laid Rabinowitz on a stretcher. They strapped him to a jeep and rushed off to Tel Aviv.

Dayan summoned signalmen to check and repair the armored car's radio. He sent for more mechanics to check the engine and suspension. A second jeep was dispatched to bring a gunnery sergeant from Qula to teach the commandos how to fire the Marmon-Herrington's two-pounder cannon.

Dayan handed Vince the old straw hat.

"You're a reporter."

"Some days."

"You risked yourself to protect my life. To save that boy."

Vince put on the flimsy hat. It barely kept out the sun.

"I don't know why I did that."

"You are trying, Mister Haas. Trying very hard."

Dayan rapped the back of Vince's arm before walking off.

CHAPTER 71

GABBI

Beside their jeep, Tarek sat with legs folded, hands joined behind his neck like a man surrendering.

Gabbi sat with her knees touching Tarek's. He had the young mechanic's blood on his trousers. She lay her palms on his thighs, on the blood, and touched her forehead to his.

He said, "I don't want to do it."

Abner squatted on his heels to bring his face even with theirs.

Gabbi said, "Tarek."

She shook him a little.

"Tarek."

"What."

"Sometimes…"

He asked, "Sometimes what?"

"Sometimes I see my mother. She's in my dreams. She's starving and cold. She goes to sleep in my arms. I have that dream one or two times a week. Then in the morning, every morning, I get out of bed without her. But, Tarek."

"What?"

"I get up."

She rubbed his leg.

Abner said, "Look. If it helps, I'll go."

Tarek shook his head. "You're a shit driver."

"No, stupid. I mean I'll go with you. On the gun."

Gabbi said, "Me, too. I'll handle the radio."

Abner said, "We'll all three go. We'll tell Dayan he gets all of us or none."

Tarek said, "I don't know."

Abner said, "We don't know either, mate. That's the fucking point."

The big South African reached down to Gabbi; he hoisted her to her feet. Both offered their hands down to Tarek.

CHAPTER 72

VINCE

Dayan clapped big Abner on the shoulder.

"Well said," Dayan told him. To Tarek and Gabbi, Dayan said, "Excellent."

Dayan called forth another young soldier, a mortarman from the second company, a mustachioed, barrel-chested, short Irishman named Michael. The four commandos were the new crew of the Arab armored car. Dayan gave them the right to name it.

Quickly, Gabbi suggested The Terrible Tiger. Dayan liked it right off. With a piece of chalk, Irish Michael climbed up to the turret. He scribbled on the two-meter-long cannon barrel, "straight to the point."

Next, a cannoneer from the Sternist company stepped up. For the next hour, he would teach Abner and Michael how to aim and fire the two-pounder gun.

Gabbi jogged over to Vince. She said, "I've only got a few minutes."

"Then you're off with The Terrible Tiger."

"I know, it's awful. I blurted that out too fast."

"You'll make it work."

She picked at Vince's clean shirt, a khaki military tunic without IDF insignia.

"The Legion might think you're an Israeli."

"Only from a distance."

"What do you think of Tarek?"

"He seems moody."

"He's a good man. He's doing the best he can."

Vince held Gabbi by the arms as if to straighten a painting.

"So, look."

"Yes."

"I'm not sure I'll see you after. Not for a while."

"Why not?"

"Malik's in Lydda. Missus Pappel asked me to go find him."

"Can you?"

"I said I'd try."

"You're Vince Haas."

"Dayan said the Eighty-Ninth is going into Lydda. That's why he wanted the armored car."

"I figured."

Vince said, "Hey."

"What?"

"After this, you should go away with Tarek. Be safe."

On tiptoes, Gabbi bussed Vince's cheek. "Be careful around Dayan."

"You, too."

❋ ❋ ❋

Dayan gathered his company commanders under a locust tree. Vince joined them. He'd grown thirsty; he picked a twig off the locust, stripped it of leaves, and sucked on the wood to put some spit in his mouth.

Dayan had assigned a few platoons of the Sternist company to stay behind, to harry the Arabs in Deir Tarif and fix them in place. Sporadic pops of fighting dribbled over the hill. Dayan cocked an ear and seemed satisfied that the Sternists were doing their job.

"The rest of us, let's head for Lydda."

The four commanders chuckled. One said, "Wait. You're serious."

"I am."

"Moshe. Lydda is no out-of-the-way village. It's a city. It's got a big population. Stone buildings, a hundred streets. The Legion's dug in there. How? We don't have the force for that."

"We're not supposed to have the force for that. We're commandos."

One officer said, fatalistically, "You have a plan."

Dayan did not hesitate. "We don't know much about the defenses in Lydda. But's it's not likely they're expecting an attack out of the east, from the direction of the Legion's lines. We'll break through from there, in a fast, concentrated strike like we did at Tira and Qula. This time we have a two-pounder cannon out front. We'll be kings."

"Moshe."

"Yes?"

"A concern."

"Yes?"

"Do we have orders for Lydda?"

"An excellent question."

"Do we?"

"We do not."

"Have you cleared this with command?"

"I have not."

Before his men could chew on this point, Dayan raised the index fingers on both hands, like a conductor to his band.

"An opportunity has opened up. We've got to move before the Legion can shift their defenses east to block us. That means today. Not tomorrow, when orders can be approved. We can do this, you know we can. The men are blooded now. No more hesitation."

A messenger arrived to call Dayan away to the signals center. He hurried off. Minutes later, he returned with his face alight.

"Gentlemen, fortune does favor the bold."

"What happened?"

Imitating a magician, Dayan clapped then spread his hands to show that something had appeared between them.

"The commander of the Yiftach Brigade just radioed. One of his battalions has run into heavy fire southeast of Lydda. They're bogged down in the orange groves there. He asked if we could provide support. I said we'd be pleased to come."

With a curling finger, Dayan cajoled his commanders to their feet.

"We roll in fifteen minutes. Regroup in Ben Shemen."

The four officers hustled off. The battalion would reassemble at a small moshav two miles east of Lydda.

Dayan hung back with Vince.

He said to Vince, almost giddy, "I'll tell them the best part later."

Vince said, "But you're going to tell me."

"If you can keep it between us for a bit."

"No problem."

"The Yiftach commander didn't know he was radioing the commandos."

"Who'd he think he was calling?"

"The Eighty-Second Tank Battalion. They left Deir Tarif yesterday. Our jeeps replaced them."

"You're saying Yiftach called you by mistake."

"He asked for tanks. That's the Eighty-Second."

"Then he'll be expecting tanks."

"He will get commandos."

"Is that the best part?"

"It is not."

Vince held out a hand as though expecting Dayan to lay a key in it.

Dayan's grin creviced his whole face, all but the patch.

He said, "Now I have orders for Lydda."

✳ ✳ ✳

Dayan twirled a finger above his head. His convoy awoke and shook the ground. The Terrible Tiger snarled like no other vehicle in line.

Dayan had a smaller strike force available to assault Lydda than he'd set out with yesterday; the battles at Tira, Qula, and Deir Tarif had pared his battalion down to eight halftracks, nine scout cars, and twenty jeeps. Instead of three hundred and fifty commandos, just one hundred and fifty would roll into Lydda.

Vince strode beside Dayan to The Terrible Tiger at the head of the column. From inside, Gabbi waved to Vince. Dayan shouted up to Abner standing tall in the turret.

Dayan pointed west. "See that tree there? On that hill? How far is that?"

Abner ducked into the turret to peer through his rangefinder. He resurfaced. "Five hundred twenty meters."

"Hit it."

Abner submerged again.

The cannon boomed flame and a perfect smoke ring. The armored car barely recoiled, so heavy was the machine. Half a kilometer away, the tree lost a fat branch.

Dayan pounded a fist on the armored car's fender.

"Go."

Tarek rolled out without a nod to Dayan or Vince, though Gabbi waved again. Tarek looked only at his hands on the wheel as if they might lead him astray.

With the convoy rumbling past, Dayan said to Vince, "Let's go find your Arab friend in Lydda."

A halftrack stopped for Dayan to climb in. He left Vince to hitchhike the column. Near the rear, a jeep with an open passenger seat stopped for him.

RAMLE–LYDDA

CHAPTER 73

GABBI

Ben Shemen
Israel

In the steel cabin of the armored car, South African Abner and Irish Michael debated whiskey and green hills, the wildness of their two nations' countrysides, and the beauty of their peoples.

Michael gestured at Gabbi.

"Austria, eh?"

"Yes."

Michael elbowed Abner. "We should discuss Austria, too, right?"

Abner donned a red-checkered keffiyeh. The point was for the locals and defenders of Lydda to see him standing in the turret and believe the armored car was one of theirs.

Gabbi touched Tarek's arm; she sensed the vibrations from the steering wheel. Driving at the speed Dayan demanded, the armored car was a wrestling match for Tarek.

She said, "Listen."

Chewing his beard, Tarek didn't glance from the bulletproof windshield.

She said, "Let's get through today."

"Then what?"

Gabbi laid fingertips on his shivering knuckles.

"Tomorrow."

✳ ✳ ✳

Ben Shemen

Seventy moshavot came out to greet the Eighty-Ninth. The settlers opened their barbed-wire gates, then cheered every vehicle rumbling past. They had no flowers to throw or food to offer, no children to hoist on their shoulders, nothing to spare here.

The convoy shut down in the center of the little village. Ben Shemen stood astride the two-mile road into Lydda's eastern outskirts. Many commandos in other vehicles wore keffiyehs the way Abner did. The moshavot inched forward to touch the dusty fenders of the convoy. The commando column, even at a third its normal length, extended far past the settlement's limits.

An order came over the radio that everyone must stay in their vehicles. Gabbi relayed this to Abner, Michael, and Tarek.

A young woman with broken capillaries in her cheeks and a kerchief over her short, mousy hair brought a bucket of water and a ladle. Gabbi thanked her.

The woman asked, "Are there others?" She peeked down the column.

"You mean women?"

"Yes."

"No."

"Just you?"

"Just me."

The woman might have been a girl who'd aged too fast on the white plain. She seemed to imagine much about one woman in a steel column of men.

Michael leaned down to ask, "May I have a sip?" When he gave back the ladle, he said, "Thank ye, beautiful." Gabbi shooed the woman away.

CHAPTER 74

VINCE

Ben Shemen

Vince's khaki IDF tunic made the moshavot of Ben Shemen think he was a Jewish soldier, even in a straw hat. They said, "Bless you," as he jogged towards Dayan's halftrack.

The Eighty-Ninth's commanders gathered beside Dayan's halftrack in the sun. Vince looked over their shoulders. Dayan diced the air as he issued his final orders.

"We will assault in column formation. The armored car will lead the way. The first halftrack company will follow, then the second. Scout cars and jeeps come last. I'll ride in the first halftrack behind the Tiger."

The commanders said, "Okay, Moshe."

"If the Tiger or any of the halftracks come up against an obstacle, or heavy fire, or the devil knows what, spread out and find a way around. Do not stop. If one of your vehicles is hit, don't stop to repair it. Pass it and continue advancing. No one but me is allowed to hold up the column."

One commander asked, "You're saying we can help no one in the convoy?"

Another asked, "No matter the circumstance?"

"Go," Dayan said. "At all costs, go."

"Okay, Moshe."

"Once we get past the Legion's outposts and we're inside the city, we'll split up. At the first main intersection, the Tiger and the first halftrack company will turn north, the second will continue south. The jeeps and scout cars will split up, too."

Dayan's eye flicked to Vince.

"Mister Haas."

"Yeah."

"This would be the time to back out."

Vince shook his head. Dayan continued with his commanders.

"If the lead vehicles in your company run into resistance, flow around them. Hit the flanks, attack from every side. Move fast and keep moving. Speed is the best use of our firepower."

Dayan let his instructions sink in. He had told them what they must do. Then he told them why.

"We are going to sow panic. The moment you enter Lydda, start firing. Shoot left and right, anything that moves. Bear down on the Arab. Run him over. Crush him in spirit and body."

Dayan raised a fist. He shook it slowly between him and his commanders.

"I intend to make Lydda surrender. They will see enough of us today to want no more. You understand this?"

"*Ken.*" Yes.

Dayan's four commanders hurried back to their companies. He and Vince exchanged no wishes for luck or safety. Dayan climbed into his halftrack. Vince had nothing final to say to Gabbi in the Tiger, so he returned to the jeeps at the rear.

Along the column, radiator shields were closed. The opening radio network twittered in each vehicle. More commandos swapped their helmets for keffiyehs, to see if they might fool Lydda before they shot it up. Vince checked his watch: 6:20 p.m.

At Dayan's signal, the convoy growled. The moshavot backed away. All the drivers revved their engines to thank Ben Shemen.

Vince's driver tied on a red Arab headscarf; he handed his helmet to Vince. Vince tucked the straw hat under a sandbag.

Tarek led the column out of the village. He veered into the fields because the farmers had mined the road.

CHAPTER 75

GABBI

The Tiger's great weight made the ride smoother for Gabbi than the lighter jeeps. Inside the armored hull, behind a bulletproof windshield, she swallowed no dust. She had no radio to balance in her lap.

Tarek gripped the steering wheel in a determined way. She thought to tell him of the child right now, when there could be no turning back, when Tarek could make no demand that she seek safety. Maybe it was the juddering cabin, the first Arab bullets bouncing off the Tiger's steel, or the radio's hiss in her ear, but Gabbi could not fashion the words. She simply wanted to carry the child into battle.

Abner tapped Tarek on the back of the neck to tell him he'd spotted targets ahead. Tarek laid on the brakes. Gabbi reached for him, but the radio squawked and she reeled in her hand.

"Tiger, Carmel One."

"Carmel One, Tiger."

"Fire at will."

Gabbi shouted the order as if it were hers.

Two hundred meters west, a pair of sandbag redoubts blocked the road; these were the Legion's first forward defenses. Abner brought the two-pounder cannon to bear using the turret's electric motor and a hand-cranked flywheel. From a rack, Irish Michael plucked a shell the girth of Gabbi's wrist, the length of her forearm. He shoved it into the breech, which snapped shut on its own.

Bullets from the Arab machine guns strummed the dirt in front of the Tiger.

Abner said, "Away." Gabbi and Tarek braced, Abner toed the trigger.

The armored car barely jerked under the blast. The recoiling breech spat out a baking casing that clattered on the padded floor. Cordite smoke and swept-up grit clouded Gabbi's view through the windshield, but it cleared in an instant. A doe-colored puff marked where one Arab sandbag bunker had been. Abner and Michael needed two more shells to dispose of the second.

Another order issued over the radio. "Tiger, advance."

Tarek gained speed. Michael and Abner shook hands over their first kills as cannoneers.

Michael leaned down to Gabbi. "Hey, Austria."

She pulled off the headset. "What?"

"Were you in the camps?"

"Why?"

"Me, I wasn't there. This big bastard wasn't, either. I doubt your black fella there was."

"What does it matter?"

"Don't worry about what gets me through my day. Were you?"

"I was."

Michael said, "Lass," and rapped a fist on her shoulder.

The Terrible Tiger surged on. The commando column rolled behind them, but Gabbi had no rearview mirror to see them. She and the three commando boys seemed to be charging into Lydda alone.

A pulse of bullets pelted the armored car's radiator plate and fenders. An order came over the radio from Dayan: to halt.

Abner and Michael loaded the two-pounder.

Three hundred meters ahead, Arab machine guns sparked from behind more sandbagged redoubts. Another order came to open fire.

Abner said, "Away." The armored car rocked. In seconds, he and Michael fired again.

Tarek jumped as if something had nipped him. One-eyed Dayan appeared beside his window.

"Stop shooting."

Tarek silenced Abner and Michael. Gabbi pulled off her headset.

Dayan said, "There's a tank ditch ahead. The road is impassable."

Tarek asked, "How big is it?"

"A kilometer wide."

"What do you want to do?"

"Go around."

"How?"

Dayan pointed at a dirt path through a field of withered wheat. "There."

"What if it's mined?"

"You'll be blown sky high." Dayan patted Tarek's windowsill and left in a calm walk.

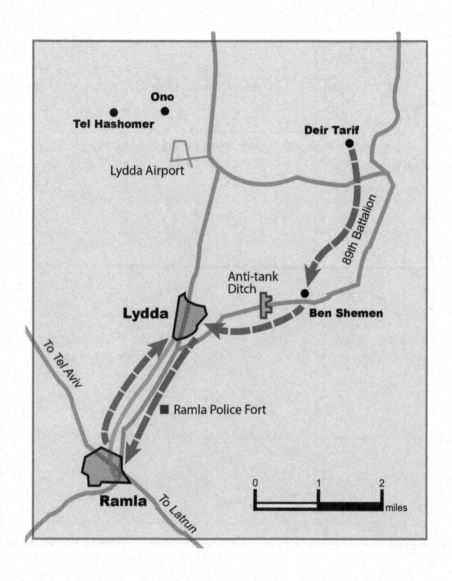

CHAPTER 76

VINCE

Lydda

The dirt lane was skinny, furrowed, and strewn with wire barriers that had to be snipped and dragged away. Dodging the Arabs' tank trap made for hot, slow going. Even with thirty vehicles ahead of him, Vince's driver worried about mines.

Four hundred yards off, a dozen legionnaires behind sandbags tracked the convoy with four machine guns. The Arabs held their fire at Gabbi's armored car, the halftracks and scout cars; they waited for the vulnerable jeeps rattling at the rear of the column, slow going with no armor, to come in range.

Once the Arabs opened up, all the jeeps traded fire with them. Between the two banks of machine guns, a field of cactus splattered in the crossfire. The late sun hovered over Lydda a mile west. Vince ducked beneath his helmet.

The ditch and the Arab gunners faded behind; the convoy picked up pace. Lydda grew closer, clearer. Vince's driver shouted over his shoulder, "Keep your head down."

"I knew that."

The driver added, "This is insane."

"You think so?"

The South African gunner standing over Vince patted him on the helmet. "What are you doing here, mate?" He didn't seem to expect an answer.

The convoy entered Lydda without another shot. Dayan may have been right; the city was lightly defended on its eastern perimeter. Perhaps the commandos wearing red keffiyehs had pulled off their trick.

Lydda was a sunbaked place, tightly packed under terracotta roofs. The buildings were one and two stories with verandas and courtyards for the cooler evenings. Goosenecked palms cast a swishing shade. Tarek led the roaring column down a quiet, pebbly road lined by limestone houses. The hundred Jewish gunners scanned high and low for targets.

Ahead, The Terrible Tiger swerved onto a broader paved avenue. The halftracks, scout cars, and jeeps closed ranks behind it.

Then Lydda erupted.

Vince's driver careened around a corner. Both MG 34s in the jeep opened up along with the rest of the convoy, firing everywhere. The rear machine gun brayed over Vince's head; its ammo belt stuttered up from the metal box. Vince held onto the gun mount and swept broiling shells off his lap.

The commandos drew fire and grenades from all sides. Their return fire flinted sparks and chipped stone on every building, around windows and doorways, raked any shadow and flicker.

A thick-walled building filled one city block ahead. From the roof, a handful of Arabs fired rifles at the column. Without slowing, The Terrible Tiger put three smoking divots in the building's face.

Shooting on the move, the whole convoy knifed deeper into Lydda. Citizens fled the streets and sidewalks. Some with guns found cover and shot back. The commandos didn't distinguish; any Arab running in Lydda was an enemy.

At the rear of the column, Vince's jeep rolled over thousands of spent casings in the road. The commandos hurtled block after block through zinging bullets and the flash and concussion of grenades. Arab men fell, some women were hit, combatants and civilians alike were targeted. Dayan's Jews fought with the wildness he'd demanded. Vince kept no tally, the column moved too fast, the streets became a blur of blasts and smoke.

The Terrible Tiger charged towards the first main crossroads, Dayan's turning point where the convoy would split up. Approaching the city center, the streets cleared, the battle paused. In the eerie lull, the column's radiators whistled and riddled tires flapped.

At the intersection, The Terrible Tiger turned sharp right like it was supposed to, headed northwest.

Behind Tarek, the first halftrack company did not turn. It and the rest of the armored vehicles rumbled south, then the whole battalion followed.

The Terrible Tiger disappeared, alone, into the heart of Lydda.

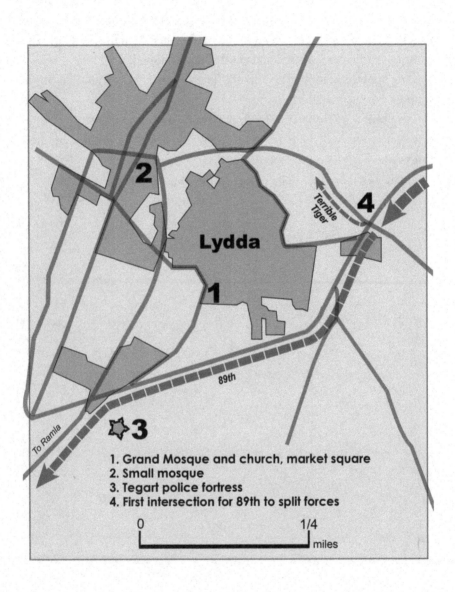

1. Grand Mosque and church, market square
2. Small mosque
3. Tegart police fortress
4. First intersection for 89th to split forces

CHAPTER 77

MALIK

Malik whirled in the middle of the road.

"Get out of the streets! Hide, all of you, hide!"

He chased a young woman and a boy into a shop, then made an old man lie behind a garden wall. Gunfire and the thumps of grenades bounded off the white walls and red roofs of Lydda.

"Run!"

A militiaman dashed up to offer Malik a rifle.

"Here. Help us."

"*Fah.*" Malik pushed away the gun. "I do not wish to die with you."

The people Malik shooed out of the street were not citizens of Lydda but refugees from the coast and the Negev. They had no walls to put between them and the Jews. Some residents opened their doors to accept those who pounded on them. Storekeepers dashed out to sweep strangers inside. The laws of Islam were suspended so men might touch unfamiliar women and hurry them into places they did not belong.

Malik stayed in the open until he was the last standing in the open. The first Jewish vehicle rounded the corner. Behind it came another, then many more.

The day was late, the light golden. Malik tugged up the hood of his robe and slipped into a slim alley. He waited there, motionless and dark to watch the Jews pass.

Vehicle after vehicle surged past, heavy and steel-armored, each one mounting multiple machine guns. Many of the Jews wore keffiyehs. They looked grim, angry to be shot at in a city they invaded.

The column passed by. Some motors steamed; the vehicles had taken wounds. At the back of the convoy came a line of jeeps, twenty roofless cars bristling with guns. One gunner caught a glimpse of Malik but traveled too fast to swing his barrel.

Was this how Israel's Jews would attack Lydda, by thrusting in this dagger of vehicles? It was an act of boldness, this little convoy. The Jews were simply showing they could do such an impudent thing as drive through the center of Lydda.

Malik turned away before the last jeeps rolled past his sunless alley.

CHAPTER 78

GABBI

Abner ducked in from the turret. He screamed at Gabbi as if she knew the answer. "Where are they going?"

"What are you talking about?"

"No one's following us. The whole damn convoy went straight when we turned right."

Michael stuck his own head out the turret.

"Oh, feck."

Abner bellowed at Tarek, "What did you do?"

Gabbi said, "Shut up." She hailed Dayan on the radio, "Carmel One, Carmel One." Tarek drove on, fiercely gripping the wheel.

"Tarek."

"What."

"You're sure that was the right place to turn."

"First big intersection."

"What went wrong?"

"I don't know."

"What do we do now?"

"I don't know."

From behind, Irish Michael said, "We have to turn around."

Abner said, "Turn around. Go after them."

Gabbi couldn't raise Dayan on the radio. When she stopped hailing, a transmission came through.

"Tiger, Tiger, Haifa Two." This was a halftrack in the first company.

"Haifa Two, Tiger. What happened?"

"Tiger, I'm not sure. Haifa One didn't turn behind you. We followed him, then everyone followed us."

"Haifa Two, where are you now?"

"Headed south. I don't know where."

"Can you wait for us to catch you?"

"I can't stop the convoy."

"Can you raise Carmel?"

"Negative."

"Okay. Keep in touch."

"I'll ty."

"Good luck. Tiger out."

Gabbi reported to the crew. Again, Abner and Michael insisted Tarek turn The Terrible Tiger around, or leave Lydda altogether.

No one fired at them from the storefronts and homes. Some Arab citizens waved, convinced this was a Legion armored car rumbling past. Others pulled the ones waving out of the street.

Tarek leaned so close to the wheel that his beard touched it. He said, "No."

Gabbi spoke gently. "Tarek."

She wanted him to bring his green eyes around so she might read them. Tarek's face stayed fixed between his hands on the shuddering wheel.

Once more, Gabbi said, "Tarek," but he waved her off.

He hissed. "Tell them to shoot."

Gabbi shouted to Abner and Irish Michael, "We're going to do what we've been told."

Michael asked, "And what is that, exactly?"

"Blow something up."

Abner and Michael both swore at her. Michael slammed home a shell, then cradled another. Gabbi stayed pivoted in her seat, glaring until Abner lowered his eye to find a target.

Tarek drove on, a juggernaut. In the next block, the road opened onto a town square. Shops ringed a paved expanse, a dry fountain at the center. A white minaret loomed above the plaza, alleys twisted away into gloom.

Tarek drove a circle around the fountain. Flimsy shanties had been thrown up in the square, shelters for refugees. Two dozen Arabs, some children, watched the armored car flash by.

Tarek yelled, "Hit something."

Abner asked, "Hit what?"

"I don't care. It's all Lydda."

Tarek drove a second circuit around the fountain. The Arabs scattered.

Gabbi said, "Not the mosque."

Abner said, "Tell him to stop."

The armored car braked. Tarek let the Tiger growl at idle.

Behind Gabbi, the gears of the turret whirred to bring the cannon into play. At the same time, Abner spun the elevation flywheel.

He said, "Away."

The Tiger jolted. One block behind the plaza, the metal cistern of a water tower exploded. Inside ten seconds, Abner sent two more shells at the structure, crumbling the cinderblocks that held the water tower high above the street. The whole thing collapsed and crashed. Moments later, knee-deep water flooded down an alley into the plaza. Wooden beams, trash, and doused cats washed around the fountain.

Tarek rolled past the soaked shanties. The Arabs in the square threw splintered wood at the windshield.

Tarek took a road out of the square, leading south into the denser part of Lydda. Abner stayed tight-lipped, Irish Michael did not cradle another shell. The two seemed to believe they'd done their job in Lydda and Tarek was hurrying after the lost battalion.

Gabbi worked the radio: "Carmel One, Carmel One."

A kilometer ahead, the broad face of a fortress dominated the next big intersection. Tarek rushed at it.

Three blocks from the fort, he stamped the brakes. The armored car squalled to a halt.

Abner demanded, "Why're you stopping?"

A bullet tapped on The Terrible Tiger's fender.

Tarek said to Gabbi, "We're out here by ourselves."

"Can you go around that fort?"

"I don't have a map. I just know we're heading south."

Irish Michael brought in his head from the turret.

Gabbi asked him, "What do you think?"

"You figure the column will come back this way?"

"It's a good guess."

Gabbi asked, "What do you want to do?"

Michael looked around the small confines of the armored car. "We've got a lot of fecking shells back here."

Abner reacted. "What?"

Gabbi said, "We do have a lot of shells."

Michael smacked Abner on his broad back.

"You don't look busy, mate. Come on. Let's introduce ourselves."

CHAPTER 79

VINCE

The battalion rolled on without The Terrible Tiger out front clearing the way. Dayan's plan had collapsed in the first minute.

Vince expected Dayan to issue the order to abort, but the commandos lanced deeper into Lydda. Their speed made them hard to hit; the Arabs who Vince spotted in windows and on rooftops shooting back were men and boys in flowing robes, full beards; they were the faithful but not soldiers, not marksmen. Their return fire was sporadic and poorly aimed, mostly at the vehicles themselves. One-eyed Dayan stayed mute in his halftrack, and his Eighty-Ninth did not slow nor pull their fingers off their triggers.

The eight halftracks out front bulled down Lydda's main avenue; their momentum swept the column along in their draft. The Israelis reacted to every flinch and flicker in their sights with a barrage. Unarmed civilians who gawped from doorways and porches were shot at. Vince kept his own head on a swivel, searching madly for anything in the crevices of Lydda that might be weapon in someone's hands. He shouted "there" and "there" at the machine gunner behind him, to keep the boy's rounds aimed at actual dangers, not the curious or stupid or children who might steal a peek at the raiders in their city.

The Israelis rushed a half mile through tight-packed buildings until the road opened up to undeveloped land at the southern city limits. Out of peril for the moment, the convoy slowed. In the abrupt quiet, the damage taken by the column showed itself. Punctured radiators sizzled, blown tires flapped, brakes lines leaked fluid. The right rear tire of Vince's jeep had popped.

A mile past Lydda, the halftracks approached a Tegart fort guarding the short road to Ramle, the sister city to Lydda. The fortress was a complex of cement walls, ramparts, and gun towers. It appeared impregnable.

The halftracks approached without a round fired. One Arab in a soldier's uniform stood just outside the iron gates. He might have heard the gunplay north in Lydda, might have wandered out for a look. When the Israelis rumbled up close enough for him to get shot at, he hightailed inside.

The lead halftrack company zoomed past the Tegart fort without trouble. But the Legion officer must have sounded the alarm.

The fortress and the rear portion of the convoy engaged in a sudden, sharp skirmish. The commandos laid on all the speed they could muster, but too many vehicles limped on busted tires and bullet-battered engines.

A grenade from a tower landed in the open back of one of the halftracks. The explosion staggered the armored vehicle, it swayed out of line and away from the convoy, trailing grey smoke.

Hemorrhaging haze and steam, spitting rubber, the back half of the convoy gathered itself to answer the fortress. Thousands of rounds beat against the high walls, chipping the concrete, yowling in ricochets.

Vince's jeep, already scuffling along on one tire rim, coughed and slowed more. Beside him, the driver urgently worked the gearshift and gas pedal. The punctured hood hinged up; flames licked around the engine, feeding on spraying gas from a severed fuel line.

The rear gunner bailed out, he rolled when he hit the street. Vince's driver put the burning jeep in neutral then pointed it, with Vince still in the passenger seat, at the fortress before leaping out, too. Grabbing his straw hat, Vince threw one leg over the side, then the other; he held onto the doorframe, running until he could let go.

A jeep at the tail of the column swooped in to whisk him away.

CHAPTER 80

GABBI

Tarek bobbed and sideslipped The Terrible Tiger, back and forward like a boxer. He stayed three blocks away from the police fort, careful never to turn broadside. Tarek paused only to let Abner fix his aim and shout "Away." The instant the cannon barked, Tarek slung the armored car to a new spot.

From inside the fortress the Arabs fired rifles and machine guns, nothing else. They had no anti-tank weapons to counter the Tiger banging on their walls. Irish Michael had ample stores of two-pounder ammo. Gabbi kept watch to be sure no one crept up on them.

Abner asked, "How long are we going to do this?"

Gabbi said, "Until the others come back for us."

"We don't know if they will."

"Then until we run out of shells."

The Irishman piped up, cherry-cheeked and enjoying himself. "That'll be a bit."

Abner smacked the hull. "Let's just go."

Gabbi said to Tarek, "Back away from the fort."

"Why?"

"We need a rest."

Tarek threw The Terrible Tiger into reverse, upsetting Abner and Michael before they could hold on. He retreated two more city blocks, taking the armored car beyond the reach of the Arabs in the fort.

Inside the buttoned-up armored car, Abner and Michael sat on their haunches. Tarek hung his head, Gabbi listened to static in her headset. Sniper potshots pattered at the armor like the first drops of a rain.

CHAPTER 81

VINCE

The column hobbled into Ramle.

No one in the city fired at them, and the commandos stirred up no trouble. They bullied their halting vehicles through the eastern corridor of the city, shambling on flat tires behind boiling radiators. The Arabs of Ramle let them go.

Outside the city, the convoy arrived at the road that would take them east to Jerusalem. The halftracks led the column into a railyard to regroup.

Vince thanked the boys who'd picked him up, then leaped out. He found Dayan marching among his troops, inspecting, cajoling. Tires were changed where spares were available, water poured into wheezing radiators. Soldiers' wounds were dressed.

Dayan noticed Vince coming and stopped to let him catch up. Dayan seemed willing to talk and explain himself.

Vince asked, "What happened?"

Dayan indicated the first halftrack, the one that had been behind The Terrible Tiger.

"Their brakes failed. They missed the turn. Everyone else stayed in line."

"Why didn't you hail Tarek?"

"My radio's dead. It's being fixed."

"Where's the Tiger?"

"The last anyone heard, still in Lydda."

"Doing what?"

"I have no idea."

"On their own?"

"On their own."

"How's the convoy?"

Dayan balled hands on his hips. He turned to encompass the battalion with his black patch and dark eye.

"Five dead. Nine wounded. We're missing a few who fell out of their jeeps at the Tegart fort between Ramle and Lydda. Your jeep burned up, I understand."

Dayan rested a hand on Vince's shoulder, to request that he not get killed on Dayan's watch.

Vince asked, "What're you going to do?"

"Turn around."

"Go back through Lydda?"

"Yes."

Vince swept a hand across the convoy that was patching itself up, cooling down, stanching its blood.

"With them?"

"Jerusalem's an hour east and the road goes past Latrun. We'll be lucky if half our vehicles can move on their own. The closest relief is in Ben Shemen. The wounded need attention. Besides, we have to go reclaim your friends in the Tiger."

The legionnaires inside the fort between cities sent a mortar round whistling their way. Vince took a step but Dayan grabbed his arm to hold him still, and tell him the shell would miss.

The round exploded close enough to the tracks to feather gravel dust over them. The commandos hastened their work with jacks, tires, gauze, and water jugs.

Dayan said, "You wanted me to take you into Lydda."

"I said that, yeah."

"I hope we've not met your friend."

"Me, too."

Dayan grinned. "Shall we drop you somewhere in the city?"

"I'll pass for now."

"Then you'll ride back with us to Ben Shemen."

"If we make it that far."

"Don't look so worried."

"Why not?"

"I have everything I need."

"What's that?"

"Just as you say, Mister Haas."

Dayan surveyed his smirched, torn up, outnumbered commandos.

"I have them."

※ ※ ※

Mortar rounds fell four and five per minute on the railyard.

Dayan told his commanders they had no hope of reaching Jerusalem. Their best chance was a return to Ben Shemen. That meant another trip through Lydda.

"The Terrible Tiger is there fighting alone. Let's go join them."

Dayan roused the convoy with his whirling finger. Three dozen vehicles answered with damaged coughs. Six dead soldiers were laid inside one halftrack, the badly wounded gathered in two others. Dayan climbed into a scout car which hobbyhorsed along on two rims that struck sparks on the road. Vince found an open seat in a jeep, again at the tail of the column.

The battalion steamed and staggered back to the Ramle-Lydda road. Turning onto it, every gunner charged his bolt, the convoy tightened up. Again, the people of Ramle raised no hand against the Israelis but watched from windows and shadows, drawn to the spectacle of the stammering convoy.

The Tegart fort greeted them from a quarter mile off; a salvo of bullets buzzed past the convoy. The commandos waited to answer. In the front seat of the jeep Vince had a machine gun at his hands but did not touch it.

The convoy lurched towards the Tegart fort. Smoke from the burning jeep obscured one corner of the citadel. Gun barrels prickled every portal and embrasure.

The leading halftracks rolled close enough for the Legion's grenades to tumble at them from the fort's towers and roof. Some grenades landed short, a few made it to the road, where they tested the armor of the half-tracks. Bullets peppered the pavement. Every moment, Vince expected the tingle of a bullet, a punch to the bone.

The Israelis gave as good as they got; seventy machine guns smoked the walls of the fortress, made the legionnaires backpedal from every opening, kept the Arabs' heads down on the roof, and dared anyone in the towers to show themselves long enough to heave a grenade.

Bullets drummed the convoy's armor. Radiators hissed, tires belched and went flaccid. The air burred with lead.

Then the convoy stopped.

CHAPTER 82

VINCE

The driver of Vince's jeep leaped out, drawing his sidearm.

He shouted at Vince, "Drive!" before sprinting towards the Tegart fort.

Behind Vince the rear gunner picked up the call: "Drive, man!"

Yelled into action, Vince filled the driver's seat. He threw the jeep into gear to edge forward with the column. One halftrack left the formation to rush close enough to the fort for its commandos to fling their own grenades over the parapet. Jeeps and scout cars scurried past the fortress while the halftracks held their ground.

Behind Vince, the machine gunner leaned back on his trigger so hard he almost sat down. The South African strafed left and right, the gun shook as if to free itself from him. The hot barrel glowed on the back of Vince's neck.

Through the battle fog, Vince caught sight of Dayan, pistol in hand, scrambling with a dozen others towards a ditch. Several wounded commandos had lain there under the Legion's sights while the rest of the column regrouped outside Ramle. The battalion unleashed everything it had to cover their leader and the rescue. Six soldiers and two bodies were hauled out of the ditch then hurried into the halftrack fighting under the fortress wall.

For five minutes, the commando convoy battled past the Tegart fort. Vince white-knuckled the steering wheel, amazed every moment at the blare and intensity of the fighting. Once the fort had faded far enough behind him, Vince checked his arms and legs, pants and sleeves, for holes, almost crying out when he found none.

In the remaining mile of open fields before Lydda, Dayan called the convoy to a halt so he might take stock.

With Vince listening, he told his four commanders that the Legion was bound to give chase. The convoy would not stop again until Ben Shemen. Dayan rearranged the column; he deployed the jeeps to the front to sweep the streets of Lydda ahead. The scout cars would come next, halftracks in the rear. Vince's driver returned, bloody from carrying the wounded and dead.

Only one out of three vehicles in the column could move under its own power. Jeeps pushed jeeps, scout cars and halftracks pushed their own.

The three dozen vehicles set out for Lydda. In the mile before the city, the convoy became a sort of accordion, stretching and contracting bumper to bumper, sharing its strength.

※ ※ ※

The surprise and awe of Dayan's first strike into Lydda was over. This time, the convoy entered the city crippled and grinding. There was no lightning, and the Arabs were ready.

The fighting grew fierce in the first few blocks. The people fired with the scent of their own blood in their nostrils. A hundred corpses littered the streets, motionless figures clumped in the alleys. Arabs kneeling over their fallen watched with plain hatred as the Jews stumbled by.

The convoy shoved itself a half mile into the city center. Each block became a new landscape of gunfire; once more, the commandos challenged any shape in every window and corridor, but it seemed as if not one vehicle in the convoy could get out of first gear. The slowed-down commandos raked Lydda even more fiercely this second time through.

Then, from the road ahead, a boom bounded at the convoy.

A cannon.

CHAPTER 83

GABBI

The radio tweeted in Gabbi's ear.

"Tiger, Tiger. Carmel One."

Gabbi raised a hand for quiet.

"Carmel One. Tiger. Go."

The one-eyed commander said, "We're coming up behind you."

Gabbi repeated this to Abner, Michael and Tarek. Abner poked his head out of the turret, looked south, then ducked in. "I got them."

"Tiger, have you been engaging the police fort the whole time?"

"Carmel One. Yes."

"Tiger, I'm pleased to see you. Report status."

"Carmel One, Tiger is good."

"Alright. The convoy is in bad shape. We have dead and wounded. Provide cover for us. After we pass the fort, take the rear."

"Carmel One, understood."

"Tiger, well done. Out."

Gabbi told the crew. Abner and Michael balled fists that they would survive Lydda. She said to Tarek, "We're getting out." Tarek nodded, his attention fixed on the fort through the cracked windshield.

Michael loaded a shell. Abner said, "I'll tell the Arabs we're coming." He fired at the walls four blocks away.

The first jeeps passed the Tiger. There was Vince riding in the second jeep, his car pushing the ruined one in front of him. Vince didn't have his hands on the machine gun mounted on the dash. Instead, when he saw Gabbi inside the Tiger, he covered his heart.

The shot-up battalion spewed steam, fluids, and fuel. Empty seats told of casualties. Abner and Michael fired every ten seconds over the passing commandos' heads. The battered Eighty-Ninth rolled through their cannon smoke.

The last halftrack growled past, shoving the halftrack in front of it. Tarek maneuvered the Tiger into the rearguard.

Approaching the police fort, Abner toed the trigger as fast as Michael could load, one after another, every five seconds. The police fort couldn't catch its breath beneath their hammer blows, and the whole battalion made it past.

Abner and Michael quit shooting; they smacked their hands as if to clean them of dust, finished with the duel. Suddenly, Tarek floored the gas pedal.

Abner and Michael could not hold on and tumbled over each other. Tarek, hands tight on the wheel, bent forward, racing something.

Gabbi focused through the spiderwebbed windshield. Straight ahead, two grenades rolled towards the road, bouncing from a long toss out of the last tower.

Tarek couldn't brake the armored car in time; if the grenades reached the pavement, he'd skid right over them. Swerving would slow him and make certain the grenades exploded close. There was no choice but to speed past before they blew.

One grenade stopped rolling before the road. The other did not.

Gabbi threw her arms around her belly.

CHAPTER 84

VINCE

Scraping along on three rims and one good tire, Vince's jeep closed the gap to the vehicle in front and pushed. The jeep behind Vince did the same for his. Up and down the convoy, every bumper was latched onto another, as though the battle had melted the column together. Only the Tiger and one halftrack could move under their own power. The rest needed a shove.

Linked like this, the full convoy cleared the police fort.

The Israeli gunners stopped shooting. Lydda stopped shooting back. The only noise in the city came from the commandos dragging themselves out.

A mile east of Lydda, the convoy re-encountered the legionnaires behind the tank ditch. The Arabs held their fire; they had little reason to risk their lives to let the Israelis leave. The convoy rattled again onto the dirt road through the ruined cactus field.

Another mile later, under the last brassy daylight, the commando battalion lurched into Ben Shemen.

Settlers rushed to the convoy to lift the wounded out of halftracks and bear them into their homes. The dead were left alone.

Vince doffed the steel helmet, snatched his straw hat, and jumped from the jeep. He hugged his driver and rear gunner; they were in his arms before he knew it. His relief almost became tears. He turned away.

Vince hurried the length of the riddled column.

Several settlers from Ben Shemen ran with Vince towards the end of the convoy, to The Terrible Tiger.

Four farm women had already reached Gabbi. Vince arrived as one tore open a gauze packet, two others rolled Gabbi onto her side, the fourth scissored away her right pants leg. Abner and the Irishman pulled Tarek off his knees beside her.

Vince stood close, but away. The farm women exposed the shredded flesh at the back of Gabbi's right thigh. Gabbi bit a knuckle and dug her nose into the dirt.

Vince moved to the Tiger. He leaned in through the passenger door. Curls of steel lipped a dozen shrapnel holes in the perforated metal floorboard.

Two women lifted Gabbi's leg so another could wrap it in gauze. Vince walked over to the three boys. Gabbi still didn't know he was there.

Abner and the Irishman took their hands off Tarek. The dark boy stood wrapped in his own arms, shaking. Vince meant to ask him what happened but the part of Tarek that might answer was elsewhere. Abner came close to whisper, "He drove over a grenade."

The Irishman squatted behind Gabbi. He gentled a hand on her shoulder.

"Vienna."

He and Abner wandered away. The mission was over, Gabbi was under care. Tarek had driven over a grenade.

A pair of moshavniks arrived carrying a door. They laid Gabbi on it and took her away. Tarek traipsed after them.

Vince trod the length of the column, gauging the damage. The convoy was wrecked but already tires were being replaced, radiators yanked off to be plugged, brake lines fixed, blood washed off the seats. The raid on Lydda had lasted forty-seven minutes.

Dayan stood over nine dead soldiers. Vince sidled up.

Dayan said, "There's sixteen wounded."

Vince said, "Seventeen."

Dayan didn't ask who. Instead, he said, "This was a victory."

"Is that what it was?"

"Ask the dead. They would tell you the same."

Vince didn't know if he would encounter Dayan again. If he did, if the war was over then and the bodies counted, he would ask the same question.

"Mister Haas, do you still want to go into Lydda?"

Vince could say no. He could tell Mrs. Pappel and Rivkah that he chose to stay with Gabbi.

"Malik's my friend."

"Ah. Malik."

Dayan said the name as if Vince were wrong to mention an Arab over the dead Jews.

"The Yiftach Brigade will be here in an hour. You can go in with them tonight."

Vince didn't shake hands. He left one-eyed Dayan alone with his victory and went to check on Gabbi. He'd stay beside her, waiting for the Yiftach Brigade and dark.

CHAPTER 85

MALIK

The sun settled on the rooftops. No calls for sunset prayer issued from the old city's two minarets, one north, one south. In all likelihood, that call would not happen again in Lydda.

In the desert, if a man finds a pool of water, he must not dip too deeply to drink or the bottom would cloud the water. The Jews had sunk their hands deep into Lydda and stirred the whole city. Twenty thousand people shuttered themselves behind doors; another twenty thousand, all refugees, drifted the streets without shelter or purpose. Malik walked with them.

No shops were open. Hunger perched over the city, but it was a quiet yearning; no one rioted or robbed another. The sun set. Arab Lydda had lived its last day. The final night arrived.

Malik walked past humble, lightless homes. The residents hoarded candles and lantern fuel, careful not to announce themselves. Many houses were dim because their owners had already left Lydda.

In the waning dusk, Malik meandered into a large marketplace. The square was empty of wares, hundreds of stalls and shelves laid bare, strung-up ropes stripped clean where yesterday carpets, copper pots, and meats dangled.

Malik approached an old man sitting against a wall.

"Father, where are you from?"

"Why do you want to know?"

"Only to know."

"Sarafand."

"Why did you leave?"

"The Jews have it."

The thin old man seemed alone.

Malik asked, "Have you nothing?"

Again the old man said, "The Jews."

"They're coming back. Tonight."

"I know."

Malik asked, "Are you hungry?"

"Are you?"

"Yes."

"Then you can imagine I am."

Malik reached down. "On your feet, Father."

"I have been on my feet. They brought me here. So did yours. What good did that do us?"

"Take my hand. I'll show you."

Malik put him on his sandaled feet. His clothes were dirty, but they were not a poor man's garb, and his teeth were fine. Not long ago this man had belonged someplace and to someone.

Malik slid the ring from his left middle finger, a gold band with an inset ruby. He laid it in the old man's palm.

"Knock on doors until you find someone who will feed you and give you a bed tonight. Give them this. The Jews will take it from them tomorrow."

Malik sealed the old man's fingers over the ring. He walked on to find eight more, only eight. No one would take Mrs. Pappel's silver ring.

CHAPTER 86

VINCE

At dusk Vince marched west out of Ben Shemen with three hundred Palmachniks. In the waning light they set out across two miles of sabra cactus and poison berries.

Vince had ditched the khaki IDF tunic for a white farmer's shirt he'd been given. He wore his old straw hat. The young soldiers he walked with asked about Dayan's commando raid. Vince told them it was brutal. That gladdened them.

Darkness fell as the Palmachniks of Yiftach slipped through an olive grove into Lydda. They avoided the Legion inside the police fort and jogged straight for the center of the old city. Vince, already worn out, straggled. He faded to the rear and arrived with the last of the three hundred.

Lydda's market plaza had been vacated. A hundred stalls held nothing but an eerie hush. Tables and chairs, tents, clotheslines, all were empty as an echo. One Israeli found a silk banner, grey in the night, and tied it about his neck like a cape.

Across the plaza stood two great houses of worship, a mosque and a church, both magnificent stone buildings at least a century old. They shared a wall and leaned on each other.

The Palmachniks established a perimeter around the market. In thirty teams of five, one hundred and fifty soldiers dispersed into the old neighborhoods. Vince accompanied one team as they rapped on doors and inky windows, ordering the residents to report to the square to be detained overnight in the mosque or the church. This was how the Palmach increased the area under their control.

Arabs filed out of their homes. The dark bones of the marketplace took on the flesh of a crowd. By flashlights, the Israelis searched every Arab man for weapons. Before midnight, a thousand were detained in the two houses of worship. Within the first hour, the women and children were released. Many women came back with food and water and to argue with the Jews.

Into the night, the residents and refugees of Lydda flowed to the square. They came beneath white flags; no violence flared in the roundup. Vince couldn't keep his eyes open. On an oval patch of grass beside the church, beneath a widespread tamarisk tree, he lay down.

July 12

The toe of a boot woke Vince.

He'd slept on his side. Sitting up, he wiped grass off his cheek. His throat was raw from snoring.

He asked, "Who're you?"

An Israeli soldier offered Vince a dirty hand. Shadows and knife-edge light told Vince the time was just after dawn.

"Captain Schwimmer. Come with me."

"Where?"

"A meeting with the city leaders. You've been requested."

"By who?"

"The Arabs."

The captain handed over his canteen. Vince rinsed his mouth, took a few swallows, and offered it back.

"Keep it for a bit, Mister Haas. Wash up."

Schwimmer, shorter than Vince, took rapid steps across the square. He didn't look back to see if Vince was behind him; Schwimmer was the sort who expected to be followed. Vince rubbed water through his hair, over his face and the nape of his neck.

The captain led him around the rim of the square. Arab men, women, and young ones jammed the cobbles, surrendering under white cloths tied to rods. The Jews herded them into the church and mosque. Schwimmer headed for the mosque.

Schwimmer led Vince to a side door that entered into a domed sanctuary. The captain took back his canteen before he vanished into the market square. Vince went into the mosque.

He walked beneath a vaulted ceiling into a marble chamber, instantly cool. Gathered on a red carpet under a crystal chandelier, five IDF officers spoke with six bearded elders and a younger Arab in a business suit.

Vince stayed to the side. In Arabic and Hebrew, the men spoke without noticing him until the Arab in the suit gestured to him.

"You are the American reporter?"

"I am."

"I am the mayor of Lydda."

He did not give his name nor a hand to shake. He asked Vince, "You are the keeper of this, yes?"

"Keeper of what?'

"What is said here. You are the witness."

Vince didn't know what he was witnessing but said, "Sure."

The mayor said to one of the officers, "Tell him."

The IDF man said, "Mister Haas."

"Yeah."

"We have offered a proposal to the Arab committee for Lydda. They wish you to be aware of the terms, I suppose as some sort of guarantee. Do you agree?"

"Fine."

The Palmach major addressed the Arab delegation. It seemed he was repeating himself.

"Israeli forces will not destroy any buildings in Lydda. We will take all measures to prevent looting, stealing, or acts of revenge. Captured fighters will be treated as prisoners of war with the Red Cross notified. Residents who wish to remain in Lydda will be allowed to do so with the understanding that they are on their own. We will not feed them or provide shelter. Those who leave the city will be given safe passage east toward the Transjordanian army."

The Jewish officer opened a hand to the mayor, inviting him to tender the rest of the terms, the Arab side, for Vince.

"We will lay our weapons on our doorsteps to be collected. We accept a curfew at nightfall. Lydda will surrender."

The officer and mayor clasped hands. Then the mayor shook Vince's hand.

Vince asked, "What about the police fort?"

The IDF officer asked, "What about it?"

"Those are legionnaires inside. This guy doesn't speak for them. Trust me, I drove by that place twice yesterday. You're not going to take it."

The officer told the mayor, "The police fort will have to surrender, too."

The mayor repeated this in Arabic to the elders. They shook their bearded heads as if this were an unfair change in the Israeli offer.

The mayor raised a palm. He spoke in Arabic and pointed at three old men, the ones who'd shaken their heads the firmest. The mayor made something plain until they were cowed.

He said to the soldiers and Vince, "We will tell the Legion to leave Lydda. Come."

CHAPTER 87

MALIK

Malik leaned against a wall in the darkest slice of a black alley. He left his cowl down to leave his hearing keen. He twirled Mrs. Pappel's silver band, the last of the rings, on his left pinky. His hands were naked but not empty. Nothing he had given away could he not get again.

He eased his bearded chin onto his chest, slid his hands into his sleeves, and stood until his own snort woke him. Grey morning light fogged the alley. Malik found a small, smooth stone to slip into his mouth to loosen his saliva. He craned his stiffened neck. Malik stepped from the alley into the market square.

People filled the plaza; a throng of Arabs walked under white flags, afraid of being shot as they appeared. Jews greeted them with rifles leveled. The soldiers turned away Arab women and children. They prodded the men into one of the two massive buildings on the square, the church or the mosque.

The Jews had come in the night, as Malik had predicted. Around the square they were not so many, a few hundred. Still, they commanded thousands to surrender. Yesterday, with even fewer numbers, they'd roared through Lydda shooting at anything that moved. With such small numbers, it was a marvel to see what the Jews could do.

A team of soldiers shouted in Hebrew for Malik to walk to the mosque.

"Go now," they said. "Inside."

Malik held his ground. The five Jews strode his way; they would take him to captivity if he would not walk there on his own. Malik nodded at an older couple walking nearby. The woman held high a white kerchief; her hair was uncovered. Malik joined them as though he'd been waiting for their appearance. The old man had a limp.

Malik called to them, "Father. Mother. *Marhaba*."

In Hebrew, he said to the soldiers, "I am going with them."

The soldiers turned elsewhere.

The woman waved her handkerchief in dainty sweeps as if dusting the air before her. She and the man looked alike, round-faced and portly, perhaps brother and sister. Malik wondered about his own sister in Hebron. Were the Jews there?

The woman spoke, quick and clever. "You are not from Lydda."

"No, Mother."

"You are Bedu."

"Yes, Mother."

"Why are you here, not in the desert? I would be there."

"I have another destination."

"If you wish to see it, do not go to the mosque."

"Why do you go?"

"Do you know the massacre of Deir Yassin?"

"Too well."

"The fighting may start again in Lydda. If it does, my husband must be safe. He cannot be in our home. What if some militiaman comes in, what if he shoots at a Jew? They will blow us up."

"They will not let you stay with him in the mosque."

"I will tell them I must be with him. He needs me."

"The Jews are going to send you both away from Lydda. What will you do?"

"We will return."

"I do not know if that can happen."

"It will. The Jews cannot win."

"They have won, Mother."

The old man walked poorly beside her.

She said, "Then it will be a short road."

Under the watchful eyes of the soldiers, Malik and the old couple moved across the square. They stopped near the long line leading into the great mosque. The old woman lowered her white handkerchief. A soldier gestured for Malik and the hobbling man to get in the queue.

The old woman told Malik, "I am going to cough. Very loudly. I will collapse, do not touch me. I will point across the square to my home where I have my medicine. I will faint. Then, Bedu, you will run from this line. Understood?"

"Yes, Mother. Thank you."

The man touched Malik's back. "Don't worry." He patted a pocket and winked. "I have her medicine."

The woman pulled up suddenly as if she'd swallowed something that wouldn't go down. She clutched her bosom. She coughed not into her hands but into the open. She coughed again and wobbled in the knees. The Arab crowd took notice, some stepped out of the line to help. Several soldiers moved her way.

The old woman barely held herself upright on her husband's arm, hacking convincingly. She rapped a fist against his chest, then aimed one heavy arm back the way they'd come.

In Hebrew, to be sure the Jews understood, she cried to Malik, "My pills. They're at home. Go get them."

Malik hesitated in mock concern, reaching to the woman as if she were a familiar, without touching her.

She shouted, "Go!"

Even one of the Jews said, "Go."

CHAPTER 88

VINCE

Under a white flag, the mayor led the way to the fort. In the road and gutters, bullet casings and bloodied clothes marked Dayan's commando raid over this same pavement twelve hours ago.

Vince walked with a dozen Palmachniks, staying far behind the mayor and his entourage of elders. Vince had no urge to encounter the police fort for a third time. Again, he followed Captain Schwimmer.

The mayor carried the white flag down the middle of the street, straight at the fort. The legionnaires took potshots at him and the elders. Vince and the dozen Palmachniks scattered for cover among the shops. The mayor bravely stayed in the street, waving the white banner. Beneath it, he yelled to the Tegart fort that he was an Arab.

The shooting quit. The mayor handed off the flag to one of the elders to free his hands. With both arms raised, he advanced another block, close enough to be heard by the legionnaires without shouting.

The mayor stopped half a block from the fortress. He spoke to the implacable, scarred walls.

As if shoved, he staggered backwards, then collapsed on the back of his business suit. A rifle's bark sailed past Vince and the Palmachniks.

Two blocks behind the mayor, the elder who held the white flag reeled and dropped it. The flag furled to the street. The other two elders caught their wounded comrade before he could fall next to the flag and ran.

CHAPTER 89

MALIK

Malik skulked in the crevices of the old city, alley to alley, through slender backstreets.

Town criers in the lanes announced Lydda's surrender. They called the citizens to put their guns outside their doors for the Jews to collect, yet not a weapon lay on any threshold.

The people stayed inside their homes. Jewish patrols swept up the refugees in families and singly, then marched them to the market square to be confined. The refugees had already lost their many towns and villages; they'd been the ones who suffered most when the Jewish convoy rampaged through Lydda. The refugees were no threat, they had no guns. They had no homes. They had not eaten.

The morning wore on. Many times, Malik held his breath to avoid being nabbed. He pressed against walls, behind downspouts and water barrels, in shadows and sunless bends. Malik waited for his chance to walk out of Lydda, go north, then east into the mountains.

Across the road a teenage boy linked arms with a grandfather. The man looked to have grown old walking. Four soldiers led him and the boy away. Six Jews stayed behind to scour the street for more loose Arabs.

Malik glided out the other end of the passage.

He emerged into a public square smaller than the city's main market. Damp blankets and planks were scattered over the flagstones around a waterless fountain. A squatters' village had been flooded here.

Malik stepped through puddles. No one else crossed the square or sat on the fountain wall. The streets and plaza were empty.

Beside the square rose a short minaret under a green metal cap. In the surrounding neighborhood, Jews knocked on doors to cull Arab men out of the homes. Malik needed to get off the street until Allah presented him the moment to slip away. He pushed on a weathered wooden door. He stepped into a small mosque.

CHAPTER 90

VINCE

No one could retrieve the mayor's body; the legionnaires shot at anyone who tried. His body and the white flag lay spilled in the sun two blocks apart, as a message: only the Arab Legion would decide if Lydda surrendered.

The Arabs coming to the plaza had slowed to a trickle. A hush fell over the city as if it were a very cold day. The Israelis were on edge. The legionnaires in the fort continued to fire at anyone in range.

Vince found Schwimmer.

"I want to go into the mosque."

"Alone?"

"You're welcome to come with me."

Schwimmer gave orders for Vince to be allowed into the mosque, then headed off to join the patrols spanning out from the market.

Inside the mosque's outer walls, the ground was bricked over. All the gardens were neglected. Stone archways connected two open-air courtyards in a compound where blue-tiled pools allowed the faithful to wash. The courtyards fed into a domed prayer hall, a great chamber of light and lingering echoes.

The Israelis had confined six thousand Arab men in a space designed for a third that number. The detainees made a pathway for Vince to walk among them. Clearly he was no soldier; they asked if he was Red Cross or a foreign diplomat. When he explained he was an American journalist, several English-speakers came forward. The word spread, and many men flocked to Vince.

He interviewed several. Hundreds leaned close to listen. Most were poor villagers with no love for Lydda; this wasn't their home, and they did not take up arms for it. They expected the Jews to send them east to the bald and bleak territories held by Transjordan. To a man they believed they would return to their homes. Many had families outside the mosque and were worried about them.

Vince spoke also with educated men, teachers, officials, businessmen, shopkeepers. These were the natives of Lydda, dating back generations. Each told Vince he believed Israel would lose the war. How could it be otherwise? A half million Jews in the middle of the Arab world dictated no other result. Allah would permit nothing less.

For hours, the Arabs shared their stories, along with baskets of food delivered by their women, jars of fresh water, citrus, and olives.

The men told Vince their fears of being murdered, the way the Jews had done at Deir Yassin and other villages. Everyone inside the mosque was afraid of the Jews.

One man said, "But there are many who are not afraid."

Vince asked, "Where are they?"

"Outside."

CHAPTER 91

MALIK

Malik entered the *musalla*, the prayer hall, through a large wooden door. He closed the portal with his hand behind him on the old doorhandle. He stepped backwards to push it shut, facing the refugees inside.

Forty women and a dozen children eyed him. Twenty old men knelt on prayer rugs in the center of the hall and did not look his way. On their knees the men's worship was very still, not like the Jews who prayed swaying like camel riders. Malik remained at the wooden door, hand on the handle, unsure if he should hide here.

The people in the small mosque did not speak to Malik or each other above the mutters of the worshippers. There was not one kind of refugee in the musalla but all sorts who, like Malik, were homeless in Lydda. They had in common only that they had come to a holy place for refuge. Among the men were chicken-necked villagers with stained teeth, dressed in the loose garb and robes of peasants. Others, fat-cheeked men, wore business clothes and moustaches. All the women had bundled their hair under scarves. The older women tended the children and watched large, dark Malik with suspicion.

From the doorway, the high dome carried his eyes upward into mosaics of gold, scarlet, and cerulean. Emerald fabric lined all the sanctuary walls. The hall was dim, without electricity. Light and air flowed through six barred windows.

None of the refugees reacted when Malik moved to the wall of the musalla opposite the door. He stood against the wall by himself.

Mumbled prayers swirled up into the hollow dome. Malik, who rarely prayed indoors, did not like the brittleness of the echoes.

Outside, Lydda remained quiet. The fountain square was empty. From the southern reaches of the old city, gunfire popped. In the musalla, nothing rustled but prayer and unsettled children.

Malik pulled up his hood to hide his face and beard; he slid his hands into his sleeves. He became a freestanding darkness, a shadow unstaked from the ground. Malik stared nowhere but at the wooden door.

CHAPTER 92

VINCE

Vince walked with Schwimmer and a twenty-man platoon down skinny, unpaved roads made for donkeys and wagons. Every few blocks, Arab criers called out to the bone-white homes that Lydda had surrendered. Curfew would begin at sunset. Schwimmer's men gathered no weapons off any doorstep. In most of the windows stood silhouettes.

Schwimmer tapped on the magazine of his Sten gun. Vince fanned himself with his straw hat. The mud walls of Lydda beamed heat.

Vince said, "This doesn't feel like a city that's surrendered."

The patrol skimmed an olive grove on the northern edge of the old city. Schwimmer's soldiers eagled-eyed the orchard and nearby houses.

The captain turned his platoon west. They moved along a paved road towards another public plaza, smaller than the main market. Five blocks ahead, a minaret dominated this northwest corner of Lydda.

Schwimmer raised a fist to his platoon, the signal to halt. Together they dropped to one knee, Vince, too. Schwimmer had heard, or sensed, something wrong.

Using gestures, the captain sent his platoon sprinting off the road. Every soldier ducked behind courtyard walls or into tight alleys. Vince ran with Schwimmer to hunker behind a stone garden gate.

Schwimmer pointed towards the olive grove and the low growl of an engine.

Two engines.

He whispered, "Armored cars."

CHAPTER 93

MALIK

At the first sounds of fighting, the refugees shifted to where Malik stood opposite the wooden door. The men kneeling on carpets raised up like hackles. They left the rugs and crowded the far wall, too.

Malik pulled his hands from his sleeves and pushed back his hood. A few refugees spoke to him as though he, the stranger, were the one who knew something of war.

"What is happening? What should we do? Should we leave?"

He said, "You are safe here. You are in a protected place."

Not far away, a clash of weapons was taking place. Automatic weapons traded with rifles, submachine gun bursts were answered by the woof of cannon fire. The Jew soldiers in Lydda were under attack.

By whom? Had the Legion come to kick the Israelis out? Had the fighters in the police fort emerged to retake the city?

The clamor crept closer. Out in the fountain square, yelling and erratic gunfire swelled. Someone shouted, "This way! This way!"

The door of the small mosque flung open. A militiaman burst in. He paid no notice to the recoiling refugees but waved madly into the square. "Come here, here!"

Automatic weapons rattled blocks away. The shouting was in Hebrew.

Four more fighters barged into the musalla. Each carried a rifle; two hefted a crate between them. The first militiaman slammed the door behind them.

Panting and urgent, the five young men checked their surroundings, the dome, green walls, crimson rugs, and seventy refugee men, women, and children huddling away from them. One militiaman flung open a door into a dark stairwell.

He asked an old man, "Father, where do these stairs go?"

The old man trembled.

The militiaman hollered, "Where do they go?"

"The roof, the roof."

Malik stepped forward.

All five militiamen raised rifles. Malik walked with care among the prayer rugs.

"You cannot bring weapons in here. This is a mosque."

Under the dome his voice sounded large.

The one who seemed the leader matched Malik's advance to the center of the musalla. He trod on the red rugs.

"There is a war outside."

Malik said, "The city has surrendered."

"Does that sound like surrender to you? Grab a gun and help us. Or go back over there to the sheep."

Malik said, "We want you to leave."

The leader, a ropey man, wore a loose blouse and woven vest. His beard was short-cropped, a brown *taqiyya* covered the peak of his narrow skull. His gaze was quick, avian. He, too, was a refugee but he'd not been forced to Lydda; he'd come here to fight. Shorter than Malik, the militiaman stopped within arm's reach. He looked up to speak.

"The Jews want me to go away, too." He flattened a hand on Malik's black robe. "I won't."

The fighter pushed to make Malik retreat. Malik did not budge.

The young Arab said, "Back away, Father. Mosque or no mosque."

"You will die here."

"I choose to be here. Not where the Jews would send me."

Malik put his back to the fighter. The refugees made space along the wall.

The five militiamen scurried about the musalla. The jittery one who'd found the stairwell opened the crate and filled his pockets with grenades. He ran up to the roof jiggling with them. The other fighters reached in, too; the crate was laden with explosives and ammunition. Well-armed, they lay their rifle barrels in the windows. One dragged the crate under a window to stand on it.

CHAPTER 94

VINCE

Two Arab armored cars emerged from the olive groves, snapping low-hanging branches. Each mounted a cannon and high-caliber machine guns. Growling, snuffling, they rolled onto the dirt lane where Vince and Schwimmer's patrol scrambled for cover.

The first car drew the Israelis' fire. The second blasted the houses and alleys where they hid. An exploded wall collapsed onto three of Schwimmer's men; a second shell blew a four-foot hole in a two-story shop. A third round at close range sent Vince and Schwimmer sprinting under a rain of roof tiles.

Bullets beat on the armored cars' steel sides, but the Israelis could do no damage without armor-piercing weapons. The Legion vehicles bulled past, then turned south towards the center of the old city. Schwimmer's patrol rushed to dig out their comrades.

Vince asked Schwimmer, "Where the hell did they come from?"

The captain poked a finger into a bullet hole though his pants leg inches below his groin. He took a moment to turn his eyes upward.

"I don't know."

"Is the Legion on its way?"

Schwimmer scanned every direction; the pair of armored cars seemed to have arrived on their own.

The captain said, "I don't think so. They might be scouts, they might just be lost. Either way, if they get into the police fort, we won't get them out."

"Then what?"

"If the Legion wants a fight and they come out with armored cars on their side, we'll lose Lydda."

The three buried soldiers were recovered alive, dusty, shaken, and bruised.

Schwimmer mustered his patrol. "We're going back to the town square. Keep your heads down."

Rifle fire sputtered in the warrens of buildings and streets ahead. Schwimmer's men hugged the walls and buildings, headed south in leap-frog. Vince shadowed Schwimmer, moving when he moved.

The patrol made progress in fits and starts. In one block, they took rounds from a mud house. The soldiers surrounded the small home; a team of three forced the door, tossed in grenades, then stormed in. The Arab shooter was silenced in seconds.

Violence picked up all across Lydda. Snaps of sniper fire and the crump of grenades sailed from every quarter. As they neared the town square, Schwimmer's squad picked up the pace. Ahead, in the abandoned bazaar, gunfire clattered. The patrol launched into a dead run towards the shooting and pealing screams. Vince, unarmed and unsure, ran with them.

Schwimmer and his men leaped into the fray while Vince stopped at the edge of the plaza. He took cover behind a low wall.

Two hundred of the detained Arabs were attacking the Jews guarding the grand mosque and church. Without guns, the Arab men threw rocks and swung chair legs as cudgels. The two armored cars were nowhere to be seen; the legionnaires inside the police fort had not come out.

Schwimmer's team flanked the crowd. On his order, they fired. Arabs dropped two and three at a time. The Israelis fended off hand-to-hand assaults and shot to kill when they had a clear lane.

The riot took four minutes to crush. Dozens of Arabs bled on the concrete while a hundred others escaped into the old city rather than return to the mosque. The rest raised their hands or dragged off wounded mates. Women who'd hurried to the market at the sounds of the melee shrieked from the edges of the plaza as soldiers pushed them away.

Vince rose from behind the wall. For this he would take notes and sketch. Lydda was a different kind of tragedy. He wanted it separate in his memory. Vince set his notebook on top of the wall and began to draw and scribble. He tried to capture the gun smoke before it thinned, the cries before they were quashed. The soldiers took casualties, too; the Jews took no joy in this little slaughter. Vince drew stunned young faces.

Schwimmer came Vince's way alone. Vince didn't stop drawing and notetaking. Schwimmer looked into the notebook. His Sten gun was still warm.

Schwimmer said, "They thought the Legion had come to help them. The armored cars."

"That would figure."

"It's what triggered them. The word in the mosque was that we were going to shoot them all. So they broke out."

"I can understand."

"They broke the surrender."

Vince said, "You don't have to explain yourself."

"Good. I won't do it again."

Schwimmer didn't return to his men but stayed beside Vince to view the square the way Vince did, far enough from the blood to see all of it.

The city continued to twitch with gunplay as the uprising spread across Lydda. A soldier hustled up to Schwimmer.

Schwimmer asked, "What is it?"

The soldier pointed north, the way he'd come. "There's a small mosque near a fountain."

"The Dahmash mosque. What about it?"

"Arab fighters have gotten in there. They're shooting and throwing grenades."

"Anybody hurt?"

"Two in my squad are dead."

"I'll be right there. Go back. Shoot at anything that moves, any clear target. Anyone on the street, in any window. Shoot. Understand?"

"Yes." The soldier took off.

Vince asked, "Any target? People on the street?"

"You said I don't have to explain myself, Mister Haas."

"You agreed to protect holy places."

"If there's guns inside a mosque, if they throw grenades, it's not holy."

Vince moved to capture the quote in his notebook. Schwimmer laid a hand on his knuckles.

"We have three hundred Jewish soldiers in this city. There's forty thousand Arabs. Stop acting surprised at what we have to do."

The captain tapped the silver magazine of his Sten and hurried off. Vince went behind him. Together they traced the contours of the sun-warmed walls leading north through the old city.

CHAPTER 95

MALIK

The five militiamen in the musalla had guns. In his sleeves Malik hid only knives.

All seventy refugees cowered against the wall with Malik, separated from the militiamen by the red river of prayer rugs. The fighter on the roof lobbed grenades onto the square to stop the Jews from coming that way. The refugees, even the children, shuddered at every explosion like rippling water. The four militiamen in the sanctuary fired at the Jews through the barred windows. The cracks of their gunshots flew up into the dome, doubled, then cast down over the tight-packed refugees.

The women pressed the children behind their hips and their skirts muffled the young ones' cries. Men stood in front of the women; even strangers did this. Malik flattened against the wall. A small fellah pushed his way to him bringing an unwashed smell.

The short man asked, "Should we run?"

"Go if you wish."

"The Jews will kill us if we stay in here. Do you know them? They will do it."

"I know them. They can do anything."

"Then run with me."

The villager turned; Malik grabbed him.

"Before you open the doors, do you wonder who will shoot you first? The Jews or the militia? We're hostages to both, friend."

The fellah tried to pull away. Malik held on.

"Stay here. I will walk with you when it's over."

The fellah pushed off Malik's hand and went back to his spot. The militiamen fired and reloaded. The prayer hall reeked of cordite and the refugees' sweat.

In the plaza and the alley, the Jews closed in on the mosque. A Jew shouted, "*Rimon!*"

A blast went off. The four militiamen fired fast into the square, spurred by the screams of soldiers in the alley.

The fighter on the roof hurried down the stairs. He pushed the little militiaman off the crate to grab more grenades, then sprinted back up the steps.

CHAPTER 96

VINCE

Grenades rained from the roof of the small mosque. A rifle sparked in each window. Schwimmer's squad couldn't cross the plaza.

Only the fountain could give cover, but the Arabs seemed to have plenty of ammo. Schwimmer stationed ten soldiers on the rim of the square, then took the other ten and Vince to find another approach.

Quickly they came on a slim alley running along the flank of the mosque. In the wall above, a single window opened into the mosque. Carefully, the Israelis and Vince drew closer.

The soldier in front whirled, shouting, *"Rimon!"*

Schwimmer tackled Vince to the cobblestones. Vince landed hard, Schwimmer on top of him. The soldiers dove to the cobblestones an instant before the explosion. Shrapnel zinged off the high walls.

With his mouth close to Vince's ear, Schwimmer said, "Next time, 'rimon' means 'grenade.'"

"Got it."

The captain helped Vince to his feet. Three soldiers had taken wounds, none life-threatening. The squad carried bandages; they wrapped what they could and braved what they could not.

A soldier reported that he'd seen the grenade tossed from the mosque's roof.

Schwimmer backed his team out of the alley. Vince asked, "What're you going to do?"

"Blow a hole in the wall. Rush in from the plaza and the alley at the same time. Go in and take them out."

"How many you think are inside?"

"Five or six."

"That wall looks thick."

"A PIAT will go through a tank."

Schwimmer sent a soldier galloping off the fetch the PIATist.

In minutes, the operator and his tube weapon jostled up. The man was a heavyset, bearded fellow greeted as Shmulik. With him came a one-handed soldier; blood soaked the bandaged stump of his left wrist. Schwimmer spoke to him, they looked to be friends. The wounded soldier showed Schwimmer how he could still manage his Sten with one hand. Schwimmer patted his comrade's chest and left him outside the alley. Shmulik busied himself cocking the spring-loaded PIAT.

Schwimmer said to Vince, "Come no closer."

The one-handed Jew stood alongside Vince. He gave his name as Yisrael. His face was ghostly white; he might still have been in shock. He knew who Vince was. Schwimmer and the strike team edged into the alley around Shmulik the PIATist.

Vince asked Yisrael, "What happened?"

"Got in a brawl with the armored cars."

"Where are they now?"

"We fought them off. They're gone."

"I'm sorry."

Yisrael held up his stump, not for Vince but for himself. He considered it, a pale man who'd made a bargain and now must live with it.

Schwimmer's soldiers stopped fifteen yards from the mosque wall. Shmulik dropped to a knee and hoisted the PIAT to his shoulder. Shmulik gave a warning, then triggered.

The wall vanished behind a boiling fireball and black smoke. A roar swept through the alley; instantly, a second, larger blast rumbled from inside the mosque.

Yisrael said, "Something just happened."

Schwimmer's team jumped into action. They heaved grenades through the hole punched by the PIAT, big enough for them to charge through one at a time. They disappeared across the broken ribs of the wall, hunched into the roiling dust. They fired Stens and Tommy guns and rolled live grenades ahead of them.

Through the smoke, the burly boy Shmulik staggered out of the alley without the PIAT. Blood sprayed from the side of his neck.

Yisrael leaped to him. Immediately he pressed his remaining hand over Shmulik's terrible gash. The recoil of the PIAT must have cut a vessel in Shmulik's neck; the boy bled like something butchered. Blood coursed between Yisrael's fingers. Clamped together, the two wounded Israelis hurried from the alley.

Vince inched closer to the opening in the wall. He put a hand on the busted bricks, felt the fire still in them. He had no intention of going into the mosque during a gunfight. He might easily be misidentified and shot down.

Deep inside the mosque, a hundred voices moaned. Vince could not step back from the wall; the scorched stench of the hole, the wails coming through it, numbed his legs.

Schwimmer exited. He smelled sour.

The captain grabbed Vince's shirt to haul him to the end of the alley. Schwimmer let him loose with a shove.

"Get away from here."

"What happened?"

The captain wiped his lips of vomit. He spit.

"I said go."

CHAPTER 97

MALIK

Malik lay face up, choked, unable to breathe. Something weighed on him. A screeching whine blocked out all other sound.

He shook to free himself from what pinned him down, to swim up and find air. He awoke sitting, gasping, churning his arms.

Malik stopped clawing, still fighting for breath, hands over his head. Around him and on top of him lay writhing bodies and the dead. A smoldering woman without eyes, another with bone showing through her cheek, sprawled across his legs. Malik gagged at the fried stench; he panted open-mouthed.

He kicked off the two women's corpses, careless of respect. With the flat of his boots he shoved away other bodies; one man kicked back. Malik rubbed his own ears to stop the whistling, but it persisted. Blood tacked his hands.

He wobbled to his feet.

The blast had splashed the refugees across the wall as if they had been a wave and crashed against it. Gore dripped down the green-papered wall, organs, every sanguine thing inside a man, torn limbs, the red prayer rugs, all were tangled in the carnage. The militiamen left no sign of themselves.

A half dozen survivors were on their feet, the few stumbling souls Allah had spared like Malik, for whom Allah still had purpose. Malik's ears cleared enough to hear how the dome gathered up every whimper, doubled it, then dribbled it down over him, the ruin, and the corpses.

His head, spine, and elbows ached. His face itched, his beard smelled singed. Malik's lungs and ribs cinched; he might have breathed in flame from the blast. The right shoulder of his robe was ripped, his right arm felt sluggish.

Jews with guns entered the sanctuary.

The soldiers crouched as if under threat. The howls from the handful of living blamed them or begged them for help. One soldier challenged Malik until Malik raised both bloody hands and the soldier moved on. The Jews staggered, too; some retched at what they had done without knowing how they had done it.

The musalla's door had been blown open. Light flooded in, haze drifted out. Malik stepped over bodies; someone grabbed his leg. He kneeled to a mangled young man, the foul-smelling villager who'd wanted him to run. Blood circled the fellah's lips. Malik scooped him off the floor, then kept his word to walk with him.

The Jews let them go out into the bright public square. Malik set the dying villager against the fountain and sat, too. Blood drizzled off Malik's fingertips; this told him it was his own.

Up on the mosque's roof, a short firefight flared. A Jew's Sten gun burped twice and the militiaman who'd thrown the grenades was killed. Did the young Arab know what lay below in the musalla, the bloodbath from his exploding crate of grenades? He needed to die last.

The fellah muttered to Malik for water. Malik dipped one sleeve into a puddle on the flagstones. He squeezed it over the fellah's lips, then his own.

Soon after, when the fellah died, Malik lifted the body. He knew of a vacant house not far away where he might bind his wounds, clean himself, and wait. No one was going to shoot a man carrying a body.

CHAPTER 98

VINCE

After the deadly riot in the market and the unexplained explosion inside the small mosque, the Palmachniks spread out again in their five-man teams. Thirty squads scoured Lydda block to block, house to house, searching for weapons and Arab men of fighting age. As before, every soldier was given the order to fire at anything that moved, any Arab on the streets, any figure in a window.

Under a scalding sun, the IDF squads searched every building. If guns were found, they drove out the inhabitants and marched them to the grand mosque or the church. If an Arab sniped from any building, that door was kicked down, grenades thrown in, the building rushed, and the shooter eliminated. Anyone else inside was endangered, too; the Israelis asked no questions when killing snipers. Weapons were taken. A body count was not.

In the late afternoon, as the temperature peaked in Lydda, the revolt was quelled.

Schwimmer stopped talking to Vince. Another soldier who'd gone inside the Dahmash mosque searched for words to describe what he'd seen. He couldn't attribute the slaughter to the PIAT shell alone. "There was something else." He traced fingertips across his lips, repeated, "Something," and said no more.

The shadows lengthened. Along with Schwimmer's team, Vince returned to the main market. Many houses had draped white sheets from railings and windows. Dozens of bodies lay in the streets and alleys. The seething heat would soon make the corpses rotten; the residents of Lydda would not come out of their homes to claim the dead. The cowering refugees had nowhere to take them.

In the market, browning stains on the bricks marked the morning's melee. Soldiers carried bodies on blankets and sheets to the Muslim cemetery. Inside the mosque and church, the crowding got worse. Thousands of detainees, like the city, kept a wary silence.

Outside the police fortress, the mayor of Lydda and the white flag still lay in the open. The legionnaires continued to shoot at anyone who approached them.

At dusk, Vince traipsed back to the patch of grass outside the mosque, beneath the tamarisk tree. He sat against the trunk to review his notebook, the pages he'd filled with sketches and facts, times and quotes about the taking of Lydda. One statement from Schwimmer looped in his head. *Stop acting surprised at what we have to do.*

Vince lay back on the grass, with arms spread as if he'd fallen there, and slept.

✳ ✳ ✳

He awoke to thunder, thinking he might get rained on. He sat up. The night wasn't humid, and the air didn't smell electric. Vince brushed grass off his shoulders, sore from sleeping one more time on the ground.

The sky boomed and jittered above the roofs in the south of Lydda. Vince walked into the dark market where the Palmachniks were bivouacked for the night. Soldiers lay on cobblestones, helmets for pillows, while guards patrolled the perimeter. No signs of life issued from the mosque or church. Only the police fort rumbled and flashed.

On the edge of the market square, a pair of mortars pitched shells high. The rounds arced and plummeted behind the fortress walls, six hundred meters away. Each blast made the citadel flicker like a campfire and sparks flash ruby above the ramparts. The Israeli mortarmen had the range; they did not miss and did not slacken.

For the next two hours the Jews bombarded the legionnaires. Vince took a seat on the dirt to watch the fortress suffer a mighty sundering. At a signal from Schwimmer, the mortars quit; Schwimmer took a hundred soldiers with him jangling away into the night.

A half hour later, at midnight, Schwimmer and six of his soldiers returned. The soldiers bore on their shoulders the body of the mayor.

Schwimmer spoke to Vince for the first time since that afternoon, at the small mosque.

"The Arab Legion is gone."

July 13

At first light, Vince arrived with Schwimmer on the doorstep of the great church. The remaining five leaders of Lydda waited. One of them wore a sling.

Schwimmer told them, "You can claim the body of the mayor."

"How did you retrieve him?"

"The Legion is gone."

The Arabs said, "This is a lie. The Legion would not leave us."

"Go look for yourself. I'll stay here."

"So they can shoot at us again?"

"No one will shoot at you."

The elder with the longest beard said, "The American will come with us."

Vince said, "I don't need to go. I was there last night. They're gone."

"You swear this?"

"Yeah. I swear it."

"Give us a moment."

The five leaders walked down the church steps to confab in the early light. They argued.

In the square, the Palmach battalion roused. They brewed coffee over small fires built with lumber scavenged out of the market stalls. The five Arab leaders came back up the church steps.

The longbeard said, "Yes."

Schwimmer said, "Understand me. You surrendered Lydda once and you broke that surrender. Don't do it again."

"What are your terms?"

"Same as before. Anyone who wants to stay can. No Arabs will be allowed weapons. The IDF will provide nothing, no shelter, food, or water. When the war is done, those Arabs still in Lydda will become citizens of the state of Israel. Am I clear?"

"When the war is done, you will be swimming back to Europe."

"So I see I was clear."

"When must we leave?"

"This morning."

"Forty thousand people?"

"Follow the road to Beit Nabala. Go east to Barfiliya. Keep going east to Ramallah. You can take with you all you can carry."

"You make us walk? In this heat? Ramallah is thirty kilometers. We have women and children."

"Women and children who can stay in Lydda if they choose."

"They will not."

"Then they'll be the responsibility of the Arab nations who invaded Israel. Tell the Legion that when you see them."

"What of the men you keep in the mosque and church? Will you release them?"

"They're free to join their families."

"And the dead? We cannot take them with us."

"They'll be taken to the cemetery and burned."

"You will burn them?"

"Gather your people. Be on your way."

The longbeard said to Schwimmer, "The people of Lydda will return."

"No, you won't."

"We will walk a thousand kilometers before we live among Jews."

"Then you're lucky it's just thirty."

The elders skittered away, still arguing as if they should have cut a better deal.

Vince said to Schwimmer, "I think I'll leave with them."

"The Arabs?"

"Yeah."

"Where will you go?"

"Out to the road. To watch."

"Why, Mister Haas?"

"I have a friend who might walk by."

CHAPTER 99

MALIK

Malik sat up naked in a house, on a mattress. His shoulder throbbed.

He might have slept better if he'd lain in the garden. The abandoned little home was breezeless and close. The corpse of the villager lay inside the front door where Malik had dumped him last night.

He unwound from his shoulder the bandage he'd made out of strips from a bedsheet. Malik sniffed the gash; a shard of stone or brick in the mosque had struck him so hard it split the flesh. The cut smelled acrid, like garbage. The wound was puffy and hot. Malik poked it and made himself wince. Bruising purpled his arm down to the elbow.

All last evening, he allowed no light in the house, not even a candle, for the Jews were out hunting. In the dark kitchen, he pumped water into a basin to clean his shoulder as best he could. He wrapped the laceration, then washed the blood out of his clothes and hung them in the courtyard.

Now at daybreak, Malik could rummage. The humble house had belonged to good Muslims, he found no alcohol to pour into his wound. In a kitchen drawer, he discovered a matchbox.

Over several match flames, Malik heated a metal spoon. He pressed the searing bowl into the swollen crevice. The meat cauterized with a fetid puff. Malik growled until the dizziness passed, then split another bedsheet into fresh wraps.

In the courtyard, he plucked his clothes off of vines. He'd hung his cotton blouse on the thorns of a twisting rose, his black robe on boughs of trumpet flowers. The overnight heat was baked in the garden wall and in the bricks under his bare feet. He'd not fully washed out the blood-stain from his undergarment. His black robe stayed damp, but it smelled renewed. The morning would be hot, and the clothing would dry as he moved through the day.

Malik dressed and grew hungry. In the garden he waited on a marble stool that had once been some ancient pillar. His shoulder pained him but singeing the wound had broken its fever.

The garden warmed quickly. Insects winged about the flowering vines. Outside the walls, mule carts creaked in the lanes, Lydda's streets grew busy. To the south, smoke curled into a tall pillar over the windless dawn. Near the little house, pans clanged and voices cried in Hebrew and Arabic:

"Lydda has surrendered! Prepare to leave. Pack what you need. Prepare to leave!"

Once the sun rose above the garden walls, Jews came through the house and into the courtyard. The trio of soldiers was well-armed, in short pants and knee socks. Malik was cleaner than they.

One soldier hooked a thumb over his shoulder, to show Malik he had to go. In Hebrew the boy said, "On your feet. Come on."

Malik answered, "I understand you."

"How do you know Hebrew?"

"How do you know God?"

"What?"

"God is like words. He comes best to the open heart."

"Is this your house?"

"No."

"Who's the dead man?"

"I don't know him. You killed him."

"You have to leave."

"I want to stay."

"You can't."

"Why can I not stay?"

"This isn't your home. Where is yours?"

"In Israel."

"Where?"

"I do not know yet. But I will have one."

"No, you won't."

Malik stood from the ancient stool.

"You do not make that decision."

The rifles of the three soldiers rattled.

The leader said, "Take that body to the cemetery. They'll burn it there."

"Ah, yes. The smoke."

"When you're done, go to the marketplace. You'll walk east to Barfiliya with the others. Don't take anything out of this house."

"So that you may?"

"Get out. Now."

Malik snipped a creamy-orange bud from the trumpet vine and drew a deep breath of it. Leaving the garden, he dropped the flower at the young Jews' feet.

✳ ✳ ✳

Malik slung the dead fellah over his good left shoulder. He was not the only one in Lydda carrying a corpse to the cemetery.

People streamed out of homes and the corridors between streets. Few had luggage for their possessions. Most wrapped extra clothes in bedlinens or potato sacks, rolled their belongings in carpets, stuffed them in woven hampers. Many brought precious things, brass from their tables, framed pictures of family and ancestors. Husbands and uncles crooked small children in one arm, bundles in the other. Wives balanced baskets on their heads. Elderly men wore linen suits and headdresses as if going off to pray. Many old men held the hands of granddaughters walking to exile on cheap sandals or barefoot. No one, Arab or Jew, remarked to Malik about the dead man he carried; the fellah was not their tragedy.

Soldiers entered houses to evict more families into the streets. The ten thousands who'd lived in Lydda could not be distinguished from the ten thousands who'd left their homes in Jaffa, Haifa, and Safed. All were refugees now.

In the town square, hundreds of men emerged from the mosque and the church in long queues. Their hands were raised like criminals. Jews marched them from the marketplace to the eastbound road. When the men had gone far enough away, half a kilometer, they were allowed to drop their arms.

Malik passed through the cemetery gates with a dozen others bearing corpses in blankets and on doors. The soldiers emptied cans of fuel on the pyre because a human was not so easy to burn. Greasy fumes twirled up from the flames, melting fat and hair; clothing did not immolate well, either. The soldiers would have done better to strip the bodies, but the young Jews with kerchiefs over their faces did not know this.

Malik carried the villager near the fire. No holy men were present to utter last words, only Jews and bearers of the dead. Malik flipped the fellah off his shoulder; the little villager lay on the ground in a twisted way that looked nothing like the living.

A soldier yelled for Malik to throw the corpse on the burning mound. Malik turned away to leave the soldiers to do that wickedness.

He left through the gates. The market square was not far. His robe no longer smelled washed; the death smoke had got in it.

CHAPTER 100

VINCE

The road to Barfiliya

Vince hitched a ride out of Lydda in one of the many trucks the Israelis commandeered. The day was hot, and he didn't have to walk, so he didn't.

Every quarter mile along the Ramallah road, the Israelis dropped off armed guards in pairs. Soldiers set up checkpoints to make sure the Palestinians carried no weapons and that they kept to the paths and roads leading to the Legion's lines.

Vince rode two miles east to Beit Nabala, then four miles south over an unpaved lane halfway to Barfiliya. Nowhere along the route was there shade, not one bush taller than Vince's waist. The land sizzled like a pan.

He got out of the truck between two sets of guards. Here, the route curved slowly east into the limestone hills of Samaria. The walk to Ramallah would be twenty miles more of this dusty, rolling, remote road with no stream or pond, on one of the hottest days of the year.

Under his straw hat, Vince sat on the blistering ground. Bugs clicked in the rocks. To his left and right, soldiers kept their vigil from high ground, unfazed in the dazzling light. The first refugees had already started out from Lydda's orchards, streets, and homes, walking into this. A few days would be needed for forty thousand Arabs to leave Lydda. Vince would sit as long as he could in this sun, then he'd be finished with Lydda. He could say in truth that he'd done all he could.

Vince put his canteen behind his back so the refugees would not see it. He would need it if Malik came this way.

CHAPTER 101

MALIK

Lydda

The Jews spurred the populace of Lydda to pack faster, pack less, leave their homes. Soldiers shouted threats and fired into the air. The refugees and residents thought the gunshots were more fighting; this made them hide, and the Jews shouted more.

The soldiers did not disguise their looting. Lydda's families were hardly out their doors before the Jews entered behind them. Malik had known the Jews as farmers and builders, then warriors. A people who would survive the world must be all of these. Then in Lydda, the Jews became conquerors. For this, Malik had little taste.

He wandered the public square. A man bumped his right shoulder; the wound made Malik suck his teeth, but it would heal if he kept it clean. He took a bowl of spiced rice he found unattended on a windowsill.

Though the Arabs of Lydda had cars and mules, the Jews made them walk out of the city, to repay them for their revolt after the surrender. The people chose which pieces of their lives would go into banishment with them, what wealth, memory, or comfort. In droves they entered the market plaza. The soldiers forced them into lines, then herded them out through the groves, shooed off to Barfiliya and distant Ramallah. The Arabs of Lydda clung to their bags and sacks as if their possessions were rafts and they might live as long as they held onto them.

Women, children, and old folk jammed the market square. Thousands of younger men had already been sent away, the ones the soldiers had held in the mosque and church.

The people did not weep. Old men walked stoically, each with stories to tell his family of his own long survival in Palestine. The women were strong under the shards of their households. Teenage boys gritted their teeth to hold back curses, girls cast their heads down but glared up through their brows. Sobbing infants were shushed. The people of Lydda would not let the Jews hear even a babe cry.

Malik could do nothing more in Lydda but go from it.

Leaving the plaza, he stepped into a line, hands tucked in his black sleeves. No one else was of his height and size. Malik raised his dark hood against the sun and like a specter walked east out of the city.

✳ ✳ ✳

Malik walked among refugees from the coast; no one around him knew where Barfiliya was. The village might be over the next hill or a destination for tomorrow.

The Jews provided nothing but the path. The Arab column stretched as far ahead and behind as Malik could see. The people had only the food, water, and medicine they carried. Two at a time, soldiers stood near the trail, hard in the sun, hard as the land, watching with arms folded over their weapons.

The first mile was an ugly stretch littered with bullet casings, a sad mile of raw earth, cactus, and scrub. The Arabs called to each other encouragement, how they would return to their homes soon.

The second mile was the same as the first, harsh underfoot, scorching, and full of courage.

In the third mile, the people grew quiet, husbanding themselves for the long trek. Malik trod on his own shadow. More and more he passed goods and furniture discarded onto the limestone shoulders of the trail. Many families veered off the path to rest; they were parents who needed to put down a child, boys and girls with stone-bruised feet, old ones who'd lost their breath to the up-and-down road and the dust.

The Jews stood on high ground. They came down, two by two, on these tired ones.

They approached the elderly first, put them on their feet and took them aside. The soldiers spoke only to the men, for the women would have answered them more bitterly. They made the men give up wallets, gold, and watches.

Walking under his black cowl, Malik willed himself to go unseen. He paused for nothing and kept his eyes on the grimy soles of the family of daughters before him.

In the fourth mile, the terrain began to rise. Malik tramped with the thousands up a steady slope; the view of Palestine became expansive in every direction. To the west lay the fields of Israel; beyond them, the blue sea. Somewhere in the brown east waited Barfiliya and the Arab Legion. North and south, miles of arid hills dared anyone but a nomad to cross.

Ahead, two more soldiers fluttered down from their perch above the trail. They halted beside the worn track and scrutinized every person passing.

One pointed at Malik. "You."

Until now, Malik had drawn no attention. But Allah would free him if he would free himself, and Allah had chosen these two Jews.

Both were boys. Had they been Arabs in Lydda they would have been locked in the mosque.

Malik stepped off the trail. He doubted he would step back on it.

He folded back his hood.

"Effendis."

The boys were not nearly so tall as him. They wore knee pants. Their skin was chestnut.

The first was a rugged sort, hatless, his hair wavy black. The second was sleek, wearing a sock hat on a sweltering day, growing a sparse first beard. They kept a few strides away, outside Malik's reach.

The sleek one pantomimed his desire that Malik take his hands from his sleeves.

In Hebrew, Malik asked, "Why do you want to see my hands?"

The Jews nodded to each other; they'd found an Arab of interest, a Hebrew-speaker. If he could do that, what more might he be hiding?

The people of Lydda hurried past. An old father hissed at his wife and brood, "Come, come, come."

The smaller soldier said to Malik, "Show them to us."

Malik produced his hands.

The slender Jew took one step closer, baited. He eyed Mrs. Pappel's silver band on Malik's left pinky.

The Jew extended a palm. He said nothing; his meaning was plain.

Malik said, "No."

The thin soldier reached for the pistol at his hip. He drew the weapon casually, with a sigh, expecting not to use it. He aimed a Walther P38 at Malik's chest. The German pistol was common, deadly at short range.

Malik said, "I cannot allow you to take this ring."

The soldier closed the remaining two steps to press the P38 into Malik's breastbone. Boredom from his duty in the sun threaded the boy's voice.

"Does it mean more to you than your life?"

To lull the boy, Malik lifted his big left palm between them. He fanned the fingers wide, showing the boy the shining ring he wanted.

Malik brought up his right hand as though he would remove Mrs. Pappel's ring. In a blink, he dipped into his dark sleeve.

Wide-eyed, the Jew raised his bearded chin on the tip of Malik's dagger.

Malik asked, "Does it mean more than yours?"

The other soldier raised his Sten against Malik.

Malik told the slender Jew, "Do not die today. That is not Allah's wish." He lowered the honed point enough to let the boy answer.

The boy said, "You can keep the ring. Keep it."

Malik said, "You may have it."

"What?"

"I will not let it be stolen. I gave my word."

"Then just keep it."

"I will trade it."

Malik nudged the dagger upward.

The thin Jew spluttered, "For what?"

"Your pistol."

"You'll shoot me."

"Allah has other lands for us to see, young man. I will not shoot you. You and your friend will not shoot me. You will let me walk away. I will disappear. Yes?"

"Alright. Yes."

"This is your vow? Before Yahweh?"

"Yes."

To the Jew aiming his Sten, Malik said, "You, too. Give your vow. Before Yahweh."

The boy on the tip of Malik's knife said his friend's name, urging him. "Ehud. Fucking vow."

"I vow." The soldier named Ehud lowered his Sten.

Malik said, "Take the ring."

The thin Jew did well, he trembled only a little to slide the band off Malik's pinky. When it was gone, with the knife tight under the boy's beard, Malik pressed down on the Walther between them.

"I will take this."

The boy let the pistol go.

Malik eased the dagger's point until the Walther, the Sten, and the knife were aimed at no one.

He slid his hands again into his sleeves. He had already shown the two Jews the speed with which he could bring them out.

Malik backed away. Lydda's people streamed by on the trail, looking nowhere but to exile.

He backed away from the two Jews, kept backing until they turned from him to accost another man.

Malik walked north into a featureless land.

CHAPTER 102

VINCE

July 20

TEL AVIV
ISRAEL
By Vincent Haas

Herald Tribune News Service

Once again, the war between Israel and five Arab nations is on hold.

The United Nations has brokered a second truce. The new ceasefire comes after a week and a half of fighting, from July 9 to July 19. The Israelis call this short-lived period of combat "The Ten Days."

Israel emerges from The Ten Days stronger than it went in. The months-old state won almost every battle on every front, and with those battles captured swaths of Arab-held territory it will not give back. The Israeli army, the IDF, swelled its ranks by ten thousand fighters, many of them volunteers from other countries. Because of the U.N.'s porous effort at policing air and sea ports, Israeli soldiers have no lack of guns or ammo.

Israel enters the truce in a truculent frame of mind. This nation of only half a million Jews mourns every death in a world where 6 million have been recently destroyed. They do not forget that they were invaded. They very much want to keep fighting.

So does the Arab street. Since the war started in May, the people of Lebanon, Egypt, Iraq, Syria, and Transjordan, 70 million of them, have been fed a diet of sound and fury at the Jews and false reports of Arab victories from the front. Their leaders have no choice but to mislead their own people, or they will be unseated by the truth. Privately, the five kings and despots are glad to have a break from the war. Throughout the invasion, their armies failed to coordinate. The results show it. Also, the Arabs haven't been as deft as the Israeli in skirting the U.N. blockade. The Arab soldier suffers from dwindling stocks of weaponry and food.

On the southern battlegrounds, Egypt maintains its grip on a strip of seacoast from Gaza to the Egyptian border. Their army failed to expand its foothold in Israel by a single village, though they fought some of the most ferocious combat of The Ten Days—like the struggle for a little kibbutz named Negba on the edge of the desert. A hundred Jewish farmers and soldiers fended off a whole Egyptian battalion for two days of ground attacks and artillery barrages. The Jews lost five dead and sixteen wounded at Negba; the Egyptians sacrificed one hundred dead and two hundred wounded, half the battalion. The Jews—a bunch of whom are guerilla veterans of the war in Europe—took to calling their kibbutz "Negbagrad."

In the north, the Galilee and Jordan Valley, both Syria and Lebanon gave ground. The Israelis pushed them back to their borders. The Golan faces a refugee crisis in the tens of thousands.

Israel made its greatest push in the center, called operation *Dani*, to force another route into besieged Jerusalem.

The first mission of Dani was to seize the twin Arab cities of Lydda and Ramle, home to forty thousand Arab citizens, swollen by refugees to eighty thousand. The two cities are ten minutes east of Tel Aviv. For Israel, taking both was a military necessity.

I entered Lydda with a commando convoy on a lightning-fast raid. After intense fighting and what will total hundreds of Arab deaths—including the unarmed, plus women and children—the city surrendered.

The Jews told the residents of Lydda they could remain, but they'd be provided neither food nor protection. Over the next two days, Lydda suffered a house-to-house battle with a Palmach battalion, grenades thrown into their homes, abandonment by the Arab Legion, curfews, six thousand able-bodied men rounded up and detained, hunger behind every door, peril in every shadow, uncounted dead and wounded in the streets. It was no surprise that nine out of ten Arabs in Lydda decided that life under the Jews was not something they wanted to try.

The IDF had no official order from the government to *goresh otam*—to expel—the Arabs from either Lydda or Ramle. Nonetheless, the soldiers did a great deal to goad the Palestinians' departure. Jews rooted people out of their houses, fired into the air, ransacked Arab homes, then robbed them of valuables on the road out of town. The Israelis made the forty thousand of Lydda go on foot, twenty miles of unforgiving road to Ramallah. This was to punish them for breaking their surrender agreement. Another forty thousand from Ramle were transported in trucks. In the two cities, only a few thousand chose to stay.

The depopulation of Lydda and Ramle took three broiling days, the hottest temperatures of the summer. I sat for two of them beside the searing east-bound trail. I had a good friend in Lydda so I kept watch should he cross my way. Shade, cool, food, water, safety, help—none of these were to be found on the way to Ramallah. Some families shed their possessions, unable to bear them in the heat over the bald white hills. Israeli soldiers stole from many. The walking Arabs were already in a weakened state; July is the month of Ramadan, of fasting. When I finally left the road, I had not found my friend. He's resilient, but I fear for him.

Hundreds died of thirst and heat on the journey east; once more, women and children were in that number. The Jews, true to their word, provided no relief, just herded the Palestinians east.

Once the people of Lydda and Ramle reached the Arab Legion, they were driven in trucks to Ramallah. Many made it as far as Amman, the capitol of Transjordan. Last week, King Husseini faced a mob that had climbed the hill to his palace. They'd come to demand that the Palestinian refugees flooding their city be sent home.

Husseini pushed past his guards into the crowd to face a man shouting for Israel's defeat. The king clouted him upside the head. "You want to fight the Jews, do you? Good. There is a recruiting station at the back of my house. Go enlist. The rest of you, get the hell down the hill."

Of the fifteen thousand fighters Husseini has sent across the Jordan to fight in Israel, one in four is dead or wounded.

I know Husseini. He's glad The Ten Days fighting are over. He's eager for the truce.

The Israelis are not. They want a decision made on the battlefield, not in a boardroom.

We'll see how long the U.N.'s fragile peace can hold these warring neighbors apart.

We'll see, too, how much stronger Israel becomes. And how many more Palestinians will be sent out of Israel.

Reporting from Tel Aviv.

CHAPTER 103

RIVKAH

July 31
Zichron Ya'akov

Mrs. Pappel stood from her porch rocker. She extended her hand to shake on the agreement before the doctor could rise.

"I'll pay you every second Friday."

Major Keisch stayed off the porch, outside the halo of bougainvillea. In the street waited a horse-drawn buckboard. The horse, a chocolate roan, appeared well cared for. The doctor, too, had a manicured look, a recent immigrant from Prague, a tattooed survivor of Auschwitz in a waistcoat and a good pair of trousers. He spoke in sure phrases as if everything were science.

Mrs. Pappel sent Rivkah inside for two thousand mil to give the doctor.

In the dining room, she went to the china cupboard, careful not to be seen from the porch. Rivkah slid open the drawer for placemats, then peeled off the bills from Malik's cash.

When she returned outside, Major Keisch had already helped Mrs. Pappel into the buckboard. He offered a strong hand for Rivkah to climb up beside her. Cheerfully the doctor sat in the wagon bed on sacks of grain. Keisch jumped on, took the reins, and clucked to the horse.

He drove east towards the early sun. The passersby of Zichron nodded to the horse cart, to the hooves and creaks in a way they would not
to an automobile.

The major asked Rivkah, "Are you sure it's a good idea for you to
come along?"

"I have a doctor and a soldier with me."

Keisch chuckled. "You have Missus Pappel."

Outside town, the white grape harvest was finished in the vineyards.
Red grapes flourished now. Farm trucks arrived in the fields, each packed
tight with Arab pickers. The villagers of Fureidis had complained to the
Zichron council about how closely their young men and women were
being transported to and from work, seventy per truck. The elders feared
harm to family relations.

The doctor whistled through the farmlands. Rivkah wondered that
any Jew who'd outlived Auschwitz could ever whistle again. Yet there he
was, and perhaps that was why.

Keisch drove north over dirt lanes between the fields, approaching
the hill of El Fureidis.

Keisch asked Mrs. Pappel, "If I may. Why do you have such a keen
interest in this village?"

"Is my interest keen, Major?"

"Plainly so, madam."

"I simply hadn't thought to explain myself to you. The army's policies have been unfair."

"From your standpoint."

"I understand that has to be your answer. But you're a good young
man, you're trying to tolerate me. So I'll tell you. I have a friend."

"An Arab friend?"

"An Arab friend."

Keisch leaned around Mrs. Pappel to lift an eyebrow at Rivkah,
inquiring if this was how Mrs. Pappel explained herself. Rivkah nodded.
Mrs. Pappel pretended to notice none of it.

Keisch's eyes dipped to Rivkah's waist.

"Please tell me if I'm overstepping."

"I will."

"You've said nothing about the father. Is he in the military?"

"No."

"The government?"

"No."

"He's not…" Keisch cut himself off.

"He's alive. An American. A reporter. He's away."

"Quite a bit, it seems."

"Yes."

"I apologize."

"Don't."

In El Fureidis, Keisch and the doctor helped Mrs. Pappel down from the buckboard. Each took an arm and she floated down like a spread-winged angel. On the other side of the wagon, Rivkah clambered out on her own.

Mrs. Pappel indicated the sidearm holstered at Keisch's hip.

"Leave that in the wagon."

"No, madam."

"Major, right now we are the safest four people in El Fureidis. If one hair is harmed on any of us, your soldiers will clear this village by midnight."

"That is true."

"So why do you need the gun?"

"If the Palestinians want to become Israeli citizens, they'll have to learn to see a Jewish soldier as their own. Not their enemy."

Mrs. Pappel feigned to fan herself.

"Why, Major, that is a remarkably clever thing to say."

Mrs. Pappel took the doctor's arm to enter El Fureidis. Rivkah walked beside Keisch.

She asked, "Where did you grow up?"

"Ein Herod."

"I saw a concert there. Leonard Bernstein."

"My parents were at that."

"It was one of the most wonderful places I've ever been."

Most of El Fureidis were in the fields working. Elders left in the village watched from stone courtyards and street corners. A few women swept the approaches to their doorways while old men in small groups debated. The Arabs of El Fureidis lived with a splendid view of the vineyards they did not own.

Mrs. Pappel and the doctor peered through windows into shops shuttered from the curfew. They admired vegetable and flower gardens and muttered to each other. They spoke gently to children too young to work the vines.

Keisch asked Rivkah, "Why did Missus Pappel want me here?"

"To see that El Fureidis is no threat to you."

"The doctor?"

Rivkah said, "Wait. It's a surprise."

The morning mule wagon from Zichron had arrived in the village center. El Fureidis could not feed itself. Children and the old ones hurried to meet it.

Rivkah, Keisch, Mrs. Pappel, and the doctor walked in the long shadow of a minaret. Beside the mosque stood a row of four red-roofed buildings, all one-story cinderblock. The war had interrupted their construction; they were just bare grey walls and window frames. Mrs. Pappel and the doctor stepped inside one. Keisch and Rivkah stayed in the sun.

Rivkah said, "She's going to ask for your help."

"With what?"

"You own these buildings."

"I do?"

"The army took them for a police station. You don't need them now that the curfew is lifted. Missus Pappel wants to buy them from the Arab owners. She needs the army to release them."

"What will she do with them?"

"The village has no school. No doctor. That building will be a medical clinic. The two in the middle will be a school. The last one," Rivkah pointed, "will have an apartment on the top floor. The first floor will be a tea shop."

"For her Arab friend?"

"He's quite a salesman."

"Is your Missus Pappel rich?"

"Somewhat."

"Rivkah. If I may."

"You may."

"If Missus Pappel was going to ask my help, why are you?"

"I don't know. I did it before I thought."

Keisch crossed his arms and beheld the four buildings.

"Then I suppose I should answer before I think."

"And?"

"Yes."

CHAPTER 104

GABBI

August 1
Tel Aviv

The women of the Kerem were slender-faced and languid. Young and old, they twittered across the neighborhood like birdsong, nothing like European women. Their clothes fit loosely, colorful as plumage, as if they were tropical birds.

Gabbi relied on the cane less than yesterday. Last week, fifty stitches had been removed from the back of her right leg. Since then, she had limped every morning among the Yemeni women, to leave Tarek's house for a few hours, away from Tarek and his sad father.

Ibrahim, the father, waited at the same bistro table where they'd sat on the day they met six weeks ago.

"You're stronger every day." This was his greeting.

Ibrahim came around the metal table to pull out Gabbi's chair and ease her into it. He motioned to a waiter.

He said, "Thank you for joining me."

"I don't like to talk behind Tarek's back."

"I needed to speak with you alone."

"We won't do this again."

"As you say."

The waiter set cups and a kettle of green *qahwa* coffee between them.

Ibrahim said, "Please," for her to pour. Gabbi did. The waiter returned with a plate of dates. The coffee smelled of spice.

He asked, "Did you know there are leopards in Yemen?"

"An odd thing to ask, Ibrahim."

"Perhaps. I have a point."

Gabbi checked herself, to not be unpleasant with Ibrahim.

"Okay."

"When I was a boy, a leopard came onto our land. It took off several of our calves. My father gave me his rifle and sent me out to hunt it and kill it. I was a strong boy."

"I'm sure."

"It wasn't hard to find the leopard. I took a young calf a kilometer from our farm and tied it to a tree. My father's rifle was good. I made a little camp for myself and waited. By the end of the day the cat moved out of the woods. It was careful; it might have smelled my hands on the calf. But it was hungry enough to step into the open. I will never forget the beast's spots, head to tail. I wondered for what purpose God would make such a creature that blended with nothing? Golden when the trees were green, spotted where the grass was straight. I did not know why then, and I do not today."

"Did you shoot it?"

"I put the leopard in my sights. I had it, you see. My hands wanted to kill it. My eyes. My duty to my family. Everything wanted me to kill it."

"But you didn't."

"I fired over its head and scared it away."

"Why?"

"That is another thing I did not know for years. In that moment, I could not obey my father, or even myself. But over the years I have learned, the heart is its own master. The leopard was simply something my heart could not shoot. This is what I told my father."

"What did he say?"

"He said he understood. He punished me. But lightly."

Gabbi opened a hand on the table for Ibrahim to take. He laid his palm on hers. Ibrahim was a handsome green-eyed widower.

"I do not want to speak without my son's knowledge. I want to stay silent. But I do not know how to obey that."

"You have another point, Ibrahim. Please make it."

"You've not told Tarek."

Gabbi left her hand in his.

"Told him what?"

"You are pregnant."

"How did you know?"

"You pee a lot. You throw up. I have had a wife. I raised a boy of my own."

"No. I haven't told him."

"Tarek is broken."

Gabbi pulled back her hand, but Ibrahim gripped her wrist.

He said, "You broke him."

She pulled harder. He let her loose. Gabbi folded her arms across her chest.

Ibrahim said, "He's my son. He talks to me. He's told me of the times you soothed him. How you whispered he was brave and showed him you are brave, too. You made him race to the front of the fight, always to the front. He was afraid if he was in the rear you might not respect him. If he hesitated. You knew this. You pushed him. He shuddered at night and you held him. You held him in the war."

"I didn't. He's a soldier."

"That is something he can no longer be."

"What did you want me to do? Send him home?"

"I understand you could not. As I could not shoot the leopard."

The scented coffee steamed as Gabbi set herself against Ibrahim. She left the coffee and dates untouched, as did Ibrahim. There seemed an agreement that neither might taste anything pleasant while their words were not.

He asked, "When are you due? February?"

"March."

Around his neck Ibrahim wore a purse. He tugged it out from his shirt and, as if opening his chest, spread it apart to show her a roll of cash. He tucked the money away, closed the purse, then took it from around his neck to lay it on the table.

"You have lied to my son before. Lie again."

"I won't."

"Tell him you're going to visit your sister. Tell him you don't love him anymore. Break his heart, I don't care."

Ibrahim pushed the purse in front of Gabbi.

"You will be showing soon. You will have to tell him. Do you know what will happen? You've been with him long enough to kill some Arabs and take his seed, but do you know what the boy will do?"

"You'll tell me."

"When Tarek sees you are pregnant he will demand you not go back to the war. This is why you have not told him. You know he will do everything to keep you and the child away from the fighting. Is this true?"

"Yes."

"You will refuse. When the truce ends you will go back to the war. Is this true?"

"Yes."

"Tarek will go with you. I will beg him, but he will not listen. If I tell him to stay because he is broken, he will hate me and go. If you say to him he must stay because he cannot fight any more, he will go and try even harder to prove it is not so. But it is, and he will die. You know it. I believe he knows it. He will die."

Ibrahim drove a finger into the table.

"Lie to me now. Tell me I am wrong."

"Your son has been a good fighter."

"Tell me I am *wrong*."

"No."

"Tarek has given almost everything. All that is left is his life. Would you let him give that? And what of me? I have lost a wife. Would you let me lose my son, too?"

"Every soldier takes that chance."

"That is not an answer."

"Yes. I would."

"There." Ibrahim lifted his finger off the table as though pulling out a knife. "You are honest."

Gabbi tried to slide the purse back to him. Ibrahim stopped her.

"I would do anything to save Tarek. I do not love Israel as you do."

"I love your son."

"Then help me save him. For his child, help me save him."

"Even if I leave, how do you know Tarek still won't go back to the war?"

"I do not. But if you take him, you will see him dead. I will have no family. Think also, he could get you killed. Would you protect his pride at such a cost?"

Ibrahim wiped his lips with a trembling hand.

"I ask you to build your nation with the living."

Gabbi asked, "What will you do?"

"Rebuild our store. Keep him busy and useful. There will be no shame. Just as you say, Tarek has fought. I will make him see he must honor his mother's death by not adding his own. You will win this war without him."

Ibrahim tapped the purse.

"There is only one chance for all to survive. Leave my house today. This money is no bribe. It will carry you wherever you must go and keep you for a while."

Gabbi picked the purse off the table. She removed only enough to pay for a bus, then tossed the purse down.

"When the war is over, I'll come back."

"You will be welcome."

"I'll tell him the truth."

"He will be here to hear it. And we will make a family again."

"I'll go from here."

"I don't want to know where. Just tell me what lie to say."

"You choose."

She used the cane to stand. Ibrahim rose for her departure.

CHAPTER 105

VINCE

August 2
Qaddura Refugee Camp
Ramallah
Palestine

Hundreds of refugees crushed in on Bernadotte and Vince; thousands more looked on. Six American peacekeepers could do little to hold back the Arabs. Vince shuffled behind the count, keeping a grip inside the man's elbow. Vince could not let go of him or they would be separated.

Bernadotte had come to the Qaddura camp with no schedule, no meetings planned, only to visit the displaced people. Word of his arrival spread, and that the mediator had brought an American reporter. The refugees shouldered close to shout at the Swede and Vince, to make their condition known to the world. Their smell was powerful. The unarmed Americans wedged a path into the Palestinian crowd one step at a time.

Canvas tents in rows seemed without end. The ground was flinty and worthless to hold anything but poverty. No trees darkened the Judean hills. The Qaddura camp had been erected on the outskirts of Ramallah, six miles north of Jerusalem, a half mile above sea level. Displaced Arabs had swelled Ramallah and the city could hold no more. A winter on this unbroken plain in these tents would be ruthless.

The Palestinians yelled at Bernadotte and Vince their hunger, thirst, cold, hard beds, their children's tears, rage. They roared, too, the many names of their lost villages and towns: Qumbaza, Lifta, Sataf, Indur, Tulkarm, Tantura, Beit Mahsir, Daniyal, Ramle, Lydda. The refugees did not stop Bernadotte and Vince from walking the camp but let them go on, even slowly, in fairness to the thousands ahead who wanted to scream at them, too.

CHAPTER 106

RIVKAH

August 5
Zichron Ya'akov

From out of the dark came the slap of a beast's unshod soles on the road, a creak of leather, and a grunt.

On one foot Mrs. Pappel catapulted from her rocker. She hopped to the edge of the steps, then turned to Rivkah, still rising from her own rocker.

Mrs. Pappel asked, "Who else would do such a thing?"

She lurched back to the chair to strap on her false foot. She secured it in moments, then trundled down the steps to stand on her walkway. Rivkah stayed on the porch in the ring of bougainvillea behind Mrs. Pappel.

Neighbors heard, too, and came out. The camel's tread sounded nothing like a horse; on the black pavement of the main street, the strides were slow, measured, desert steps.

Malik rode up in moon shadow to Mrs. Pappel's house. The camel said hello, or complained, as it folded to lower him. Someone on Mrs. Pappel's street called to her; she answered, "I'm fine."

Malik dismounted. With a riffle of robes he stepped onto Mrs. Pappel's walk, barely lit by the lantern in her window. He was massive.

He halted in front of Mrs. Pappel and pushed back his cowl. His eyes and beard were black, but his hand was somehow white as a pigeon. Malik touched fingertips to his brow, then his heart, then reached for her. He wore no rings.

Mrs. Pappel took his hand. "I'll get you some tea."

She passed Rivkah on the porch, dabbing her eyes.

Malik held his place. The resting camel stayed collapsed at the curb.

Rivkah asked, "Do you have a poem?"

"No, child. I have been busy."

She eased down the steps; Malik spread his arms. When his robes enveloped her, she felt as though she'd stepped into a second night, safe and good.

She cupped a hand under his wiry beard. "Go on the porch." Malik's face had lost some of its fleshiness. "Prepare yourself."

He flowed up to the porch. Rivkah went to the street to pet the camel. The beast bent its neck and batted its long lashes. Rivkah scratched the bristly chin.

She whispered, "Well done."

On the porch Malik stood with a teacup and saucer, dwarfing both as he sipped. He would not take a chair, claiming he'd been in the saddle for days. Mrs. Pappel asked if he'd brought her a poem. He said he was working on one and raised a cautionary eyebrow at Rivkah.

Mrs. Pappel said, "I sent Vince to find you."

"To Lydda?"

"He wrote about it. He said he didn't find you."

"I hope he was not hurt. Have you seen him?"

"Not since June. After Hugo was killed."

"I am sad to hear that. Little Hugo was your friend."

Mrs. Pappel said, "He was."

"When will the child arrive?"

"Six weeks."

"Vince will come."

"I don't know."

"It saddens me, also, that you do not know. But he will."

Malik set the cup and saucer on the porch rail. He stood before Rivkah and Mrs. Pappel, broad, blocking the view of the street and the summer moon. He slipped his hands inside his sleeves.

He told them of Lydda.

He spoke first of the commando convoy, the one made famous in Israel. From their speeding cars the Jews fired at everything, Malik said, everyone. He shook his great head, said no more about it, and this said enough.

Following the raid, the city rose up. The Jews put down the revolt, always with a smaller force.

Lydda surrendered.

Malik left the city. He walked scorching kilometers with thousands of Palestinians. On the trail, over dusty hills on a furnace of a day, the Jews fired over the refugees' heads to urge them on. The Jews robbed the Palestinians on the road and gave them no aid. Dozens of Arabs collapsed from hunger and thirst, too old, too young, on the path to Ramallah.

Mrs. Pappel asked, "Did they try to rob you?"

"They did."

"Of your rings?"

"No. Those I gave away. I had only yours left, Missus Pappel. I did not let them take it."

"You should have let them."

"It would not have been a ring they took from me. You understand."

"I do. Where is it?"

"I traded it."

Mrs. Pappel clapped beneath her chin as if she'd just heard an amazement.

"Oh, Malik. For what?"

"A gun."

He raised a bare finger.

"I traded the gun for a good horse in Birzeit. The horse I traded for another, a swaybacked nag in Nablus. The nag for a mule in Jenin. The mule for food from Jews in Gesher. Then on foot to Degania on the Jordan River."

"Why did you go there?"

"I promised a farmer I would return for my camel."

"Be honest. You promised your camel."

"True."

"Then you came here."

"I would have arrived sooner. I traveled only at night. But I did not steal, Missus Pappel."

"I believe you."

"I have remained worthy."

At this, Mrs. Pappel could not keep her seat in the rocker. Malik could not keep his hands in his sleeves.

CHAPTER 107

VINCE

August 10
Tel Aviv

Six UN observers carried the casket. The coffin was pine, the handles of rope. The bare box had been cobbled together recently enough to smell the sap beneath the French flag draping it.

Count Bernadotte saluted with the back of his hand to his forehead in the British fashion. He'd served in no military, and Vince could have told him that a military salute from a civilian was improper. Bernadotte should have simply removed his hat instead. But Vince kept a proper distance behind Bernadotte and the pallbearers. As an American marine, he saluted the Frenchman going home.

The pallbearers paused in front of Bernadotte. The count didn't speak but cast his icy eyes far away. When Bernadotte dropped his salute, Vince did, too, along with thirty French UN peacekeepers on the runway, gathered to say farewell to their countryman who'd stepped on a land mine.

Once the coffin was on the transport plane, the peacekeepers left for their white jeeps. Bernadotte turned to Vince when the plane's propellers began to spin,

Vince asked, "What was his name?"

"Labarrière. Major Labarrière. I believe he called Toulouse home."

"Where did it happen?"

"Not far from Negba. On the Egyptian front. Will you write about him, please?"

"Yes."

"Let's see if we can find a drink, Mister Haas."

✳ ✳ ✳

Bernadotte had no personal guards. He said he lacked the manpower for his own security. He could not in good conscience pull peacekeepers away from duty at the seaports, airports, and front lines so they might guard him instead.

The count measured two pours of tawny sherry into beer glasses. The big glasses bore the logos of British pubs; they were all that could be found in the airport lounge. The bottle was a stroke of luck.

Bernadotte raised his rubied glass. Vince matched him. The count made no toast, perhaps he had too much to say. They drank and the port went down well.

Bernadotte set down his glass.

"I am reminded today of what I established during the end of the war in Germany. The work in the service of peace and humanity is often extremely dangerous."

Vince sipped and kept quiet. Bernadotte wanted to muse.

The count asked, "Did you know the last British officer to sail away from Palestine at the end of the Mandate occupation spit on the dock?"

"I did."

"That, I think, is the single most representative act of the great powers in this land. When I accepted this task of mediator, I was promised three hundred observers. I have less than half. Most arrived in the past five days. None are armed. It is impossible, as you have observed, to supervise the truce if I do not have sufficient staff and equipment. Now my men are dying. Last week, I attended the departure of another casket, a Norwegian shot by a sniper in Jerusalem."

"What are you hearing from the Israelis?"

"What do I hear? Laughter. Israel considers the United Nations a joke. They flaunt the embargo and the truce. Ben-Gurion himself takes pride in rejecting every one of my proposals. Do you know what he calls the United Nations Organization?"

"No."

"UNO schmoono."

"I can hear him saying that. What about America?"

"No help will come from America. Your President Truman is too busy with the Berlin airlift and his reelection." Bernadotte fluttered his lips like a horse. "America is too fascinated with its own politics. This does not bode well for your ability to intervene in future world conflicts."

"What about the refugees?"

Bernadotte rotated his glass in a slow circle, as if it were a smaller, better fit for the port. This might have been Bernadotte's gift, to see what he believed.

"I have made the acquaintance of many refugee camps. Never have I witnessed more suffering than what you and I encountered in Ramallah."

"You're not serious. Worse than Europe?"

"In Europe, the Jews could choose whether to return home or not. At the end of the war, the great powers were sympathetic, even cooperative. By contrast, the Palestinians are a forgotten people. They are forbidden from homes and fields that have been taken by a people not their own. They've seen their villages destroyed or renamed and repopulated, their crops go down in flames. No Arab nation welcomes them, particularly the ones who invaded. The Jews did not face this after the war in Europe. Yes, I believe the Palestinian condition is worse, for they are forgotten."

"What're you going to do?"

"Continue to press for the refugees to return. If Israel and the Arabs will not negotiate, or the UN makes it too difficult to enforce the second truce, I shall resign and go home myself. With regret."

"Speaking of home, how's the family?"

"Patient. And what of your family, Mister Haas?"

"Mine?"

"The one I understand you may have here in Israel."

"I suppose our situations are very similar." Vince raised his glass. "Here's to us, Count."

CHAPTER 108

GABBI

August 15
Jaladiya
Contested Palestine

Jonny said, "Fire over their heads."

Gabbi loosed a burst from her MG 34. The bullets flew above the wheatfield and the hundred women reaping it. The rounds landed a kilometer away in the Negev dunes.

At the sound of gunfire, half the women left the field. They fled east towards Jaladiya, Sawafir, and Beit 'Affa. The starving Palestinians in these three villages would not quit trying to harvest their grain. Gabbi and the jeep company had orders to stop them.

At Jonny's hand signal, the four jeeps edged forward. Dozens of women in black *chadors* did not run off, the way crows were hard to frighten.

Jonny halted the platoon at the edge of the field. The stalks had grown tall in the hot summer; the women were visible only from the chest up. The sky glowed clear blue, the wheat dun, the Arab women dark-robed and coal-eyed.

Jonny climbed out of his jeep. He shouted, "*Dahaba.*" Go away.

The farmwomen did not stop cutting and binding sheaves.

Jonny had no other Arabic. He switched to Hebrew. "You are on land that belongs to the state of Israel. This field is no longer yours. You must leave it. Now."

The women may have understood but none lifted their heads to Jonny, the jeeps, or the machine guns that could scythe them all.

Gabbi climbed out from behind her machine gun. Jonny motioned for her to keep her seat; some of the boys in the other jeeps, too, told her to stay put.

Her limp was gone but not all the pain. The scars on the back of her leg had not stretched and still stung.

Wheat tassels brushed the pistol on her hip. The first woman Gabbi approached swung her sickle with practiced hands. Another scooped up the felled stalks and held them like a bouquet. Both gazed down at their labor even as Gabbi stood before them.

"Dahaba," she said. "*Min fadlik*." Please.

They ignored her. Gabbi pushed through the wheat to another woman kneeling, gathering the fallen grain.

In Hebrew, Gabbi said, "These men will shoot you."

The woman, head down, said, "I have a child."

Gabbi spoke to the black crown of her hijab.

"So do I. It does not matter to them."

The woman's hands froze on the shorn wheat. She stood, shorter than Gabbi.

"They would shoot women trying to feed their families?"

"Don't make them do it."

"Is that what you will say over me? That I made them shoot?"

The fifty reapers in the field watched Gabbi. Because she was a woman, surely she would help. Gabbi turned back to the jeeps. She shouted for Hillel to shoot again over the Arab women's heads.

Fifty more rounds ripped above the grainfield, but the women would not go.

Jonny ordered the drivers out of the jeeps. Hillel and the other gunners stayed at their weapons. Gabbi climbed into her jeep but did not touch her machine gun.

At Jonny's order, the drivers lifted red petrol cans from the rears of their vehicles. The four of them broke into the wheat, striding through the stalks like hunters. Jonny and the drivers splashed gasoline among the fifty Palestinian women, daring them to hold their ground or be drenched.

The women shouldered their sickles and blew from the wheatfield like low, black kites. Jonny struck the first match. The gas and the harvest-ready grain gulped the flame.

A rifle barked. Gabbi reached for the grips of her machine gun just as a second rifle shot snapped above the crackle of the spreading fire. Standing tall in the back of the jeep, Hillel opened up with his MG 34. He didn't fire over the wheat but into it.

Thirty meters out in the grain, a figure bolted. Hillel walked bullets through the stalks, slicing the tassels until he knocked the man down. Four more young Arabs leaped up from where they'd been hiding. They'd come to guard the women, but the women were gone and they were left in a burning field. The four Arab boys popped off a few more rounds, then dashed.

Hillel and the jeep gunners killed them. Jonny and the drivers sprinkled the red cans and threw matches without regard to where the bodies of the boys fell.

CHAPTER 109

VINCE

August 20
Tel Aviv

Vince had a scotch and dinner alone in the Kaete Dan dining room.

Afterwards, on his veranda, the full moon lit the dead *Altalena* in the shallows. After half a pack of cigarettes, Vince went inside to begin his column.

A knock interrupted his typing. He didn't answer.

The knock repeated. Vince read the opening lines to his column, an opinion piece on the UN, including Bernadotte's harsh comments and mentioning the killed Frenchman. The first paragraph didn't grab. Vince shook the cigarette pack. The pack was hollow; he crushed it. He pushed back his chair, faced the door, and was going to yell if someone knocked again.

A boy's voice came through the door. "Mister Haas?" Barefoot, Vince opened up.

A bellhop, someone's fourteen-year-old, offered him a folded piece of paper.

"Vincent Haas?"

"Yeah."

"I was told give this you."

The bellboy's accent was a bramble, he was some Eastern European kid right off a boat. This was one of the many hopes of Israel.

Vince dug a mil out of his trousers. He traded it to the bellboy for the paper and shut the door. The note read: *We must talk. Downstairs.*

If he'd had another cigarette or a scotch, if he'd liked the opening lines to his column, Vince would have stayed in his room. In two more hours the moon would peak; the *Altalena* would cast no shadow and rest on a platter of pewter. He'd sit on the veranda, look away west for a while, and come in under the ceiling fan if the night stayed hot.

✵ ✵ ✵

Down in the lobby, a pair of bronze young men waited in khaki shorts and white shirts. They had a cleanness that smacked of zeal. The desk clerk took pains to look elsewhere.

The two shook Vince's hand and invited him out for a coffee because they had something to say. They identified themselves as Spiro and Cohen. Both were South African immigrants. Spiro, the taller one, told Vince not to bother remembering their names because they were phony.

In silence, they walked two blocks to a café. Only a little traffic plied Tel Aviv's coastal road, a few strollers took the night air. Along the way, Spiro and Cohen never glanced at the charred hulk of the *Altalena*. Vince guessed they were not Irgun.

He sat with them around a bistro table on the coffee shop's unlit patio. The café was ready to close but Spiro went inside. The seashore had no breeze and the night felt like a held breath.

Vince said to Cohen, "You're Stern Gang."

"Yes."

"What do you want with me?"

"We'll wait for the coffee."

Spiro returned with three mugs, then went back in for three glasses of *raki*, a Turkish anise. The Sternists touched their shot glasses, neither made a toast nor included Vince. They drank, and he drank after them.

Spiro said, "You know Bernadotte."

"I do."

"Well enough to get him a message?"

"Depends on the message."

"Tell him we're going to kill him."

Vince stood from the table. With the backs of his knees he pushed away the chair.

Spiro asked, "Walking away, mate?"

"I shouldn't have walked this far."

Cohen, apparently a calmer man, extended an arm. "Sit down. We only want you to warn him. That's fair, right?"

Spiro dipped his head at Vince's chair, a promise to contain himself better. Vince sat.

"Why the hell are you telling me this?"

Both Sternists sipped coffee. They looked to each other to see who would answer.

Cohen said, "You know we'll win the war, yeah?"

"I figure."

"Bernadotte doesn't seem to get that."

Vince raised a finger to make a point but lowered it quickly. These were dangerous boys.

He said, "You do something like that, the rest of the world's going to come down on Israel."

Tall Spiro leaned in. He gestured with big hands.

"Come down on us? Tell me something. Where was the rest of the world when the Jews were burning in Europe? Where was the goddam UN while we threw out the British? When the Palestinians started a civil war with us? When Egypt and the Muslims invaded us? Where was the world, mate, eh? Now the UN sends some Swede Gentile to dictate terms to us. Let's be clear, right? The rest of the world doesn't spill one fucking drop of blood every time the Jews are attacked. We've got our own state because of Jewish blood. No one else's."

"There's been plenty of Arab blood, son."

Cohen reached out to compel Spiro back into his chair. Cohen was cool. He had the feel of a trigger man.

Vince asked, "Like I said, why are you telling me?"

Cohen replied, "Because we shouldn't have to do this. The UN ought to be rising up on our account. Only they're not."

Vince hadn't touched his coffee; the mug steamed, slow, like Spiro, to cool in the warm night. These two assassins were the future of Israel, too. What would that bellboy grow up to be?

Cohen said, "Tell Bernadotte that what Israel wins on the battlefield won't be given back at some council table. We'll never hand the Negev to the Arabs. We'll never let Jerusalem be an international city. As in fucking never. Tell him to do that to Stockholm."

Big Spiro pushed back his chair, ready to stand as if they were done. "Make sure he knows."

"Funny thing. He does."

"Then for fuck's sake, tell him to walk away. Do what the UN did before, just leave it alone. We'll settle it between ourselves and the Arabs."

"The UN can't walk away."

"Why not?"

"This is their first peacekeeping mission. If they screw this up, no one will listen to them again."

"No one's listening now."

Cohen asked, "What about Bernadotte?"

"He'll stay."

"Even if he knows we'll kill him."

"Even if."

"Why?"

"This isn't his first death threat."

"It's the first from us."

"He's a brave man."

Spiro said, "I'll give him that."

"What's the point of killing him?"

Cohen answered. "Israel's four months old. You get that, right? We're a fucking child, we're still weak. Like you said, Bernadotte's got the UN behind him, probably the rest of the world. Maybe they'll overcome Ben-Gurion, we don't know. But if Bernadotte won't back down, if Ben-Gurion starts cutting deals, we'll put everyone on notice that the people of Israel won't tolerate it."

Vince said, "You're going to make everyone think Israel's made up of extremists."

Cohen sat back. "It is. One way or another."

Together, Spiro and Cohen, whoever they were, folded tan arms across their white shirts. Spiro bit his lip, shaking his head. Even angry, he didn't seem eager to be a murderer.

Vince would address the two Sternists one more time, then he'd leave them at the dark café that was waiting to close, with no night wind off the sea to cool or ruffle anything about them. On his walk back to the Kaete Dan, he'd find a shop for more cigarettes. Then he'd sit on his veranda to watch the moon fall.

He asked them both, "Were either of you in the German camps?"

Cohen said, "Me, no."

Spiro said, "After the war. I recruited for the Haganah."

"Then you saw."

"Yeah. I saw."

"How can you do that to another people?"

"It's not the same."

"It's close enough for me to ask."

Spiro knit big fingers as he leaned again onto the bistro table. Cohen stayed out of the conversation. He was a man with his path already chosen.

Spiro said, "The Palestinians' misery is their own. Ours is ours. No need to compare."

"Fair."

"I know you, Mister Haas. I've read you. I wanted to meet you."

Vince tried to thank him, but Spiro said, "Shut up, mate."

"Right."

"Listen to me. Nature made you, made everyone else on earth. But it didn't make the Jew. History did. From the start we've been tooled to survive, and to do it alone. Egypt, Rome, Germany, Britain, Egypt again, fuck all. History's been a bastard to the Jew."

Tall Spiro stood.

"We've survived it all. We will this time. Go tell Bernadotte he won't."

Cohen rose, too, nodding as though his partner had finally come around.

The duo walked away. The café lights went off. Vince bummed a few cigarettes from the shopkeeper as the man left.

Vince would finish his column in the morning. He'd write nothing about Spiro and Cohen. He wouldn't notify the Tel Aviv police or mention the Stern Gang's threat to Bernadotte.

They'd picked the wrong messenger.

CHAPTER 110

GABBI

August 28
Tell as-Safi
Contested Palestine

Jonny slowed the jeep on the fertile bottom of the Wadi 'Ajjur. When he stopped, he climbed from behind the wheel; freckled Hillel eased down from the rear gun mount. Gabbi swiveled out of the front gunner's seat. Each carried a canteen.

They walked not far through thistles and wild mulberry. Hillel's stride had a small hitch from the hole shot in his calf two months ago. Today was his second day back with the commando company.

A stack of rocks marked a meter-wide hole in the ground. A rusted wheel and a bucket on a suspect rope dangled over the well. On her knees Gabbi peered down; an ancient cool breathed back.

Using the creaky handwheel, she lowered the bucket until it splashed. She let it fill, then cranked it up. Jonny and Hillel walked away to piss facing the parched Judean hills ten miles east and, a mile away, the rocky mound of Tell as-Safi.

The three dipped their canteens in the bucket, drank the clean water, and topped off. Jonny knew of this well because last month the jeeps had chased a dozen Arab women away from it.

They clambered back into the jeep. Jonny took off up the wadi's sloping bank, then out onto a rising plain of tinder-dry brush and knobs of chalk and limestone that looked as if the bones of the earth were showing through. The one-mile drive east to Tell as-Safi gained a hundred meters in altitude. Jonny picked his way between the outcroppings, careful of mines so close to the front lines.

Gabbi, Jonny, and Hillel patrolled alone this morning. The four other platoon jeeps were two miles north checking on Mughallis and al-Tina, two other emptied villages along the Wadi 'Ajjur.

Jonny crested the ridge. He drove the plateau north across a slow grade, down to Tell as-Safi. Blanched rocks and the ruins of an ancient watchtower broke the mossy height. This elevated ground would be impossible to cultivate but had once been ideal for the Crusaders to overlook the wadi and the lowlands west and south.

Hillel and Gabbi kept their hands on their machine guns out of routine more than threat. A week ago, Tell as-Safi had been home to twelve hundred Arabs, with a mosque and marketplace, homes of stone and mud brick. Most of the structures were gone now, the mosque, too. The IDF had dynamited them down to the foundations to stop the Palestinians from returning, or even hoping they might. Only sixty houses out of three hundred were left standing in Tell as-Safi.

Jonny halted at the edge of the village. Hillel started to shuffle out of the rear of the jeep but Jonny stopped him.

"Gabbi can do it."

Skinny Hillel protested. Jonny told him he was limping too much and would take too long to clear the village. Hillel carped that Gabbi had a bad leg, too.

"She'll do it faster than you." Jonny told Gabbi, "We'll be right behind you."

She scooped her Sten off the floorboards, then stepped out of the jeep.

Gabbi walked at a good clip; her right leg worked fine. Jonny shadowed her twenty meters back on the dirt lanes. Hillel stayed at his rear-mounted gun. The army's explosives teams had done a better job of rubblizing this village than centuries could do. The remaining homes were the most solid ones; they'd been preserved to serve later as dwellings for the immigrants flooding into Israel from around the world.

Gabbi kept a loose hold on her Sten gun. She sniffed for cookfires and keened an ear for talk in the unwrecked houses. She expected to find no one in Tell as-Safi. She poked the Sten's barrel into every third building. Gabbi found scattered clothes and rubbish where the Palestinians had been run off too fast, cupboards left open, wooden toys on earthen floors, birds' nests in the rafters.

The August morning wore on, lengthy and stifling. The dust of Tell as-Safi's destruction coated Gabbi's tongue, adding to her thirst. She drained her canteen before turning onto another dirt street. Jonny had taken to idling at corners. Hillel sat on his sandbags in the rear of the jeep.

On this block, only one house was still intact. Gabbi approached, Sten relaxed but ready. The door was ajar; she stepped in out of the sun. As in every other house, the first room was bare. The soldiers before her had trucked away all the furniture and utensils. Gabbi stepped over broken clay pots and withered flowers. The concrete floor had been painted green like grass. In the middle of it sat an Arab child.

The little boy didn't cry or speak. He raised both dirty arms. Gabbi lifted her Sten to firing position, tight to her shoulder. She circled the child, checking for tripwires. The boy rose to his bare feet to keep his dark eyes on her. Following the Sten, Gabbi cleared the rest of the house, two more blank rooms. She made sure nothing more was involved here, then picked the boy up off the green floor to carry him outside.

From the end of the block, Jonny came spurting up. He skidded to a halt in front of Gabbi and the child.

"What the hell is this?"

In her arms, the little boy covered his eyes with one pudgy hand, the sun was too sudden for him.

Behind his machine gun, Hillel said, "There's no way that kid's alone."

Gabbi hefted the boy, a gentle jiggle.

Hillel swiveled for enemies in Tell as-Safi. Jonny drew his sidearm.

She asked the boy, "You have a mommy? Where is she?"

The Arab child had looped one arm behind Gabbi's neck. The other hand he took from his eyes to stick fingers in his mouth. Gabbi pulled them out, his hand was too dirty.

"Let's find your family." Gabbi jostled him again to keep his attention. She pointed. "There?" She tried different directions. "There?"

Her hand swept the village. When she indicated north, to a footpath leading down the hill to cereal fields and an olive grove, the little Arab boy said, "*Na'am.*"

Yes.

✳ ✳ ✳

Jonny crashed through the wheat field, a fast, crazy course to scare up anyone hiding. Hillel fired bursts through the stalks, but no heads popped up. The tasseled tops were bent; the wheat was overripe and heavy; it should have been harvested weeks ago.

Gabbi held the Arab boy tight. Likely he'd never ridden in a car before or been so close to a firing machine gun. The boy clung but did not cry. He smelled sour from hunger and days without clean water. He stunk like a soldier.

Jonny carved figure eights in the field. When he raced down the western edge of the wheat, the little boy's eyes snagged on a stand of olive trees.

Gabbi said, "The orchard."

Jonny wheeled around. He eased the jeep out of the field, then entered the shade beneath rows of old-growth trees. A hundred grey trunks twisted out of the ground like fat smoke; the olive grove was ancient. The thinnest branches bowed under swelling fruit. In another month the rains would signal the picking season, perhaps the first season in a thousand years with no one in Tell as-Safi to pick.

Jonny drove down an old wagon path. In Gabbi's lap the child squealed at shadows that lie ahead. Jonny slowed. The shadows shifted.

Jonny and Hillel cursed at the same time.

Beneath a knurled and kingly olive tree huddled a group of Palestinians. Most were elderly men, faces as worn as the olive bark.

Five old women sat on the grass in black chadors. Eight toddlers sat, slept, or wriggled among the women.

One woman approached the jeep. The rest stayed under the dipping limbs of the tree. The woman reached for the child. The boy's tiny hands forgot Gabbi in a moment. The old woman rested him on her hip. The boy stuck filthy fingers in his mouth.

In Hebrew, the woman said, "Thank you. He wandered off."

Jonny asked, "Why are you here?"

"We are from Sawafir. The Jews came. They told our village to go east. Seven hundred of us walked away. We could not keep up. This is where we stopped. The others went on."

"How long have you been here?"

"Three days."

Jonny said, "You need to go."

The old woman blinked slowly, owlishly at Jonny. She gestured to the people under the tree.

"All the other women are blind." She touched the little boy. "All the men walk with a cane. The children are as you see. We are not here because we want to be."

In English, Gabbi said to Jonny, "They'll die."

"What do you want me to do?" He motioned to his jeep. "Where do you want me put them?"

Gabbi reached behind her seat for the boxy radio. She handed Jonny the mic.

"Call a truck."

Jonny radioed the base at kibbutz Gevim. Quickly a farmer agreed to bring his cattle truck twenty kilometers north to Tell as-Safi, then take the Palestinians another ten kilometers east to the truce line. The sighted woman informed the others. They took the news as if it were another unfortunate thing.

Gabbi sent Jonny and Hillel back to the well in the wadi to fill canteens and bring back the bucket full of water. She sat with the Arab child, tried to play clap-hands but the boy would not. He put out a small palm for her to give him something, but she had no food or gift. He sat beside her, not sad but blank, and waited along with Gabbi for the jeep and the water.

When Jonny returned, the Palestinians drank not greedily; they shared the bucket when Hillel set it in their midst. Jonny handed out the canteens. Some men drizzled water over their hands and put themselves on their knees facing east to pray. The blind women closed their old, wild eyes to rest after they realized they would survive the day.

When the cattle truck arrived, the kibbutznik and Hillel helped the Arabs into the bed. The women went on first, then the lame men, the children last. Gabbi carried the boy to the truck to hand him up to the sighted woman. The boy reached back for Gabbi as the farmer closed the rear gate.

The truck pulled away; the little boy extended both arms through the slats. He did not know what a Jew was.

Once the truck was gone, Gabbi said to Jonny, "When we get back to Gevim, I'm going to take leave for a while."

Jonny didn't object, only asked why.

"My sister's having a baby."

The three got into the jeep. Jonny drove out of the orchard. Gabbi tipped her machine gun skyward, Hillel sat on his sandbags. Tell as-Safi was empty now.

CHAPTER 111

MALIK

September 2
El Fureidis

Malik stood beneath fresh pine joists inlaid to the cinderblock walls. The aroma of sap was sticky and green. The flooring for his apartment would be hammered on top of these beams. Malik imagined himself lying on his floor, sniffing through the boards for these clean, new joists. He'd never in his life smelled such trees in the Negev. Israel had forests.

Gabbi came to stand beside him. Both mopped their brows. Over the swash of saws, the chink of hammers, she said, "Someone's here."

Vince left his duffel in the sun. He stepped inside the construction site, over the dross of building the new bakery. Ten Arab workers around and above Malik paid Vince no mind. He looked more gaunt than when Malik had last seen him. No pencil was stuck under his straw hat.

Vince waggled a finger at him and Gabbi. "Frick and Frack."

Malik asked, "Who is that?"

Gabbi said, "He means we match."

Malik said, "Missus Pappel gave us these clothes. For the work."

"They're called overalls."

Gabbi said, "Shut up," and stepped into Vince's arms.

The two whispered, then he lifted; her boots came off the ground. Vince swung Gabbi so she might dance a moment on the air, then put her down.

She said, "I'll see you at dinner," then walked away.

Vince said to Malik, "I looked for you."

"In Lydda. I was told."

"I'm sorry I didn't find you."

"I'm glad you did not. I needed to stay. To see."

"I think I did, too."

Malik said, "My friend."

Vince clasped Malik's hand. "I've never seen you out of your robes."

"I have lost weight."

"You're still a big fucking man."

"I feel unclothed. Have you seen Rivkah?"

"She's in Tel Aviv at the doctor. Missus Pappel told me I'd find you here."

"Your child is due soon."

"Three weeks."

"You came."

"Yeah. I did."

"Did something happen?"

"No. I was going to come back at some point. I guess that point arrived."

"Everyone will be relieved. Rivkah most of all."

"Malik, I'm not a son of a bitch."

"I know that phrase."

"It's bad."

"A dog. To be a dog's son."

"Malik."

"Why is this bad?"

"Malik."

"Yes, of course. But I like this phrase. I may use it in a poem."

"Don't."

"No?"

"Just don't."

"As you say. Now you are here, will you stay for the birth?"

"I don't know what's going to happen."

Malik clamped Vince's shoulder. "There is a saying in the desert."

"Of course there is."

"We say when a man moves, his eye is on the horizon. When he camps, his world is the fire."

"What does that mean?"

"You are here. Be here."

An Arab worker brought in Vince's duffel from the street. Vince looked around at the demolition of old plaster, concrete pads and walls, everything hammered to bits, carted away, then built new.

Vince asked, "She put you in charge of all this? Masons, carpenters?"

"Yes."

"You don't know a thing about construction."

"No. It is of no matter."

Malik drew a proud breath against the straps of his blue overalls.

CHAPTER 112

RIVKAH

Rivkah stepped through the opening that would soon be the front door for the schoolhouse. Arab workers roiled dust as they poured a fresh bag of cement into a wheelbarrow, then water, then stirred with a rake. Brooms, hammers, and shovels flung up more dust. Vince, bare-chested in his straw hat, shoveled at a pile of broken concrete. A bandana covered his mouth and nose.

Rivkah stopped ten meters behind him. Vince's ribs stuck out; his exertion had turned the bullet scar in his shoulder pink. She'd touched every knot in his back, every bump of his spine.

Rivkah coughed, not for his attention, but from the dust. She said his name as he turned. "Vince."

His shovel clattered on the cluttered ground. Vince came to her, looking at his boots as if he might stumble. He took off the straw fedora, pulled down the kerchief, then gestured to his grimy, sweat-streaked self.

He said, "Not sure I should hug you."

"You're here."

"Malik put me to work."

"He told me you would come. So did Missus Pappel."

"You didn't believe them?"

"I hoped."

"And now?"

"I hope you'll hug me."

Rivkah curled a finger to beckon him. Vince dropped his straw hat to slide his hands around her roundness. Rivkah pressed her cheek into his sweaty chest. Vince was dirty and glowing; this made him even more present.

She said, "You could have written."

"I did."

"I mean letters."

Vince kissed the top of her head, then eased her away. They faced each other, close enough to touch again.

He asked, "Everything okay?"

"The baby is fine."

"You look magnificent."

"You do, too. An honest day's work suits you."

"Can I be honest?"

Rivkah laughed. "I can't tell you the number of times I've wished you couldn't be."

"Every column I wrote. I knew you'd read it."

"I did."

"I figured if I wrote things important enough, you'd forgive me for being away."

"You're Vince Haas."

Rivkah ran a finger down his abdomen. The gesture was intimate; it left a streak on his front.

He said, "Malik's a tough boss. I'll be washed for dinner."

Vince returned to his shovel. Rivkah left the schoolhouse but stayed outside in the light to watch him heft rubble into a wheelbarrow. She'd seen Vince shovel many times, in the citrus orchards, in graves, trenches. The child, she thought, will have that strength.

✳ ✳ ✳

Zichron Ya'akov
Israel

A year had passed since they'd been at the same table in Massuot Yitzhak.

Mrs. Pappel raised her glass first. "Hugo."

Rivkah sat to Mrs. Pappel's left, Vince on her right. Gabbi and Malik faced each other at the other end. Malik wore an ebony button-up tunic with long sleeves. A black headdress curtained his neck and shoulders. His beard and hair were combed. He smelled scrubbed. With Mrs. Pappel, all of them toasted Hugo.

Gabbi asked Malik if he had a poem for the occasion.

Malik seemed to deem this a challenge, that he was becoming too civilized. His poems came from the desert, and if he had not a poem, perhaps he had not the desert. He raised a finger.

"Child, you will have a poem before you sleep."

A roasted chicken simmered on a platter; vegetables had been baked in the juices. Wine was poured for all save Malik. Candles made the meal seem a holiday.

Mrs. Pappel asked Vince, "Will you carve?"

Vince's clothes had been washed and ironed, he'd bathed and shaved, but he remained a scarecrow. He did not stand at Mrs. Pappel's request, but only gazed at the table. The last time Vince had been in this house, Hugo's corpse lain between these candlesticks.

Mrs. Pappel leaned on her cane to stand. She swept the backs of her hands at the table.

"Shoo. Shoo. All ghosts go away now."

She returned to her chair and quietly leaned her cane against the tablecloth.

"That's done. Vince, if you would carve, please."

The meal began. First the conversation focused on Rivkah and her doctor visit, did it go well? Yes, she said, routine. Rivkah told Gabbi that she liked the pediatrician in Tel Aviv and when Gabbi's time came she should go to him. Malik reported that the construction of the school, shop, clinic, and apartment in El Fureidis was faring well. Malik called Vince a good worker. Mrs. Pappel reminisced about the first time she'd put Vince to work in Massuot Yitzhak, filling a water bucket to irrigate an orchard of plum saplings at the bottom of a hill.

She said, "I had to walk by every hour to make sure he wasn't sitting on the bucket."

Rivkah covered Vince's hand. He took the ribbing well and did not pull away.

The sun set slowly. When the food was eaten and the wine gone, Mrs. Pappel made tea. The house's west-facing windows stayed aglow. Darkness held off. Had night fallen faster they might have left the table with wishes of a good evening. Rivkah wanted them to go; the time together had been perfect.

Then the talk of war began. Vince asked about Tarek, how he was faring? Gabbi said things she'd not said before. Tarek was finished with fighting. He'd done a great deal for Israel in the war, but the fear never left him anymore. It built until it made him unreliable. He knew it, his father knew it. Even so, he accepted it as long as Gabbi was beside him in his father's house. But the war was going to come back, and when it did she'd return to the commando company, even pregnant. Tarek would never stay behind.

Malik, who did not know Tarek but knew men of every kind, said, "No. He would not."

Gabbi admitted she wouldn't stop him. He had a right to fight for Israel; she would never take that from him, or from Israel. But in the war again, Tarek would try to protect her and the child. He was no good anymore in the fight: too quick, too nervous, unpredictable. He'd likely die or cost Gabbi her own life. To save Tarek the only way she could, she took the child without telling him and went away. She let him believe they were finished, she did not love him. When the war was done, she'd go back to him if he would take her. If he would forgive her.

Rivkah reached for her sister's hand; she held it as the sunlight faded to its end and the talk turned to Lydda.

Gabbi, Malik, and Vince had all been there. Gabbi had been wounded there. Vince described Moshe Dayan's commando raid. Gabbi told how she and Tarek and the armored car had fought their own battle in Lydda. Malik explained how he emerged from the city with no rings. He claimed he'd stolen nothing. Vince spoke of a small mosque where refugees were killed.

Malik asked, "You were there?"

"In the alley."

"I was inside."

The two shut down their talk of the small mosque. Perhaps if they'd been alone, they might have shared more.

Rivkah stood. The child rising with her gave her a sort of command.

"I'm getting tired, so I thank you all. Malik, go to the porch. Light your pipe and write Gabbi's poem. Missus Pappel and Gabbi will wash. Vince and I will clear the table."

She clapped in a way that meant now.

By the time the meal was cleared, full night had fallen. Malik smoked and muttered on the porch. Rivkah walked Vince to the back-yard, to a bench among Mrs. Pappel's black-eyed Susans and purple coneflowers. The plants were perennials; Mrs. Pappel said she would never live in another house.

Vince asked, "Where do you want me to stay?"

"Interesting word. Stay."

"Where does Malik sleep?"

"In a tent."

"Shit."

"Stay with me."

"Okay. I'd like that."

"Vince."

He put up a hand between them.

"Can we not? I'm sorry." He touched fingertips to his forehead, then jerked the hand away to show it held nothing. "There's a lot. Can we just sit? Tonight?"

"Yes."

Vince pinched a coneflower, sniffed it, then tucked the bloom in his shirt pocket. He'd done the same in the citrus grove of Massuot Yitzhak when they'd met, their first talk. He'd plucked an orange leaf, smelled it, and kept it.

CHAPTER 113

MALIK

September 4

Vince and Gabbi arrived early with the Arab laborers. Malik greeted them with a wave.

Hammers thudded in the tea shop, bringing down a wall for the expansion of the kitchen. Gabbi took up her wheelbarrow and headed that way. Vince shouldered a sledge and followed. Malik followed both.

In his straw hat, Vince stepped up with the Arabs to pound the old blocks of the wall. He battered tirelessly, barebacked, throwing his long limbs into every swing. Gabbi trundled in and out, load after load. She and Vince never exchanged a word. Both seemed satisfied, shedding something through their sweat. Malik left them to it.

✳ ✳ ✳

When the workday was over, Gabbi walked by herself down the footpath between Zichron and El Fureidis. She disappeared into the trees like a spirit. Vince lingered at the work site with a cigarette. A dozen Arab laborers joined him, Malik too. They sat cross-legged on the ground. Malik in his overalls translated for Vince, who shared his cigarettes.

The Arab men were literate. All spoke Hebrew but no English. Before the war they were not pickers of grapes and olives but shopkeepers and tradesmen: a grocer, a blacksmith, a leather tooler, a cooper, one man knew how to make cheese. When the peace returned, they would go back to their professions.

Vince showed curiosity for the Arabs he'd toiled alongside all day without speaking to them, but he had seen the honor in their toil. Though he was a stranger to them, his questions were not simple.

He asked, "Why do you stay when so many others have villages have gone?"

"El Fureidis is our home. Our children's home. Why should we go?"

"Don't you fear the Jews?"

"Only as an enemy."

"Do you hate them?"

"We've not made them our enemy."

"You're Muslims."

"Yes."

"Isn't this a holy war?"

"Some say it is. That is not the truth of Islam to us."

"Do you believe you can live with the Jews?"

"Think of your question. We have lived with them for a thousand years."

"What about Palestine?"

"What was Palestine? It is a name for land. It was no country."

"Can you live in a Jewish nation?"

"For five hundred years this was a place run by Turks. Then the British. Now the Jews. The Jews may yet be the better of the three."

"What if they're not?"

The Arabs pointed to each other. "That is my brother." "He is my father." "He is my cousin."

Malik said, "They mean they will be together. Here."

One Arab indicated Malik.

"He is Bedu. He is the desert. He has no brother in El Fureidis, no property. He has found a reason to stay."

Malik pressed a hand to his coveralls over his heart; he inclined his head to the shopkeeper who said this.

The Palestinians departed with wishes for a good night's rest. In crisp amber light, Malik and Vince walked together down to the ravine, up to Zichron Ya'akov, dirty and late for dinner. With their hearts on their tongues, they finally talked about what happened in Lydda, when the Jews raced through the city, the small mosque, the road out.

CHAPTER 114

RIVKAH

September 12
Tel Aviv

On Sunday morning, Rivkah asked Vince to take her to Tel Aviv. She wanted to see the *Altalena*. She'd read all his columns about the fighting. After tea and toast, he drove her south.

Vince parked at the Kaete Dan, then walked Rivkah to the sites of the battle.

Strolling the boardwalk along the beach, he pointed out where the Zahal's forces had been arrayed. A few hundred guns here and there, machine guns here, and here. There on the beach, and there, the Irgun ducked behind crates of weapons. "See how close," he said, amazed and sad.

On the beach, at the closest point to the blackened ship, he said, "I jumped in the water here."

She asked, "Where was Hugo?"

Vince walked not far across the sand. He pointed down to the white grains that, like the blue water, could hold no memory.

Weekend swimmers and surfers paddled out to the freighter. They touched the scorched hull and would say for the rest of their lives they'd done that. The *Altalena*, a black wound on the waterfront, had become a curiosity and history.

Jew had killed Jew here. Rivkah had seen too many Jewish deaths, Gabbi even more. Hugo more than all of them. The child would replace one, only one.

Vince escorted Rivkah past The Red House, Ben-Gurion's headquarters. Ben-Gurion could have watched the *Altalena* burn from his windows. Rivkah held the bend of Vince's elbow to slow his long gait.

After a mile walk along the seafront, they reached the Kaete Dan. Rivkah's back and feet had tired. Vince took her inside. At a table in the guesthouse bar, he pulled out her chair below a wicker ceiling fan.

"I'll get you a water."

"What are you having?"

"Whiskey."

"I'd like one, too."

"You're due next week."

"The child will have water. Whiskey for me, please."

A crowd of newsmen milled in the Kaete Dan bar. Cherry paneling lined the long room, the polished bar top gleamed. The bartender was an African. West-facing windows opened to a terrace and a view of the bright sea.

The reporters were sloppy men, or natty and tucked, bearded or shaved, portly and waddling, hawk-eyed and thin, coughing from cigarettes. Israel had marked them all. They walked on the balls of their feet, none sat at the tables or resided on stools. They stood along the bar, as though in a moment they might need to pounce elsewhere. The press were a hunting pack, not resting or lounging in the Kaete Dan, but waiting.

On his way to the bar for the drinks, Vince accepted pats on his bony back. The reporters congratulated him, a few pointed at Rivkah. The top of her belly rose higher than the table. Vince smiled toothily, he seemed to know them all. Rivkah was the only woman in the bar.

None of them was a Jew but her and the bartender. Rivkah had never seen Vince among anyone but Jews and Malik. The journalists in the Kaete Dan moved like him, nimble, gossamer, even the fat ones. They were Europeans, Soviets, Americans from cities other than Vince's. They were in Israel without roots, they blew back and forth across his path as he tried to return with the whiskeys.

❋ ❋ ❋

Rivkah stepped out of her dress and petticoat. Vince picked them off the floor then spread them over a chair.

She said, "I liked your friends."

He sat on the bed to unlace his boots and peel off his socks. Rivkah eased down on the opposite edge of the mattress, facing the bathroom.

"Not sure they're my friends."

"They drink a lot."

"It's the only hobby a reporter can have."

"I'm certain when they're home they collect things and build things in garages."

"No. They drink."

Vince's belt jangled when he lowered his trousers. He tossed the pants on the chair beside her petticoat, then his white shirt. In britches he climbed on the bed to sit against the headboard and a pillow. The Kaete Dan's mattress was bigger than the one they shared in Zichron.

Rivkah had never stayed in Vince's space, not like this. When they'd lain together, it had always been in her bed or under the trees of her kibbutz's orchards. Once they shared a trench, another time a blanket, but never his own room. His typewriter, notebook, pencils, a stack of paper, and an ashtray covered a table in a corner. All the things on the table staked their claim to Vince. He'd tidied up the room, but he was not a tidy man, and the neatness felt contrived.

He cut off the lamp on his side; she cut off hers but did not lie back. Rivkah needed to pee, but she didn't want him to be stretched out and asleep when she came out.

He said, "I'll wait."

On the bathroom sink rested a comb, razor, bar of soap, and a shaving brush. Behind the mirror door she found nothing.

In bed, Rivkah cut off her lamp. She lay beneath another whirling ceiling fan, under the slanting light of a three-quarter moon, and Vince's hand.

She rolled to her side, belly against his hip, her forehead on his bare chest. The smell of the briny sea ghosted through the windows. The night water was quiet, but Vince's slow breathing sounded like the sea.

He ran the pad of his long thumb over her shoulder. Rivkah sensed he was looking down on her.

They lay a long time not sleeping. Vince tapped his thumb on her shoulder over and over. She imagined him at his typewriter tapping like that, thinking what to write.

Later that night, Rivkah woke alone in bed. She moved to the open door to the veranda. Vince was standing out there in his trousers, with a cigarette, rapping his knuckles on the railing.

The moon, low to the sea, hovered right above the *Altalena*, as if it had come down to study the ship with him.

CHAPTER 115

MALIK

September 17
El Fureidis

Ten wheelbarrows waited in the alley behind the tea shop. Grey mounds of concrete powder filled each barrow, waiting to be stirred with water, then poured into the new slab for the kitchen floor. Three men kneeled inside the shop, waiting with trowels.

Malik stood to the side. He held no tool, did no work. The Arabs had no need to see him as an equal. At his signal, water buckets were dumped into the first four wheelbarrows.

An Arab hurried into the alley to find Malik. He said the Jewish girl was searching for him.

"She does not look well."

Malik cut through the tea shop, stepping past the trowelers, across the bare dirt. Out front, in the street and sun, Rivkah stood alone. She seemed burdened, as if stricken ill on the path to El Fureidis.

"Do you need to sit, girl?"

"I need to see Vince."

"What is wrong?"

"I have to tell him something."

"What is it? Is it the child? Missus Pappel?"

"No."

"Good. Praise Allah."

"Malik, where is he?"

"Can you tell me first?"

"It's terrible. It's going to make him leave."

"Vince will do what Vince will do. Come here."

Malik guided her by the elbow to a stack of cinderblocks in the shade of the tea shop. He eased her down to sit.

"Tell me what happened."

"The radio."

"Yes."

"Count Bernadotte is dead."

"Dead? Do you mean killed?"

"Yes."

Rivkah told him the few details available. The news was fast-happening, sketchy, ruthless, bloody.

She said, "I have to tell him."

Malik said, "I will do it."

In the tea shop, clinic, and schoolhouse behind them rang hammers.

Rivkah asked, "Why you?"

"Because if you are the one to tell him, you will be linked to it forever. We cannot have that. You know Vince. This is how his mind works. He remembers everything."

Rivkah stood from the stacked blocks. Malik lay a soft hand on her shoulder to tell her, gently, that she should not question. He was going to do as he said.

She said, "Thank you."

"Rivkah, do not go home."

"Why not?"

"When I tell him, he will leave here and go to Missus Pappel's house. Then he will go somewhere, and he will do something. Do not make him say goodbye to you or explain himself. You will see him when he returns tonight."

"Will he come back?"

"Do not act like he is a stranger to you. Yes. Now go."

Rivkah retreated. She faced Malik for several steps before she turned for the path out of El Fureidis.

Malik found Vince inside the clinic, slapping mortar on cinderblocks to build a new wall for the entryway. He labored by himself.

Vince hefted a block in place, then rapped the butt of his trowel on top to set it into the mortar. Artfully he swept away the excess. Vince mopped his brow in greeting of Malik.

Malik said, "Come here."

"Why?"

"Come." Malik pointed at the trowel. "Leave that."

Vince brought the trowel anyway.

"What's up?"

"Bernadotte is dead."

Vince did not drop the trowel. He blinked at the news. Or he was recalling something.

He said, "The Jews did it."

"That is what is being said."

"When did it happen?"

"An hour ago."

"Where?"

"Jerusalem. His car was ambushed."

Vince turned his back to Malik. He set the trowel on top of a stack of blocks for the next man tomorrow, then walked off.

CHAPTER 116

VINCE

Tel Aviv

Soldiers surrounded The Red House.

The streetlights of Hayarkon jittered before they came on, like lightning. The beachfront was vacant in the warm twilight.

At the first roadblock, Vince showed his credentials. A young soldier refused the booklet.

"I'm sorry. No one gets in tonight."

Vince pushed his press ID on the soldier. "Give this to your commanding officer. Ask him to take it to the prime minister's office. Tell Ben-Gurion I'm out here and I'm not leaving."

Vince waited twenty minutes while darkness fell. On another Friday night, Tel Aviv's seafront promenade would be swollen with families, soldiers on leave during the truce, boys and girls courting, new immigrants taking in their new city. Tonight, Tel Aviv was on edge, staying inside by the radio, waiting for the next move and wondering who would make it.

An officer arrived to escort Vince through doubled security to the entrance of the government house. Inside, one of a dozen guards pointed Vince to the staircase. At the top of the steps, Ben-Gurion's secretary hooked her thumb at the prime minister's door.

Vince knocked, then stepped in without a call to enter.

Behind his desk, Ben-Gurion sat with arms folded, his face in the half-light of a table lamp.

"Mister Haas. I am never surprised to see you."

Ben-Gurion did not rise. Vince took the leather chair before the desk.

"Did you do this?"

Without uncrossing his arms, Ben-Gurion nodded, shifting the light that fell on his white corona of hair.

"In a way."

Ben-Gurion stopped bobbing his head.

"You understand, if I had ordered the death of Bernadotte, you would be the last person I would tell. Since I did not, you will be the first. No. I did not do this."

"Then it was the Stern Gang."

"An hour ago, letters were left at consulates in Jerusalem. A group that calls itself The Fatherland Front claims it was they who carried it out. We suspect that's a cover for the Sternists."

"I know it was them."

"How is this?"

"Let's just say I know."

"Did you know in advance?"

"Yeah."

"Truly? And you said nothing about it? No report to the police? Not even an article?"

"No."

"Why?"

"I've been trying to stay out of your fights."

Ben-Gurion left his desk for the open leather chair.

Vince rattled his head at himself; some part of him told him to get up, walk out, and keep walking.

Ben-Gurion asked, "But?"

"I've got a kid on the way."

"Perhaps having a Jewish child will help you understand us."

"Maybe."

Ben-Gurion waited before he patted Vince's knee.

"Feel no guilt, Mister Haas. Count Bernadotte ignored every reality, every warning. He sealed his own fate."

"In a country like this."

"Yes, in a country like this. Shall I tell you something for what I suspect may be one of your last columns about Israel?"

"Sure."

Ben-Gurion indicated his desktop.

"I have there Count Bernadotte's second proposal. It was submitted yesterday. Would you care to take notes?"

"I got it."

"As you wish. Bernadotte insisted again that our boundaries be approved by the United Nations. This flies in the face of our military gains. It achieves for the Arabs what they cannot get on the battlefield. Bernadotte demands the Negev be made Arab territory. That Jerusalem be an international city. Haifa an open port. He requires that the refugees be allowed to return to their homes and to receive from Israel. These were ridiculous the first time Bernadotte presented them."

"So he was murdered one day after submitting it."

"Frankly, I'm surprised it took that long."

"Are you that big a bastard, Prime Minister?"

"Oh yes."

"What is it about you Jews? You can't take criticism. You can't consider any view but your own."

Ben-Gurion chuckled.

"It's true, we're a sensitive people. How can we not be? Too many times we've opened our hearts only to receive a knife in the back."

"That's politics. You want to be a grownup country, get used to it."

"No, I think we will not. The British were our friends when the Balfour Declaration promised us a Jewish state. They reneged for Arab oil and became our enemies. America was our big brother when you guided us through the United Nations to become our own nation. Then you gave us not a sharp stick to defend it. The UN did nothing to protect us from an Arab invasion. King Husseini was our friend, then sent tanks across the border."

Ben-Gurion tapped the side of his own head.

"You must see that a Jew weaned on the Polish ghetto might be slow to accept a friendly gesture unless it comes from a Jewish hand? Can you understand that a German who took off his yellow star three years ago might be a little prickly over criticism from anyone but a Jew? Now that we have a little muscle of our own, we're enjoying hitting back a bit."

"Is that what Bernadotte was? The Jews hitting back?"

"No. Bernadotte is a tragedy for Israel. Make no mistake."

"How'd they do it?"

"This afternoon, the count returned to Jerusalem from a visit to Ramallah. In the Katamon neighborhood, a military jeep blocked the road. Four men in uniform left the jeep. They found Bernadotte in the second car of his convoy beside a French observer. I have been told that four years ago Bernadotte saved this Frenchman's wife from a German camp. One assassin fired a submachine gun through the open window. The Frenchman leaned across Bernadotte to protect him. He and Bernadotte were killed. The count was struck six times in the chest."

"Did you ever meet Bernadotte?

"Briefly."

"He was a good man."

"This room is not big enough to hold the names of the good men and women who were murdered because they were Jews."

"What are you going to do?"

"Round up and disband the Stern Gang."

"Will you catch the killers?"

"They will be difficult to find."

"So you're going to do nothing."

"They will, as I said, be difficult to find. Bernadotte's killing will be a worldwide black eye for Israel. Here, however, the man was not loved."

"What about the refugees? They're not going away because Bernadotte's dead."

"If anyone had told me at the outset of the war that one day we would expel the Palestinians, I would have thought it madness. But it has happened in the course of a war the Arabs started. The Palestinians abandoned their villages as much by the invaders' own words and deeds as anything Israel has done."

"There's half a million refugees."

"There's *more* than half a million. Why does no one consider the Jews displaced by the war? The ones who lived in the Arab territories of Palestine. So far there have been sixty thousand. We take responsibility for them. We welcome them."

"Good for you."

"And what of the Jews living in the countries of the Arab invaders? Jewish shops are being looted in Egypt, Jews are arrested in Lebanon, molested and hanged in Iraq. The hatred they endure is forcing them to leave their homes, as well. The number fleeing the Levant will also be half a million. Have the Arabs offered Jewish refugees compensation? Did Bernadotte demand it in his proposal?"

"I'll guess he didn't."

"Not a word. And see how differently the Arab and the Jewish refugees are being treated. In Israel we do all we can to help every Jew become a citizen. What do the Arab invaders do with the refugees they have created? Clump them into camps. Leave them to starve and freeze. Do you honestly believe the Palestinians will ever call Egypt, Syria, or Lebanon home? No, Mister Haas, the Palestinian people will live on the hard rocks the invaders will maroon them on as they go home themselves. The Palestinians will be left on Israel's doorstep. Four hundred million Muslim Arabs will do nothing to rescue the refugees from suffering. Why? To threaten our security, yes. But more importantly, to blame Israel for the Palestinians' misery."

Ben-Gurion stood, the signal that his next remark would be his last.

"The Palestinians who have left cannot return to their homes inside Israel. There are too many of them. How can a Jewish state exist where the Jew is a minority to the Arab who despises him? This is a clock that cannot be turned back."

Vince rose, too.

Ben-Gurion asked, "Have I made all my points, Mister Haas?"

"You have."

"Good. Now. I've told you what I will do. What of you?"

Vince offered his hand. "Goodbye, Mister Prime Minister."

They shook. Ben-Gurion took Vince's hand in both of his.

"Vince."

"Yeah."

"You wish for a gentle Israel. You've seen for yourself. A gentle Israel cannot exist."

Ben-Gurion opened the door, then closed it behind Vince with a muted click.

CHAPTER 117

VINCE

Zichron Ya'akov

Mrs. Pappel found Vince in Rivkah's room packing his duffel. She hugged him.

"That was from Hugo."

For herself, Mrs. Pappel kissed his cheek.

"You're an intelligent man. I assume I can't say anything you haven't thought of."

"No, ma'am."

"You are loved in this household. That will not change, and never forget it. I will leave a cupcake on the kitchen counter for you."

She left Rivkah's room without a glance back. He listened to Mrs. Pappel lurch down the staircase, heard her fiddle in the kitchen, then from the window watched her leave the front porch on Malik's arm. Both stopped in the dusky street to look up at him. Malik touched his forehead, then his heart. Mrs. Pappel covered just her heart. Together, they walked in the lane into late, quiet Zichron.

Vince carried his duffle bag downstairs. In the kitchen Gabbi had eaten his cupcake.

She said, "I'm pregnant."

Gabbi crushed him in an embrace. When she let go, she stepped back.

"Do you have to go?'

"No. I don't have to."

"Then don't."

"Gabbi."

"What."

"You'll have a beautiful green-eyed child."

"I want a bunch of them."

"Take care of everybody. There's no one better for that."

On the porch, Vince laid his duffel next to the empty rocker. He turned the chair to face Rivkah in the other rocker. She gazed a long moment at the duffel.

"You almost stayed."

"Almost."

"Was it Bernadotte?"

"That was the last straw, yeah."

Vince tilted forward. He opened his hand for hers. Rivkah gave it. She asked, "Does it matter that I love you?"

"No more than it matters that I love you."

Vince let go of Rivkah's hand and rocked back.

"I knew they were going to assassinate Bernadotte."

"What do you mean?"

"A month back, the Stern Gang sent two of their thugs to see me. They wanted me to warn Bernadotte they were going to kill him."

"My God. What did you do?"

"Not a thing."

Rivkah covered her mouth. She asked though her fingers, "Nothing?"

"No."

"Tell me."

"I didn't think it wasn't my problem."

"What's happened, Vince? You've done so much for Israel. How can you turn your back on it?"

Vince rattled his head. "I just can't stay here."

She held out a hand, not for him to take, but to ask, Why?

"I'll always question."

"Israel needs that."

"Something Ben-Gurion said to me."

"What?"

"It has to come from Jews."

Rivkah didn't reel in her hand but left it extended. She worked her fingers for Vince to put his hand in hers. He did.

She asked, "Can you stay a few days until the baby's here?"

"I can't."

"Why not?"

"How strong do you think my heart is?"

A hushing breeze made the trees swish. The town was firm and safe, shuttered for the evening, it didn't know Vince was leaving. Zichron would be a good place for a Jewish kid to grow up.

Vince let go of Rivkah's hand. He stood and shouldered the strap of his duffel.

He stepped to the edge of the porch. Zichron Ya'akov smelled of the sea and the good soil.

"I'll send money."

"Don't. Missus Pappel has plenty."

"You'll always know where I am."

"And you will know we are here."

Rivkah set her hands to the arms of the rocker but did not push up. She didn't stand, as if to play no part in his leaving.

Vince came back to kiss her forehead. He spread his palm wide over the orb of the child.

Then he stepped off the dark, flowered porch.

CHAPTER 118

October 2

AQABAT JABR REFUGEE CAMP
ARAB-CONTROLLED PALESTINE
By Vincent Haas

Herald Tribune News Service

From where I stand just outside Jericho, everything is windswept, barren, and ancient.

Only the Dead Sea glimmers, a one-hour camel ride south. Three miles east, the Jordan River winds between the Dead Sea and the Galilee. If I want, I can cross the river into Transjordan. But that's forbidden to the people around me, the twenty thousand displaced Palestinians of the Aqabat Jabr refugee camp.

This morning, I rode a camel down to the sea with four camp boys. These lads, two sets of brothers, have adopted me, they keep me safe. The residents of Aqabat Jabr who live in peaked tents, sleep on brush mattresses under Swiss-cheese blankets, in squalor and hunger, have been known to vent their frustrations on visitors in Western clothes.

The days are warm, as they tend to be on this blank pan of the Jordan Valley. The Dead Sea is a quarter mile below sea level. Its remarkable salinity makes the water sterile; nothing can live in it. The

sea is so dense with salt that I floated on the surface
like I was in an easy chair, arms and legs in the air.
A blister on my hand stung like nobody's business.

Sunning on the rocky bank, the boys told me of
a shopkeeper from Haifa who two days ago took his
own two sons, friends of theirs, out behind his tent
and shot them through the head, then himself. The
boys said it was the Jews who killed the man, made
him confined, penniless, made him watch his children's stomachs bloat.

I've come to Aqabat Jabr after several days at
another refugee camp, a big one outside Ramallah.
Before that, I spent time at Ain al-Hilweh camp in
Lebanon, and another in Gaza. There are fifty such
camps for the Palestinians outside Israel. The story
the boys tell of the Haifa shopkeeper is particularly
disturbing, but his despair is not extraordinary among
the half million stateless Arabs.

The second shaky truce has allowed both sides to
rest, rearm, and plot. But the peace has done very little to achieve meaningful negotiations between Arab
and Jew. The Israelis, for their part, have offered to
repatriate one hundred thousand Palestinians, adding
them to the seven hundred thousand Arabs who've
chosen to stay and become Israeli citizens. The Arabs
responded by snubbing this and every Jewish proposal. They reject anything that might smack of rec-
ognition of Israel's right to exist.

Without intending it, the Arab nations have
done a great deal to assist Israel's growth. By starting a war, then refusing all overtures from the Jews
and the U.N., including the Bernadotte Plan, they've
handed Israel a golden opportunity to conquer territory it could never have gained otherwise.

This spectacular and unexpected expansion of Israel's borders has resulted in Israel taking dominion over hundreds of Palestinian towns and villages they did not anticipate they would control. Whether to become an Israeli citizen or remain Palestinian became a choice many Arabs had to make, often in minutes, with guns bearing down on them.

The result is the refugee camps.

Four hundred thousand Arabs who fled the conflict in central Palestine are now stranded west of the Jordan River. Two hundred thousand more are clumped in a strip of seafront territory stretching twenty-five miles from Gaza south to the Egyptian border. Another hundred thousand Arabs cluster in northern camps dotting Lebanon and Syria. The Palestinian refugees receive only threadbare care from the nearest Arab army or country, or the United Nations.

What will happen to them?

First, what's going to happen in the war?

For now, the truce is sticking. Israel's in a holding pattern; no war, no peace. But the assassination of the U.N.'s mediator Count Folke Bernadotte by Jewish extremists may have turned the diplomatic tide against Israel. The U.N., including America, is so angry they might try to force Bernadotte's plan down the Jews' throats. If that happens, Israel will find her immigration and borders restricted, Jerusalem and the Negev in Arab hands, and the Palestinian refugees granted full rights of return to their homes.

But Prime Minister Ben-Gurion is a pugilist in all things regarding Israel. His best defense is to punch back. For example: the U.N.'s truce headquarters is in Tel Aviv at the Kaete Dan guesthouse. This morning, Ben-Gurion had Bernadotte's limou-

sine parked there, in plain sight. Hundreds of Israeli
citizens crowded around it. The crusted blood of
Bernadotte and the French peacekeeper murdered
beside him still caked the backseat. A row of bullet
holes stitched the upholstery chest-high. Not a single
Israeli peeking inside the limo windows expressed
remorse, shame, or regret for the murders, at least not
for the hour I stood there.

Ben-Gurion doesn't want to give the U.N. time
to punish his little country for Bernadotte's killing.
Look for Israel to find ways to provoke the Arabs
into breaking the truce. This will, of course, restart
the war. Israel will win. When they do, the final battle lines, not any U.N.'s map or moralizing, will be
the enduring truth of Israel's borders.

How can such a small, newborn country defy
the United Nations? The same way they've dared
five Arab armies, two truces, an embargo, world
opinion, and the odds. Defiance isn't just in Jewish
politics; it's in the character and myth of the people.

It's too late to parse who has the moral right to
belong in Israel. That issue's been decided here as it
has been around the world, throughout time: by force
of arms. To be honest, I can't imagine anyone mus-
tering the kind of force necessary to make the Jews
relinquish the homeland they're winning.

This means over a half million Palestinian
Arabs will not be allowed to return. Why did they
leave their homes in the first place? One of four rea-
sons: hatred of the Jews; fear of the Jews; driven out
by the Jews; or, they trusted the word of the invading
Arab nations who told them to step out of the way so
the war could be won quickly. This last cause turned
out to be the most frequent, and it's not Israel's fault.

By sheer numbers alone, the return of the refugees would destroy a Jewish homeland. The Arabs might again fortify their villages, setting the stage for another civil war. Also, by weight of sheer numbers, their return would put the Jews into a political minority in their own country, swamping the very notion of an independent Jewish state.

When the war is over, the five invading, defeated Arab armies will go home. The Palestinians will not be invited to follow. Egypt, Lebanon, Iraq, and Syria will slam the door in the Palestinians' faces. Only Husseini of Transjordan offers citizenship in his country to the refugees. But he doesn't want them on his side of the Jordan River. Husseini will abandon the Palestinians on this pallid land with a view of the Dead Sea.

If Israel will not allow the refugees to return, and the Arabs will not host them, the Palestinians will remain in all the awful, bleak places they are now. This is not a recipe for a lasting peace.

What of Israel?

This past year, 70 percent of Jewish immigration into Israel has emanated from Arabia: Israel has accepted a quarter million new citizens from Tunisia, Yemen, Algeria, and Morocco. One of the great challenges ahead for Israel will be to feed themselves. This calls for the reclamation of conquered lands, much of it desert. Before you can have milk and honey, you need cows and bees.

A lot of Americans and Europeans have taken one look at the labor required for Israel's agriculture and construction and said no thanks. Westerners want city life, not sunrise on a remote kibbutz. To date, Russia has allowed just one immigrant to Israel, a multiple-amputee war hero. The hardier Jews from

Muslim countries are a better fit for the tough lands
of Judea and the Negev. It's not a little ironic to see
North Africans in flowing Arabian garb alongside
Jews in khaki shorts.

While Israel sows and reaps her own future, the
squalid refugee camps will plant only hatred. It's a
crop that will be reseeded every harsh winter, every
droughted summer, by every distress, every haunting
tale of a businessman from Haifa.

Israel will call the war a victory. The Palestinians
already have a name for it. The *nakba*. The disaster.

And what, finally, of me?

This will be my last dispatch from the Middle
East. After I leave Aqabat Jabr, I'll head back to New
York and rest. I'll let the city become my home again.

I leave the war in Israel behind, but it will follow me. Ben-Gurion once told me I wished for gentleness. He warned me against it. I fear that, like the
Arabs and Israel, gentleness will elude me.

I leave a great deal of good behind in Israel, too,
more than I will say here. She reads what I write, and
she will know.

Reporting from Aqabat Jabr refugee camp.